Olivia is a former software  romance. She lives in Atla two naughty cats (Hairy I she enjoys traveling and most of the time, she end because her family has a limit on how much they love her.

She is a member and volunteer at the Atlanta Writers Club. Olivia is represented by the lovely Helen Lane.

www.oliviajacksonbooks.com

instagram.com/oliviajacksonbooks

... an engineer who writes contemporary romances ... lives with her husband, two kids, and ... (Houdini and Bess). Besides writing ... experimenting with cooking, and ... ends up eating the new meals herself ...

DIGGING DR JONES

OLIVIA JACKSON

One More Chapter
a HarperCollins*Publishers* Ltd
1 London Bridge Street
London SE1 9GF
www.harpercollins.co.uk
HarperCollins*Publishers*
Macken House, 39/40 Mayor Street Upper,
Dublin 1, D01 C9W8
This paperback edition 2025

1

First published in Great Britain in ebook format
by HarperCollins*Publishers* 2025

A catalogue record of this book is available from the British Library
ISBN: 978-0-00-872965-3

This novel is entirely a work of fiction. The names, characters and incidents portrayed in it are the work of the author's imagination. Any resemblance to actual persons, living or dead, events or localities is entirely coincidental.

Printed and bound in the UK using 100% Renewable Electricity
by CPI Group (UK) Ltd

For Burke, the love of my life.

Thank you for proving every single day that happily ever after exists in real life. I love you.

Playlist

Dreams - The Cranberries

Close To You - Gracie Abrams

Island In The Sun - Weezer

Hands To Myself - Selena Gomez

goodnight n go - Ariana Grande

Miss Americana & The Heartbreak Prince -
Taylor Swift

Heaven - Niall Horan

BIRDS OF A FEATHER - Billie Eilish

Bed Chem - Sabrina Carpenter

Slow Burn - Kacey Musgraves

I Like Me Better - Lauv

Wonder - Shawn Mendes

Cornelia Street - Taylor Swift

Undiscovered - Laura Welsh

Risk - Gracie Abrams

Pray - JRY

The Night We Met - Lord Huron

Vertigo - Griff

Little Freak - Harry Styles

Love & Liberte - Gipsy Kings

What If I Love You - Gatlin

West Coast - Lana Del Rey

Breakaway - Kelly Clarkson

Carry You Home - Alex Warren

Daylight - Taylor Swift

Chapter One

My karma wasn't mean, she just had a quirky sense of humor. She strategically placed jackasses in my path so I wouldn't grow bored. She messed with my personal and professional life, and every time I thought I was in the clear, she'd surprise me in the most peculiar way.

Today was my second day at a ritzy, all-inclusive Costa Rican resort, and everything was going well when a hotel staffer delivered a package addressed to me. It wasn't my birthday, and it was two months past Christmas. I ripped it open anyway—blame it on cocktails at lunch. A bulky gold bracelet embellished with elegant swirls around four green stones fell out of the box. No note. It sparkled in the early afternoon light, beguiling me, and of course, I snapped it on.

My Apple Watch vibrated with a message.

WILLIAM

Hurry. The Mr. Sexiest Legs contest is starting

I grabbed my purse and, like any sensible thirty-three-year-old, I rushed to have drinks with my brother.

The Triton bar was the indoor/outdoor extension of the main restaurant. It had a tropical vibe and offered a full panorama of an infinity pool and an extensive list of hand-crafted cocktails that could quench anyone's thirst. I found William perched on a stool at the bar with a prime view of the lineup of contestants.

I sidled up next to him. "Thanks for finding great seats."

"Only the best for you."

"You and I both know it had nothing to do with me." I smiled and leaned on the counter to catch the eyes of the busy bartenders.

"I already ordered us—Wowza!" William grasped my right hand and brought it up to examine the bracelet. "When did you go on a shopping spree without me?"

"I didn't. It was delivered to our room a few minutes ago."

"Two days at this resort and you already have a secret admirer. Bravo, Adriana."

A strawberry daiquiri and a margarita on the rocks materialized in front of us. Without a toast—we did plenty of that yesterday—we took a large gulp of our drinks.

"I doubt it," I said. "But it is weird. Who knows we're here?"

The contest host's booming voice reverberated around us, snapping William's attention to the front of the pool.

For the next two hours, I enjoyed people-watching, my foot swinging to upbeat merengue music, but after the third or maybe fourth cocktail, the truth finally hit me.

"Son of a gun," I said, with my margarita midway to my

lips. "This isn't a gift. It's a bribe to let him back in on the deal."

William, staring at a group of men with abs that should be used in an anatomy class, finished his drink with a loud slurp and turned to me. "Huh?"

"This bracelet." I thrust my hand at him. "It's from Jeff. Don't you get it? He wants back in as my silent investor."

He glanced at the bracelet, and then his hazel eyes focused back on the washboards. "I like my secret admirer theory better." He sucked on the straw even though there was nothing left in the glass. "But it could be him."

"I'd rather live in a cardboard box and eat maggots than partner with him again." One week plus some blurred days ago, Jeff had left me in total WTF-ery. "I might be jobless and carrying a Texas-size mortgage loan, but my dignity is bigger. I'll throw this thing away."

"That's the spirit." William clinked his empty drink glass to mine.

I finished my margarita and *tried* to concentrate on anything that could hush the Itty-Bitty Shitty Committee chanting in my brain. But my rah-rah attitude ran its course, and my anxiety took over.

"I'm a total failure." I folded my hands on the polished stone bar and pressed my head into my forearm. The bracelet's center stone jabbed into my skin.

"You aren't a failure," William said. "Think of it as stepping in dog crap while jogging. It sucks. It stinks. But like all big girls, you wash your shoes off—or better yet, buy a new pair—and the next day, you run again."

I lifted my head, and William grinned at me. I wished I had

his *let's-stay-positive* personality. Did he inherit it from our father? What did I inherit from him? I'd never know.

"Is Jeff the dog crap?" I asked.

I met Jeff through my work at Salzburg Wine Distributing and pitched him my idea to open a boutique store selling wine, olive oils, and vinegars supplied by women-owned businesses.

"Who else would I mean? That jerk left you high and dry. Who does that?"

"The jerk who had different motives." I sighed.

Jeff's only stipulation was for me to own the property—so I'd have some skin in the game, he said. That was fair enough since he would be the one investing hundreds of thousands of dollars into renovating the building and buying all the initial inventory. It wasn't easy to get a loan, but I managed, scrapping the bottom of my savings and retirement funds to make a down payment. I just wished I hadn't overlooked the line stating both parties could break the contract at any time.

A bartender placed two tequila shots in front of us. We raised our glasses in a toast, licked the salt off the rim, tossed down the spicy liquor, and bit into fresh limes. As the hot liquid went down my throat, I cringed at the taste. William gently patted his lips with a napkin while I wiped mine with the back of my hand.

"Now," William said, "you promised not to ruin our trip by talking about your minor issue."

I vaguely remembered making that promise in exchange for a paid-by-him vacation at a luxurious resort. After a day of hysterical panic, followed by three days of not being able to get out of my bed, followed by rage at every human with a dick— my brother excluded—I needed this break.

4

I raised my right eyebrow and scoffed. "How is being a million dollars in the hole a minor issue?"

William stubbed his finger above my raised eyebrow. "You need another round of Botox. When we're back in Atlanta, come by my clinic."

Annoyed that William wasn't taking me seriously, I swatted away his hand. "I have much bigger issues to worry about right now than my wrinkles." I should be grateful and not annoyed. He was only trying to take my mind off my dumpster-fire life. "Plus, I don't have money to waste on something like that."

"First, taking care of your beauty isn't a waste. Second, since you refuse my help with your money problem, Botox will be my treat."

He was thriving as the owner of Atlanta's highest-rated non-surgical beauty treatment clinic, but I couldn't take a penny of his hard-earned money. It wasn't my pride, but rather my fear of dragging him down into my financial hole.

William unlocked his iPhone and pulled up our itinerary for the next two weeks. "So, tomorrow, we have a sunrise yoga class on the beach, followed by a detox breakfast."

I didn't need a green smoothie. I needed to sell an empty shell of a building or quickly find money to pay the bills that were already piling up.

I planted my elbow on the bar to prop up my heavy head, the tequila shot warming my bloodstream. "Are they serving Bloody Marys? It's basically a salad in a glass. With *protein*, if they add bacon."

"I don't know if they do, but we can certainly find some after." He scrolled down to the next item. "Then we have

5

nothing to do, so we can be lazy bums until dinner time, which is … a barbecue at six and dance lesson by the pool."

I felt bad my glum mood was ruining our vacation. William wanted to have fun, and all I wanted to do was crawl into a hole and die from wallowing in self-pity. I'd bring a book with me, just in case it took a long time.

William looked up from his phone and leaned back in his seat. His lips shaped into an O as he stared over my shoulder for a few seconds. "OMG. Superman is *in* the bar."

"Oh yeah?" Without turning to check out the guy, I wiggled my eyebrows—well, the right one at least. "Is he wearing a tight blue spandex costume and a red Speedo?"

His gaze slowly traveled up and down. "Nope, just a white button-up shirt and beige trousers, but he'd look great in a Speedo."

"No one looks great in a Speedo."

"I do."

"Not even you."

"Rude." William's eyes went wide, and he bumped my knee with his. "He's coming over here."

"Hello," the man said in an English accent. "I'm Dr. Andrew Jones. I'm afraid there's been a mistake."

My eyes rolled so far back in my head it hurt. Why did so many men use cheesy conversation openers? Usually, I'd kindly brush off whoever hit on me, but in the current contingency, I was exhausted from dealing with men.

"Save your pickup lines for someone else." I dismissively wave my left hand to flaunt my false princess-cut diamond engagement ring.

"The bracelet on your wrist is not yours. It's mine," the man said, voice edged with vexation. "Please take it off."

What the actual fuck? Was he politely robbing me?

My mouth dropped open, and I spun in my seat. "What?"

This man with the face of a god walking amongst mere mortals looked to be in his early thirties and sported brown, wet-out-of-the-shower hair and a lopsided smirk. His green eyes … no, wait, blue eyes—how drunk was I—glared at me. I squinted. I was sure the iris of his left eye was a different color than the right one. Wild, but beautiful.

"No!" I said. "It's mine. I just got it today."

Dr. Jones' jaw clenched tight, and he took a deep breath, his wide chest expanding. "I don't have time for this. How much do you want for it?"

I glanced at my hand. The bracelet wasn't my style and was cheaply made. Its gems weren't set well and kept depressing slightly under finger pressure. I didn't want it, but out of principle *or spite*, I said, "It's not for sale."

"I'll give you a thousand dollars for it," Dr. Jones said.

A cocky smile grew on my face as I met his intelligent eyes. "Five grand, and it's yours."

"Deal."

For real? I was thunderstruck.

But why did he want it? And did I care that much to question him? Nope. This money was a drop in my debt ocean, and right now I was unemployed, living on William's couch and cramping his lifestyle. Anything was welcome.

"Don't do it," William whispered to me. "It's some pyramid scheme."

"I don't think you understand how a pyramid scheme works. And don't you want me out of your condo?"

William peered over my shoulder. "You'll need to Venmo it to her account."

I twisted around and faced my brother. "You said you liked our bonding time."

William made a puppy face. "We can still bond. Only at the end of the night, you can go back to your own place."

My eyes widened with pretend hurt. "Let me remind you"—I poked his arm—"I came with a case of very expensive wine."

"More like overpriced wine, and there's now only one bottle of it left."

Dr. Jones cleared his throat again. "Please provide me with your contact information to complete the transaction."

"Who are you exactly?" I gave Dr. Jones a once-over, trying and failing to find anything incriminating about him. Instead, I found myself admiring his fine-cut features and downright intimidating confidence, which I found impossibly sexy in men.

"I'm an associate professor and academic director of Archaeology at the University of Cambridge."

"That's a lot of big words people shouldn't say during happy hour." William pushed my shoulder, sliding a cocktail napkin with my name, phone number, and Venmo username on it across the bar.

"William! Seriously?"

I exhaled an irritated breath, but my left hand went to the bracelet. I twisted it a few times but it was impossible to find the fastened clasp among the intricate engravings of serpentine vines, which now looked more like jagged lines than scrolls.

"How do I take it off?" I tugged on it, trying to pull my hand through the band.

"May I try?" Dr. Jones said, a smirk pulling at the corner of his lips.

I held out my arm to him.

His feather-light touch on my skin sent shivers down my spine and made me exceptionally aware of his closeness, the heat radiating off his body. He carefully rotated the bracelet, pausing a few times to examine it. While concentrating, he chewed his bottom lip, his eyebrows drawn together as his fingers applied pressure on the stones. Being so close to him, I couldn't help but take a deep breath and enjoy the lingering scent of the hotel's lavender and lemon soap mixed with a hint of sunblock. It had been too long since I'd felt a man's weight on my body, enjoyed the smell of sweat and sex, or been touched in the way no battery-operated boyfriend can.

Dr. Jones cleared his throat. He rotated the bracelet some more, then pressed on the largest blue stone. Nothing happened.

"Hmm." He raked his hand through his hair.

"Hmm, what?" I stared up at his face. The man was taller than I'd initially thought. I was five eleven, and he must have a good six inches on me. "You don't know how to open it?"

"I need more time."

"Let me try to pull my hand through it again." I broke our eye contact and tugged hard on the bracelet. Why in the world did I put it on? Embarrassment crept up my neck and then morphed into hot anger. I took a deep breath, seized the stupid golden thing in a vice-like grip, and yanked it.

"Stop." Dr. Jones grabbed my arm. "You could damage it."

"Maybe if we put some lube on it, it will slip off?" William chipped in.

"I didn't bring any," I hissed through my teeth.

"I did," William said. *Of course, he did.* "Lube will work. Let's go to our room and try it."

"It's worth an attempt," Dr. Jones agreed.

In awkward silence, we rode to the third floor and walked to the end of the hall. When we entered our suite, William disappeared into the bedroom, and I made my way to the bar, selected a mini tequila bottle out of the refrigerator, and found a glass.

"Do you want a drink, Andrew? Or do you prefer Dr. Jones?" I asked the handsome stranger who stood in the middle of my suite, typing on his cellphone, the right side of his mouth quirked in concentration.

"No, thank you." He glanced at me and gave a tight-lipped smile. "And Andrew is fine."

I studied the liquor bottle in my hand, thought better of it, placed it back, and grabbed a club soda. Years ago, a man like him—highly educated and striking—was my heart's Achille's heel. But, once bitten, twice shy, and now I was immune to his type.

"How did you know where to find me?" I asked.

"When the bracelet didn't arrive, I checked with the receptionist, and we quickly figured out the issue." He regarded me for a moment. "You are a very memorable woman. After a brief investigation, I was directed to the Triton bar."

William returned, holding a box of Kleenex and a large bottle of lubricant.

"Let's do it." He poured a generous amount of liquid onto his palm and massaged it over my wrist. "Okay. Try now."

I gripped the bracelet and tugged it as hard as I could. My skin wrinkled, turning red. "It doesn't want to come off. We need to cut it."

"No!" Andrew barked so urgently that my insides performed a backflip.

"Jesus, don't give me a heart attack. You can pay me half of the money and take it to a jeweler to fix it."

"It's worthless if it's damaged." He glared at me as if somehow this was all my fault.

I yanked a couple of tissues out of the box and vigorously wiped my wrist and hand. "Why don't we find a jeweler who can help us open it?"

Andrew walked to the floor-to-ceiling glass door that opened on to a terrace with a view of white sand and turquoise water. He linked his fingers together behind his neck and groaned.

"It's not so simple," Andrew muttered. "Christ, why would you put it on?"

"Um, because it was a gift for me?"

Andrew stared at the vast view. "No, it wasn't."

"It was delivered to *my* room with *my* name on it," I said, incredulous.

"It had *my* name on it." He turned. "Someone delivered it by mistake to *your* room."

"You're wrong, and I can prove it." I strode to the powder room and fished the package out of the garbage bin. "See, right here." I pushed it into Andrew's hands. "It says Ms. Adriana Jones. That's my name." I pointed at the smeared writing with the first part of the name mostly gone, leaving only an "A" somewhat visible and only the last part with the surname Jones recognizable.

Andrew's eyes flicked to me, then again at the writing on the paper. His smirk spread into a shit-eating grin. "Look closer, and you'll see my name," he said. "Dr. Andrew Jones."

"No, I won't."

With confidence, I turned the package around and concentrated on the name. Andrew pushed the torn paper edges together. My stomach sank low, realizing that I was a total dipstick. It was Andrew and not Adriana. And what I thought was Ms. now looked more like Dr. I let go of the box, lowered myself onto the couch, and leaned my head back, closing my eyes.

"Okay, maybe it *does* say Dr. Andrew Jones. I really thought it was for me. There was no note." The sting of embarrassment burned my nose, and I scrunched up my face, not wanting to cry. "I tried it on, and then William texted me…" The tears streamed down my face. "I'm such an idiot."

My pity party must've been too much for Dr. Jones. One moment he was by my side, the next he was headed for the door.

"Let me think more about how to unlock it. I'll be back." Andrew started to leave, but then he ducked back inside, a warning on his face. "No matter what, *do not* cut or damage that bracelet."

By dinner time, the bracelet was still an embarrassing weight on my wrist. The television was on but muted, showing an overly dramatic soap opera. I sat on the couch and flipped through a resort magazine full of advertisements, my foot tapping to the distant sound of Latin music coming from the direction of the pool. On the balcony, William Facetimed with someone. Multiple notes in Andrew's handwriting were scattered over the coffee table and Andrew himself was slumped in a chair, his head clutched between his hands, his elbows pressing into his knees.

When Andrew had returned to our suite, he'd asked for a quiet moment so he could concentrate. That moment had stretched into sixty long, boring minutes as he held my hand while turning the bracelet repeatedly, pressing four stones in different sequences. Other than his name and profession—and the knowledge that he must have an abundance of money, to offer so much to me for this bracelet—I knew nothing about this stranger. At some point, he had rolled his sleeves up to his elbows, exposing cords of taut forearm muscles. On his left wrist, he wore a banged-up Swiss Army watch with an age-softened espresso leather strap, its metal bezel and crystal glass showcasing numerous scratches. It wasn't enough to know someone, but somehow it made me like him. I found myself wondering if he was a sentimental man as a fancier wristwatch would have suited Dr. Jones better.

With a groan, Andrew leaned back, tipping his head over the back of his chair and extending his long legs under the coffee table. The fabric of his pants hugged his thighs, outlining firm muscles. Was I ogling? I wasn't. I was just observing.

"Christ." He rubbed his face with his hands. "You'll have to come with me to Colombia."

WTF? Did he just say Colombia?

One look at his face told me he wasn't kidding. I bit back nervous laughter. "Excuse me?"

"Please hear me out." Wide-eyed, Andrew sat up. "It shouldn't take long. One day there, and one day back. I'll reserve the best hotel." His hair was disheveled, making him look boyish. It was cute, and I couldn't help but smile. "Good, you're smiling, so you agree."

"No," I said, pulling on a serious face. "I don't care how many days it takes. I'm not going to Colombia. William and I are on vacation, and there are twelve days left to enjoy it before I need to…"—*beg for my old job back, fix the burning hole in my savings account, avoid a potential foreclosure and ruined credit, all because I purchased a building and couldn't afford to make the payments*—"face reality."

"I'll pay," Andrew said with a solemn expression.

I snorted. "It would take much more than an extra few thousand dollars for you to convince me to—"

"Twenty thousand," Andrew said, dead serious.

William stepped into the room. "Twenty thousand what?"

Paralyzed with shock, I didn't move or breathe.

"Adriana, what's he talking about?" William's gaze ping-ponged between Andrew and me.

"I need her to go with me to Colombia, and I'm willing to pay for the trouble that *she* created." He threw me a dirty look. I rolled my eyes.

"Why Colombia?" William rested his butt on the couch's armrest.

"In Santa Marta, we'll meet with the director of the Museum of History, Dr. Carlos Garcia, and then, if my assessment is correct, we'll use the bracelet as a key to unlock a trunk."

Getting a buttload of money just to go somewhere with a stranger to unlock a chest sounded too easy. And I'd learned nothing came easy in life.

I shook my head. "This is a stupid idea."

"Shh. Let the man explain," William said to me. "What's in the trunk?"

"Don't shush me." I glared at my brother. He motioned with his hand for me to shut up.

"A group of archeologists believe the trunk might contain a map to the location where pirate Augustine Pérez hid the Asiento de Padua treasure."

I swore William's ears perked up like a cat's at the sound of a tuna can opening.

"Oh good god." My head dropped backward as I groaned.

I already knew what the evening ahead held for me—William being a total child, ignoring the stranger-danger red flag and begging to go to Colombia. He would go for free too. When I was at the University of Georgia and he was doing a rotational internship at a hospital, he dragged me on a three-day road trip to Key West so he could visit the Mel Fisher Maritime Museum, home of a sunken Spanish treasure. Nobody else wanted to ride thirteen hours one way in his crappy car with a broken air conditioner, so he trapped me with a guarantee of endless seafood and the Hemingway house tour. It worked.

"In 1757, a ship named the Asiento de Padua set sail from Lisbon to Rome carrying gold, silver, tapestries, and jewels," Andrew explained. "Two pirate ships attacked the Asiento de Padua near Cartagena, Spain. The first pirate ship, captained by Augustine Pérez, made a clean getaway with most of the treasure. But the second ship was captured and the crew was hanged except for two officers, who were sent to prison. Two years ago, a group of French archaeologists discovered a diary written by one of the officers. In it, he mentioned Pérez had most likely sailed to Santa Marta, Colombia. As a fundraiser for the museum, Dr. Garcia collaborates with several Latin American private antique collectors, and this past weekend, he held an auction at the museum. At the last-minute, a chest that had allegedly belonged to Pérez—who was notorious for hiding his stolen valuables in the most secure places, in large chests with elaborate locking systems—was added to the list of items being auctioned."

"Who *are* you?" William asked with awe.

An ATM and Wikipedia page.

"I thought we already established that? I'm a professor of Archaeology at the University of Cambridge, and I also work for the Octavian Global group, a network of wealthy and powerful people devoted to protecting cultural heritage by ensuring irreplaceable artifacts find their way to museums rather than private collections, and preventing the wrong people from getting their hands on them."

"Jesus." William's hand went to his mouth. "Which wrong men?"

"Careless and entitled rich people who don't know how to care for newly found historical objects and would lock them up in their private homes and not let the rest of the world study and enjoy them," he said with exasperation.

This favor sounded too risky of a venture, even for twenty thousand dollars. I wasn't an adventurer or a risk-taker. Look at what had happened to me when I'd taken a calculated gamble with my career.

"That's very noble of you," I said, rising from the couch, "but I'm not going. I don't want to play sidekick to Indiana Jones."

"Oh, honey." William turned to me and grinned. "You won't be a sidekick. You'll be the leading lady."

"Still don't care." I walked toward our bedroom. "Tonight, I'll figure out how to take this thing off, and tomorrow morning, you'll have your bracelet."

"Give us a minute," William said to Andrew in his most placating voice, the one he used with fractious clients. He followed me into my room and closed the door.

"Why are you being so stubborn? The man offered you a lot of money for a little trouble. And an adventure." He pressed his hands together in a prayer, his face showing too much stupid glee for my liking.

I removed my gold hoop earrings and dropped them into a jewelry travel case on the side table. Then I yanked off my hair tie, letting my hair fall down my back. I ran my fingers over my skull, slightly digging my nails into the skin and chasing away some of my tension.

"How do we know he really has the money? What if he's a

criminal who kidnaps us and holds us for ransom?" I gave William a *you-didn't-think-about-that-did-you?* stare.

"Who would pay our ransom?" He burst into laughter as if I had told the funniest joke. "A father we haven't seen since god knows when? Or our mother, who calls only when she needs money?"

William was right. We had no other siblings, and we'd been so busy running like squirrels looking for a nut—aka making a living—we'd neglected to make any close friends. We'd only had each other since we were kids.

"He doesn't know we're our entire family." I point at the closed door. "We *are* at a fancy resort, after all."

William pulled his iPhone out of his pocket. "I already looked him up on the university website." His fingers tapped on the screen with the speed of light. "He's telling the truth." He turned the phone for me to see.

The screen had a headshot of Dr. Andrew Oliver Jones dressed in a suit and sporting the smirk I'd now become familiar with. Underneath his name and title were his areas of expertise in Classical Archaeology & Ancient History, Museum Studies, Material Culture, and Cultural Heritage. Had he crammed every possible title into his degree out of boredom?

"Doesn't mean he's not a creep." I rested on my side of the bed, leaning my back against the headboard, and stretched my legs. I was tired of dealing with men and their business propositions.

"Jeff was a creep, and you wanted to work with him."

I tensed at the memory of Jeff's hand on my thigh the day we'd celebrated closing on the historical building I'd bought. With his fingers digging into my leg, he suggested we move our party to his hotel room. Battery acid ate through my stomach when I removed his hand and, in a confident tone, explained we were only business partners, and that was all we'd ever be. I thought he'd taken it well, and we'd finished our dinner, talking only about our store. A week later, my sweet dream come true had turned into a total nightmare when he terminated our contract, leaving me in monstrous debt.

"He was…" I tilted my head up and looked at the ceiling, searching for the right word. I sighed. "He was a successful businessman and a tad creepy, but I can fend for myself."

I wasn't sure how to win this argument with my older brother. He knew I needed that money. *I* knew I needed that money. But a sudden change in any plan was never a good sign. Even those carefully outlined over the course of many years could fail. I needed to email my real estate agent and tell her to relist the building. The thought of officially giving up on my dream stung but it was the best way out of my predicament.

"I don't want to go." I twisted the bracelet as if it was a fidget toy, its stones faintly pressing under my fingers. "Colombia is nothing but a jungle."

"You're in the middle of a jungle right now." William gestured at the window with a view of the lush green vegetation.

"What about vaccinations?" The excuse sounded weak even to me, and I knew my protests were running out of steam.

"I'm sure what we got to come here covers the whole of South America. Adriana, please," William said. "It's only for two days. Let's go on an adventure. You know how much I love pirate treasures."

He moved closer to me and took my hand in his. "Please think about it. The *hot* professor in the next room offered you a stupid amount of money simply to accompany him on some college project. We'll go together. You won't be alone. Just think of what you can do with that cash." He smiled sheepishly. "You can take your time to find a decent job … or better yet, you'll have money to make payments on the store for several months while looking for a new investor. You've talked about this shop for the past four years. Think of all the companies you contacted and already had agreements with. Those women count on your support."

William could persuade a stranger to do whatever he wanted. I had no chance.

What he wanted most right now was to go on a *treasure* hunt, and what I wanted most was to own a shop and bar where people could find the best olive oils and vinegar, wines, take pairing classes, and hang out with their friends after work. Somehow, those two goals were aligning today.

Andrew's offer circled in my mind. The money could only cover four months of loan payments, but it was four months I didn't have before.

"I don't know. It's not enough, but it buys me some time." I smiled at William. "I could talk to the Small Business Administration again and see if they can help me."

"There you go." William squeezed my hand. "And your shop will be fabulous."

"You're just saying that because you got excited at the mention of treasure."

"Not true. I'm excited at the idea that you'll move out of my place because you're messy, and I don't do messy."

"I'm not messy." I threw a pillow at him. "You just don't have enough space to store all my things." I was untidy, but in my defense, for the past month, my life had been nothing but chaos.

"What about this vacation and the things you have planned?" I asked.

William shrugged. "Meh. It's just two days out of twelve. Adriana, please," he pleaded. "If not for you, do it for me. This short pirate treasure trip will be so good for me."

My phone pinged with a new email. I checked it, and my heart sank when I opened the attached PDF. Four logo proposals for my future shop.

"Aw … these are so eye-catching." William pressed his face closer to mine, his hand adjusting my phone so he could see the images better. "How can you pick just one? Hun, this is the sign that you must go."

"*This* is the sign I have more bills to pay now." I released a heavy sigh.

Even if I didn't find a new investor or secure a business loan, I had to pay for these. Crap. There went a month of loan payment.

"So?" William nudged me with his foot.

My loud sigh morphed into a groan. "I guess we can go. But he needs to send us the money first."

———

Andrew was talking on his phone when we returned to the living room. "I'll see you soon. I need to go." He hung up. "Are you coming?" he asked, his voice edged with worry and eyes full of a silent plea. And at that, something broke inside of me, and a stone rolled off my erected defense wall.

"Yes," William said with way too much enthusiasm. "But I'm going to accompany her."

"As any good brother should," Andrew said, with a slight nod.

I folded my arms over my chest and leaned on the balcony door. "Could you please tell us your exact plan?" I asked, hoping my voice sounded more determined than anxious. "Do we need visas? When are we leaving?"

"Well…" Andrew said, his face turned serious.

Oh no. No great plan started with the word *well*.

"Hold on." I held up a finger. "Is there a plan?"

"Well, yes."

That word again. Andrew had no plan. Or he thought he had a plan, but he was questioning it.

"He has no plan," I blurted out and faced William. "We're not going."

"You just said you would," Andrew said.

I spun back round to glare at Andrew. "That was because I thought you had an actual plan, but you don't."

"You didn't even let me speak—"

"You started it with '*well*.'"

"So what?" Andrew's eyebrows drew together.

With a roll of eyes, William released an exaggerated breath. "My sister has this theory that if someone starts their sentence with 'well' when they explain something, that means they're bullshitting."

"Christ. Fine. No more 'well.' But the plan is simple. Tomorrow morning, we fly to Santa Marta, meet with Professor Garcia, and hopefully unlock the bracelet—"

"Hold on," I said again. "What do you mean *hopefully*?"

"Well…" Andrew coughed. "I mean, there is a chance the bracelet won't unclasp."

"And then what?" I snapped. "I get to wear this bracelet like a prisoner in handcuffs? For how long?"

"Nobody asked you to put it on." Andrew's voice rose an octave.

I was about to tell him to fuck off and fetch me a bolt cutter.

"Hey, guys," William said in a calm voice, "can we go back to talking about tomorrow's plan?"

"I'm sure it will come off the second we unlock the chest," Andrew said, his eyes never leaving mine. "And then you'll never see me or it again."

With my hands planted on my hips, I turned away and focused on the indigo skies with orange hues on the horizon, my heart beating faster than it should have been. Going somewhere on the fly, especially to a country I knew next to nothing about, seemed like a bad idea. Was my karma playing a trick on me again? Too soon, even for her.

Chapter Two

At eight in the morning, the pool was mostly empty with only a few parents occupying lounge chairs while watching their kids splashing in the shallow end. William and I sat in the Triton bar outdoor area, having a carb-loaded breakfast—calories didn't count on vacation—and avoiding any mention of last night. We had done enough talking yesterday while we packed. William had presented me with his ridiculous, romanticized ideas about Dr. Andrew Jones and me. To the point that he had already married me to the man just so I wouldn't have to change any of my legal documents because our last names were the same.

Most people didn't think we were siblings. We were both tall, but William had hazel eyes, sandy brown hair with professional highlights, and a bowlike mouth, and I was green-eyed with chestnut hair and had a mouth that was often compared to Julia Roberts. Or a horse. I preferred the former. But the main difference between William and me was that he fell in love easily, just like our mother. An army of people did not have enough fingers to count how many lovers our mother had had, and the same went for William. Whereas I didn't care to fall in love at all. Been there once. Done that. No more, thank you.

"Hot professor alert." William wiped his mouth.

I looked over my shoulder. Dressed in a light-blue button-up shirt and oat-colored chinos, Andrew strode past the lifeguard, greeting the young man with a nod. The top two buttons of Andrew's shirt were undone, and his sleeves were rolled up to the elbow. Keeping my face blank, I did a one-shoulder shrug. I'd never admit this out loud, especially to William—because I'd never hear the end of it—but, my god, Dr. Jones was hot. My stomach fluttered, and I ignored it.

Andrew approached a petite blond woman wearing an enormous sun hat and oversized sunglasses, who was reading a book. A girl about six years old with dark curly hair in a ponytail emerged from the pool and ran up to him. Was that his family? His wife was pretty and slim, sporting a sexy white one-piece swimsuit. Andrew crouched next to the child and listened intently to whatever she babbled about while showing him her mermaid doll.

I felt the familiar ache of sorrow in the pit of my stomach. "Would you recognize our dad if you saw him today?" I asked, without taking my eyes off the young family.

"Probably not. Mom trashed all his pictures."

"How could a grown man leave two kids with the words 'Well, I'll just run out to get some smokes. You kids want anything?'" I picked up my newly refreshed coffee and took a slow sip. The bitter taste jolted me. *Yuck.* I stirred in a spoonful of sugar and added a splash of cream.

"Twenty-five years later, I'm still waiting for my M&Ms," William said.

"I'm not sure if I'm mad at him for leaving us or for leaving us with Mom."

"Why are you thinking about him now?"

"I don't know." I shrugged. I turned and surveyed Andrew and his daughter having an animated conversation, him holding the doll, no doubt saying something about mermaid treasures hidden at the bottom of an ocean. I bet he told amazing bedtime stories. "Sometimes I wonder … if our father had never left, would our life be any different?"

"Probably not."

Not able to resist, I glanced over my shoulder again. The little girl hugged Andrew, and he closed his eyes, wrapping his strong arms around her tiny body, not caring that her wet swimsuit soaked his shirt. He held her for scads of heartbeats before he pressed a sweet, long kiss to her head and then rose to his feet. She waved to him as she speed-walked to the deeper end of the pool and cannonballed into it. Andrew continued to chat with his attractive wife. Did she mind him going on a trip with another woman?

Last night I hadn't noticed whether Andrew wore a wedding band, but a man didn't have to wear a solid circle of gold to be a good husband and father. When Andrew and the woman finished talking, she reached out her hands to him, and he leaned into her.

I averted my eyes and shifted in my seat, not wanting to see them kiss. I shouldn't have been watching him and his family. I shook my head, trying to shrug off a strange feeling of disappointment. Why was I upset? Envy for not growing up in a family like his? Or was it guilt because I didn't want to have a family, fearing that I'd inevitably become like my mother?

"Why are you shaking your head?" William asked, his eyes glued behind me, no doubt watching the handsome couple.

"It's nothing."

William gave me his *I don't believe you* look.

"Are you done? We promised to meet him at the front of the hotel"—I checked my watch—"in ten minutes."

"Don't think I didn't notice your look." William smiled his Cheshire cat smile.

Dropping the linen napkin beside my plate, I rose and picked up my canvas tote bag. "Oh, wipe that stupid smile off your face. You noticed nothing."

Forty-five minutes later, we walked out of the hotel's main entrance. Behind us, a bellboy pushed a luggage cart overstuffed with designer suitcases. Leaning against the trunk of a taxi, Andrew waited for us, his arms folded over his chest. As we approached him, he took off his sunglasses and watched us wide-eyed.

"That's not all yours?" Andrew asked.

I stopped next to him, my small, blue and white polka dot Tumi suitcase by my side. Andrew said he would need us in Colombia for two days, so I chose minimum make-up, one extra pair of shoes, two pairs of panties, and two dresses. I only ever packed dresses for a beach getaway, in different sizes. Smaller and fitted for the beginning of vacation, and larger and more forgiving towards the end in anticipation of overeating and drinking.

"*This* is mine." I tapped my heel on my carry-on bag. "*Those* are William's."

"We're only going for one night." Andrew's surprised expression was adorable.

"You should have seen how much luggage he brought when we went on a two-week Mediterranean cruise. The ship barely stayed afloat."

"Reporting for duty," William chirped as he joined us by the car.

"You can't take all that." Andrew pointed at the cart. "The plane we're taking barely has enough space for us. Pack only what is necessary for today and tomorrow."

"It's all necessary," William said. "I can't go without any of it."

"Then you have to stay behind." Andrew placed his sunglasses back on his face and turned to me. "Are you ready?"

"I'm not going without him." I planted my fists on my hips.

Andrew groaned. "William, please pick only two bags." He slid into the front passenger seat. "Two *small* bags."

An hour later, smothered by heat and the reek of burnt jet fuel, three of us—and four of William's suitcases—stood on the tarmac in front of something that couldn't possibly have been considered a plane. The twin-propeller, six-seater aircraft resembled a mechanical Frankenstein pieced together with parts probably found at an airplane graveyard, the weathered paint struggling to do its chore to cover up the assembly job.

flab·ber·gasted | ˈflabərˌgastəd |

ADJECTIVE: My current state with my mouth agape, rooted to the spot.

ORIGIN: Right now, in front of our next ride.

"What's that?" William dabbed his forehead with a Kleenex.

"The finest plane I could find on short notice," Andrew answered, his voice lacking its earlier confidence.

William scoffed. "I'd hate to see the worst."

I faced Andrew and pulled off my sunglasses. "We're flying in that to Colombia?"

"Apparently so." Andrew's expression held equal halves of shock and terror.

I wasn't sure if I was happy or petrified that he was just as surprised as I was.

"I thought you were super rich or something," William said.

I wasn't a woman with high expectations, and any luxury I had in my life had been earned by hard work. By me. But if I had to be honest—and I wouldn't ever admit it out loud—since it seemed Dr. Andrew Jones had no issues throwing big wads of cash at us, I was expecting a private jet, a nice one, like the ones I saw in movies or on Instagram.

Under the false pretenses of a usable plane, this tin can probably had engines held together with duct tape. A short, tubby, middle-aged man with triple thick glasses on his nose, walked up to the plane. *Dear god, please don't let that be our pilot.* But my prayer went unanswered as the man opened the door and climbed into the front seat.

I shook my head slightly, then more vigorously. "No. No. No."

No way we were getting in that.

"Deal's off." I grabbed William's arm and turned to leave.

"Where are you going?" Andrew asked.

I swirled around. "Back to the resort."

"We have an agreement. You promised to go."

"And you promised a plane. This piece of junk is an impostor. Are you honestly expecting me or my brother to get in that thing? It should be sold for scrap."

"Yes. I agree it's not the nicest, but it works. Besides, we had a deal. I paid you." Andrew's large eyes seemed to double. "You can't back out now."

Who the hell did he think he was? Anger oozed out of my pores, mixing with my sweat.

I crossed my arms over my chest. "Do you think you can just buy me?"

"Don't be ridiculous. I'm not buying you," Andrew said, his ever-present, infuriating smirk tugging at his lips, but his eyes swirled with fury.

"You did offer money for her company," William chimed in. "It's like *Indecent Proposal.*"

I glared at William. "It is *not* at all like that movie."

William bit his bottom lip and nodded. "True. Robert Redford paid a million dollars."

I rolled my eyes, then returned my focus to Andrew. I wasn't angry with him. I was pissed at myself for harboring a small hope of saving my store.

"Dr. Jones." I took a calming breath. "I'll wire your money back to you, but we aren't going unless you provide something not piloted by Skipper, Kowalski, Rico, and Private."

"Who?" William would look confused, but his eyebrows didn't move due to Botox.

"Penguins," I said.

"Adriana, you're making a bigger deal of this than it is," Andrew said.

"What penguins?" William still didn't understand.

"*Madagascar*," Andrew and I parroted.

At that, I smiled. I was impressed he knew right off the bat which cartoon I meant. I adored *Madagascar* and had seen it a hundred times. Andrew had probably watched it with his daughter, whereas I'd enjoyed it alone, with a glass—fine, a bottle—of wine.

"Look." Andrew wiped the sweat off his forehead with the back of his hand. "I wouldn't have to deal with you if you hadn't put on a bloody bracelet that wasn't meant for you."

"It was sent to my room with my name on it."

"For the tenth time, it was my name, not yours," Andrew said in a controlled voice, but his face seethed.

"Yours. Mine. Whatever. It was delivered to me!" I spun and pulled on William's shirt sleeve.

William and I marched several yards toward parked taxis

outside the fenced-in area before Andrew ran around us and raised his palms.

"Don't make me beg. If you think something is wrong with that…"—Andrew waved his hands toward the scrap of metal behind him and pushed a word out of his mouth with difficulty—"plane, then we won't take William. For his safety. And ours." He exhaled. "God only knows, the weight of his luggage might plunge us from the sky."

A smile tugged at my lips again, but I pressed them together.

"I'm sorry, but my answer is no. That thing…" I turned for another look at the aluminum death trap. Nope. "That thing shouldn't be allowed to fly."

Andrew's head sagged, and so did his broad shoulders as we made our way around his tall figure. I understood the project was important to him, just like my store was to me, and he was enthusiastic about the possibility of discovering some great treasure, but I couldn't risk my life or William's. The best thing to do was to wire back the money I'd received this morning, return to the resort, enjoy our vacation, and then go back to my messed-up world so I could get my life together. To my—

"Fifty thousand dollars." Andrew stopped my thoughts in their tracks.

Shit. Shit. Shit.

That was a lot of money just for one night of my company. Wait. That didn't sound right. For two days of my help. That wasn't right either. I wasn't helping Andrew. On the contrary, I was a hindrance to his work. Either way, I wished I had more time to think about it. Could I run my business without a partner? Was it possible to figure out the interior design by myself, be my own marketing team, and even get an initial inventory on credit? No. This new offer wasn't sufficient to remodel the space. But it guaranteed enough time to look for a business partner or investor. This offer was intoxicating.

I scrutinized the plane one more time. If I closed one eye— or better, both of my eyes—it didn't look that bad. If it managed not to lose any vital parts in mid-flight, and we safely landed in Colombia, we could find a better plane to return on.

"How long is the flight?" I asked.

"Two and a half hours."

I shut my eyes. "Dadgummit."

Chapter Three

Each of us muttered obscenities as we crammed into the six-passenger aircraft. The interior was worn-out but thankfully clean and so small that Andrew's tall frame barely fit. His head touched the ceiling, and his knees crowded mine. He sat across from me, and William picked the seat to my right while all his luggage—secured and bundled together by a rope—occupied the space in front of him.

"Do you always travel in such luxury?" I asked, tightening the seat belt and then pulling my skirt as far down as it would go to my knees, which were pressed together and inserted between Andrew's spread legs, way too close to his crotch. To call this situation awkward was an understatement.

Andrew threw an unwelcoming glance my way, his face glistening with more sweat. He leaned his head back, taking in deep breaths through his nose and exhaling through his mouth. His phone rang, and a picture of the little girl from the pool filled the screen, with the name "Lulu" on the top.

"Hey, Little Mermaid," Andrew answered, his voice warm.

A high-pitched voice prattled something into his ear, and he smiled wide. "That sounds fabulous... Yes... Of course, I'll get you some when I come back... All right. I miss you, too."

There was a brief silence on the phone, and then a different, lower voice began saying something. I busied myself with setting my iPhone to airplane mode. I was curious to hear what was being said, but it was hard to understand. And most of all, I shouldn't care.

"That's good," Andrew said into the phone. "Yes, I will..." He looked out the window, listening. "Charlotte, you know I'll support anything you decide to do. Yes... I'll call you when I land. I love you, too." He hung up and then turned off his phone.

Charlotte. Silently, I rolled her name on my tongue. The name suited the beautiful, posh blonde. Where did they meet? Perhaps at an artsy-fartsy gala, or at a fancy fundraiser where only the wealthy or celebrities were invited. I'd attended many events like that for my job, and only when my then-boss, the CEO of Salzburg Distributing, couldn't go. I'd sweep into the charity event convinced my designer dress would help me fit in, but after an hour, it was obvious mine came from a rack whereas the other women had had theirs tailor-made. A knot tightened in my stomach as I remembered Greg's, my college ex, words that had engulfed my soul like an oil slick in the ocean, killing every living thing: no matter how successful I'd become, among people like Andrew and Charlotte, I would always be an impostor.

I had tried to make something out of my life and failed. My blood turned cold at the thought of the crazy mess I'd left in Atlanta, which I could now potentially avoid thanks to

Andrew having dropped into my world. Perhaps "dropped" was a bad word to think of as the plane picked up speed down the runway, creaking and shaking too much for my liking.

Andrew closed his eyes. More sweat covered his forehead, and his large hands gripped the tiny armrests, sunlight reflecting off his watch. This behavior was familiar to me. This man wasn't a good flier. Flying wasn't a fear for me, but I had many other phobias. Living off cereal again. Sleeping in unwashed bedding. Falling in love.

"So, Cambridge, fancy school," I said. "Did you go there?" Small talk could take his mind off his fear and give me some insight into the man I was about to spend two days with.

"Yes," Andrew said, not opening his eyes.

"William has a Bachelor of Science in Nursing from Emory University." I tightened the belt over my lap one more time. Talking about William was easy since he'd accomplished noteworthy things in his life. "It's a big university in Atlanta. Have you heard of it?" Andrew nodded. "He worked in a hospital for a couple of years until he and his buddy opened a prosperous skin and body clinic."

Turning the bracelet on my wrist, I waited for Andrew to inquire about William's clinic, but he was quiet. Okay. So, chatting to him would be as painful as blisters after wearing cute but ill-fitting shoes. The plane jerked, lurching us side to side for a second, and Andrew visibly swallowed, eyelids pressing together even harder.

"Your watch." I nudged Andrew's knee with my hand, needing him to focus on me. "It's old, isn't it?"

His eyes met mine. "Yes."

"Where did you get it?"

"It was my grandfather's."

The engines roared in my ears, making it harder to hear Andrew.

"That's neat," I said, shifting in my uncomfortable tiny seat. All I got from my grandparents was … nothing. My parents had met at a foster house when they were teenagers, and I guess they never cared to look for their families. I couldn't fault them for that. William and I cut Mom out of our life for failing as a mother. Her self-absorbed behavior ruined our childhood and drove our father away. We didn't care about her and not once did we try to find him.

"So, are you going back to the resort once we're done in Colombia?"

"It depends on what's inside the chest," he said, studying my face.

"And what would you guess is inside?"

"I'm not at liberty to discuss it."

I rolled my eyes. Fine. It didn't matter to me.

The airplane wheels left the ground, and the plane tilted up its nose, inching into the sky. The shaking stopped and the previous racket hushed, leaving only the muffled thrum of the two engines.

"Why'd you bring your family on vacation just to leave them behind?"

"I didn't plan this. My family and I were on holiday in Costa Rica." Andrew shifted in his seat, his thigh making brief contact with mine. "Two mornings ago, I received a call from Octavian Global regarding the chest, and was told to expect the bracelet with instructions."

"Why you? Is it because you were already in Central America?"

"No. I specialize in Latin American studies during the colonial period, with an interest in piracy in Spanish America."

"And you couldn't put it off until your vacation was done?"

"No. I couldn't." Andrew swallowed hard again.

Workaholic husbands and fathers weren't the worst, but not the best either. However, they came back to their families after they finished their work, unlike *some* parents. Soon after our father left, we started to receive a few hundred bucks in the mail twice a year with no note or return address. The donations came for six years and then stopped. Did our father die—if it was him—or did any love he had for us run dry? I didn't want to know. Even as kids, we knew keeping it a secret from Mom was better for our stomachs. Digesting expired cereal was easier than the brand-new pair of shoes or make-up she would have bought.

The plane tilted sideways as it turned, shifting our bodies with its movement. My left hand found an armrest, and I grabbed onto it.

"How were you able to arrange everything so quickly?"

The plane straightened its course. Andrew released the armrests and rubbed his hands up and down his thighs a few times. "I didn't. It was arranged for me."

"By oooky spooky Octavian Global group?" I whispered conspiratorially.

He nodded. The pale color of his face brought out the green in both of his irises. He looked vulnerable, and for an odd reason, I wanted to hug him and promise him everything would be fine.

"Is there a deadline to get the case unlocked?" I didn't care if there was one. All I cared about was returning in the promised time frame—preferably in one piece—and having him deposit the rest of the money.

"Yes. It's time sensitive."

"Why?"

"Do you always ask so many questions?"

"First." I crossed my arms over my chest. "You're dragging me along, so I feel like I'm entitled to ask as many questions as I want. Second, I'm trying to make conversation to take your mind off the fact that we're flying."

Andrew held my gaze for a long time before he relaxed *some*, dropping his shoulders. "I need to get to the chest before it's shipped to its auction winner tomorrow in the early afternoon."

"What are you planning to do with whatever is inside that box?" I moved in my seat, carefully avoiding touching his legs. "Doesn't it belong to the highest bidder?"

Andrew looked out the window. Was Andrew a sophisticated and educated burglar? I bit my tongue to stop myself from asking anything else. The less I knew, the less I had to lie about if this adventure led me to jail.

The engines hummed as the plane soared over slow-passing land. The densely populated areas turned into a green grid of farmland dotted with red-roofed houses, towering palm trees, and horses, but soon, the landscape transmogrified into rugged mountains blanketed by an untamed jungle.

William crunched on crackers. I stretched my hand to him

and flexed my fingers. He handed me a bag of trail mix, then rested his head against the headrest. Talking to him was out of the question, too. He had a minor fear of flying, and he dealt with it by listening to a suspenseful thriller—carefully picked with no airplane crashes. I offered my snack to Andrew first. He shook his head. We had two and a half hours before we'd reach our destination. This was going to be a long flight.

The aircraft bumped once, then dropped unexpectedly, shaking us in our seats. My heart jumped to my throat, practically bringing my snack with it. Did we lose the plane's tail? I gulped in a deep breath. *Whoosah*. Two out of three of us already had a fear of flying, no need for me to freak out, too.

I studied Andrew's classically handsome features with that sharp jawline. Even in his unsettled state, the teasing smirk still pulled at the corner of his lips, and for the first time I noticed a thin, barely noticeable scar zigzagged amongst his dark stubble. Was that why he always looked that way?

"What happened to your mouth?" I asked.

Andrew clenched his hands into fists, then relaxed them. "When I was a kid, I trespassed and entered an abandoned house, fell through a rotten wooden floor, and ripped my face from here to here." He inclined forward as he pointed a finger to the middle of his cheek and traced it to the corner of his mouth. "The scar is mostly faded, but the cut damaged muscles inside."

I leaned in to examine his face and was struck by how sensual and strawberry-red Andrew's mouth was. My traitorous fingers itched to touch it to find out if it was also soft. His lips parted slightly, and a warm tremor ran down inside my ribcage. My ability to pick out scents was crucial for my old job, but at the moment, it threw me off my axis. Andrew smelled delicious, bold, and masculine with a touch of sweet bergamot. Pheromone and testosterone.

Wait. Were those even fragrance notes?

I glanced up at his eyes, and he was staring at me. A coy smile pulled at his lips. He gazed at me for a long time, and my heart stuttered, my entire body shimmered with giddy delight. This feeling was so wrong. He was a married man, and there was nothing to swoon over but the idea of saving my store.

We moved back in our seats at the same time.

"I bet you got a lot of 'wipe that smirk off your face' growing up?"

Andrew smiled. And damn it. The cabin was chilly a second ago, but now I needed a fan.

I knotted my hands on my lap. "Is there anything you want to ask me?"

He tilted his head and zeroed in on my fingers. "How did you meet your fiancé?"

"This isn't real." I pointed at the ring. "I mean, it's a genuine diamond, but there's no fiancé attached. I got a bargain during a jewelry store closing sale."

"Why?" Andrew's eyebrows pulled together.

"I bought it to reduce unwanted sexual advances from strangers. It's my man repellent."

"And it works?"

I shrugged. "I didn't do an extensive study by going out with and without this ring. A magazine article suggested it. I guess it works sometimes, but some men are pure pigs and ignore it."

"Why did you buy a diamond instead of cubic zirconia?

You could have gotten a bigger stone. The size of it would intimidate men."

I laughed and spun the ring on my finger. "Believe me. Size doesn't matter. They just don't care."

"What if this ring keeps away your true love?" he asked, his voice deep and earnest. His sincerity went straight to a void in my chest, stirring the familiar ache, but I ignored it and laughed again.

"Call me a cliché," I held his stare as I spoke, "but I don't believe in love. I did once, but not anymore."

Andrew frowned. I could have explained my reasons and defended my motives, but did I care what he thought? Nope. After this two-day trip, we'd go our separate ways. I dumped the last of my trail mix into my mouth. Once I was done chewing, I lifted my right arm, which had the bracelet. "Am I keeping this once we're done with the chest?"

He arched an eyebrow. "What do you think?"

"Its strange beauty has grown on me. I'm afraid I might actually miss it."

"It should unlatch at the same time as the chest unlocks."

The plane jerked, then banked, jolting my heart. Andrew squeezed his eyes shut. The aircraft leveled itself, and I slowly blew out a breath.

"You know," I said, my body tightening, and I struggled to keep my voice calm, "they have drugs you can take before a flight. It takes your mind off the fear." I wouldn't mind having some myself.

Andrew nodded. Sweat visibly built up on his forehead again. "It works on flights for over seven hours, and I need a clear mind when we land. The medication makes me drowsy."

"Good thing England has a great train system. You can get from London to pretty much anywhere in Europe." I crumbled the empty snack wrapper and hid it in a side pocket of my bag. The aircraft dropped again. What the hell? I knew it was a bad idea to get on this piece-of-shit plane. Andrew's nostrils flared as he breathed in and out.

"Do you want me to stop talking?" I asked and hoped he would say no because I felt a *tad* anxious about this flight and needed to ramble.

He shook his head, deepening the crease between his eyebrows. "Keep talking."

"Okay…" I tapped my fingers on my thigh. I could give him a pitiful childhood story about how our father had left us when I was seven, and we grew up basically without a mother because she was busy dating men like she was training for the Olympics. Or I could talk about my old job.

"How about wine? Do you want to learn about it?" I gently bumped Andrew's knee with mine, and he looked at me. The line between his eyebrows disappeared, and his eyes focused on me. I tucked a loose strand of hair behind my ear. He watched me with that almost smile, in a way that no other man had ever looked at me before. Not a predatory peer that gave me an unsettling feeling, not a piercing or judgmental stare that made me feel like dirt. His eyes reflected a curiosity as if he had just noticed me for the first time. My skin grew warm under his regard.

He blinked. "Sure."

I launched into a history of wine production, starting with ancient tribes from China making fermented rice and honey and fruit wine. For Andrew's sake, I kept it brief, and then I dove into a deep explanation of vinification. I loved talking about wine production, educating people about types of wine, and how to become better at choosing one. Most people grew bored with me and changed the subject after fifteen minutes, but even after an hour, Andrew wasn't strapping himself to a parachute and searching for an exit door. He was a hundred percent engaged in this discussion, listening with rapt attention and asking questions I gladly answered.

Toward the end of our flight, without volunteering details about why the contract with my investor had fallen through, I shared my business idea and how, because of the Colombian trip, I could now look for a new investor and hopefully avoid having to execute a painful decision to sell the building. The more I talked about my store, the more I became grateful for meeting Andrew. Of course, I wasn't sure if he felt the same way. He was losing money by dragging William and me on this trip, and we were liabilities, too.

"Why did you offer me so much money?" I shifted in my seat, searching for a nonexistent, comfy position. "Are you so rich that you don't know what to do with your money or is there someone sponsoring your trip, carelessly tossing cash around?"

"Octavian Global and I have worked together for a long time. We believe rare historic objects belong in a museum, and recognize that making that happen can be a costly endeavor."

"Are you saying you don't have a single thing in your house that is historic and unique?"

"I own a few things, but they aren't necessarily extraordinary or..." He sighed. "What I'm after is a fortune that was hidden from people for hundreds of years."

A stupid grin grew on my face. "Tell me," I said, leaning forward in my seat, "do you own a whip?"

"What?" Andrew's eyebrows went up.

"And a brown Fedora?"

He stared at me as if I had turned into an ogre, then smiled. "For a moment I thought you were changing the subject to some fetish you have."

My face lit on fire, but I said, "You didn't answer my question."

Andrew laughed. "No, I don't own either."

"Too bad." My lips stretched into a huge smile. "I think you'd look good in it."

I was flirting with him. That wasn't me. I wasn't a flirtatious person. This must have been the result of constantly fearing for my life during this flight.

The pilot yelled something in Spanish.

"What did he say?" I asked.

"We're out of fuel," Andrew deadpanned.

Say what?

I gaped at Andrew; my muscles tensed so hard they hurt.

"You should see your face." Andrew chuckled, shaking his head. "He said we're approaching the airport and should land in the next five minutes."

"Oh my god! You're such an asshole." I smacked Andrew's arm.

The landing felt like coffee beans shaken vigorously in a can.

We were the beans. Nonetheless, we landed. And any landing I could walk away from was a great one.

Andrew turned on his phone, and dings of incoming messages poured in like a melody. I left my mobile on airplane mode to avoid the fifteen-dollar daily charge. I'd check my email when I found Wi-Fi. Andrew pressed his phone to his ear.

"Hi. We just landed," he said, looking out the window. "It was fine." He laughed weakly. "Yeah, not as bad as St. Helena… I'll talk to you later. Kiss Lulu from me. I love you." He hung up, faced me, and caught me staring.

Crap.

I averted my eyes, pretending to peer over his shoulder at a sun-beaten yellow and orange control tower.

We wheeled our luggage on an uneven cement sidewalk toward a one-story blue building with a few white pickup trucks parked next to it. As soon as we walked inside an air-conditioned space, my eyes immediately watered from heavy cigarette and cigar smoke. I hoped we didn't have to stay long. A hefty man, wearing a dark green uniform and a sour attitude, sat in a booth behind a tall plexiglass wall that had a narrow opening at the bottom for documents. He barked something in Spanish and Andrew replied warmly, sliding our passports into the opening, a thin stack of money squashed between them.

WTF! Was that a bribe?

Of course not, right? Andrew was just purchasing our visas. Was Colombia one of the nations that issued a tourist visa on arrival? Nausea roiled in the pit of my stomach, and I wiped clammy hands on my dress. It could have been nerves or the nasty air.

After what seemed like forever, the Colombian officer stated something, then gave me a long stare, then William. Andrew spoke again, his beaming smile never leaving his face. With a loud boom, the man stamped all three passports and slid them back. Andrew thanked him and nodded for us to follow him outside through the main entrance.

"Is everything okay?" I hurried after Andrew, who was marching in the direction of a row of parked cars. "He didn't look pleased."

"Everything's fine," he said as he strode toward the only yellow cab.

Power lines zigzagged above the busy road. People crowded the street, carrying grocery bags, sitting in plastic café chairs, or scrolling on their phones while standing at a dingy bus stop. Shops and cafés were painted in shades of yellow, blue, and purple, and in different stages of deterioration. Some buildings were in better upkeep than others, but all had iron bars across windows and doors, and some had circular barbed wire on their roofs. *Lovely*. Hopefully, wherever we stayed tonight would be in a nicer part of town.

"Last night, I read that tourists are supposed to arrive at Medellin or Bogotá airport to go through immigration," I said. "This place doesn't look like either of those cities. Did you bribe that man?"

We stopped at the car and a man climbed out to stand beside the open trunk.

William pulled me into a side hug and stretched out his arm, holding his phone. "Our first selfie in Colombia. Say cheese." He grinned at the camera while I scowled at Andrew, who was showing the driver a piece of paper, presumably explaining where we needed to go. The man nodded and climbed back into the driver's seat. Andrew loaded his bag, then took hold of my suitcase, but I didn't let go.

"Explain your questionable behavior with border control, or I'll be happy to fly back to Costa Rica."

"There'll be time later to answer your questions. Now, please let go of your bag."

We both knew I was bluffing. Damn it. I needed that money. I relaxed my grip, marched around the car, and slumped into the back seat. William helped Andrew load his luggage, then slid in next to me.

"This looks like a cute town," he said.

"I don't have a good feeling about this." My stare bored into Andrew's back as he stood outside and typed a message on his phone.

"You said the same thing when we flew into Moscow," William said, looking for a seatbelt and then giving up because there wasn't one.

My hand nervously twisted the bracelet on my wrist. "We didn't have to bribe anybody to enter the country."

Andrew took the front passenger seat and said, "¡Vámonos¡"

Never in my life had I wished more that I'd paid better attention in Spanish class in high school.

Chapter Four

The taxi zipped through the traffic as if our driver was making up the driving rules as he went while simultaneously rattling nonstop in Spanish. Perhaps he prayed because he was scared of grazing cars, jumping into oncoming traffic lanes only to swerve back into our lane, nearly missing a collision, and making me squeak *"fuck!"* each time. Wind from his open window tore through my unsecured hair, thwacking it against my face and making me eat some of it, too. My hands grabbed the oh-shit handle with so much force that I was sure with the next turn it would rip off.

Someone's phone rang.

Unfazed by this death-on-wheels situation, Andrew fished his phone out of his pocket and swiped to answer.

"Hi, care bear," he answered with a smile in his voice. "Well, that's exciting. Did you enjoy it?" He listened, his body hardly swaying with car movements as if he were riding in a Rolls-Royce, whereas I was inside a tumbling dryer. On a roller coaster. Sideways.

"We are on our way to a museum," he said. "Yes, similar to the one we visited in London." He was quiet for some time. "I love you, too. Send my love to your mum."

My heart expanded with warmth at how sweet he was to his little girl, and then it shrunk back to its prune size. If my father had ever expressed any love for me, I'd been too young to remember it. Andrew hung up, looked out the window, and took a deep breath.

For another ten minutes, we flew down narrow streets until the taxi made the last turn onto a cobblestone street and stopped next to a prominent three-story building with massive columns. Andrew spoke to the driver for several seconds and then twisted in his seat to face us.

"We shouldn't be long. The driver will wait for us," he said, then threw the door open and exited the car.

Oh, for crying out loud. I would rather walk than have another ride with that crazy chauffeur. I ran my fingers through my hair a few times, trying to calm down the outer— and inner—craziness the previous twenty minutes had produced. On shaky legs, I plodded to where William and Andrew were waiting for me.

"Are you okay?" William asked me as I got closer. "You look a bit pale."

"I think I need to see a surgeon to untangle my organs after that ride," I mumbled.

His eyes went wide. "Wasn't that fun?"

I shot him an *are you out of your mind* glare. "That was *not* fun at all."

William gripped my forearm and leaned in. "Just kidding.

I'm in serious need of new underpants. If only I'd been allowed to bring all my luggage…"

Leaving the taxi idling on the street, we went up the grand stairs and entered the Museo de Historia. The hallway we filed into had little conditioned air, if any. The time-worn parquet extended down a long corridor with various doors to the left and right and a staircase at the end. The building appeared to be empty, just like its ticketing counter, but then swift steps resonated, and a stubby, round, older man with dark eyebrows and a gray, neatly trimmed beard and hair marched in our direction, his right hand stretched out in front of him.

"Dr. Jones, great to see you again," his voice echoed over to us. "So glad you could come on such short notice."

Andrew clasped the man's hand with his own. "Dr. Carlos Garcia, this is Adriana and her brother William. Adriana, William, this is Dr. Garcia, my father's great friend and one of my best mentors. Carlos and I have been on many memorable journeys."

Dr. Garcia laughed and tugged on his bow tie. "Yes, many wonderful adventures. Some of us thought we would never see our loved ones again. Good times." He took off his glasses and wiped his eyes. "We can catch up over dinner tonight, and I'll tell you about some of them. Now, Andrew, did you bring the bracelet?"

Andrew cleared his throat and turned to me. With his eyes, he indicated to me to show the bracelet to Dr. Garcia. "Yes, but…"

With a squeamish look on my face, I outstretched my arm.

The old man put his glasses back on, took my hand into his soft one, and examined the bracelet. "Marvelous work, just marvelous. I just have one question." He straightened. "Why did you put it on?"

My cheeks turned hot with embarrassment, and my eyes jumped from him to Andrew, then back to him. "There was a bit of confusion with the delivery. I thought it was for me, and I was wrong, and then Andrew couldn't figure out how to take it off and—"

"I believe we can open the chest while it's on her," Andrew said. "According to all the information I was able to find, keepers wore it on a wrist, and just as the chest unlocks, the bracelet unlatches too."

"For security reasons, wouldn't they want it on their wrist all the time?" William asked.

"No, they needed to be able to pass it to the next keeper." Dr. Garcia pursed his lips, his focus on the bracelet. He moved his head from side to side, humming as if thinking about what Andrew had just said, then smiled. "All we can do is try. Follow me."

We shadowed him through a gallery with sculptures of many sizes, then we turned and proceeded through a huge room with collections of tapestries and textiles. He stopped by a massive door and fished a key ring out of his side pocket. Selecting one, he unlocked the door and ushered us down the stairs into a basement office overstuffed with stacks of paper, crates, and shelves that groaned under the weight of thick books and binders.

Dr. Garcia pushed his way between us and stopped at a large desk. "Here is the chest," he said, puffing.

In the center of the desk sat a massive black metal box decorated with an intricate network of carvings. Four serpent-like creatures coiled their bodies around it, their heads coming to the top and resting at an indentation in the center. It was nothing like what I was expecting. In my mind, it should have been a wooden trunk with a dome top like I often saw in museums or pirate movies. This box was intimidating, with an aura of menace. I wouldn't touch it with a ten-foot pole.

"Now, Adriana, come closer, if you don't mind." Dr. Garcia motioned to me. "This should be simple. You need to turn your arm and press this part"—with his index finger, he touched the crown on the bracelet—"inside this indentation here." He pointed to a spot on the chest.

Simple enough.

I gave my purse to William and walked over to examine the mysterious box.

"It seems so unfriendly." I circled it, checking out the wondrous artwork. Fifty thousand dollars might not be worth me losing my arm. The snakes' heads could snap at my wrist, breaking it, or their venom dissolve my skin and bones. Or worse, suck the life out of me and turn me into a shriveled body like Imhotep in *The Mummy*. "These things look like they can come alive at any moment."

"Nothing will come alive," Andrew said.

He was right. I knew I shouldn't let my imagination get the best of me, but I had a very real fear it would explode if I did something wrong.

"What if it's booby trapped?" I glanced over my shoulder at Andrew.

"It's not," Andrew and Dr. Garcia said in unison.

With my heart rate up a notch, I glanced at each man in the

room. They all waited on my next move with an air of expectancy. Even William seemed to hold his breath.

"Okay." I exhaled, leaned forward, reached my arm over the box, and then lowered it with the center stone pointing down. The bracelet snugly fit into the cold crater. One second passed. Two seconds passed. Nothing happened. And nothing sprang to life.

"Now what?" I asked.

"Now press on it." Andrew moved towards the table and pressed his hands on the edge of it as he took a closer look.

I did what he said. There was a faint click. My breath caught in my throat. William took in a sharp, loud gasp.

And nothing.

No sound of turning metal wheels. No clicking of unlocking locks. No movement of scaly bodies.

Andrew bent his knees until his eyes were on the same level as the top of the metal box. William brought my purse to his chest and hugged it, biting his bottom lip. *For real?* Was this that exciting to him?

"William?" I said. "Remember to breathe."

"I just can't wait to see what's inside," he squealed with the thrill. I rolled my eyes.

"Aren't you a tad curious?" Andrew asked.

It took me a second to realize he was talking to me. I met his gaze, and my stomach fluttered. His stare held an emotion, but I couldn't identify it. Was he hoping I cared about what was inside this darn box? Would I hurt his feelings if I said no?

At this precise moment, I should have been on a beach holding a coconut cocktail. Instead, I was in an air-condition-less building, with my wrist pressed against a threatening-looking box—that might or might not be booby-trapped.

I smiled my liar smile and said, "Of course, I'm curious."

"Why is it not doing anything?" Dr. Garcia pulled a handkerchief from the inner pocket of his jacket and wiped his forehead. "Dr. Jones, do something." He sounded more frustrated than the situation called for.

"Keep your arm in place," Andrew said. While still squatting, he moved sideways and bumped my thigh with his shoulder. I shimmied aside, giving him some space. His left hand came over my wrist, and he applied pressure to the bracelet. The warmth of his touch radiated through my skin, traveling up my arm and spreading over my body. I closed my eyes for a moment, relishing this forgotten sensation.

There was a metallic click and then another. My eyes went wide, and I stared at the box. My pulse racing with ... did I dare to say with excitement?

Another click.

And then one more.

And then nothing else happened.

"It didn't open," I said.

"Thank you for pointing out the obvious," Andrew mumbled, with a deep crease between his eyebrows.

"I don't understand." Dr. Garcia scurried to the table and peered at the box. "Something should have happened."

"Are you sure you have the right bracelet?" William said.

"Yes," Dr. Garcia said. "Augustine Pérez had several chests like these, and the only way to open them was with the bracelet he made as a key for his wife, Maria." He sunk into a reclining chair, dropping his arms on his lap. "I don't understand."

Andrew's hand was atop my wrist, and he shuffled more, pressing his shoulder against my thigh. I would have moved away, but my arm wasn't long enough to reach the stupid box.

"How long do I need to stand like this?" I asked.

"Just a few more seconds." Applying pressure to my wrist, Andrew rose to his full height, and with his right hand, he pulled a desk lamp closer and turned it on. He scanned different parts of the chest, his eyebrows drawn together. While he was studying the mysterious trunk, I studied him.

My mouth went dry.

"Adriana," he whispered without looking at me.

"Yes?" I whispered back.

"You're staring at me."

My nose twitched.

Dang it.

My nervous tic was back. Growing up, I twitched so much that kids teased me on a daily basis and gave me the nickname "twitchy". As I got older I got better at controlling it, so today was the first time it had twitched like this in many years. I turned away, pretending I had to wipe my nose.

"Don't move." Andrew's right hand came over my wrist before he removed his other one. "We need to keep a steady pressure on the bracelet as I go to the other side."

His words were so close to my face, they caressed my cheek and released an army of goosebumps. Keeping the weight on my wrist, Andrew brought his left arm above and around me, enveloping me in a partial hug. He shifted behind me, brushing his chest against my back, his—

Holy Mary, sweet mother of God. I couldn't breathe as my brain focused only on the spot where my largest body part— my butt—and Andrew's … most likely large body part, came in contact.

Time slowed, then halted, tipping the earth on its axis. This was so inappropriate. This was wrong on so many levels. And I enjoyed it.

This lovely, married man was just doing his job, trying to find the priceless treasure to share with the world, and here I was, mapping out where his body touched mine. I was *sooo* going to hell for this. When did the room become so freakishly hot? Heat rose from the tip of my toes to the top of my head; a couple more degrees and my skin would fuse to the bracelet. I should have stopped any unnecessary touching, but since my brain ceased to function, I stood statue still.

"Quite a dance you're doing there," William commented, and I could hear suppressed laughter in his tone.

I sucked my stomach in and pushed my hips forward. Andrew cleared his throat and finally passed by me. He reached with his left hand and rested it on the bracelet before removing his right hand.

"As we apply pressure, we also need to press these stones," Andrew said, pointing at smaller gems on the bracelet, "in a certain order, like pressing buttons on a security panel."

"Okay, so start pressing them," I said when my brain rebooted, and my vocal system worked again.

Andrew's fingers pushed on the gems in various ways before they stilled, and he stepped back from the table, his hand leaving my wrist, cold instantly replacing his touch. "I don't know the pattern," he said. "Or this is the wrong bracelet."

"But it can't be." Dr. Garcia got to his feet. "All the research papers, along with the interpretation of Augustine's diaries we have, point to this chest and this bracelet."

Andrew faced a wall with a narrow window opening to a sidewalk.

"Let me get the papers." Dr. Garcia hurried to a cabinet and threw a drawer open. "The pattern should be mentioned somewhere. We can figure it out. We just need more time."

"Which we don't have," William said with a voice of authority as if he was part of this conversation. My hand was pressing into the chest since I wasn't sure if I could move or not.

"Can someone *please* tell me what you think is inside?" I said.

"A map, my dear," Dr. Garcia said while rummaging through the filing cabinet. "Directions to the location of a great treasure."

Apparently, Carlos *was* at liberty to share this information, unlike another professor in this room.

"We'll read through these again. The answer has to be here." Dr. Garcia lifted a hefty plastic bin onto the desk and pulled out folders. "You and I can go over everything," he said to Andrew. "Stay up all night if we must. We have until tomorrow at one in the afternoon before they collect the chest."

Andrew returned to the desk, picked up a manila folder, and opened it. He paused when he glanced at me. "You can remove your hand."

Relieved and disappointed at the same time, I stepped back and took my purse from William. "So, what do we do now?"

"Wander for a few in the museum," Andrew said, scrutinizing the papers in his hand. "I'll find you soon."

———————

For an hour, William and I meandered in and out of halls, enjoying different Colombian historical artifacts and artwork, eventually making our way into a gallery dedicated to Augustine Pérez. It displayed a collection of jewelry, locks and keys, parts of shipwrecks, old notebooks, letters, and much more. Several beautiful pencil sketches along one wall drew my attention. These sketches held so much detail that, at first, I thought they were photos. One atmospheric drawing with lifelike intensity illustrated a town square with a church in the middle and rolling hills in the background; another depicted a ranch with a large house in the Spanish style with horses running before it; the third portrayed a palace at the base of a towering mountain, and the fourth displayed a tall waterfall surging into a small lake. Details of the waterfall were so vivid its roaring sound almost reverberated in my ears, but the rest of the sketch was incomplete with faint lines of what appeared to be the beginning of tree branches. I fished my iPhone out of my purse and snapped a photo of each artwork.

"This is fascinating," William said, staring up at a carved wooden figurehead from the bow of a ship. "But all the information is in Spanish, and I don't understand what it says."

"The gift shop has a book in English about Augustine Pérez," Andrew said, his voice startling me.

"Hey." I turned, hiding my phone back in my purse because I had no clue if we were allowed to take pictures in this museum or not. In my defense, I didn't use the flash. "How did it go with the Pandora's box?"

But I knew the answer by the way he stood in the doorway with his shoulders slumped forward and a disappointed expression on his face.

"Not well," Andrew said, shaking his head. "We need more time to go over Augustine's journal to identify the pattern."

"How many more hours?" I checked my watch. It was past two in the afternoon, and hunger and boredom had replaced my earlier excitement.

"You should go to the hotel and enjoy the rest of the day."

"And you? Are you coming with us?"

"We only have until tomorrow afternoon, so every minute counts. I might stay here all night." He ran his hand through his hair. "If something surfaces, I'll come and get you."

Andrew walked us to the taxi, briefly stopping at the shop where he purchased the book about Augustine Pérez for William. Outside, he explained to the driver to take us to the Complejo Del Gran Castillo Blanco resort.

I never thought I would offer a quick thank you prayer for traffic, but because of jammed roads, our driver drove slower and calmer this time around. Well, the word "calmer" was a stretch. The frequent bursts of Spanish words accompanied by enthusiastic hand gestures meant he wasn't happy about the line of cars in front of him.

As we traveled farther from the museum, down streets rich with history and the finest example of Spanish colonial architecture, my eyes fed on the beauty of the variegated buildings, bougainvillea draped over their balconies.

A few minutes later, we passed through a set of gates, the driver raising his hand to greet a security guard, and continued meandering through sanctuary-like, lush grounds. After a crapshoot plane, I feared Andrew's promised "nice" hotel would be the Colombian version of Motel 6. And god, I was glad to be wrong. The resort was superlative with a state-of-the-art hotel with spellbinding white-sand beaches flanked by palm trees.

Once we checked in, William and I stored our luggage in separate rooms, ordered the most popular Colombian cocktail with Aguardiente—it turned out not my favorite because it tasted like licorice (gag)—and explored the property.

Later that evening, waves calmly rolled onto the sand below a restaurant deck where William and I enjoyed chilled Chardonnay and mouth-watering seafood paella with saffron rice cooked in lobster broth.

"This adventure has turned out to be a delightful addition to our Costa Rica vacation." William stretched his legs under the table, the retiring sun casting a warm glow on his face. "The resort is amazing, the food is out of this world, and OMG, look at that view."

"Please don't call it an adventure. This is strictly an opportunity to make easy money."

"I get no money out of this deal, so I can call it whatever I want." He gave me a cheeky grin.

While he was pleased with the breathtaking sunset and local cuisine, my brain was an Instant Pot on the verge of a blowout. Earlier in the hotel room, I'd connected to the free Wi-Fi, and my inbox had exploded in front of my eyes with emails from Roswell Planning & Zoning Department, an interview request from a local newspaper, and bills from the interior design agency, marketing group, and engineering firm totaling nine thousand dollars. I finished my wine in two gulps. What if Andrew wasn't able to unlock the chest because he couldn't figure out the code? Or what if it was the wrong bracelet altogether? Was the deal off? I needed the promised fifty thousand dollars. Without it, as soon as I returned to Atlanta, my building—gosh, that sounded so good, *my building*—would have to be placed back on the market. And who knew when it would sell? I had some savings, but barely enough to cover one month's mortgage payment. An involuntary shiver ran over my body. I'd have to return to Salzburg Distributing and beg for my old job back. My previous salary—presuming I got it—was enough to not default on the loan and get me a small rental, so William could get his condo all to himself.

"Do you think…" I bit off a cuticle. "Even if they can't open the chest … do you think Andrew will still pay me?"

William sent me an unsure look, then his expression changed, and he smiled. "I'm sure he will. You did your part. It's not your fault he can't unlock it."

"What if it's because I put the bracelet on?"

"Think about Pérez, the pirate, who, by the way, according to the book Andrew bought me, was quite a romantic and madly in love with his wife, Maria. Because of severe motion sickness, Maria could not travel far, so, on some trips, Augustine returned with an extra ship packed with gifts around the world just for her: Greek statues, French furniture, ivory carvings from West Africa, and even an ancient Roman mosaic floor. What a murderous sweetheart." He waved his hand in the direction of the ocean. "Sorry, I got sidetracked. Back to your worry about the bracelet. Maria wore it on her wrist, and it's not in a grave, so it came off somehow."

Yes. That made sense.

"But," I said, "she also knew the correct pattern. What if she unlocked the bracelet, took it off, and only then used it to open the chest?"

William linked his hands behind his neck and stared out at the sunset. "Possible. But Andrew strikes me as a person who would honor his word no matter what."

"I hope you're right."

Chapter Five

I n the morning, I found Andrew on the same restaurant patio where William and I had eaten dinner. A warm sunrise had replaced the breathtaking sunset. I wore a white cotton flared dress with tiny blue flowers on the bottom, whereas Andrew wore the same clothes from yesterday, his previously crisp shirt now wrinkled. His hair was disheveled as if he hadn't even run his finger through it this morning to make it presentable, but he'd shaved.

A somber expression clouded Andrew's face, his eyebrows drawn together and his lips turned into a frown. Even his smirk wasn't happy. He read a menu and sipped his coffee. As I approached the table, he glanced up. His mouth curved into a full-beam smile that reached his beautiful eyes, softening his tired look. A pleasant sensation passed through me at his reaction. My presence had taken him out of a dark place and brought him into the light. I did that. I've never seen a man respond to me in the same manner. Should I leave and come back again, just so I could watch it one more time? And then annoyance slammed into me harder than an out-of-control bus. Why was I even enjoying this? He was married. And even if he wasn't married, I shouldn't toy with the idea of… Best not even go there.

Maybe the look meant he'd found the pattern so we all could return to our lives.

Me to my mess. Him to his lovely family.

My smile wanted to fail me, but I kept it on.

"Good morning." I reached the table, and Andrew got up and pulled out the chair for me. "Thank you."

"How was your night?" He pushed the chair in as I sat and took his spot to my right.

"Fine. And yours? Were you able to get much sleep, or were you up all night breaking into the chest?" I picked up the menu and scanned the English side, seeing no words as my brain struggled to play catch-up. All I saw was Andrew's expression when he'd noticed me.

"Where's your brother?"

"He's on his way. So, what did you find out last night?" I lowered the menu. "Or do you want William to be present so you don't have to repeat yourself?"

"We don't have to wait for him. I'll tell you now."

A server appeared and hovered over us, pouring coffee for me. Andrew pressed his full lips together, waiting for her to leave so he could speak.

"Could you please bring a mango nectar for my brother?" I said to the young lady, pointing at the empty seat. "He's running late."

She nodded and then left. Andrew cleared his throat. "I don't need to open the chest," he said, defeat tinging his voice.

"Why not?" I added a splash of cream and a spoonful of sugar to my coffee. Worry burned a hole in my gut. What did it mean for our deal?

"Augustine commissioned several types of bracelets—some for chests and the rest for other purposes. After a further comparison of Dr. Garcia's research papers and mine, we detected the cryptanalyst's errors and concluded that they had deciphered the letters incorrectly. Augustine meant 'a trusted person' not 'a secured trunk' has the treasure. The most trusted person would be his brother, Jorge Pérez. Jorge had enough influence to smuggle and hide all Augustine's treasure under everyone's noses."

"What about the chest? You no longer need it?"

"Augustine and Maria had two sons, Simón and Gabriel. This particular chest was a wedding gift from Augustine to Gabriel. It could contain something from the Asiento de Padua ship, but most likely it's empty."

I stirred the coffee, brought it to my lips and sipped. My god. Compared to this heavenly juice, coffee back home was made of NFL players' sweaty underwear. I closed my eyes and moaned. "This is so good. I could stay in Colombia just for this coffee."

"I'm glad to hear," Andrew said, wary, "that you might be persuaded to enjoy it for a few more days."

I stilled, my mind refused to process the words that had come out of his gorgeous mouth. Did I call Andrew's mouth gorgeous? No. Not gorgeous. It was just a mouth. My brain had no business adding any adjectives to it. I took another sip of liquid gold. I would happily drink it all day long, even though it might cause me to have a heart attack.

"Adriana, are you paying attention?"

My eyes snapped open, and I gave Andrew an unruffled stare. The face staring back at me was tired but hopeful. "You said something about how you'll continue your search but will send William and me back home with bags of this coffee so I can enjoy it for a few more days."

Andrew shifted in his seat, his knee gently bumping into mine. "I know we agreed on two days, but I need more time. Just a couple of days."

I moved my leg to avoid unnecessary contact, folded my arms on the table, and leaned toward him. "Dr. Jones, you're breaking our verbal contract. We agreed you'd pay me fifty thousand dollars for two days. And now you want me to stay for a few more?"

He angled toward me, mirroring my pose, his elbow touching mine. "Yes."

"And if I don't agree?" I said in a low voice.

"Then I'll have to press charges against you because you stole the artifact from me." A playful smile tugged on his lips.

He was bluffing. There was no way he would do it. Would he?

"I'm sure I could convince the jury it was a misunderstanding. I'd play innocent."

"Are you? Innocent?" He bit his bottom lip, raising an eyebrow.

Starting from the point where our arms met heat raced through my body. Jesus. Were we flirting? This was wrong, but somehow it felt so good.

I was a bad person.

Stop this immediately.

Sometimes, my conscience needed to mind her own business.

"All right," I said, unable or unwilling to move. "Where would we go next, Dr. Jones?"

"We need to visit San Antonio Church," he said. "I think it has an undisclosed vault where Jorge might have hidden Augustine's treasure for his brother."

"You *think*?" I cocked my right eyebrow to mimic him.

He nodded slightly.

"And where is this church?"

"San Sierra. It's a village about five hours' drive away. Before you say no, I have a proposition for you. I'll pay twenty-five thousand for each extra day. It's not in my interest to lose money, so I promise you, I'll try to finish my research as fast as I can, and then you'll never have to see me again."

For some maddening reason, his last sentence caused a faint twinge somewhere in the vicinity of my heart, but I ignored it.

Wait, did he say twenty-five more? Per day? That was a lot of money for basically nothing.

I had two choices: I could spend another ten days at the posh Costa Rican resort where I would wake up every morning in a cold sweat, freaking out about my failed business because the fifty grand that Andrew paid me for these two days would hold me afloat only for a few months; or I could spend an extra few days pretending to be Short Round from *Indiana Jones*, enjoying Colombian culture, their wonderful food and coffee, and getting paid a lot more money. If I were to stay here for four more days, I could *possibly* keep my building, renovate it *and* purchase—minimal—initial inventory. I could *possibly* finish what I started but on my own, without a partner or investor.

It was all *possible*, but it also sounded too good to be true.

We sat in the same position, our faces a foot apart, our eyes not losing contact. This sent my pulse into overdrive. To the outside world, we probably appeared as if we were talking dirty.

"What's the catch?" I whispered.

Andrew's smile increased. My heart rate increased, too. Because of the money, of course. Not because of being so close to him, inhaling the scent of his lemon and bergamot soap and noticing how full and long his eyelashes were. Men should pay extra taxes for having such beautiful lashes.

"There's no catch." His eyes searched mine. "I work, and you just need to stay near me."

In such proximity and in the bright morning, his irises were like two mysterious, unexplored planets. One was nothing but a green jungle and the other a bottomless blue sea. I could get easily lost in both unfathomable places.

"Doctor Andrew Jones," an unfamiliar voice with a British accent boomed next to us.

We straightened in our seats, and Andrew's grin fell, a bleakness replacing his playful expression.

A middle-aged man with an arrogant face and a cynical twist to his smile stood at our table. He resembled someone who had recently pledged a college fraternity with his blond hair parted on one side and glued to his skull with an overabundance of gel.

"Richard," Andrew said with so much disgust he might as well have thrown shit at this man.

"We don't ever run into each other in Cambridge, and yet we meet in Colombia of all places. What are you doing here?" he said, leaning on William's empty chair.

Andrew's jaw ticked. "The usual: buying coffee beans at wholesale prices."

Richard's gray gaze fell on me, and his smile widened, exposing large and long canine teeth. "Are you going to introduce me to your companion?"

"Adriana Jones, meet Richard Head." Andrew's hand gently curled around my right wrist, covering the bracelet and enveloping my skin with warmth. I gave him a quick questioning look but didn't pull away. Was he trying to hide the jewelry? Or was he grasping at anything just to keep himself from jumping at the man's throat? I didn't need to know these men or their history to understand that the tension between them was stretched wire thin.

I sized up the man standing by our table and rested my left hand on top of Andrew's. "Did your mother dislike you, Richard? She would have to, to give you that name."

Andrew chuckled quietly.

Richard's eyebrows pulled together in confusion, but then his eyes dropped to my ring, and his eyebrows shut up.

"Andrew, you finally tied the knot. Holy shit. Brie will be delighted to hear that someone finally made an honest man out of you."

I opened my mouth to correct the misunderstanding—

Andrew's fingers tightened around my wrist. "Too bad the same never could be said about you."

Was he fake marrying me at this moment? What about his actual wife?

"Don't tell me you're on honeymoon?" Richard narrowed his eyes at Andrew. "And shame on you. You can afford a much bigger stone than that."

"Congratulations, Richard," Andrew bit off, "you have ruined our breakfast. You can leave now."

"So much for a friendly hello. Does he treat all his old friends like this?" Richard turned his attention to me.

"No. Only dickheads." I grinned and leaned my head on Andrew's shoulder.

A human Barbie doll, only about five feet four, with dirty-snow-blond hair walked up to Richard and snaked her arm around his. She wore a tight white shirt and cream-colored satin pants. I sat up straighter. Dr. Jones wasn't my man, but the way this blue-eyed doll gazed down at him, I instantly wanted to yank her high ponytail.

"Andy, so good to see you," she said with a posh (you guessed it) British accent on a half-sigh, her mouth turning into a bright smile.

She was a happy-go-lucky ray of fucking sunshine, but Andrew's face went ashen as if he had seen an image of his own death.

"What is Brie doing here?" he asked, a bitter edge to his voice.

I had so many questions now. Why did he go pale at the sight of this woman? Who is she? Why didn't Andrew like this guy? And why was Andrew pretending to be married to me?

"I'm standing right here. You can ask me directly," she said. "Spanish is one of the six languages I speak. I'm here to help." She focused on me with a squint of annoyance. "Are you also working at Octavian Global? Is that how the two of you met?"

If I were going to play along pretending to be Charlotte, it was best to stick to the truth as much as I could. How many years would it have been since Andrew and I met and got married? I tried to calculate how old Lulu was. Six. Maybe seven years old.

"No. We met on vacation. Eight years ago," I said.

She peered at Andrew, her face awash with confusion. "Is that true, Andy?"

Andrew stared at me with a perplexed expression and mouthed. "What?"

Perhaps I'd made a mistake in my calculations. Sweat started to build up under my knees. I should've kept my mouth shut.

Andrew let out a heavy sigh. "Is there something you two need from us? We would like to get back to our breakfast."

A sneer spread across dickhead's face. "Come on, darling, the car is probably ready."

"See you later, Andy," Brie said, wiggling her fingers over her shoulder as they strode across the patio and disappeared through the open doors. Why did she keep calling him Andy? That sounded so personal, so touchy, so clingy. I didn't like it.

The smile slipped off my face and I tugged my hand away at the same time Andrew relaxed his grip.

"Next time, let me do the talking," he said, picking up a glass of water and taking several gulps.

My earlier warm protective feeling had twisted into irritation. "Next time, give me a briefing on our marriage."

Andrew's jaw muscles spasmed as he clenched his teeth. I waited for him to explain who those people were and what had crawled up his ass.

72

William sauntered onto the patio just then wearing a Cuban collared shirt peppered with pink cocktails and beach umbrellas and white shorts that matched his wide, bright smile. He waved to us.

"Cheer up, love, it might never happen," William said with a bad English accent as he slipped on a chair across from Andrew. "Isn't that what you chaps say in the UK to everyone who looks like ... well, like you right now?"

When neither of us said anything, he leaned back in his seat, rubbing his chin. "What did I miss?"

"I got married," I said.

"WTF? And I wasn't invited? Who's the lucky guy?"

I nodded to my right. "Apparently he is."

"I approve." William removed a decorative red flower from his mango juice and dropped it into his glass of water. When had his drink appeared? Was I so fixated on Andrew's face I'd missed the server? "Now, tell me all the dirty wedding night deeds."

Andrew rubbed his face and gave a tired groan. "I apologize about Richard."

"Who is Richard?" William asked.

"Andrew's rival stopped by," I said, "and Andrew pretended we were married and politely told him and his ... wife?"—I glanced at Andrew—"to go squat in a cactus patch."

"Draaaama." William smiled and expectedly gawked at Andrew for clarification. "Come on. Give up the good stuff. What happened?"

"Dr. Richard Head and I—"

William burst out a loud laugh at the name, his head thrown back. I smiled and watched a ghost of a smile pass over Andrew's face. William waved his hand. "I'm sorry, go on."

"Richard and I worked together and then…" Andrew looked where Richard and Brie had disappeared inside the restaurant. "We had a disagreement, and our interests ran in opposite directions."

"That isn't the good stuff," William said. "It's a summary. What. Happened?"

"We met in Cambridge. Worked together. Now he's a black-market antiques dealer who works for private collectors and always tries to beat me in getting to what shouldn't be his in the first place."

"And has he?" William asked.

Andrew's teeth grazed his lower lip, his gaze remained pinned at the same spot. "Once."

"So, he's after Augustine's treasure too?" I said.

"Yes." Andrew glanced at me, his eyes full of apology. "I'm sorry I touched your wrist. I had hoped to hide the bracelet. Only a few people know about it."

I brushed my thumb over the spot where Andrew's heat penetrated my skin. "That's fine. I knew that's what you were doing." Of course, I did. He had a wife; there wasn't any reason for him to be so touchy. Unless he was a pig. And I had a strong feeling he wasn't. "Why did you pretend to be married to me? You could have just said the truth."

"I was going to, but you interrupted." He shook his head. "It doesn't matter. I don't care what they think." Really? What if someone told his petite, blond wife that they ran into Andrew, and he was with a tall, chestnut-haired, green-eyed wife? Sometimes, I truly didn't understand men's logic. "Not now I know Richard works for Nicolai Kolesnikov."

"Kolesnikov?" My jaw hit the table. "*The* Nicolai Kolesnikov? The second wealthiest oligarch in Russia?"

Working for Salzburg Distributing had allowed me to learn a lot about wealthy people around the world, since they often hunted for the best or rarest bottles of wine. Some utilized professionals like myself, and some traveled personally to auctions and exhibitions. On several occasions, I'd sat at the same table with people whose weekly spending equaled my yearly salary. *Side note:* my salary was great. Like six figures great. Damn it! It was dumb of me to quit my job.

The server returned with coffee for William. We placed our order, and she collected menus and left.

"And how do you know Richard works with Kolesnikov?" I asked.

"Two weeks ago, Nicolai approached me, wanting my help to lead his team for a new exploration. I turned him down. He must have turned to Richard."

"Why did you turn him down?" William asked.

"Artifacts belong in a museum and not on some asshole's private yacht."

"Very Indiana Jones-y," William marveled.

"If that's how you feel, why are you okay with the chest going to the private collector?" I asked.

"I have to focus on saving the irreplaceable ones." Andrew rubbed his eyebrow. "Since Richard is already here, there's a slight change in our plans. We need to leave immediately." He stood up. "Have your breakfast and let's meet"—he glanced at his watch—"in thirty minutes in the lobby."

"Oh, yes." I turned to William. "Something else you missed. I'm staying with Andrew for a few more days. You don't have to. You can go back to Costa Rica."

I hated for William to miss his luxurious vacation, and I was sure he'd have fun without me. He was an expert at finding someone special anywhere he went.

"And miss all the fun?" William pointed his glass of juice at me. "Besides, you need me for security. I go where you go."

Warmth spread in my chest, pulling my lips into a smile. William was always protective of me. When he was about to start university, he considered not going on my account. He didn't want to leave me alone with my mother and her constant revolving door of men. But after a serious talk, he changed his mind. At fifteen, I knew how to take care of myself. I was the only girl in our twenty-trailers *dreamland* neighborhood, and the boys taught me many quick ways to bring someone down to the ground. When William finally moved out, there were only a few nights when I had to push my bed against my bedroom door as one extra layer of protection from my mother's *here-today-and-gone-tomorrow* boyfriends.

"Andrew, you should eat breakfast," I said. "A few minutes won't change much."

"You'd be surprised," Andrew mumbled but returned to his seat.

"So." William leaned back in his chair. "What did you find out last night about your pirate?"

"The next logical place to visit is at Iglesia San Antonio, the church where Jorge Pérez was a priest and is buried. For a ruthless pirate, when it came to his family and friends,

Augustine was kind and loyal. As long as they were loyal to him, of course. Augustine's right hand was his brother, Jorge, and some notes hint that Jorge temporarily stored Augustine's treasure in his church. We don't know when and for how long. It might be still there."

I thought of every movie I'd seen where people had to break into the floors in old churches and crawl among skeletons. Shivers ran down my arms. I wouldn't want to do that. It was creepy and disrespectful to the dead.

William's phone dinged, and he fished it out of his pocket. Frowning, he pushed his chair out and got up. "It's my clinic. I'll need to call them back."

"Don't you think by now someone would have read their letters and notes, and found the treasure?" I said after William disappeared into the restaurant's indoor dining room.

"It's not that simple. Anything important, Augustine wrote in hieroglyphs. While you received the bracelet, I received an unfinished chart and a few other items which I might be able to use to partially decrypt any additional messages we come across."

"Who are these Octavian Global people anyway? Have you met any of them?" I pressed my elbows on the table and cupped my chin, curiosity rising inside of me as if I was getting excited about this journey. I wasn't, I told myself. I was simply making a conversation. Only the prospect of getting paid excited me.

Andrew leaned closer. His eyes sparkled with mischief. "If I tell you, I'd have to kill you."

I shifted, making the space between our faces even shorter. "I'd like to see you try."

A smile tugged at a corner of his lips, and his gaze did this slow sweep over my face, carefully lingering on my lips for several heart beats and finally returning to my eyes, but not before a pleasant feeling spread through me, making my toes tingle. I shouldn't have, but I enjoyed that look.

I should stop. Starting now.

"OMG." William returned to his spot, pulling us apart. My face was on fire as if I'd swallowed ghost pepper. I picked up the glass of cold water and pressed it against my cheek. "I just ran into the most gorgeous man with a sexy accent. Maybe Australian? We only had a brief chat, but he was so cute." He twisted in his chair and glanced over his shoulder at the restaurant. "Shoot, I didn't catch his name or where he was from."

"You should go catch him," I said.

"Nah, he was in a rush leaving. If it's meant to be, we'll run into each other."

Everything I tried at breakfast was out of this world good. The sausage had unique spicy seasoning, sweet bread rolls melted in my mouth, and the small, orange, round berries were so remarkable I moaned when their tart, tangy flavor exploded in my mouth.

I closed my eyes and enjoyed the moment. "What are these?"

"Physalis peruviana or golden berries," Andrew said. "They're native to Colombia."

"From now on, this is my favorite fruit," I said.

"Every fruit is your favorite," William said. "Adriana spends most of her money on wine and fruit."

"Don't forget cheese and bread." I pierced the last berry on my plate.

"How could I?" William chuckled. "The key to this woman's heart is to shower her with superb wine, cheese, and fresh bread."

"Noted." Andrew pushed his chair out, dropping the napkin on the table. He'd only eaten an omelet and fruit, leaving his sweet dessert rolls untouched. "I'll see you in the lobby in twenty minutes."

"Wait," I said, and he turned to face me, "I only brought clothes for two days. I need to go shopping."

"We can find a store later. Right now, we need to keep moving."

Chapter Six

Fifty minutes later, William and I found Andrew in the lobby near the exit, talking on a phone. He noticed us and nodded to follow him outside, his iPhone pressed to his ear. "They're here," he said to whoever was on the other side of the line. "Kiss Lulu for me." He ended the call and slid the phone into his pants pocket.

"I'm sorry we're late," I said.

"Next time, I'm docking your delay from the agreed-on price."

"Hey, don't be a dick to her." William dabbed his sweaty forehead with a napkin. "I couldn't find the sunscreen."

We stopped at an old, red Jeep Wrangler. Andrew hoisted my luggage into the back of the car next to his bag.

"Is this our ride?" William stepped back and scrutinized the open-top car.

"Yes." The muscles in Andrew's back strained against his shirt as he reached for William's first suitcase. I knew I should turn away and not stare. But I didn't want to. "Is it a problem?"

"Well, yeah." William deadpanned. "With all the money you're throwing around, this is what you rented?"

"Dr. Garcia let me borrow it."

"Oh Jessezzz. Too much sun. I need my hat if we're going without a roof." William pressed his fingers to his temples. "I just don't remember which bag it's in."

Andrew took the next bag and piled it on top of the others. "You'd better hurry and check."

William closed his eyes and wrinkled his nose. To avoid ogling Andrew's *despicable* forearms as he secured ratchet straps around our bags, I climbed into the passenger seat and waited for William to inevitably discover that he hadn't brought a hat.

"Shoot," William muttered. "I didn't bring one."

There it was.

"I can't go without a hat."

"You're welcome to stay here. I'll pay." Andrew got into the driver's seat and slid the key into the ignition.

"Tempting, but you know I can't do that." With pleading eyes, William glanced between me and the hotel. "The resort store opens at ten. We can get a hat there."

I turned to Andrew. "We're already late. What's another thirty minutes? He needs a hat."

Andrew's eyes bored into mine, and his jaw ticked. He groaned, got out of the car, and marched towards a group of workers trimming flowering bushes. After a short exchange, he pulled his wallet out and handed them cash.

"Oh no," William whispered. "He is not doing what I think he's doing."

"It looks like it." I smiled.

Andrew returned to the car with a gardener's straw hat in hand.

"Here you go. A hat." He held it to William.

William shook his head. "I'm not wearing it. Are you mad? It's dirty and has someone else's sweat and oils on it."

Andrew pulled a cotton handkerchief out of his pocket and offered it to William. "It's clean. Wear it underneath the hat. Please work with me. Once we get to the town. You can buy a new one."

"Freaking Mr. Darcy," William groused. "Who in this century carries a hanky?"

With an exaggerated sigh, my brother unfolded the handkerchief and placed it on his head. I swallowed the laugh that wanted to burst out of me. If I laughed, we weren't leaving until the store opened. Cringing, William turned the hat a few times and then set it on his head.

"I should get a cut of your money for doing this." He pointed at me and climbed into the back seat.

The car came alive with a loud roar, and Andrew wheeled it out of the hotel parking lot onto a busy road.

"How long is the drive?" I placed my sunglasses on, grateful I'd applied SPF 50 all over my body.

"If everything goes well, we should be there by three," Andrew said, paying attention to cars zooming by. He changed gears, and the Jeep made a choking noise.

"Aren't you worried this car … um … won't make it far? Did you hear that struggling sound?" I asked and pulled a chunk of my hair out of my mouth. One of the things I didn't like about cars like this was the constant whipping of my hair around my face and then arriving at the destination with a bird's nest of frizzy hair. I pulled my purse onto my lap and rummaged inside for a hair tie.

"Not at all." Andrew pulled the Jeep onto the highway, and the wind worsened as the car accelerated.

I made a messy bun on my head, certain that my presentation wasn't the prettiest, but I wasn't here to impress anybody. I was here to help to find a priceless treasure ... or whatever.

It was hard to carry on a conversation with constant noise around us, so for four hours we drove without exchanging a single word. At a small gas station, we used the dirty bathroom, where I had to drop paper towels on the floor to protect my shoes as I edged to a questionable hole in the ground with flies buzzing above it.

Before we continued, Andrew bought us lunch wrapped in banana leaves from a food cart next to a thatched house. Colombian tamales were out of this world delicious. Flavors of braised salty pork, potatoes, and carrots swaddled in sweet masa danced on my tongue. I wished I'd asked for two.

At three thirty in the afternoon, Andrew made the last turn, and we entered the center of a town with cobblestoned streets lined with buildings painted with vibrant murals, bright flowers on windows and by front doors, a few outdoor cafés, and a couple of bars—judging by neon beer logos. Andrew parked in a quiet, sleepy alley and turned off the engine.

"I'll go to the museum alone." Andrew pushed his

sunglasses off his face to the top of his head. "If I need you, I'll call you. Please keep your phone on."

"Can you just text me?" I said. "I don't get charged for incoming texts."

"If I message you, I won't know if you got it or not. I'd like to call you. I'll reimburse you for any expense." Andrew grabbed a small notebook and flashlight out of the center console and jumped out of the car, before veering around the corner.

"I need a stiff drink," William said, wafting the hat in front of his face. "That drive was so not good for my skin." He gently touched his cheek and then glanced at his finger. "So much dirt. My pores are crying right now."

"And a drink will help you how?" I unfastened the buckle and twisted in my seat to face him. I needed to stretch my legs too, but we couldn't leave our stuff unattended in the car.

"It will numb my immense disappointment about this trip."

"I thought you were having fun." I arched an eyebrow.

"I was wrong."

"Someone needs to stay here," I said. "If Andrew calls, I'll have to go to the church, so that leaves only you. Your drink has to wait."

William pooched his lips. "Fine, but can we sneak out for a second and take a selfie in front of the church? I thought we could post a reel about this trip later."

Our surroundings appeared safe and clean, and the houses had no iron bars on windows or doors. I guessed it wouldn't hurt.

For the late afternoon, the town seemed very quiet, with a

few people outside and practically no cars on the road. I wandered to the middle of the road and snapped a picture of San Sierra's main square. The orange Iglesia San Antonio, with pieces of plaster crumbling off in some places, dazzled against the green mountain with a rounded top. A row of bright-colored colonial buildings with intricate carvings stretched on each side of the cathedral. Minus a few mopeds parked along the street, it resembled one of Augustine's pencil drawings we'd seen at the museum.

"This is the place Pérez sketched." I stared at the photo. William lifted his sunglasses and squinted at my phone. I zoomed in. "I recognize all the buildings and the church."

"I thought the one in the museum looked like the cathedral in Cartagena."

"I'm telling you it's the exact place. I can prove it."

I swiped my screen until I found the photo of the pencil drawing. It was remarkable. The details were so vivid it could easily pass for a black-and-white photo. Next, I opened the Layout app, selected the sketch with the church, and then picked the last photo I took. I arranged one atop the other for comparison.

"See. It's the same." I glanced up at the church.

Did Andrew know about it? Was that why he'd picked this place to find a clue? Andrew said he and Dr. Garcia had talked about a collection of letters and diaries in the church's museum, but he hadn't mentioned this drawing. Should I tell him that Augustine had sketched this place anyway? It could mean nothing, of course. Maybe Augustine always sketched places he had been to or that were dear to his heart.

"What if his sketches had a special message?"

William shrugged. "It's just a drawing."

He must have been really worn out after a five-hour drive in the sun to be so disinterested. It was his idea to go on this treasure hunt in the first place, and here I was searching for hidden meanings in old artwork.

My phone rang with an unfamiliar phone number.

"Yeeeellow," I answered and ambled to the sidewalk.

"Can you come to the church right now?" Andrew said.

"Okey-dokey." I hung up. "I'm summoned."

"Okay." William smiled, but his shoulders slumped. "I'll be guarding our stuff in the car." I didn't miss the hint of sadness in his voice.

"Are you okay, handsome?" I asked gently.

"Yes. Just tired. Go. Dr. Hot Bod is waiting for you."

I landed a kiss on his cheek and made my way to find Andrew, my chest aching with worry that something was off with William.

The church's massive door didn't open when I pulled on it. I yanked on the handle again. Nothing. How in the world was I supposed to meet Andrew inside if the doors were locked? I pulled my phone out of my purse and was about to dial the previous number when Andrew stepped out from behind the corner of the building and beckoned me.

I hurried to him. "The doors are—"

Andrew grabbed my hand and pulled me through the wooden gates into a cool, shadowy, narrow alley. He shut the door behind us. "Church is closed today," he said in a low tone.

"Why are we whispering?" I spoke in a hushed voice too.

"We're not supposed to be here."

I was afraid he would say that. "I'm getting a feeling you're often in places where you shouldn't be. Should we come back tomorrow?"

"No." We trotted along the building, his hand holding mine, my long legs barely keeping up with his strides.

"Jesus, what's the rush?"

"I don't want anyone to notice us." He stopped at steps covered in moss and vines with tiny green leaves, leading to a door the size of a compact refrigerator I used to have in my college dorm. "We go through this door."

I assessed Andrew's tall frame. He wasn't a gigantic man, but his shoulders were twice as wide as the opening, and his height was enormous.

"Are you going to fit through?" I pulled my hand out of his grip. "I'm five eleven. You're what? Six five?"

"Six six." He gestured to the entrance. "Ladies first."

"Is it even open?" I descended the four steps, and as I got closer to the door, the fresh fragments of broken wood near the handle were my answer. "Ignore that," I said over my shoulder. What had I gotten myself into? If we were arrested, my story would be that Andrew was a deranged man who had kidnapped me.

I swooped my skirt up before squatting, pushing the door open, and crawling inside. Andrew followed me as soon as I squeezed through the door frame and we crammed into a small room with weak daylight streaming through a lancet stained-glass window far above. Shrouded in darkness, the space was jammed with rolled banners, stacks of candles, boxes, books, and now two figures that shouldn't have been there.

"Are we searching for anything in particular here?" I peered at the stacked boxes. "Should we check these?"

"No. It's with Jorge Pérez."

"What is *it*? And how do you know?"

"It's my job to know."

"You said the same thing about the bracelet, and yet you haven't taken it off, and you couldn't open the chest, and—"

He scowled at me, and I didn't need much light to properly see his unappreciative expression. "On the way here, I kept thinking about the last notes Dr. Garcia gave me. Jorge was so loyal to his brother, he wouldn't allow anybody to see his journal. He said he took all Augustine's secrets to his grave." Andrew pulled a door ajar and peeked through the gap. After a few seconds, he opened it wider, and we slipped outside the room.

The musty yet floral old church scent enveloped us as we passed through a narrow, windowless hall and stepped out into the nave. I wasn't very religious, but I always loved the smell of burnt candles and the woody scent of frankincense.

The church was quiet with not a soul in sight. Well, maybe it was full of souls, but they were invisible and mute. Andrew moved quickly to the right, and I shadowed him. He turned after the first column, briefly stopping and looking back, then slid behind it. *Jeez, so much suspense.* I rolled my eyes and kept after him, my heels making a low clunking noise that echoed from stone wall to stone wall and rose to a vault.

"Christ." Andrew turned and looked at my feet.

"What?" I stepped back.

"Could you make any more noise?"

88

"What would you suggest?" I said, frowning. "I go barefoot?"

He raised his eyebrows and a smile played on his lips.

"Seriously? Nobody is here."

"You don't know that."

"You said it's closed today."

"It doesn't mean people aren't here."

"Fine." I rolled my eyes again and pulled my shoes off.

Under the judgmental gaze of stone statues, we continued down the corridor, my feet quiet on the cold marble floor. Andrew stopped in a hall with crypts on both sides. He ran his fingers over words that were carved into the stone, brushing away cobwebs from some places. Then, out of his back pocket, he pulled his notebook. He leafed through it, his eyes lingering on one page longer than the others. He glanced up at the wall, then back at his notes, and finally said, "This is it."

I moved next to him and peered at the crypt wall. It had engravings with swirls and flowers, something written in Spanish, and the dates 1733–1785. The concrete surface had minimal cracks and a brighter color than the surrounding areas. "It doesn't look ancient in comparison to the neighboring stones. It seems like someone tried to stain it so it would appear to be weathered."

"I noticed that too." Andrew pocketed his notebook. "I'm afraid someone seems to have beaten us here."

"What do we do now?"

Andrew checked his watch, then walked toward the end of the corridor and picked up a large standing candelabra. He returned with it and jerked his head to the side. "Step back."

I moved away several feet. "What are—"

The church bells thundered, and he swung the candelabra wide and hit the stone right in the center, across Jorge's name. My heart jumped to my throat. The loud bang racketed from wall to wall and in my ears. And he'd complained about my shoes? The man had lost his mind.

"What the fuck are you doing?" I whisper-yelled at him. "What if someone hears us?"

The bells rang again, and Andrew swung and landed another hard whack. I turned to see if anybody was running in our direction.

After another hit, the stone gave way, and a small opening appeared. Andrew grinned and brought one last good blow to the wall as the bells tolled a fourth time. A large piece of the crypt fell, landing next to his feet. He lowered the candelabra and tore the rest of the pieces with his hands, creating a considerable opening.

Out of his front pocket, he fished out a small flashlight and peered inside the hole. "That's what I thought."

"What is it?" My heart hammered just as loud as the racket Andrew had created seconds ago. I inched closer to him, but his massive shoulders blocked my view. A new draught wheezed around us, its ghostly fingers pulling on my loose hair strands.

He straightened his back, and his lips curved into a sly smile. "Do you know what happens next?"

"We go to prison?" I hissed at him.

Andrew harrumphed. "I hope you don't mind skinny bald guys with a toothy smile."

I drew my eyebrows together. Had he lost his marbles?

He gave me a sideway glance, then stepped away. "Ladies first."

What the hell was he talking about?

He motioned with his hand to the hole.

No. No freaking way.

Eyes wide, I backed away until my back pressed against an opposite crypt wall. A chill ran down my spine, either from the cold touch of a stone or the thought of…

"You aren't suggesting what I think you're suggesting. Crawl inside of that?"

"There's an opening on the other side. It's a passage."

"Passage to where?"

"The only way to find out is to…" He pointed the flashlight at the hole and made a low whistle. "If I go first, you'll never follow me. So, you go first, and I follow."

He is a lunatic.

"I didn't sign up for this."

"Yes, you did, when you agreed to come with me."

A good whack with that candelabra on his head would serve him right, if I could manage to lift it. I exhaled sharply as I slipped my wedges back on. I stepped towards Andrew, so close his body heat radiated through my clothes. Andrew was too tall for me to stare him squarely in the eye, even in my three-inch heels, so I shot a peeved glare up at him, pressing my finger into his hard chest. His stupid grin fell, leaving only that permanent smirk tugging at his lips.

"I don't like you at all." I yanked the flashlight out of his hand and leaned in to check out the black gap.

night·mar·ish | ˈnīt͵meriSH |

ADJECTIVE: The next disturbing and
bothersome minutes crawling through a
dark crypt over a skeleton while not
dying to do it and wishing you had a
few or five tequila shots beforehand.

ORIGIN: Iglesia San Antonio.

The crypt was deeper than I thought. I didn't know what I'd imagined, but this one was at least ten feet long. On the opposite side from me, there was an opening, but I had to creep over a dead guy covered in ancient dust and cobwebs. I wasn't afraid of bones. Life was full of alive people that I had to worry about every day, so I didn't believe the dead could haunt or hurt me. But still. It was beyond creepy. And disrespectful.

I tossed my purse in and poked my head inside, but then stopped. After this, my white dress was a goner. There was no way to clean the crap that was about to get on it. I groaned inwardly.

"Don't follow me until I tell you. I don't want you to turn into a peeping Tom. And you're buying me a new dress."

Andrew's laugh was short and deep. "If we find Augustine's treasure, I'll buy you hundreds of dresses."

I moved the flashlight around to ensure there weren't any tarantulas or rats. "I thought you didn't do this job for money."

"Octavian Global pays me a small percentage of the total value of the find."

It must have been nice to live a life where you get paid for a *fun* adventure, and my guess, it was a nice payment too. But this type of life wasn't for me. With my old job I traveled a lot, but after doing it for ten years it got tiring to never be in the same place, never having a chance to make my home feel like an actual home, decorate it with more than just the novels I'd picked up at airport bookstores over the years. Maybe even get a pet. I'd always wanted a cat, but it would've been unfair for it to be left alone for days or weeks.

I pushed my shoulders deep into the cool space, holding the flashlight in one hand and moving cobwebs with another. A musty and damp soil smell replaced the fragrant church one. I crawled farther, my hands and legs spread over the skeleton, my knees painfully pressed into small rocks. I hit my head on the ceiling a couple of times before I faced Jorge's shocked expression, his mouth agape.

"Yeah, buddy," I mumbled. "I'm just as surprised as you are to find myself on top of you. Don't get a boner. Okay?"

"Who are you talking to?" Andrew's voice sounded way too close. I glanced over my shoulder. Andrew was staring at me.

"Andrew!" I snapped. "I told you not to look."

His face disappeared out of my view. "Sorry."

I reached the end of the crypt, now the skull happily faced up my skirt between my spread legs. Never in my wildest dreams had I imagined myself in this odd and sickening position. Whatever was at the end of this tunnel had better have all the treasure. I was done with this adventure. Of course, the end of the journey meant the end of the payments. But how much more of this *outlawish* behavior could I take? It was always fun and games until someone had to go to prison. Was my business worth going to jail? In Colombia?

I waved the flashlight in the darkness, the light running over a curved stone-walled tunnel that disappeared into shadow.

"What do you see?" Andrew asked.

"An arched passage leading somewhere, but I can't see exactly what's there."

"I'm coming. Move."

I shone the light down to check how far the ground was. I was about five feet off the floor and couldn't go forward without completely nosediving. *Literally.*

"Give me a minute," I said.

Like a cat in an empty tight box, I twisted to the side, accidentally pushing on the skull. It made a crunching sound. "Oops."

I pulled my knees close to my body, shifted to my left, turned, and finally pointed my ass in the right direction. Andrew's face was on the same level with mine, our noses practically touching.

"Hi, you," he said, not letting go of my gaze.

"Hi."

His gaze did a slow sweep over my face again, stopping a second too long on my lips, and then finally went up to my eyes. My heart skipped a beat. Stupid heart.

"You're in my way," he said teasingly, his breath mingled with mine.

I moved backward with the speed of light, carefully finding

the floor with my feet, then finally getting out of the crypt. I shook my arms and head, trying to shake off the creepy feeling that I was in a tomb and the buzzing feeling that Andrew awoke in me when he stared at my lips. I pushed my hair off my face, along with several nasty cobwebs.

Somehow Andrew had no problem reaching the floor with his long arms and walking out on his hands until he'd completely pulled his body out.

"I can't believe I crawled over a skeleton," I said. "You should be ashamed of damaging the crypt's wall and ruining a piece of history."

"I'll send them an anonymous donation as an apology." Andrew rose to his feet and gestured for me to pass him his flashlight. He neared where the tunnel turned and stopped. "There's a staircase."

"Of course, there is." I groaned, pulling the strap of my purse onto my shoulder.

Chapter Seven

W e crept down a stairway barely wide enough for Andrew's shoulders to fit and then came around a sharp corner to a stone landing about ten feet by ten feet. Andrew clicked the flashlight button once more, boosting the intensity of the light and revealing an enormous underground chamber before us.

"Is this a catacomb?" I asked.

"I doubt this was used for burial reasons. This is where they stored smuggled goods."

My eyes roamed over the empty space. "Someone should tell them that they were robbed."

"We need to get lower." Andrew knelt near the edge, then he shook something at his foot. "This should hold."

"What should hold?" I crept closer to him but kept my distance from the edge.

"The ladder attached to this wall." Andrew grasped the flashlight between his teeth, turned around, and descended down a fucking threadbare wooden rope ladder. The heavy corded fibers screeched under his weight, and my stomach spasmed.

"You're out of your mind. It's been here for hundreds of years. What if it breaks?"

He mumbled something incoherent. Yep, that was exactly how I envisioned the thoughts in his head: incoherent.

Andrew landed on the lower-level dirt floor without breaking any of his bones. He pulled the flashlight out of his mouth and ran it over the room, briefly stopping at another goddamn passage leading somewhere else. He looked up at me. "Now it's your turn."

I peered down. The drop was maybe one and a half to two stories high. Would I die if I fell, or would it just hurt really bad? Why did I put the stupid bracelet on?

"What are you waiting for?" Andrew said, his tone hushed and impassioned.

I took my wedges off. "I should hurl my heels at you."

"What did I do?"

"You dragged me into the abode of the dead."

Andrew chuckled. "Once again, you did it to yo—"

I lobbed the right shoe at him.

"Hey, watch it." He jumped aside. "You almost hit me."

"You mention again that it was my fault, and the next one *will* hit you." I stuffed the other shoe into my bag. "How far is it?"

"Thirty feet at most. Are you afraid of heights?"

"No. I'm afraid of decaying ladders."

"You'll be fine. It held me. It should hold you. Drop me your purse."

I did as he asked, and he caught it.

Fuck. Fuckity fuck.

I lowered to my knees, turned, and inched backward. My hands gripped the ladder's sides, while I searched with my right foot for the first wooden bar. Then my left foot found the second bar, my fingers digging into the rope on this piece of crap ladder. The cool air snaked up my legs. "Andrew, look away."

"It's too dark. Even if I wanted to, I can't see up your skirt."

"Look elsewhere anyway."

I made another two steps down and carefully moved my hands to the next bar. The ladder seemed to be securely fastened to the wall. I didn't even want to think how. I pressed my forehead to a stony wall, breathed in, and breathed out earthy air. I was halfway down. Everything was going fine, until I realized … once we were done, we had to ascend the same ladder. Well, shit.

The bar under my feet yawped a faint crack, and my skin doused with cold sweat. The brittle structure made a ripping and crunching racket, and everything below my feet crumbled. My heart lurched up into my throat as my body dropped.

"Shit!" I tightened my grip on the bar, my feet desperately searching for some footing on the *apparently* smooth wall.

"Hold on!"

"I'm trying!" My arms quickly grew tired. I peered down. How far was the ground? Andrew dropped the flashlight and stepped to the wall below me. An additional feeling of horror rose up my neck. "Andrew. Don't. Look."

"Christ, Adriana. This is not the time to worry if I see your backside."

"I'm sure Charlotte wouldn't approve of this."

"Charlotte?" he said with bewilderment. "Why would she care?"

Really? Why would a woman care if her husband checked out another woman's ass?

"Let go. I'll catch you."

"It's too far. I'll pull myself back up," I lied through my teeth. There was no way I could do it, and my arms were only getting weaker. Terror ripped my heart apart. I didn't want to get hurt. I didn't want to crush Andrew, either.

Damn it.

"This is all your fault!" I yelled, glancing down at him.

"Do you want to chat about whose fault it is, right now?" Andrew pinched his chin. "Fine. Let's chat. Do you want your shoe so you could throw it at me again because—"

"Andrew!"

He raised his arms toward me. "Let. Go."

I squeezed my eyes shut until white dots appeared.

Fuck it.

My fingers relaxed, and I dropped. My skirt flew up to my neck, and a moment later Andrew's hands wrapped around my torso, catching me. His warm forearms pressed hard into my bare stomach. He stumbled backward, his arms not letting me go, and we crashed onto the ground, our bodies pressed tight, my bottom on Andrew's crotch, my hands on the ground on each side of his legs, my back against his rising and dropping chest. His heart drummed hard against his ribcage, its beat vibrating through my body. Electricity coursed through me, making me aware of every point of contact between Andrew and me, of every inch where his hot skin was touching mine.

Andrew pressed his forehead into the back of my head, snorted once and then he erupted with a healthy laugh, and the sound of it went straight into my bloodstream and right into the center of me.

A chuckle bubbled up in my throat too, and I burst out laughing.

"That was graceful." I quietened my laugh and wiped the tears that had formed in my eyes.

Andrew drew in a deep breath. When he released his breath, it skimmed the side of my neck. "Your hair smells like roses."

Butterflies fluttered in my stomach. "Stop smelling my hair."

"Your hair is in my face. I'm merely observing a fact."

The dress bunched up above my waist, covering Andrew's arms. My dishabille state *should* have mortified me, and I *should* have pulled my skirt down, but the flashlight lay several yards away from us, tossing its light into a dark void. Andrew shifted, and his thigh muscles flexed beneath me. I shouldn't have been in this situation, in his arms or on his lap. But I couldn't deny how good it felt to be pressed against him. I didn't want to move. And dang it! It was so wrong to want that. Just for a split second, for that one short second, I wanted to believe he was free, and I could relax into him and pretend that I hadn't simply crash-landed on him, but that he'd hugged me, wanting to be close to me.

"I don't think your wife would appreciate us sitting like this," I said, and my voice came out like I was sharing a secret with him.

"My wife?" he asked his breath a whisper against my exposed skin.

I nodded. "The beautiful woman by the pool? I saw you with her the morning we left."

"You think Charlotte is my wife?" His question was tinged with humor.

"Yes. And your daughter, Lulu, who seems to like to call you a lot."

He chuckled. "Charlotte is my sister, and Lucille is her daughter."

I wanted to let out a sigh of relief but held it in. "You aren't married?"

"No."

"So, you don't have a wife?"

"That's what unmarried means, usually."

I cleared my throat. "You go on vacation with your sister?" Why was I talking like I was an idiot? I met Andrew during my vacation with my brother. Families went on trips.

"Yes. Three of us. It's always three of us."

"And you aren't married?"

"We already established that."

Of course. Where did my smart brain cells go?

"Hmm…" I nodded slowly.

Oh. My. God. I was so fucked.

Figuratively speaking.

"Hmm. What?" Not letting his arms go, he shifted again, as if trying to look at my face. Which I was sure was red with embarrassment. Good thing it was dark in here.

"Why did you say *always* three of us?"

Andrew's chest expanded with a deep breath.

"Her husband, Louis, was a pilot. Seven years ago, he was flying his plane with my parents on board." He swallowed. "They crashed over the Alps. Charlotte was five months pregnant so she hadn't gone along on the trip."

My heart pitched hard with sadness. Poor Charlotte, what a horrible thing to live through, especially when pregnant.

"I'm so sorry." My words came out low.

"There were some scary moments, but she held on to the only thing that was left of Louis. Since then, we've always stuck together. After their accident, she moved in with me so I could help her while she was pregnant. Once Lulu was born, I didn't feel there was any need for them to move out. My home has enough space for all of us. And I needed them as much as they needed me."

"You love that little girl very much, don't you?"

"She is the most important person in my life," he said, and I heard a tender smile in his voice.

"I can see that. You never miss her calls."

"I never ignore people who are important to me."

That was nice to hear that there was a man who didn't disregard a little girl, who didn't mind taking their time from his busy life to listen to what she had to tell him. Andrew wasn't even her father, but he made Lulu his priority. I wished I had parents or *a* parent like that. A parent who gave a damn about how my day in school had been or if I had eaten anything, let alone what I had to say.

"Andrew?" I looked over my shoulder.

"Yes?" His breath brushed against my face, and goosebumps swooshed over my skin like a tsunami.

"I'm safe now. You can let go of me."

Even though I'd asked him to release me, for irrational reasons, when Andrew eased his grip and moved his arms away from me, it left my skin cold, and I already missed his touch. I tugged on my dress, pulling its skirt down to cover my thighs. He stood, picked up the flashlight, and offered me his hands. With a light yank, he hauled me up.

"I only caught a glimpse of your rump, and…" He wolf-whistled.

I smacked his shoulder, my face turning hot. "I told you not to look."

"You shouldn't have worn a dress." Andrew bent and grabbed my purse.

"How was I supposed to know I'd be hanging on a broken ladder?" I accepted my bag from him and looped its straps over my shoulder. "Plus, I only pack dresses for vacation."

"Maybe tomorrow you should buy some pants."

I tilted my head to see the platform above us. "How are we going to get back up there?"

Andrew ran the light up the wall with the missing ladder. "We aren't." He shone the light around the space, stopping on a dark tunnel. "That's our way out."

Perhaps it wasn't the first time Andrew had ended up many feet below the ground, in an ancient building, amongst the dead. He was, after all, an archeologist, and my guess, one of the best ones since someone apparently paid him a whole lot of money to chase a lost treasure and break laws.

From the stories Andrew had told me about the treasure, this room should have been filled with a lot of massive chests and crates, but the room was vacant.

"So, no treasure here." I dusted the dirt off my feet and put my shoes on. "Should we keep moving?"

"It seems we won't find the Asiento de Padua cargo. But something is here." He surveyed the walls towering over us with markings and words carved deeply into smooth stones.

"By the way. Yes. Look…" I fished my iPhone out of my bag and found the collage of images I'd made. "Augustine sketched this church." I held my phone out to Andrew. "When I took this photo today, I immediately recognized the town square."

Andrew's warm hand enwrapped mine, bringing the screen closer to his face. "Where did you see this sketch?"

"At the museum."

"This is good." His smirk turned into a smile. "Before he died, in his last letter to Simón, Jorge wrote that Augustine's artwork conveyed more than just the beauty of the world he saw. It told stories. Sometimes, it's a love story, and sometimes, it's a message deeply hidden that only select people can grasp its true significance. I presumed it was a poetic way of saying how incredible of an artist Augustine was. But now it makes more sense that what he meant was Augustine left actual messages in his sketches."

"The museum only had four drawings on display. I have photos of them."

"May I see them?" Andrew's eyebrows narrowed.

I pulled my hand out of his touch and found images on my phone. "If you scroll to the left you'll see an unfinished waterfall, a large house, a palace, and this village square."

Andrew was staring at my phone, unblinking, a satisfied

smile spreading on his face. "I need to ask Carlos if they have more in the archives."

"Do you know what message he left in this sketch?"

"This could be it." Andrew pointed the flashlight at the wall in front of us. Carvings showed rural life with figures working in fields, riding horses, ships battling sea serpents, and a jungle with large cats and snakes hanging off trees. In the center of it all was a structure with angels above. Maybe a church? This church? I wasn't an artifacts expert, but in movies, these kinds of engravings usually carried a message.

I opened the camera app and snapped a picture, illuminating the area with a bright flash.

Andrew studied the wall, slowly moving the flashlight's beam over it in a kind of pattern. Deep in thought, he looked even more intelligent. The dim light underlined his sharp and confident profile, making it extra noticeable how handsome he was. And he was single.

Well, unmarried, at least.

An old feeling I hadn't allowed inside me for such a long time pushed all the air out of my lungs. I wasn't sapiosexual, but I knew well the type of guys that attracted me like positive ions to negative ones. I tended to fall hard for highly educated, intelligent men. And here I was in the company of a man who ticked all boxes. On top of everything, he had a sexy accent. But a man like Andrew wouldn't fall for a woman like me. I have worked enough with people in high society to know I was too far outside Andrew's socioeconomic class. Men like him seek partners who share their affluent lifestyle, education, and cultural sophistication. I had none of those. And if I kept reminding myself about it, I could control my growing interest in him.

"These look familiar, but I need my notes from the car." Andrew's voice yanked me out of my daunting personal rabbit hole.

"Then we'd better leave," I said. "William is probably worried."

"Not just yet." Andrew stepped to the wall, retrieved a pocketknife, and scraped around the rock at the bottom of the churchy structure.

"What are you doing?" I asked.

"This stone is protruding slightly," Andrew said. Tiny particles of dirt fell on the ground as he grated. "We're in the lower part of this building. If I'm correct—" The knife blade slid inside. He placed the flashlight into his mouth *again*, and pivoted the handle side to side, slowly pushing a stone out.

"That can't be good for your teeth," I said as I gently removed the flashlight.

Andrew sheathed his knife and slipped it into his side pocket. Grasping the stone, he blew a slow breath and cautiously wiggled it out. We exchanged rock for flashlight, and he shone the light into the hole. He broke into a wide smile, making my heart skip a beat.

"What's there?" I asked, breathless.

"Possibly the answer to where the treasure is." He reached inside and withdrew a worn, leather-bound book, then his hand went inside again and extracted a dusty stack of yellow papers. "Now we can leave."

Chapter Eight

Andrew placed the stone back into the wall, and without opening the book or leafing through the papers, waved for me to follow him into the dim tunnel. I would have peeked inside, but that was me, and maybe that wasn't how archeologists acted when they found a new clue. Perhaps he needed special rubber gloves or clean hands before paging through it.

"What are those papers?" I asked.

"Letters from Augustine. The wax seal has a ship battling a sea serpent and the inscription '*Non timeo. Inveniam viam meam ad vos*'—I'm not afraid. I'll find my way to you. It's Pérez's monogram."

We made our way down the stonewalled corridor; Andrew's small but powerful flashlight and my phone the only two light sources. The passage wasn't as narrow as it'd first appeared, and Andrew and I could have walked side by side, but we didn't. Instead I let him lead the way just in case there was some danger or booby traps. He was also great at removing thick gray curtains of cobwebs that hung across our path.

"What about the book?"

"I don't know. It could be Jorge's Bible."

"It could also be a hollow-book safe with a cutout to hide things."

"Could be."

"Don't you want to check it now?"

The curiosity boiled up inside me to the point that I wanted to rip the book from under his arm and check it myself.

"Yes, but I'll go over everything once we're in a safer place."

"Can I help?"

The words slipped out before I could stop them. Where did that come from? I didn't know how I could help him. I had no knowledge of Augustine's history, besides what little Andrew had shared, but a small part of me wanted to be involved more with this—I cringed at the thought of what I was about to call it—adventure.

"Yes, but not here," Andrew said. "Don't forget we left a mess and probably should leave this town in a hurry."

I checked my watch. It was five after five. *Oomph*. I smashed into Andrew's hard body, dropping my phone.

"What's wrong?" I picked up my phone and peered around him. The tunnel split into three. "Well, shit. Is this a maze?"

"I don't think so." Andrew tilted his head to the left, then to the right.

"So there are just different routes of escape? Where do they lead?"

He glanced at me with a smile. "Let's find out." After a beat, he went straight. I hurried after him.

"Why did you pick this way?"

"I don't know. Just a hunch."

Andrew was a confident man. Except for this morning when Richard and Brie had stopped at our table. The change in Andrew wasn't just anger. There was some underlying alarm. Or maybe even hurt. Andrew had said Richard was looking for the same treasure, but my gut feeling was there was more to the story. It wasn't only about the money or who discovered the historical artifacts.

"What's your problem with Dr. Dickhead?" I said as we trekked through the tunnel. "And you're in a church, so you can't lie."

"We're no longer under the church. We're under a different building now."

We continued moving through the dark passage. Tree roots started catching my hair and grazing my bare shoulders, and my shoes caught on a few stones on the floor.

"Are you not going to answer my question?" I jabbed my finger into his extensive back.

"Are you not going to drop it?" A hint of irritation threaded through his voice.

"Nope."

"Christ." He shook his head, and I could practically hear his eyes rolling back. "Richard decided to make money by working for private collectors. I believe that certain, if not all, discovered artifacts should be displayed to the public to share knowledge of history. Unfortunately, most of the time we're searching for the same things."

"You already told me that story. I don't think that's the reason."

He released a grumbly sigh. "And he slept with my girlfriend, then married her."

I sucked in a breath. "Oh, shit."

"Yes," he said. "Total shit."

The puzzle pieces began to fit in place, and just one was missing. I knew the answer but had to ask. "Was it Brie?"

Andrew slowed and removed stubborn cobwebs off bulkier roots. "Yes. But I moved on."

Obviously not.

The passage veered to the right, and we came to an avalanche of dirt and rocks from the collapsed ceiling. No way to go around it.

"Fuck," Andrew muttered. "We should try one of the other ways."

I shadowed him back to where we started. "How long ago was it?"

"It's ancient history. Let's keep moving."

"But you're happy now, right? Do you have—"

Halting, he turned to face me. "I'm happy." He stared down at me, his lips pulled into a flat line. "Please, let's move on."

Wow. It was clearly a sore subject, but so many questions buzzed in my brain. How long ago had it happened? How had Andrew and Brie met? And apart from being a bitch for cheating on Andrew, I wanted to know what she could possibly find attractive enough in Dr. Dickhead to let Dr. Andrew Oliver Jones go. *Andrew's name even sounds better.*

I shrugged. "Okay."

Andrew and I returned to where the tunnel branched and picked the tunnel to the right. For a few minutes, we zigzagged in heavy silence until we discovered a dead end. We retraced our steps, tried the left turn, and soon came to a solid wall again.

Well, shit. Was the broken ladder the only way out?

"We must have missed a hidden door or a turn." Andrew slid by me and marched in the direction we came from. "If you hadn't distracted me with your questions, we wouldn't have missed it."

"I was trying to get to know you." I rushed after him. "We're stuck together for a few days, so we might as well learn some things about each other. Is there anything you would like to know about me?"

"Where is your mute button?"

I huffed. "Don't be a di—"

"Shhh." He raised his hand and stopped. A low hubbub of laughter, shouting, and a music boom reached us. "You hear that?" he whispered. "We must be getting closer."

We made a few steps, and a turn to our left appeared out of nowhere. How in the world did we miss it the first time? The noise of a crowd was unmistakable now. Before long, we made another turn and reached a small space with steep steps leading up to a trapdoor and walls boarded with planks like old mines in Western movies. Andrew stepped up and leaned his shoulder into the door. After another try, something heavy slid on the other side, and the trapdoor opened.

Andrew went first, and I climbed after him into a storage room full of boxes of different food cans, cases upon cases of liquor, and the noisome stench of cigarettes. He lowered the panel, and its outline vanished from the view in the grimy floor.

"Wow." I stepped around it, my eyes searching for the secret door contour. "This is incredible." I leaned down and traced my fingers over the grooves and cuts on the wooden floor. "All this time it's been here, and nobody knows about it?"

"Someone knew about it since they took everything hidden under the church."

"Not everything." I nodded at the leather book and letters securely wedged under Andrew's arm.

"True." Andrew walked to the only door in the room and cracked it open.

I tried to dust off the dirt of my dress. It was pointless. My white dress was ruined, and I was sure I bore a resemblance to a corpse bride.

We walked into a dim hall, stale cigars and the reek of cigarette clogging my nose. Andrew shut the door behind us, and at that moment, a door on the opposite side swung open. A lanky man with heavy stubble appeared, zipping his jeans. He stopped and threw us a questioning look. Andrew gave him a short nod. The man mumbled in Spanish and went past us. We followed him into a seedy, dark pub with mismatched tables and chairs occupied mostly by men. William was a head taller than everyone else, so I quickly located him. At the bar, he was carrying on an enthusiastic conversation with a bartender, six shot glasses between them. Four were empty, and two were filled with a dark liquid. What the hell was he doing here?

A frustrated groan left my mouth.

William's hazel eyes met mine, he grinned and said something to his new friend. They picked up glasses, saluted, and took a swig.

Andrew grasped my hand, threading his fingers with mine, and led me to the bar. At his firm grip, a longing I never imagined I could feel for this man shot through me, from my heart to the tips of my toes. And I didn't know what to make of the foreign feeling, but I welcomed it.

"Here is Rick O'Connell and…" William paused scrunching his nose, "what's the woman's name from *The Mummy*?"

"William?" I hissed. "What the hell happened to watching our stuff?"

"No worries, I found a trustful boy to keep an eye on our car." He gestured to two empty seats near him. "Care to join me for a drink?"

"We need to leave. Now." Andrew withdrew several bills from his wallet and dropped them on the bar.

When we stepped outside, it was to find that the sun had made its way around the mountain, dazzling the skies with brilliant colors of orange and blazing red. The streets had got busier with people, relaxing at cafés, chatting near shop doors, or rushing somewhere, carrying grocery bags. The delicious aromas of grilled meat and fried food flooded the air and my senses, making my stomach growl. Strangers threw us concerned glances as we marched in the direction of the alley where William had left our car with a boy to whom he'd apparently given fifty dollars to watch our stuff.

"OMG. Adriana, look at yourself." William's eyes bugged out as he saw me properly in the light, and he slapped his hand over his mouth. "Did you crawl through a graveyard?"

Pretty much.

I glanced down at my dress, and my body deflated like an old balloon. My once-white dress had streaks of black and brown, twigs stuck to its fabric, and a small tear at the hem.

Fuck.

"It's not so bad." I sighed.

I liked this dress a lot. At whatever hotel we found to stay at, I'd soak it in the water and scrub it with soap to ease dirt out of the fabric. In the past, I had removed much worse things from my clothing, like red wine, blood, and someone else's puke. Dirt didn't scare me.

Andrew settled behind the steering wheel and slid the found book between the driver's seat and the console. To my surprise and great relief, our suitcases were untouched.

"Can we find a store and buy club soda?" I said, opening the passenger door. "I want to get some spots out before I wash it."

Andrew gave me a once-over. "Try gasoline."

"Really?" I stared at him with confusion. "It works too?"

"Yes." His smirk deepened. "With a match, you light it on fire."

I scowled at him. "You owe me a dress."

William reached out and dusted something off my head. "You have cobwebs in your hair."

I sighed and swore under my breath. I probably had cobwebs in other places, too.

Chapter Nine

"**I** have bad news." Andrew returned from the hotel desk dangling two keys in his hand. "They only had two rooms."

We'd found a small hotel three towns away from the San Sierra—best to keep a good distance from a crime scene. It was an old Spanish colonial home with uneven wood floors and plaster walls. If it wasn't so rundown, it'd be charming, but the hotel was in need of some serious TLC. Still, it was what it was, and I've spent nights in much worse places than this. All I needed was a clean bed and a hot shower.

"Adriana, you can have your own room." Andrew handed me a key. "William and I can share the other. It has a bigger bed."

I was touched that Andrew was trying to be a gentleman and let me have some privacy. And I liked that he didn't mind spending a night in the same bed with another man—a man who hadn't sobered up during our thirty-minute ride. Judging by the alcoholic fumes wafting off of him, William needed a longer shower than I did.

"No worries." I pressed the key back into his palm and snatched the other one. "William and I shared a double mattress until he went to Emory. We don't mind splitting a room."

I would have bet money that mattress was in the same shitty trailer my mom was still living in, and that the *Toy Story* sheets hadn't been washed since the day I left for college.

Andrew's confused face begged for an explanation, but I had no energy to share details. William's and my miserable upbringing always brought up many questions, turning simple answers into a wearisome and dreadful story.

"We were dirt poor and had to share everything." William pulled up the handle on his suitcase. "I'm hungry and in the mood to celebrate whatever you guys discovered today. Let's meet there in a few." He pointed at a restaurant and bar adjacent to the hotel lobby.

"Does our room have an en suite?" I asked.

"Sort of." Andrew hoisted his bag onto his shoulder and took two of William's suitcases while I picked up mine and another of William's. "It's shared with the neighboring room, but there's a lock. Remember to unlock it when you're done and lock your door when you return to your room."

Yikes.

Our room was bleak but clean, with yellow walls, a chair, a double bed, a stack of clean towels on top of it, and a nightstand with a lamp. A window, covered with threadbare curtains, looked out on the street where we'd parked our Jeep.

The bathroom had a basic shower, a small rusted-out sink, and a toilet that at some point in its life had been white.

William quickly washed, changed into a bright Hawaiian shirt and grey shorts, and skedaddled to the bar. A warm shower was god's gift to me to scrub off the crypt's dirt, cobwebs, and dead man leftovers. As I ran a bar of soap over my body, the memory of Andrew's arm pressed hard against my torso made my pulse beat harder in my throat. I shouldn't think about it, but my lascivious brain couldn't help itself. I pictured Andrew's hands and what they could do. I closed my eyes, and my hand slid over my breasts, down my stomach, and finally reached—

Nope.

If I let my mind wander in a valley of sexual fantasies, it might journey into a territory of *why don't you find out*? And I didn't need that. This was strictly a business affair.

With my hair wrapped in a towel, I did my best to save my dress. I applied mascara and burgundy lip gloss, and changed into yesterday's floral dress with a sweetheart neckline, a fit-and-flare skirt, and cutouts on each side of my waist.

The hotel's pub had a homely atmosphere, dimly lit with decorative hanging lights here and there, its walls covered with vivid artwork, and twinkling tea candles on the mirrored bar amid the bottles. I found William and Andrew in the furthest corner, a small chandelier dangling over their table.

William was scrolling on this phone while sipping from a glass containing brown liquid, and Andrew held one of the newfound letters in one hand and a pencil in his other. His sleeves were rolled up and his hair was wet from the shower. Oblivious to the loud pop music, clatter, and shouting around them, Andrew looked lost in his thoughts. With his eyebrows pulled together and mouth in a flat line, he wrote something in his notebook, then read more. He flipped the paper over and glanced up, his eyes immediately locking with mine. His face relaxed, and the corners of his mouth turned up as he lowered the paper. And there it was, the look he had had this morning when he'd seen me. A warm spring burst into my heart and my chest expanded as if a million flowers had bloomed inside of me.

"Any new interesting discoveries, Dr. Jones?" I slid into a chair beside him.

"Yes." He placed his journal on the table and pointed at his last note. "In one of the letters to Augustine, Jorge mentions his return from a construction site, but it's not clear where it was."

"Another church?" I asked, scooting my chair closer to him.

Heat radiated from Andrew's body, and his citrusy bergamot and powdery coumarin scents beguiled me. Was that how his bed smelled after he slept in it? Had sex in it? A hum went through my body, pooling low in my core. Some people you just knew would be amazing in bed. I bet Andrew was a master at using his fingers and his sultry mouth to unravel women and make them come undone…

"Judging by the details," Andrew said, yanking me out of his bed and back into the present, "this space should be cathedral size." He peered at me half-amused. "You okay? You look flushed."

"It's a little hot in here," I said with as much conviction as I could muster, pressing my hand to my cheek. "What about the book?"

"A collection of short stories. It was specially bound for

Jorge Pérez since it has his monogram." He planted the tome before me.

Gold flowers and vine swirls on both sides decorated the black leather-bound book. In the center was a circle with the same motif that was on Jorge's crypt. The interwoven JP and a cross above it. Five raised bands divided the spine into four compartments, each crowned with a different image: sun, cross, ship, and star. The inside pages were printed in two columns, with blue chapter initials three-lines high, embellished with red ornamentations. Notes, markings, and doodles in someone's handwriting annotated passages.

I brushed my hands on my skirt to get rid of sweat, then traced my finger over the penciled inscription. "What does all this mean?"

"I'm not sure yet. But we have tonight to figure it out." Andrew smiled. "Would you like to see the letters we found today?"

We. He said it as if we were partners in this venture.

I nodded like a sugar-high child, beside myself with excitement, though over *what* I wasn't sure about yet.

Andrew slid the book aside and set the letters in its place. "Some of them don't make much sense to me." He picked one up and laid it flat on top of the others. "They start with the usual family greetings, and then list these." He ran his finger over a sheet that looked like a page from merchant trade records. It had two columns. One with strings of numbers separated by periods, and the other with words.

"What are the words?"

"Description of goods. And this one is especially perplexing." He took a paper out of his journal. "Dr. Garcia thought this note from his archive might be helpful. It's from Augustine to his son and it has one line similar to these." Pictographs of vegetation and fragments of architectural plans dotted the sheet. The bottom had a line with three numbers and one word.

"Do you know this word?"

"Horse."

I looked at Andrew. "Horse?" He shrugged. "That's not very helpful."

Andrew passed me the next letter. "This is a drawing of a security system Augustine designed." The page had ground plans and elevations of some apparatus, with pulleys and cog-wheel mechanisms, with accompanying notes. "Here he talks about the great device, which came to him in a dream. Also, something about him wanting to bring a skillful carpenter from Portugal."

"Where was he planning to build it?"

"He doesn't say."

"William." I glanced at my brother. "Do you want to look at these?"

His eyes flicked to the letter I held, then to his phone. "Not really."

Smitten with today's events, I had forgotten about the strange mood William had fallen into this afternoon. Guilt squeezed my heart. I should've spoken to him earlier in the room and figured out what was wrong. We were on a treasure hunt. He should be happy. I could ask now, but he wouldn't be honest in front of Andrew.

The server stopped by our table to take our order. William and I ordered corn flour *arepas* stuffed with beef and vegetables, and Andrew asked for *ajiaco*, a chicken soup made with four different kinds of potatoes and *guascas*. When the dinner arrived quickly—thank goodness—Andrew hid the book and letters in his backpack. At first, we wordlessly dug into the food, then with our hunger sated, Andrew told us more about Augustine Pérez's life.

"During his first successful robbery of a Portuguese ship," Andrew said, pushing the empty plate aside, "Augustine spared one officer's life. Francisco Ferreira was a cryptographer for the Portuguese military. He and Augustine became friends, and he taught Augustine code writing and helped him develop new codes, which Augustine used in his letters. Unfortunately, seven years later, his friend died."

"What happened to him?" William gulped the remains of his rum and coughed, then lifted a hand, signaling to the server for another round. I was glad he was finally getting his curiosity back. Over dinner, while Andrew talked, I had watched emotions shifting across William's face, from indifference to sadness to finally interest.

"He drowned in a shallow puddle of water."

My hand went to my chest. "Did he pass out drunk?"

The server collected dirty dishes and cleaned our table with a wet rag.

"No. He was drugged with *daturas* by a thief." Andrew wiped the table dry with the paper towels the server had dropped off earlier, and I couldn't help admiring his sculpted forearms as they moved. He unrolled the protective canvas and placed his journal and the letters on it. "The drug comprises all the parts of the flower Datura. It stuns and disorients its victims. In high dosages, it induces a state of psychotic delirium, amnesia, and a burning thirst. Many drown as they try desperately to kill their thirst."

A chill ran over my body, and I shivered despite the warm room. "That's awful."

"Yes," Andrew said, dropping his notebook, the letters, and the book back in front of us. "Shall we continue?" He arched an eyebrow, his lips pulling into an inviting smile.

Even though I was tired, I wanted to stay for a while. I hadn't contributed anything helpful, but nevertheless, I was having fun. "I was afraid you wouldn't ask."

Apart from the three of us, there was hardly anyone else left in the restaurant, the servers having cleaned all the tables but ours. From time to time my knee would knock Andrew's, and eventually, it stayed pressed against his. Andrew's shoulder flattened into mine as we sat close, looking over the sheets we'd found. Or maybe I ended up leaning against him? At some point, we huddled so close Andrew wrapped his arm around my back but quickly corrected his mistake and rested his hand on the back of my chair instead. Working with him as if I was his true partner and feeling the warmth of his body next to mine made me realize how lonely I had been for a while now. My entire adult life, really.

"Have you noticed how Augustine's handwriting is different in some of the correspondence?" I reached over to take a letter from Augustine to Simón, leaning into Andrew and stealing as much of his touch as I could. My hair was in his face and he inhaled deeply, and I had a sudden urge for him to move my hair aside and trace his lips slowly over the back of my neck.

I returned to my seat and opened the letter. "You see how some words starting with M or S have more swirls." I pointed at the sheet in front of me with a much-rigged capital M. Every spot of my body tingled where our knees, thighs, arms, and fingers were touching. I sure as hell knew half of my brushing against him was on purpose, and I couldn't shake off the feeling that his was too. "And compare these Ds and Ls. His handwriting is the same in all of these except for some initial letters. And only," I said with a triumphal grin, "to his sons."

Andrew hummed, his gaze tracing words, then his mouth parted, and his eyes locked on mine. "You're a diamond, my dear."

Time slowed as we looked into each other's eyes, and even though we came from different backgrounds and our lives would never fit together, the soft breeze in my chest turned into a gale as we shared an unmistakable connection. I wasn't sure what to do with the longing that flared inside me. I didn't want it, but it was there. I resisted the need to run my fingers across his stubbled cheek, to feel the fullness of his lower lip. There was a glint of challenge, an unspoken question in his eyes, which made me wish he would kiss me, made me want to mouth *please*.

Andrew blinked and leaned away to root around in his backpack. He must have realized that acting on our attraction would only lead to complications. He pulled out a gilt brass ring with letters and handed it to me.

"This is..." Andrew cleared his throat. "This is a broken cipher, but it's likely useless to us. The top dial is missing."

My pulse seemed to echo in my throat. Swallowing my relief and regret, I asked, "Where did you find it?"

"The cipher arrived with the rest of the items my trusted *friends* sent to me in Costa Rica. It belonged to Simón, and it was most likely used for these letters."

I turned the heavy brass, examining it, then passed it back to Andrew. "Well, then we focus on these numbers and their meanings." I gestured at the sheets in front of us.

"It's probably like the Arnold cipher used in the War of Independence," William slurred. His elbow was propped on the table, his cheek leaning heavily on his palm, eyes half closed.

"What?" I said, twisting in my seat. William was so quiet all this time, I nearly forgot he was with us. No, I actually did forget.

"Gosh," he sighed, "for someone with such great memory, you sometimes surprise me. To find an encrypted word, you need a page number, a line number, and a word number on that line." William waved his hand in my direction. "Remember you watched *National Treasure* with Rai and me? Well, the Ottendorf Cipher they mentioned is pretty much the same as the Arnold."

A wave of sadness passed over me. This was why William's enthusiasm had dimmed, and why he'd drunk so much since we'd arrived in San Sierra. This trip reminded him of the one who got away. William's love of treasure hunts and his ex's love for history had brought them together. When their four-year relationship ended, it destroyed William.

"Rai loved that goddam movie," William said in a whisper almost to himself, looking away. He finished his rum and set the glass down with more force than was necessary, stood up, and swayed.

Time to go.

I pulled my lips into a kind smile and calmly said, "Honey, we should probably go to bed."

It was a few minutes before ten, and I wanted to stay with Andrew, but my brother needed me.

———

I led William up the stairs and through the corridor, his arm thrown over my shoulder and mine around his waist, supporting his drunken body. I unlocked our room, and the two of us wobbled to the bed where William crashed face first on the pillow. Andrew waited in the hallway, holding my purse.

I walked out, quietly closing the door behind me. "Tonight was fun."

"I enjoyed it too," he said, handing me my bag. Tingles cascaded down my spine at the brush of our fingers. "Thank you for your invaluable help. You're a natural at this."

That was an absurd statement.

"Whatever." I laughed, rolling my eyes good-naturedly.

"And I'm very sorry about your dress." He wore a shy smile and rubbed his neck. "You looked beautiful in it."

My heart did the same jolt from this morning, only this time stronger, and it vibrated somewhere in my core. The small hallway we stood in seemed to shrink in size, and the surrounding air went up several degrees. Heart pounding, I stared intently at him. I watched him swallow, his Adam's apple bobbing. Andrew's smile vanished, but his eyes were full of invitation. We were back to that moment earlier at the restaurant.

"Adriana," Andrew said, his voice uncertain. His eyes swept over me, and my pulse turned into wild drumming. Something fierce and determined flashed over his face, and he wetted his lips. And I swear that was the sexiest thing I have ever seen. My stomach twisted with anxiety and hope.

"Yes?" I swallowed too. My whole body hummed with need. I wanted Andrew to haul me into his arms and kiss me. Not gently. Hard. Could I throw myself at him?

My back pressed the door and pushed it open, making me stumble back. The universe was giving me a sign to back away, not to muddle this trip.

The phone in Andrew's palm rang, and a picture of the attractive blond woman hugging the little girl filled the screen.

"I'm glad we cleared up that you don't have a wife." I backed into my room.

"Me too. Good night, Adriana." He inclined his head politely and brought his phone to his ear. I liked how my name sounded when he said it; smooth and seductive, like lazy morning sex.

With a last hungry glance at Andrew, I shut the door and pressed my back to it. My heart pounded so hard its sound vibrated my body. This morning Andrew was a smart, intriguing, and heartbreakingly handsome, unavailable man, and now he was a smart, intriguing, handsome, sweet man with a kind heart that stirred emotions inside of me I had no business having.

Chapter Ten

The sexual hum hadn't ceased as I scrubbed my face and teeth, and changed into pajama shorts and an old university t-shirt. The fabric was so worn that in a certain light, it was almost translucent in some spots. I climbed into the bed beside William, who snored as loud as an aggravating next-door garage band on a balmy fall night. Tomorrow he'd regret passing out without taking care of his face. I groaned and turned the nightstand lamp on.

After a few minutes of wrestling with his limbs, I removed his shoes, shorts, and shirt, and returned to the bathroom to rummage in his beauty bag. I plucked cotton pads, a balancing cleanser, and a conditioning night lotion. William had a ten-step cleansing routine, but this would do.

Smoothing William's hair off his forehead, I gently ran the wetted pad over his skin. His sandy brown hair took on a warm brown shade in the dim light. His snoring stopped, and his lips twitched at their corners. He was such a beautiful human inside and out, and it hurt to know he was as lonely as me. After Rai left, for two years my *heart-of-the-party happy-go-lucky* optimistic brother turned into someone unrecognizable, a workaholic who would gag at the word love. He even stopped watching rom-coms. When William came out of his depression, he started having a new *special someone* almost monthly, and I wondered if he was desperately trying to find The One or merely the one to replace the ghost of Rai. I kissed his forehead and said a silent prayer that soon he would meet someone who would do both for him.

I dropped the used cotton pad on my lap and added lotion to my fingers. I reached out to his face and gently rubbed it on, the bracelet catching the lamp's light.

My hand paused, and I stared at the etched lines on the bracelet that were no longer *just* lines. The bases the stones were pressed into took the shape of the foot of a mountain, and the swirls around it looked like rivers branching out. A few years ago, I went to an Atlanta Art Museum exhibition on light sculptures that form beautiful images when viewed at a certain angle. I rotated my wrist slightly to the right, and the landscape vanished, becoming again just gems and carved swirls. I turned my arm where it was a few seconds ago, and the hills and river returned.

"Oh my god." I stood up, and the bottles fell on the floor with a racket. William stirred, and his eyelids fluttered but never fully opened. He mumbled something and turned to his side.

I had to tell Andrew. I checked the time. A quarter to eleven. It was late, but Andrew had said he'd stay up working. Wait. Was I doing this to help Andrew beat Richard, or was I taking any excuse to see him again?

I'd debate it later.

Barefooted, I stepped out of my room into the quiet hallway. Before I could lose my nerve, I crossed the hall in one step but didn't knock. My heart began its odd beating again. Perhaps waiting for the morning would be a better idea. What could he do with my new-found information in the middle of the night?

As I contemplated what to do, the door opened wide, and Andrew's broad figure filled the frame. A well-after-five-o'clock stubble highlighted his sharp angles. He wore gray cotton pants and a cream shirt. The top four buttons of the shirt were undone, revealing some chest hair. My mouth went dry.

"Everything okay?" He leaned out, turning his head left and right.

"How did you know I was here?"

"I noticed a shadow lurking under the door." His eyes perused from my face down to my breasts, lingering there a beat longer before meeting mine once again. Uh, yeah, no bra.

"I wasn't lurking. I was standing and thinking."

Andrew dropped his hand off the door. "Do you want to think in my room?"

With my heart boomeranging in my chest, I maneuvered around him. His bed was made, the overhead light was on, and the breeze from the open balcony door played with a sheer curtain. The lamp on a writing desk cast a bright light on his journal, the book, and the letters we'd found today.

Andrew closed the door and pressed his back against it, crossing his arms. "Are you here to help with the Arnold Cipher? William was right, by the way."

"You were able to decipher the code?" I didn't know what to do with myself, so I crossed my arms too.

"Yes. I used Jorge's book."

"And?"

"They planned to move the cargo to the palace when it was completed. I had no idea Augustine was building something like this."

"By any chance, did they mention the location?"

"No. This is something we'll have to figure out. And in the last letter, Augustine planned to visit his old ranch in March to see love birds. That's all I got so far."

I arched an eyebrow. "Love birds?"

He pressed his lips together and shrugged.

"Could they be talking about the palace in the sketch?"

"I'd assume."

"So earlier, when you said Jorge returned from a cathedral-size construction, maybe that's what they were building. And the complicated mechanism with pulleys and wheels could be a security system to store the treasure at the palace."

The corners of his mouth turned up. "Exactly my thought."

I stayed calm but wanted to squeal, giddy with excitement. We'd made progress. The puzzle pieces we started with were connecting. I was sure some elements were still missing, but I had no doubt we would find them with time.

"So why were you in the hallway?" Andrew uncrossed his arms and slid his hands into his pants pockets. I'd gotten so wrapped up in his news I forgot why I was here in the first place.

"I also have something to share. If you hold the bracelet at a certain angle, it becomes a geographic layout."

Andrew arched an eyebrow. "A map?"

"Yes. I'll show you." I approached him, raised my wrist, and slowly moved it. "Do you see it?"

"No." He pushed off the door and narrowed his focus on the gold band. "We might have too much light." Andrew's hand found the switch on the wall and flipped it off, dowsing us into semi-darkness.

"Now?" I asked, peering at his face, which was somehow even more gorgeous in the dimness.

Andrew chuckled. "It's too dark now. Let's try it with the table lamp."

We moved to the desk, and I had no doubt my t-shirt was turning transparent in this light. Andrew took my hand into his, the warmth of his touch fused with my skin. His gaze drifted to my breasts, and the heat spread all over my body. How much could he see? Did I want him to look? At that thought, my traitorous nipples turned painfully hard, making this situation even more awkward. Andrew cleared his throat and dragged his eyes to the bracelet.

I watched him, holding my breath, waiting for his face to flash with exultant recognition as he steadily rotated my hand. I could practically see the wheels turning inside Andrew's head, just like when we were under the church. Lines on his face changed, his mouth twitching a bit, and his jaw muscle shifting ever so slightly as he bit the inside of his cheek. He was a handsome man, but when he was concentrating, he was fucking gorgeous.

"You're staring at me again," Andrew said, attention on my wrist.

Of course, I was. He was hard not to ogle.

My face turned warm. "No, I'm not."

"Yes, you are, like you did when we were in Iglesia San Antonio."

What the hell? Did this man have eyes in the back of his head?

"I wasn't. I was waiting for you to share more of your thoughts."

"And you were staring." A cocky grin grew on his face, but then it fell, his beautiful eyes widening. "Christ."

Excitement rippled through me. "Do you see mountains and rivers?"

"Yes. There's more than just those. This is stunning. And it's been with us all this time."

Without releasing me, Andrew bent to check something in this journal, turned the page, and ran his finger down the sheet.

"What else is there?" I asked.

"Come, sit with me." He picked up his notebook and his phone and sat on the bed.

I dropped next to him, hands on my lap, my hip pressing into his. I didn't have to sit this close, but I wasn't about to move.

Flipping a few pages, Andrew paused on one with sketched crests and hallmarks. Then he took his phone and found the photo of the ranch with horses that I'd airdropped him earlier in the bar. He zoomed in, then pivoted his phone to me. "What do you see?"

"Um…" I said and leaned a bit, my arm flattened against his—I might have done that on purpose—and looked at a blurry image of two horses and a rising sun.

"The crest on this photo is the same as the one on your page."

Andrew brought my hand close to his face and slowly turned it. "It's also here." He pointed at a small spot carved into the gold with a pencil. "See it?"

Pulling my hand out of his hold, I leveled the bracelet with my eyes and concentrated, turning it slowly. The same crest appeared in the curve near the smaller stone in a river bend. If I'd blinked, I'd have missed it.

An unexpected thrill ignited my heart.

"I see it," I whispered and faced Andrew.

His hands remained at his sides, but his gaze skimmed over my face before stopping on my parted lips.

"You found a map," he murmured with a coy smile, his eyes turning up. He held my gaze, unblinking, and a wave of desire coursed inside me, muddling my senses. I ached for him to kiss me. One kiss. To celebrate this discovery. It would be fine. I would be fine. I was in no danger of falling for Andrew. There wouldn't be enough time. We had a map now, and in a few days, the bracelet would be off. Our paths were going in different directions and would never cross again.

"Map to where?" I could barely form the words. My breathing was shallow, and my heart was in my throat.

The air was hot and thick as his eyes were intent on me. God, why wouldn't he lean in and kiss me already?

The phone on his lap rang. The display showed that Dr. Garcia was calling.

"I'm sorry," he rasped. "I need to answer."

"Of course."

I hate that phone.

Andrew brought the phone to his ear. "Carlos." He looked down at the floor. "I got your email but might no longer need the scans. Adriana uncovered a map on the bracelet." He could have taken full credit for the discovery, yet he didn't. He paused, listening. "I'm not sure yet. It has Las Loma on it. Yes. Just like we discussed." He nodded, raking a hand through his hair. "Yes, I can do it. You should have it by the morning."

He hung up, and the quiet groan that escaped him was genuine frustration. He turned to me with a sad smile, the fire in his eyes gone. And maybe it was for the best.

"I know it's late, but do you mind staying for a bit longer?" Andrew said, his voice jaded with disappointment. "I need to copy these details and send them to Carlos."

"Sure, no problem."

"It might take me a while..." Andrew scanned the room, then dragged a chair to the bed and set the lamp on it. "If you can lay and place your hand under the lamp...?"

"Is Las Loma ranch one of the sketches?"

"Yes. It's Augustine's childhood house." Andrew grabbed his notebook and a pencil, then he dropped to the floor next to the bed, crisscrossing his legs. "While Augustine lived near the ocean, his sons, Simón and Gabriel, resided on the old ranch with their families. Usually, the sons came to visit their father's house, but based on the messages that we found tonight, Augustine went there not long before he died. There's a letter from Simón to Jorge in which he mentioned their father arriving in March with carts carrying large chests."

"Do you know where the ranch is?"

I followed his directions and lay on my back, stretching out my arm. The lamp's heat warmed my skin but wasn't nearly as hot as Andrew's gaze on me a minute ago.

"Yes. A decade ago, a resort chain bought the ranch and converted it into 'Erizo,' a luxurious B&B. We'll go there tomorrow."

"Are we staying there?"

"We could if they have rooms available."

For a while, Andrew sketched in silence and I studied water stains on the ceiling, trying my best not to think about how we'd almost kissed. At least I thought we were going to kiss. Did Andrew answer his phone as an excuse to stop the head-on collision? He could have called back Dr. Garcia later. I turned to look at him. His long lashes cast shadows against the curve of his cheekbones as his gaze traced the movement of the pencil. Maybe he had someone waiting for him in Cambridge. Should I ask?

"Adriana," he said.

I rolled my eyes. "Yes, I'm staring at you."

He chuckled. "That wasn't what I was going to say."

"What were you going to say?"

"Thank you for coming with me on this trip." His eyes had a glint of appreciation.

A warmth rushed through me, and something like hope swelled inside me. I wasn't sure why and what to do with it, so I shrugged a single shoulder to cover up whatever that feeling meant. "I only came because I need money."

Andrew's expression dimmed. "Of course."

My smile faltered at his reaction. "But I'm enjoying this trip ... and your company." Too much. But it was the truth.

He glanced at me, then went back to sketching, his lips quirked. "I like you, too."

"I didn't say I like you," I mumbled.

Andrew hmmed, like he knew I was lying, his smile wider. Probably because he came from a planet of breathtaking hunky stallions who were accustomed to women turning into wet goo in his presence.

"Tell me about your childhood," he said.

I groaned and tore my stare from him back to the ceiling. "Why?"

"From brief comments you and William have made, I've gathered you had a difficult upbringing."

"We were fine." That was a stretched truth. "Our mother's narcissism drove our father away. She blamed him for our poverty even though she has done *absolutely* nothing to save money or tried to find a better job. So he left us when I was seven, and William was ten. Our mother only wanted us when no one wanted her. She sometimes abandoned us for weeks at a time. Once she left with a new friend around Easter and returned mid-July."

He stopped sketching, and worry creased his already-scrunched brow. "How did you manage to live like that?"

"You know the saying it takes a village to raise a child? In our case, it only took one sweet neighbor, Mrs. Rudy. She helped us when she could. Anyway," I stifled a yawn, "why don't you share with me how you grew up to be what you are now?"

"My granddad was Dean of the College of Archaeology at Cambridge. And when I was eight, he took me with him to what was supposed to be the location of Sodom and Gomorrah in Jordan."

I stared wide-eyed at Andrew. "At eight? Your parents allowed that?"

"I'd traveled with my grandparents since I was five."

"Wow." I didn't leave Georgia until I was nineteen. "Are they still alive?"

"Yes. Are yours?"

"No," I said. "Well, I don't know. My parents met in a foster home. They didn't know their parents."

"Do you know what happened to your father?"

"Nope. William and I are too pissed off to locate him." I sighed heavily. "I don't even bother to keep in touch with my mother." I knew I should have felt pain or regret or guilt for saying those words, but I didn't. I felt more empathy for a homeless person on the streets than for my own self-loving mother.

Andrew's eyebrows pinched in a sad arch. "Why?"

"Our mother wasn't interested in us. To this day, she only calls us when she needs cash. Sometimes I don't even answer. But…"—I pulled a weak smile—"I keep in touch with Mrs. Rudy, so I know mom is alive and changing jobs as quickly as her boyfriends."

"Was she unkind?" he said, the concern clear in his voice.

I shrugged, trying not to move my extended arm. "She didn't beat us or anything like that. She just didn't want to be a mother. As a child, I craved her love, and any insignificant attention from her was a big deal, but as I grew older, I didn't like her. William and I have been running a household since before we were teenagers. We had no childhood." The old anger rose in me at how many weeks we'd spent left alone without a parent. Wearing the same dirty clothes and eating cereal for days. Kids complained about school food, but to me it was the best meal of the day. Summers were the hardest because of the two-month break. William and I lost our breakfast and lunch.

"If not for Mrs. Rudy's help, we probably wouldn't have survived." I scoffed and rolled my eyes. "Okay, we would've survived, but we would've been pulled into the foster system, probably separated, and I'm not sure it would've been any better. We had classmates who were in foster care, and the horrors they told us haunted my nightmares. It was for the best we were left to fend for ourselves."

Andrew placed the pencil on his lap and studied me with an unsettled expression. "Did this Mrs. Ruby have any kids? Why couldn't she foster you both? Was she old?"

I took a deep breath, expanding my lungs to their maximum. "At the time, she was in her early fifties, but she had a criminal record, so she wasn't a *perfect* fit. She's the nicest woman I know and would have been a great mom to us. She knew telling authorities about our parents wouldn't do any good so she helped as much as she could. She took us to a doctor when we were sick, and she taught us all the things we needed to know to make our situation work."

"What about school?" Andrew peered curiously at me. "Didn't they notice your mother wasn't there ever?"

"Maybe they did; maybe they didn't. We were honor students and never bothered anybody. William and I were both valedictorians."

"I'm sorry you had to grow up like that."

"What doesn't kill me makes me stronger, right?" And a little bitter. I grinned to cover the old pain.

"You are strong. Look at everything you and your brother achieved in your life with nobody's help."

I laughed without humor. "William, yes, he achieved a lot. Me? Well, I'm not sure yet. So far, I'm a homeless and jobless owner of a building that needs thousands of dollars to become a store and my home. Money that I don't have." First, Dr. Garcia's stupid call and now my mopey life story had totally dampened the mood. "When did you decide you wanted to become an archeologist?"

"When I was eight years old, I climbed inside an abandoned manor about a mile away from where we lived." Andrew reached out to my hand, and the pads of his fingers pressed into my skin as he rotated the bracelet.

"The same place where you got the scar on your face?"

"Yes. I explored it for a while, and then I fell through the rotten floorboards and landed in a cellar. The door wouldn't open no matter what I tried, so I was stuck there for fourteen hours."

I sucked air between my teeth. "Ouch. Fourteen hours? Were you scared?"

"Not really. The aftershock of pain vanished—I didn't even know how bad it was until I saw my mother's face—and I knew someone would find me eventually. I got thirsty, and there were several cases of unopened wine bottles."

"Oh god." I wrinkled my nose. "Don't tell me you drank some of it?"

"It was disgusting." Andrew gently changed the angle of my arm. "Hold still."

"How much did you drink?"

"Enough to put me to sleep and not hear my parents calling out my name when they came looking for me that evening when I didn't return for supper. Eventually a sniffer dog found me. The paramedic team had to pull me out through the same hole because the wall in the basement outside the cellar had collapsed and blocked the door."

"Did you get in trouble for trespassing and getting drunk?"

"No. I was dirty, inebriated, and blood covered my face. My parents were so happy to see me alive that they forgot to lecture me. My poor mother, I can still picture her expression." His hands stilled, then he released a heavy sigh. "Anyway, the morning after I decided I wanted to become someone who always explores unknown places and searches for treasure, I asked my grandfather to take me on his next dig."

Having grown up with parents who loved him, Andrew's childhood was the polar opposite of mine. The closest William and I got to those Hallmark happy family moments was when our mom returned after some loser dumped her. We would watch a show on our crappy TV set, snuggling up on a worn-out couch, eating cheap Little Caesars Pizza, and drinking up all the attention we could get from our mom before it inevitably disappeared again. That would last for a week or two until our mother met another douchebag that swept her off her feet, and our snuggle time was gone for an unknown period.

Andrew went quiet again, sketching with a vacant smile on his face, no doubt thinking about the adventures his grandparents took him on. I didn't even go on a school field trip because there wasn't enough money. While Andrew explored decaying manors for lost treasure, I was brawling with the nursery of raccoons outside our crumbling trailer. The biggest adventure I had in my childhood was when Mrs. Rudy took us to a Six Flags theme park for William's fifteenth birthday.

My eyes grew heavy, and I fought hard to keep them open, but eventually, I lost that battle.

Sometime later, I rapidly blinked while my mind figured out exactly where I was.

In Andrew's bed with a thin blanket thrown over my body, drool running down my cheek. *Great.*

I wiped my face, propped myself up on an elbow, and surveyed the room. The desk lamp was on, illuminating Andrew where he was slumped in the chair, his head resting on his folded forearms, his eyes closed. His broad back slowly rose and fell. He was even more handsome when he was asleep. The fluttering in my chest was back again.

Careful not to wake Andrew, I threw the blanket off and got up. The bed made a measurable squeak, and he opened his eyes.

"Sorry," I whispered. "I should go to my room."

He dragged a hand over his face and then over the back of his neck, groaning. "Thank you for staying."

"Did you get everything you needed off the bracelet?"

With a tired but triumphant smile, Andrew turned the notebook my way. "We have half of a map."

Chapter Eleven

When I told Andrew that we should hit the road early in the morning, I didn't mean before daybreak. Still, he knocked on our door before the sun even tried to reach this part of the planet.

Dazed and half asleep, I pushed on William's shoulder. "Time to get up, handsome." He mumbled a string of curses. "I agree." I yawned, rubbing my eyes. "But we need to keep going. The treasure awaits."

I checked the time and moaned: 5 a.m. Leaving the overhead lights on, I shuffled to the bathroom. When I was done washing my face and applying make-up, William pushed past me and turned on the shower, letting it warm up. His hair resembled a bird's nest, but there was no hint of a hangover on his face.

"How are you feeling?" I passed him his toothbrush.

"Tired." He stared at his reflection. "This can't be accurate."

"What?"

"My skin. God, it looks awful."

I wanted to roll my eyes. William could spend a month with his face in the dirt, and his skin would still be better than anybody else I knew. "I tried to clean it a bit."

He picked up the toothpaste. "Yeah. I saw bottles by the bed. Thanks."

I pressed my hip against the door, holding my make-up bag. "Do you want to talk about it?"

He glanced at me through the mirror. "About how you don't know a simple skin cleansing routine? That was the morning cleanser."

Now I rolled my eyes. "No. About what was going on with you yesterday."

"There's nothing to talk about," he said and began brushing his teeth.

"It's about Rai, isn't it? This whole trip reminds you too much of him."

I waited for him to finish brushing. He spat and washed his face.

Tentacles of panic grasped my stomach. I wasn't sure what had changed in William, but this was new to me. William and I were more than brother and sister, we were best friends, sharing everything, and never keeping secrets.

He hooked his fingers into the waistband of his boxers. "Are you going to stay here and watch me undress?"

"I'd need to bleach my eyes if I did." I collected my dry dress and left the bathroom.

If William needed some time, I would give it to him, but now he knew I was worried about him, he should open up soon. Wouldn't he? He told me about Rai's decision to move to California without him the same week it happened. I was at a winery in Oregon on a work trip, but I cut it short and flew home to be with William. I was his rock just as much as he was mine. Was William keeping his feelings to himself because my life was a dumpster fire and he didn't want to bother me with his troubles? Or was our relationship changing and he no longer wanted to confide in me? I swallowed the hurt and anxiety that had become a hard lump in my throat. I couldn't bear the thought of not being Williams's best friend. If I lost him, I lost everything.

———

Andrew was in the lobby when we arrived, his tall figure leaning against the supporting beam near the restaurant entrance, holding two coffee mugs. He looked way too good for six in the morning, with only a few hours of sleep. He gave me a warm smile and my heart flipped. Was it going to do it each time I saw him?

"Hey, for the first time, you aren't late." Andrew handed us the paper cups. "How are you feeling, William?"

"Hungry," William said, accepting the cup.

I sipped the warm coffee, noticing it was made as I liked it, with one spoon of sugar and a splash of cream. Andrew had remembered.

"We'll eat in the car." Andrew pushed off. "I already got us a to-go breakfast."

The sunrise over the Colombian coastal route had the intensity of flawless beauty. I unsuccessfully tried to capture it on my iPhone as we drove up the highway. The early morning air was cool and whipped around my face and bare shoulders, raising goosebumps on my skin.

"How many days are we staying there?" William called from the backseat. He was browsing the Erizo at Las Loma resort website.

"When I called this morning, I secured three rooms only for one night," Andrew said.

"Bummer," William said. "It sounds amazing. It has sunrise *and* sunset horse rides, *and* a huge pool."

"And what exactly are we going to do there?" I asked, my finger playing with the bracelet stones.

"Explore," Andrew said.

"No shit?" I said with mockery. "Could you please elaborate?"

Andrew chuckled. "I don't know how much has changed since the renovations, but I hope to find out what Augustine meant by visiting the love birds. It could be anything. Maria adored birds. She painted them and made sculptures. Augustine brought her many birds from around the world and built her a large bird sanctuary."

As we drove south, the scenery of the land changed with each passing hour, from the rugged mountains with their peaks disappearing in a veil of mist, to sloping hills with adobe houses scattered on the ground, their tin roofs reflecting the sun. With only one hour left, we found ourselves stuck in bumper-to-bumper traffic in a village, breathing car exhaust, and baking under the hot sun, sticky sweat and black ooze coating my skin.

"If only we were driving a car with air-conditioning." William pressed a handkerchief to his mouth and nose and threw his head backward.

Without a breeze and with so many running cars, the air quality had dropped from bad to terrible. I peeled my thighs off the seat and rose, trying to check what the hold-up was, but the truck a few cars ahead of us blocked my view. With a groan, I plopped back down.

The car line before us moved several yards. Once we turned the corner, the explanation of what had caused the traffic presented itself. A skinny dog with enlarged nipples was making circles around the gutter on the road, jumping in front of cars, then bolting back, barely avoiding being hit. Cars moved slowly around her, going onto the opposite side, creating a logjam for incoming traffic.

Andrew wheeled the car to the side and went over a curb.

"What are you doing?" I asked, my hands grabbing the dashboard.

"The dog has lost its pup." He parked the car and unbuckled his seatbelt.

Andrew got out of the Jeep, signaled for the oncoming car to slow down, and carefully approached the dog. Cars behind us honked, and drivers yelled—my guess—profanities in our direction. One blessing of not knowing the language. To help Andrew, I jumped out of the car and hurried to him. He neared the dog and it growled, then fled to nearby bushes. I wasn't sure I could help but I could shoo the dog if it made to attack him. Andrew lowered flat on his stomach on the ground and pressed his face into the opening.

"I can hear it." He stuck his hand inside the hole.

"Aren't you worried there are snakes?" I asked, my gaze frantically jumping from the moving cars to the dog to Andrew.

At last, Andrew pulled out a small puppy. He stood up, cradling the pup to his chest. He whispered something to it as he approached the distressed mom and gently lowered her baby. The mother wagged its tail, visibly shaking from fear or excitement, grabbed her pup by its neck and disappeared into the bushes. My heart melted into a hot puddle and trickled down somewhere between my thighs. My attraction for Andrew was undeniable and overwhelming. I ached to kiss him. It took a lot of effort not to do that.

"You're the sweetest man I know," I said as we climbed into our car.

"Any decent person would have done the same." He started the car and waved his hand out to let the car behind us know he was getting back on the road.

"No one helped, but you." I buckled up and pulled my sunglasses on my face.

In my ribcage, someone released butterflies that were high on cocaine. I was in big trouble.

Surrounded by green hills and set at the edge of a lush jungle, the "Erizo at Las Loma" retreat was nothing like the ranch in the pirate's drawing. Only the front of the main building resembled what Augustine had captured. Manicured trees dotted the property grounds, water splashed in a large fountain before the manor entrance, and expansive grassed lawns stretched on each side of the gravel driveway. A perfect place to disconnect from the fast-paced world and relax in paradise on earth. Based on the resort's outside appearance, my guess was that the inside would be mind-blowing, like something out of a luxurious travel magazine.

And I was right.

A stunning terracotta floor and high, wood-beamed cathedral ceiling opened before us, and cool air with a hint of orange and jasmine enveloped us. William's and my jaws unhinged when we walked in.

The hostess presented us with cucumber water—*yuck*—and an old-fashioned heavy metal key with a blue ribbon. A super cute touch, but how could a modern woman fit it in her tiny cell phone purse?

Our rooms were on the first floor, down the corridor, past an indoor fountain in the large living area, a seating room, and finally down another corridor. It was a workout to reach our room. I surveyed the décor for signs of birds but there were none in the paintings or sculptures.

"Since you might be staying longer on this trip," Andrew said to me as we walked side by side, my high heels making a clickety-clack noise. "You need to buy different shoes. No heels."

"I like wearing these. The average male height is five-eleven, so I can look any man straight in the eye if not down when I wear them. You're a gigantic exception to the rule."

"This is me." William stopped at the door and slid his key into the lock. "I want to take a long shower and then let's meet in the restaurant to grab something to eat before we go on a bird hunt. Say an hour?"

We nodded and continued down the corridor.

"Why is that important?" Andrew and I neared my room.

I faced him and craned my neck to capture his gaze. "Level eye contact is intimidating, causing the opponent to feel studied and uncomfortable. Let him be fooled we have the same height, or I might even be taller, and somewhere in the back of his mind he already fears me."

Andrew's lips curved up, a move I discovered made my pulse thump out of rhythm. "I think your long legs with that seahorse-shaped birthmark just above your knee that matches the one on your wrist is enough to intimidate any man."

For a split second, our worlds collided. A bouquet of hummingbirds replaced the earlier butterflies, and they all congregated in my chest. My fingers relaxed, and the heavy key fell out of my hand. Andrew was quick to pick it up. I had a strong wish for him to run his hand over my legs as he slowly rose to his full height. He extended his hand, holding the key.

His eyes, full of mirth, lingered on mine before dropping to my mouth, the mirth replaced by yearning. His Adam's apple bobbed as he swallowed.

So what if this man was tall, and handsome, and smart, and has a huge heart, and probably other huge body parts? I needed to get a grip on myself.

"What are you thinking about?" Andrew's voice was husky and low, and he regarded me as if I was a complicated Bauhaus statue.

I smiled and arched an eyebrow. "My secret plan to steal Pérez's treasure."

Andrew gave a sardonic snort. "Sure, that's what you were thinking." He grabbed his bag off the floor. "See you soon." He turned and strode to the neighboring door, and before he entered his room, he gave me another stunning smile.

My room was rustic but glam, with sumptuous furnishings enclosed in pale green stucco walls, and an abundance of light that came through two large windows offering panoramic views of a mountainous landscape. But the best feature of this space was the ornate, tiled flooring and the high ceiling with exposed wooden beams.

I kicked off my shoes and raced barefoot to check out the bathroom. And oh my god. As soon as my gaze landed on the lion-clawed tub next to another massive window, I had a craving to fill it up with warm water, dump in the entire complimentary bottle of rose oils, and sink into magnificence. Of course, there was no time for that right now. I needed more than an hour to indulge in such luxury. But later tonight, I had a date with that tub and a bottle of the best champagne the hotel could offer.

And oh, hello! It had a mobile showerhead. Fingers crossed pressure was strong. After what Andrew did today to my insides, without a doubt I would use it.

But for now, I turned on the shower, returned to my room, stripped naked, and laid my dress on the gigantic bed. I dug out my underwear from my suitcase and took them to wash. I *really* needed to buy more clothing.

As soon as the warm water hit my head, I released a sigh of relief. God, it felt so good to wash off road dust and exhaustion muck. The resort's shampoo smelled of almond and honey, and the sugar scrub left my skin feeling like silk. My hand glided over my body, and when it reached my breast, I pictured Andrew's large hands cupping me instead.

Should I try out that handheld showerhead now? No. No time.

I washed my panties, hung them over the tub's long faucet, then wrapped myself in one of the complementary soft robes. I towel-dried my hair, then pulled it into a messy bun on the top of my head. Over the years William had imparted all kinds of horrors about how bad make-up was for the skin, so I tried to follow his advice. My usual daytime make-up was minimal— no foundation, no powder, always sunblock, a touch of concealer, mascara, blush, and occasionally eyeliner. Something nudged me to add more color to my eyes to make them stand out more so I applied silver-copper eyeliner that complimented my green eyes. Did Andrew like women with lots of make-up or did he prefer more natural? I shouldn't care, but just in case, I tapped berry lipstick lightly on my lips.

I tossed the lipstick tube into my make-up bag but missed it. It clacked on the floor and rolled under the sink, stopping on a tile with a design of entangled flowering branches with two small blue birds, facing west and east. I leaned in to examine it. I'd seen a similar design in the Museo de Historia, and Andrew had it somewhere in his journal too. Only, this time the birds were facing each other. Someone knocked on my door, and I straightened, hitting my head on the vanity top.

"Shit, that hurts." I grabbed the top of my head. The impatient asshole knocked on the door again. It was probably William needing something from my bag. "Just a second," I yelled.

When I cracked the door open, I found Andrew standing in the hall with his wet brown hair in total disarray, a wavy lock stuck to his forehead. I had to admit, he looked even sexier than before. He wore the same khaki pants and light green Oxford shirt as earlier, both visibly wet, as if he'd dressed without drying himself after the shower. In his hand, he clutched his leather notebook.

"Has it been an hour already?" I glanced at my watch. Forty-five minutes had passed.

Andrew blinked once, then again, and he had an expression as if he didn't recognize me. He opened his mouth, then closed it. His behavior confused me.

"Is something wrong?" I asked.

Then, as if someone had clapped their hands, he snapped out of his weird trance. "Can I come in?"

I pulled my robe tighter and stepped aside to let him enter. He paced to the window, then to the dresser, and then to my bed, his stare in constant contact with the floor. A water drop ran down my neck, tickling my skin. I wiped it away. Maybe my chaotic hairdo was the reason Andrew had lost track of his thoughts when I opened the door. Or my too-open robe.

"Are you searching for a tile with birds?" I untangled my bun and braided my hair.

"Yes." He stopped and focused on me.

"I found one near the tub just as you were trying to break down my door."

Andrew marched into the bathroom. A moment later, he came out, a pink hue coloring his cheeks. "It's not it."

"You have one in your notebook. Can I see it again?"

He strode in my direction and handed me his journal. "Maria designed it. An oak tree and Tabebuia rosea. Strength and beauty."

The drawing was of elaborate swirls that linked branches with acorns and flowers, in the center two small birds faced each other. It was a remarkable pencil sketch.

"All right, we need to find a tile with this pattern." With my finger I traced the drawing in the notebook, memorizing its curves and twists. I glanced up at Andrew, who was studying the tiles around my feet. When our eyes met his face again flashed an expression of wonderment. Or stupidity. Those appeared similar when there was no explanation provided. Did he also hit his head? "Andrew, are you feeling okay?"

Andrew placed his hands on my arms, his fingers curving around, sending an electric sensation inside of me. "I need to see what's under your feet." At least that was what I think he said, because my mind heard *I need to see what's under your robe.* He gently pushed me to the left.

He looked down, and his face expressed disappointment. The tile had a similar design, but different birds faced opposite directions.

"What happens when we find it?"

"We check under it." He stepped to my bed, dropped to all his fours, and peered under it.

"Let's check William's room too." I grabbed my dress off the bed.

"I already did. We didn't find anything. The only original room left is at the end of the hallway."

I hid in the bathroom and quickly changed into my dress. "Okay, can we find out who booked it and talk to them?" I walked out. "We could explain our situation and ask if we can check it out."

"We can't." Andrew stepped to one of the windows and pressed his hand over the panels. "I saw Brandon Pines leaving the room."

I slid my feet into wedge sandals and bent to fasten them. "Who?"

"A museum curator who works with Richard."

My heart sank. I was hoping we were beating Richard and Brie at this.

"Dickhead is good at his job," I muttered, angry on Andrew's behalf.

"But not as good as we are." Andrew tugged on the window clasp, then pushed in the center where the panels met. "These are original to the house. Only some of the glass squares are new."

I bit the cuticle on my thumb. If they hadn't figured out where to look, they would soon.

Absentmindedly Andrew tapped this journal against his palm, his eyes narrowing on me. His right eyebrow lifted. "Did you do something different with your make-up?"

"No." My cheeks heated, and I pretended to search for something in my purse. Did he not like what he saw? He must be used to high-class, glamorous women.

Andrew stepped around, catching my eyes and dazzling me with a heart-melting smile.

"I meant to say whatever you did is nice. Maybe it's your wet hair, or I don't know, but you look more beautiful…" He cleared his throat. "Sexy."

His cheeks flamed with color. Oh god, this confident man blushed when he complimented me. That was way too cute. Would it be too much if I squished his face between my hands and kissed him?

"Brandon is a drinker, so he'll be in the bar right about now. So…" Andrew bit his bottom lip as his eyes swept over me. Oh, Jesus, I knew where this was heading.

I crossed my arms over my chest. "No."

"You could distract him while I sneak into his room." He grinned. "Would you?"

"You're good at reading signs." I pointed at my annoyed expression. "What does this mean?"

"I'm not asking you to sleep with him," he said with a playful tone. "Just flirt a bit."

Maybe it wasn't that big of a deal to chat with someone. But what would I say? I couldn't think of a single time I'd intentionally toyed with someone. Sure, I flirted during a conversation, because it was a natural reaction of one human to another when there was attraction, but how to flirt on purpose? Loop my hair around a finger and bat my eyelashes? Better not. Or I'd appear I was a few clowns short of a circus.

My stomach twisted in the same sickening way as it did when Jeff slid his hand on my thigh and asked me to go to his room with him. Would Andrew have asked me to do this if he'd known the story? Probably not.

"Fine." I jabbed my finger into Andrew's hard chest. "But if he touches me or does something I don't like, I'm not responsible for my actions." I grabbed my purse.

"Adriana." Andrew wrapped his hand over my forearm, stopping my hand and reaching for the doorknob. "Promise me that at any moment you don't feel comfortable, you'll walk away, and find me."

I didn't feel comfortable now but I wanted to help, so I had to do it. "I promise."

Chapter Twelve

The restaurant had a bright and inviting area with a white stone and weathered wood bar stuffed to the brim with various liquors. High-top tables and standard tables spilled into the open outdoor terrace. Many people were lounging inside and even more outside. No Richard or Brie in sight.

"Pretty busy," I said, searching for my target. Which one was Brandon? I secured my braid with the black tie that I wore on my wrist. A red mark left by the tie on my skin stung, and I rubbed it nervously, then my fingers found the bracelet and turned it, gently pressing on the stones.

"You ready?" Andrew's hand was on my lower back, his breath a warm flutter against my neck.

Nope.

"Yep."

"Brandon's wearing a blue polo shirt and staring at his phone. Keep your phone close. I'll call you when I'm done or if I need more time."

Brandon was of medium build, with wavy brown hair, and glasses. He was cute enough, maybe even resembled Ryan Reynolds. I liked Ryan. I could do it.

I stepped out of the view of the bar, my skin cold from where my wet hair had left the fabric damp. "What do I say to him?"

Andrew gaped at me. "I don't know. Whatever you say when you want to start a conversation with a guy you like."

"But I don't like him. And usually, guys approach me and start to chat."

"Great." Andrew smiled wide. "Then use whatever they've said to you."

I narrowed my eyes at him. "Hmm, that should be easy." I tapped a finger on my chin as if I was thinking hard. "Should I say 'Are you a bank loan? Cuz you have my interest.' or 'If I could rearrange the alphabet, I'd put *U* and *I* together.'"

Andrew's lips pressed into a tight line, his face expressing marginal annoyance.

"Or wait, here is my favorite of all time." I folded my arms like a genie. "'Well, here I am. What are your other two wishes?'"

"There are my love birds," William said, coming toward us.

Not funny, William. I shot him a look.

"Any luck with the tiles?"

Andrew faced William. "How would you start a conversation with a stranger if you needed to toy with him for an hour or more?"

Confusion passed over William's face. "Are you serious? With your sultry façade—"

"Not me. Her."

William's hazel eyes cut to me, and he barked a laugh. "Her? Flirting?"

I blew out an irritable puff. "What is that supposed to mean? I can flirt if I need to flirt. Actually, I don't even need to say anything. I can do this."

My hands unfastened the top button of my dress. My medium-sized breasts were nicely pushed together—thanks to bra magic—and my skin had enough tan to radiate against the white fabric of my dress. Andrew's gaze dropped to my now more ample cleavage, but he quickly averted his eyes.

I took a bracing breath and squared my shoulders. This was such a bad idea.

"I can do this," I mumbled, but my feet stayed rooted to the floor.

William stepped around me and peered into the restaurant. "Which one is your prey?"

"The—"

"OMG!" William gasped and brought his hand to his heart. "The handsome guy from the Santa Marta hotel is at the bar. What are the chances we meet again?"

"Who is he?" I asked, staring at the bar.

"In the blue polo shirt," William said.

"That's the prey."

William waved his hand in the air. "I got it."

"Wait," Andrew said. "He doesn't know that you're with us. Richard and Brie only saw Adriana with me. Just make up a story about who you are and why you're here."

"Gotcha." William winked and strolled in Brandon's direction. He placed his hand on Brandon's shoulder, said something to him, which made Brandon laugh, and the next second William was on the chair next to Brandon, carrying on a conversation. How in the world…? No wonder William's clinic had more clients than it could handle, with people parking their names on the client's waiting list.

"No time to waste." Andrew gently took me by my elbow and moved us toward the doors leading to the terrace.

As if we were on a pleasant walk, Andrew and I navigated through the spectacular grounds. I scanned our surroundings, searching for the short Barbie doll and her troll husband. At the end of the garden, Andrew pushed through the opening of bushes, and I did the same. Here the grounds were lower, and the building appeared much grander from this view. We weaved through trees, made our way around the building, and soon came to a stop.

"That's his room." Andrew pointed up at the tall windows about six feet in the air.

"Okay. Now what?" I craned my neck to spy our point of entrance.

Bribing cleaning staff would have been much easier. But here we were.

Andrew studied four windows, then lifted his arms and pushed in the center where the panels met. The window moved but didn't open. He applied more pressure, rocking panels several times. The sound of wood snapping punctured the air, and then the window was ajar.

"How did you know it would open?" I turned to make sure no one was nearby. The coast was clear.

"These aren't original to the building, but about two centuries old. I checked our rooms, and they had the same weak latch." Andrew grabbed onto the windowsill, pulled himself up, and peered into the room, his shirt doing nothing to hide his taut shoulder and back muscles underneath the fabric. And at the sight of his tight ass, a hot tremor flowed over my body.

"Seems like no one is inside." Andrew dropped to the ground and stepped back. "Ladies first."

"Why should I go first?"

"Because I need to push you."

The top of my head didn't come close to the window. I could reach a lower part of the casing, but there was no way I could pull myself up. My eyes searched the manicured lawn and flowering bushes near us for anything to stand on, but I came up empty.

And of course, I was wearing a dress.

"Fine, but don't you dare glance up." I pointed my finger at his face.

Andrew closed his eyes, shaking his head. "You should either get a pair of pants or get over yourself."

"Get over myself?" I said incredulously.

"If it makes you feel better, I'm not into small-bottomed women who like lacy panties with a yellow trim," he said with a straight face and in a matter-of-fact tone. I gasped. I had worn yellow trim panties the day we'd played grave robbers.

My cheeks burned, and my nose twitched, but I ignored it as I sucked in the air. "You said you didn't see anything in the church," I whisper-yelled at him. "And for your information, my *bottom* is not small. It's a very nice size, fuck you very much." I planted my fists on my hips. "Oh, and you maybe should stop asking me to do stupid shit like crawling through the windows into someone else's room."

One of his eyebrows arched, and a hint of a lopsided grin grew across his face. "Are you done?"

I glared at him without blinking. "If you give me a second, I'll come up with more."

"While you're thinking, grab onto the windowsill, and I'll lift you."

My palms grew damp, and swallowing my anxiety about breaking-in, I turned to the wall, stretching my arms up. My fingers barely touched the wooden frame. Andrew stepped to me, and the heat of his body radiated through my cotton dress. The whiff of his lemon soap and musk cologne set off a shiver down my spine first, and when his large warm palms settled on each side of my waist, a different feeling knocked my anxiety out of the way and took control of my nervous system, igniting it and readying my body to burst into flames.

"Were you a cheerleader in high school?" he said low into my ear. The closeness of his lips to my skin and the hum of his voice made me unbalanced. I should be pissed at him, but instead, I had a mad desire to lean back and press my body against his, tilting my head sideways and exposing more of my neck.

I finally registered what he'd asked and I scoffed. "Oh god, no."

"Why did you say it like that?" Andrew's fingers shifted; his grip got firmer, but not restricting.

I peered at him. His face was too close to mine. An inch more and I could rub my nose against his. Involuntarily, my gaze dropped to his mouth, and when I dragged my eyes back to his, he was staring at my lips.

"Cheerleading requires a lot of money and after-school time." I turned away. "I didn't have either. Now let's do this."

I used every muscle to push off the ground at the same time Andrew lifted me, and as I gained momentum, my arms worked hard to pull up. Andrew's hands gripped my ankles, and with his extra shove, I hoisted my body over the window ledge.

I walked on my hands the rest of the way until I was entirely inside the room. Before I had a chance to stand, Andrew appeared in the window like a limber feline. An attractive cat that every cat lady would like to keep.

"How do you crawl through the window so effortlessly?" I said, breathless, standing up.

"It gets easier each time." He brought the window panels together, closing them. "There's no time to fix the lock, but at least it'll appear shut."

The room had a slightly jarring wallpaper with large, bright green palm tree leaves, a four-poster king-size bed with unmade white bedding, and a man's shirt carelessly thrown on top. A couch and two side tables separated this area from the living space.

We roamed the suite, focusing on the floor and studying its tiles. Andrew crawled under the bed while I flipped the floor mats on each side. Then we moved the nightstands, and after that we migrated to the living space. We moved the sofa and glass coffee table out of the way and pulled the rug. Our search yielded no results. We pushed everything back in its place, and Andrew disappeared into the bathroom. I checked the small closet and double-checked the same exposed tiles we had already been over.

"Bollocks." Andrew returned. "I was so sure it would be here."

"Is it possible that, while renovating this hotel, the tile was damaged, and they replaced it and found the hidden place?" Or maybe Andrew was wrong, and we should have been looking for something else. "What if it's not a tile?"

Andrew took in a deep breath.

"It said to kneel before love birds…" he muttered, running his hand through his hair. "The floor is original. We're in the east part of the house. This was Augustine's and Maria's bedroom. He often wrote to her about how much he enjoyed watching the sunrise with her in their bed. The view out of these windows matches the description. This is the correct room."

Something banged on the wall inside the closet. Then the sound of a door slammed shut. In the hallway, women's voices chatting in Spanish grew louder. The sound of footsteps stopped outside Brandon's room. Fear clawed up my throat. On the other side of the thick wooden door, the metal keys rattled. They knocked and called out something in Spanish. Housekeeping? We shouldn't be in here. Metal keys clanged again.

A turn of a key.

My blood froze in my veins.

Click.

I looked at Andrew, and his face was a replica of my fear.

Time stood still as the door creaked open.

Chapter Thirteen

I dashed to the closet first, and Andrew rushed after me, quietly shutting the door behind him. My heart drummed erratically, pushing the hot blood through my body. Two women came into the room, their silhouettes visible through the louvers. Why hadn't Andrew or I called out to them to come back later? They didn't know what each guest sounded like, did they? One crew member stayed in the bedroom, and the other went to the bathroom.

Fear burned a hole in my gut, and sweat began to bead all over my body, the snug space quickly turning into a brazing pit of fire. We stood flush against each other, my face into Andrew's chest, inhaling his cologne, which had by now become familiar. My hands were by my sides, itching to wind around his waist. For no other reason, but to keep me stable, of course. Andrew wrapped his left arm around me, the corner of his notebook digging into my lower back.

Swallowing, I glanced up and whispered. "What if they find us?"

"Shh." His arm tightened, pressing me closer.

Oh my god. What if his niece called him? What if William called me?

One of the women came to the door, and my breathing ceased to exist. Brandon had left his shirt on the bed. What if she decides to hang it? How often have I returned to a hotel room to find my make-up and toiletries neatly stacked, my shoes lined up, and the clothes I hastily threw on the floor folded on the bed or hung in the closet?

Through the slits, I could see her standing near, her voice vibrating in my bones. Her shadow moved. A hand reached for the handle.

This was it. We were busted. I shut my eyes and pressed my forehead into Andrew. *Okay, if she saw us, we should say we were playing a sardines game, and invite her in. Yeah. That would go well.*

A pull of the door.

Another tug.

The woman muttered.

I opened one eye. Andrew held the handle with his hand, not letting the lady in. She tugged again. Grumbled and sighed. A walkie-talkie beeped. Static crackled. She quickly rambled. After a bit, there was muffled hubbub, some more static noise followed by a man's voice replying back to her.

"*Gracias,*" she said.

Ha! I knew that word.

Her shadow disappeared, and both women chatted in the bathroom. I didn't understand what she said on the radio, but I sensed the worst in my gut.

"What did she say?" My voice quavered.

166

Andrew lowered his lips to my ear. "She needs Alejandro to come in and fix the door again."

I'd have liked to focus on the brush of Andrew's lips on my ear but... *Houston, we have a problem.* Panic rose inside me quicker than water after the second flush in a stopped-up toilet.

"What if they wait for him here? What do we—"

Andrew let go of the handle and pressed his fingers to my lips. "Shh."

My breath hitched from unexpected contact. Our eyes stayed locked, and he slowly dragged his hand away, his fingers brushing gently over my mouth and catching on my bottom lip. His hand caressed my shoulder and slid down my arm. The sensation of his touch was too much. My body tightened and stilled, my brain momentarily forgetting about cleaning ladies and some guy coming over to check the door. I was glad the hotel didn't splurge on making this space any bigger because I loved being pressed against Andrew's broad body. Was this the original wardrobe in the house? What about the bathroom? Did the hotel sacrifice some space to add both of these spaces? When we stood outside under the windows of Brandon's room, there were four windows. But when we were inside his room, there were only three. Two large ones in the bedroom and one in the bathroom.

"Where is the fourth window?" I whisper-blurted.

"What?" Andrew's eyebrows pinched together.

"When we were in the garden," I whispered, "there were four windows, but inside there're only three."

Andrew was quiet for a minute, his eyes searching mine, and then his full lips curled up. "You're brilliant," he whispered and pressed his lips to the top of my head, and the entire Keukenhof garden blossomed in my chest at once. This kiss was the most action I'd gotten in almost two years.

"I concur," I said, a bit breathless, but hey, we were in a stressed situation.

The water stopped running in the shower, and the cleaning ladies' voices emerged from the bathroom and passed by our hiding spot. They lingered for a while, and then the main door banged shut. The lock clicked once, then twice.

Besides our heavy breathing and the loud heart beating, the room fell into silence.

"The coast is clear," Andrew said and walked out. I shadowed him.

I pressed my palms to my chest, inhaling deeply.

"Oh, my god. That was *not* fun." I wrapped my hands around my middle and bent, breathing in and out. "That was something I don't ever want to repeat."

Frankly, it was a lie. I wouldn't mind being crammed into a small space with Andrew again.

Andrew pressed his ear to the room door, unlocked it, and cracked it ajar. He peeked out, then slid into the hallway, beckoning for me to follow him.

"How are we going to lock the door?" I shimmied out.

"We aren't." He took my hand.

Pulling me after him, Andrew stepped into a darker connecting corridor, a red sign with the words "*Salida de incendios*" was above a door. To the right was another door. Without hesitation, Andrew opened it. He fumbled with his hand on a wall and turned on a light.

Well, my wish came true.

It was the housekeeper's storage area. The hotel had apparently boarded the window to make an extra room with storage space. Shelves lined all three walls, full of linen and towels, and plastic bins filled with hotel toiletries, paper products, and amenities supplies. In the corner was a vacuum cleaner, a mop, and a bucket. Andrew and I jam-packed into the limited space, and he closed the door. A low *tick tick tick* sound counted down minutes to automatic light shut off. The room had no air conditioning, and sweat quickly coated my skin, or maybe it was again the proximity to Andrew's body.

"I just realized that being stuck with you in tight places is becoming my new norm," I said, unable to hide my tiny grin. This situation, today and over the entirety of the past four days, was so bizarre, but I was enjoying it.

"Is that a complaint?" Andrew glanced at me with a twinkle in his eyes.

No.

"The jury's still out."

Andrew gave me a teasing smile before crouching on the floor and studying the tiles. I lowered onto the floor too, my bum bumping his as I checked under the selves, moving boxes out of the way. Tiles in this space were faded and tarnished, some worse than others, making it hard to make out what symbols they had. The light above our heads went off, leaving us in total darkness. I was about to get up and turn it on again.

"Don't bother. I'll use my phone," Andrew said, and a second later his phone gave out dim light, illuminating his face. He turned on the flashlight app. I did the same. We shone both phones on the floor and continued to explore.

"What do you think about this one?" Andrew traced a

finger over the discolored outline of what could have been two birds facing each. He pulled the pencil out of his notebook and traced faded lines, giving them more definition. It was remarkable to watch him expertly revitalize the old artwork.

I moved sideways so I could see it from his angle. My hip pressed against Andrew's leg and my body's temperature skyrocketed. I was confident we were looking at the correct birds. "We can't break it. Can we?"

Andrew set the pencil aside, handed me his phone, and produced a pocketknife. He dug the blade into the grout around the tile and scraped it. The dust particles danced in the light as Andrew continued his work.

"How did you find Octavian Global?"

"Saw a job ad in a newspaper." Andrew flashed me a quick smile, sweat glinting on his face, then returned his attention to his task. He fell quiet. Maybe he wasn't allowed to share that information? But after a minute, he finally said, "One doesn't find them. They find you. They recruited me when I was in my first year at uni. At that time, being part of an exclusive and honorable society was fascinating and exciting, and they paid well."

"If money is good, why do you work at the university?"

"It's not MI6." He wiped his forehead with his sleeve. "They only reach out when they need my expertise, maybe once a year. On rare occasions twice a year. I needed a day job, and I enjoy teaching my classes more than doing this."

"Are you the only one from Cambridge that works with them?"

"Octavian Global doesn't organize Christmas parties yearly for everyone involved to meet. Dr. Evans, a professor at the

University of Oxford, is the other person I know who is with them. Well, Richard was too, but he left."

"What about Dr. Garcia?"

"No, he's just an old and loyal family friend. This is his first time being so involved with my assignment."

I wiped off the sweat above my top lip. "How did Brandon end up working with Richard?"

"My guess is money. Richard hired him a few years ago. Brandon is a pleasant and intelligent man, but a museum curator's salary doesn't allow for a lavish lifestyle. And money can easily change people and their principles."

We again fell into silence, the blade's scratch on the grout filling the small closet.

"I think you would make a perfect secret MI6 agent. Ambling around, wearing a black tux, seducing beautiful women, and using sex as your weapon to get secrets out of them. Instead of your name, they'd scream classified codes as they climaxed."

I might have gone overboard here with my imagination. I didn't have any top-secret information, but I'd probably give up my Netflix password. Heat crept up my neck as an image of naked, worn-out Andrew lounging in a bed with silk sheets, materialized in my mind.

Andrew's hands came to a stop, and he glanced at me, his eyes twinkling with mischief. "Any secrets I need to get out of you?"

My heart somersaulted, and my jaw went slack. "What?!"

I gaped at him.

He stared at me.

I wanted to kiss him.

He cleared his throat.

"Sorry, a poor joke," he said and returned to scraping.

Now it was my turn to clear my throat. "Um, what do you think is hidden here?"

"Not a clue. It could be nothing, or it could be a map, journal, correspondence, or heirloom, or a piece of a broken vase."

"Sounds like you've found all of those items before."

"I have." A bead of sweat dripped down his face.

I observed him carefully push the blade along the tile edge, admiring his sculpted forearms, cords of his muscles flexing and dancing with each movement.

When he'd dug most of the grout out, he set the tip of the blade at the edge of the tile and pressed on the knife's handle, lifting the tile up. Catching the tile by its edges, he moved it aside, and adrenaline in my body surged to a record high when a hollow space underneath came into view. We grinned like idiots at each other, my chest rising and falling with a rapid speed. Andrew broke our eye contact and shone the light inside.

He frowned. "It's empty."

"No!" I leaned forward, hitting my forehead on his cheek.

"Ouch." He chuckled, rubbing his jaw. "I'm kidding. I see something." He reached into the space and pulled out a bundle wrapped in a stained cloth.

I could have exploded with excitement.

He carefully unraveled the dirty fabric and exposed a mahogany box. Inside, on a stack of light-brown, folded paper sheets was a bracelet like the one I had on my wrist, but instead of green stones, it had dark blue gems. The box also had a brass cipher composed of two disks, and a similar book with a collection of short stories with an Augustine Pérez monogram in the center.

"Do you think this is the cipher we need to read messages in his letters to his sons?" I asked, turning brass rings.

"We'll find out soon." Andrew took his phone and shined it on the gold bracelet. "This is unexpected."

He moved it slightly, catching the light.

"Do you see the map on it too?"

"Yes." Andrew smiled. "This should complete the map we already have."

My phone buzzed with a message.

WILLIAM

> Brandon and I are going to the pool. He's going to change first in his room.

> It's fine. We're in a closet.

> His room?!!!

> God, no! I'll explain later. You don't have to hang out with him anymore. You can leave him.

> r u kidding me? This is the best thing that's happened to me on this vacation. He is soooooo hot. I want to spend time with him. R u ok?

> Fine. Don't tell him anything about what you know and that you're with us. Remember he works for THE dickhead.

173

"Is everything okay with William?" Andrew asked as he set the tile back into its place.

"Yes. They apparently bonded and are off to the pool."

After last night, I was happy William had found some happiness on this trip, even if it was with the enemy and would probably be short-lived. What cover-up story had he come up with? Actually, William didn't need to come with much, he just needed to omit his last name, and that he was with Dr. Jones.

Andrew took a clean washcloth off the shelf, wiped his face, and then dusted off the floor. He moved a bin with tiny lotion and body wash bottles to mask the crime scene. Holding the wooden box in one hand, he hauled me up and opened the door, letting in cool air around us.

I peeled my dress away from my sticky back. I needed a shower.

We exited the dim corridor and curved into the main hall where our rooms were located. Thankfully there wasn't a soul in sight.

"For the last six years," Andrew said as we neared his door, "I have worked alone. Working with you has reminded me of how nice it feels to share the excitement of uncovering something new with someone else."

I shook my head, not believing what I was about to say. "This trip is the most ridiculous fun I've ever had in my life. I'm glad the package was delivered to me."

"Me too." Andrew smiled. "Would you mind if I mentioned you and William in my research papers?"

I hoped I mirrored his sincere smile. "Only if you promise

we'll be invited to the opening night of the museum exhibition?"

"You can count on that."

I turned to go to my room.

"Adriana?" Andrew called out.

I whirled. "Yes?"

"Would you like to help me with these?" He lifted the box in his hand.

I wasn't sure if it was the idea of spending more time with Andrew or that he thought I could help him, but my heart surged in my chest as I stepped in his direction.

Chapter Fourteen

Andrew's room was a mirror of mine except it overlooked the pool and had a view of the green mountain range as the backdrop. Below us, guests relaxed on white loungers, drinking expertly mixed cocktails. The room didn't have a desk or table, so the only reasonable option was to settle on the bed. I tried my best not to think that Andrew would be sleeping here tonight, under fine cotton sheets, wrapping his arms around soft pillows. My mind wandered to what he slept in. Did he wear pajama pants, or would he perhaps be completely naked? My stomach fluttered.

Andrew pulled his backpack from the closet and dropped it next to the foot of the bed. Then he lowered onto the tiled floor and began pulling items out of it. I pushed off my shoes and settled on the opposite side of him, crossing my legs and pulling my skirt over them. We spread everything out between us.

"Where would you like to start?" I picked up the brass cipher we'd found and examined it. The outer ring had thirty-three sections with uppercase letters and several numbers in no particular order, and the inner one had twenty-nine lowercase letters.

"Do you know how to work that?"

I shrugged. "I've watched enough movies. You turn the discs, and they point to the correct letter."

"Yes, only you need to know where to start." He stretched his arm out and waved his hand to give him the cipher. "This one resembles the Alberti Cipher, invented by a Renaissance polymath. We could try its method first. This ring," he said, pointing at the outer disk, "is the *stabilis*. It's fixed. And the smaller one that we can rotate is called the *mobilis*. The sender and recipient agree on the index letter. Let's say 's.'" Andrew turned the smaller dial until the small "s" went under "L" in the outer disk. "'L' is now the start of the ciphertext. Once the recipient receives the message, they use the same cipher and do the reverse decoding." He lifted an eyebrow at me. "Does it make sense?"

I nodded. "How do we know what they agreed on in the first place?"

"Uh," he said, "that's a great question. We don't know."

"So our best way is trial and error?" I gave him a stern look. "In this case, I won't be very helpful because I don't know Spanish." Slight envy about Brie being multilingual pinched me. How many languages did she say she knew? Six? I only spoke two: good English and bad English. I also couldn't help sketching the second bracelet's map because I couldn't draw a cartoonish house to save my life. I was useless. I shouldn't have agreed to help him. Why did he even ask me?

"What's wrong?" Andrew said in a low voice.

"Nothing." I swallowed, picking dirt from under my nail. "I'm just not sure what I can help you with. I can't draw. I can't read their language. I should probably go and let you do your job."

"No. Stay," he said with so much urgency that it was almost comical. It made me smile.

"Why?"

"Because I need your help."

"You'll be fine on your own. I didn't go to school for all this."

"You don't have to go to school to do what I do. You have a great talent for memorization, and your attention to detail is astounding."

I scoffed and rolled my eyes. "Yeah. It's got me so far in my life."

"Why are you insisting on putting yourself down? You're the one who pointed out that Augustine used different handwriting in his letters to his sons. And using this cipher now we can read what messages he sent. You discovered the map. And you saw that there was something special about the sketches."

"Again. Pure luck."

"It wasn't pure luck," Andrew said, his word firm. He picked up Augustine's book and the stack of letters. "You can help with these. You don't need to know Spanish to find words corresponding to the numbers."

"Okay. I can do that," I said, trying to hold on to my emotions and not let my voice break, as appreciation and excitement blossomed inside of me, not because I could be more helpful, but because Andrew had stood up for me against my judgmental bully, against my worse critic—me.

Andrew took a pencil, then tore the middle pages from his notebook and handed them to me.

"Do you know how an Arnold Cipher works?" he asked.

I leaned back against the foot of the bed, pulled the book closer, and unfolded the first letter, which resembled merchant trade records with one column containing strings of digits separated by periods, and the other column having words separated by commas. "My wild guess is the first number is the page, the second is the line, and the third number is the word in that line."

Andrew grinned. "You got it."

An hour later, I was done with my task, but Andrew was still working with letters he'd copied from the sheets, rearranging them and turning dials, then dragging a line across the words and trying again.

"What should I do next?"

He bit his inner check, thinking, then he gave me his iPad. "Thirty-one zero one. Could you research any palaces or ruins of large mansions in Colombia? We need to find where Augustine was building it."

When I unlocked the iPad, I wasn't surprised to see a picture of Lulu as his background. She was grinning, one baby tooth missing, face covered in chocolate ice cream. A longing I never imagined I could feel pulled at my heartstrings. "How old is she here?"

Andrew glanced, and his lips turned up. "Five. It was the first time Charlotte had ever left me to look after Lulu on my own. I have never been more nervous in my life than I was on that day. Of course, she'd lived with me since her birth, but Charlotte had always been there. I took Lulu to spend a day in London. We visited the Natural History Museum and then a playground in Kensington Gardens."

"I'm sure you did just fine. She looks like she had the best day of her life."

I could only imagine how many women clutched their hearts while watching handsome Andrew playing with a little girl, giving her rides on his broad shoulders in the park.

"We had a good time." He returned his attention to the page in his hands.

I wondered if he wanted to have a family and kids of his own. He would be a great father, and most likely a perfect husband. I wouldn't mind one day settling with a decent man, but as for kids, I didn't want them. Each time I thought of becoming a parent I pictured my own mother. What if I didn't have what it took to be a mother? My grandparents abandoned her, and she deserted William and me. Seemed to me that the neglecting gene ran in our family. I didn't want to take a risk. I wouldn't forgive myself for ruining my kid's childhood. The iPad went dark. I unlocked it again and tapped on the Safari app. *Focus.*

Colombia had several palaces, but none of them resembled the sketch. I searched for ruins of historical buildings, and only found two, but the footprint wasn't large.

Andrew absentmindedly pinched his bottom lip as he stared at his notes. He exhaled sharply, let go of his gorgeous mouth, and scribbled something on the paper.

"Breakthrough?" I asked.

"The earliest message says, 'The twin bracelet is done.' The next one is a year later and says, 'The requested trunk from the Ángel Hermosa has arrived.' This one says, 'Vault is ready.' And the last one says, 'Stop construction. Pay the agreed price in full. Everyone needs to leave.' It's dated a day after Maria died." He dropped the notebook and groaned, stretching his arms above his head.

"Does this mean there is no palace?"

"I guess not."

It made sense. In three hundred years someone would have noticed a huge building, even in the middle of a jungle. I twisted the bracelet on my wrist.

"Is Ángel Hermosa a town?"

"No. I don't know. It translates to 'my beautiful angel.'" Andrew closed his eyes and tilted his face to the ceiling. "I have heard it before somewhere." He reached for his notebook and paged through it. "It's the waterfall where Jorge secretly married Augustine and Maria."

"Why secretly?" I cocked my head.

"Because her family was opposed to their relationship."

"Oh. How old were they?"

"She was fifteen, and he was eighteen."

"Oh wow, young. How long were they married?"

"Twenty-nine years," he said, lost in his thoughts.

It must have been nice to find the love of your life at such a young age. Too bad they didn't grow old together.

Andrew bit his bottom lip. "I could've sworn Augustine used those words somewhere else. Where did I see it?" He grabbed a green plastic folder and plucked a stack of photocopied letters. Two pages enclosed in transparent laminated sheets fell out of the folder and landed between us. I whisked them up and peered at them, trying to make sense of what they were. Both papers had faint combinations of dotted lines that went up two-thirds of the sheet, with dashed lines branching out left and right, stopping and continuing a few centimeters up the page. Squiggles or maybe letters were marked in some places. One sheet had a short railroad track-looking scribble almost at the center and an inch to the right. Everything looked as if it was drawn in an unsystematic way. One page was in better condition than the other, its lines more defined and not smudged.

"What are these?" I asked, turning them both upside down. They still didn't make sense.

Andrew directed his attention to me. "That I don't know yet. Dr. Garcia gave them to me right before I left him. What do you think?"

"Are these also Augustine's work?"

"We're not sure, but they were found among other items that belonged to him."

"Some of this looks like stairs or maybe … shoot, I don't know … but it looks to me like an incomplete architectural foundation or floorplan drawings maybe? Like, it's as if whoever made them was just sketching out ideas on a napkin. Version one and version two. Look at this one. If you flip it, it looks like a fountain maybe? Could it be a garden plan?"

After Andrew didn't answer, I looked at him. He was immersed in reading the letter he held. He scanned the page, then he picked another, and another until he found what he sought. "Here, Ángel Hermosa. It's from Augustine to Maria. It says … hmm…" Andrew slowly nodded, biting his lip as he read. Then his eyebrows shot up, and his lips parted. He concentrated even harder on the sheet in his hands.

"What?" I straightened and peered at him. "You know where it is?"

"Not exactly." Andrew shifted in his spot, lifting and adjusting his shirt collar on the back of his neck. "No. It does mention the waterfall." He hesitated a moment, as though not knowing what to say next, and a blush had crept up his neck. "He says he loves her dearly."

"Aww." I cooed. "What else does it say?"

Andrew scratched his forehead. "He's in Portugal right now," he murmured, and brushed a hand through his hair. "And he misses her," he said, so quietly that his voice was barely audible.

I observed him, amused. What had gotten into him?

"Oh my god. I would rip that paper out of your hands and read it myself if I knew how." I laughed impatiently and pushed his thigh with my foot. "Why are you mumbling?"

"Well…" He rubbed his neck, his eyes flicker to mine and then back to the paper. "He's talking about how beautiful she was the day he kissed her for the first time behind the waterfall."

Seriously, that's what made him so squirmy?

I sighed. "I remember my first kiss. I was in ninth grade." It was awful. The boy stuck his tongue inside my mouth and just stood there not moving. A minute later he stepped away, shrugged, and said my tits were too small. *Asshole*. I was only fourteen. Not a first-class introduction to the male species.

Andrew scoffed and scratched his forehead again, the blush on his face deepening. "This is not the kind of first kiss he is talking about."

I blinked at him. "What do you mean?"

"I mean, it's the..." His face turned red. "It's the other kiss."

I arched an eyebrow. "The other kiss?"

How many kisses were there?

"For the love of god, Andrew. Read the damn paragraph out loud. In English."

"No."

"Why not? It's their first kiss."

His eyes drifted around the room, then fixed on my face. "It's not their first kiss. He talks about the *first* time he kissed her *there*."

He sat still, holding my gaze, then lowered his chin a little, his gaze landing on my skirt, somewhere in the proximity of where my thighs touched.

Ah, crap, I couldn't just drop it.

I gasped and slapped my palm over my mouth. And then I giggled. Yep. That was me when I was embarrassed.

"Just for the record," I said, waving my hands in front of me, "I was not kissed like that in ninth grade."

Andrew chuckled, holding my gaze. "I figured."

I wiped tears from under my eyes. "I'm curious now, what else did he write there? Is it in poetic prose or pure porn?"

Andrew slid the sheets back into the folder. He swallowed. "Augustine doesn't go into details."

He stared at me, his startling eyes dark and heavy as if he was pinning me underneath him right here on this floor, on these old letters. If I were standing, my knees would buckle. Thirty years from now I might not remember all the details of a sexy stranger who dragged me to Colombia, but the way he looked at me right now would stay with me forever.

Heat surged from my toes to the top of my head as my imagination plummeted into the dangerous territory of Andrew nudging my knees apart, running his tongue up my thigh, his lips gently sucking on my swollen center, his face smug with wetness around his mouth, his hair disheveled by my fingers. My nipples began to harden to sensitive peaks.

"All right," Andrew said, breaking my daydream. *I'm a wreck.* He gave me a questioning look. "Where did you go?"

"Nowhere," I said, my voice embarrassedly thick. I needed a cold shower.

"We have another mention of the waterfall," Andrew continued, his pupils dilated. I had the distinct sensation that he was trying to keep himself from leaping like a wild animal at me. I wouldn't stop him. "The place where they got married. If he stopped construction on the palace, he most likely didn't move the loot from its original location."

Right. We were back to the business. *Concentrate.*

"And the note said one trunk arrived from Ángel Hermosa. Does this mean there are more trunks left?" I picked up his iPad and google searched waterfalls in Colombia. Too many results came up, we couldn't possibly check all of them. Well, we could, but it would take us weeks. We could narrow the list down by this sketch. "So far everything Augustine has drawn has been a missing piece of the puzzle. It only makes sense to go there. The question is, do we know where *there* is?"

"Let me call Carlos." Andrew pulled out his phone, tapped

the screen a few times, and mouthed *One sec*. He got up and strode over to the window.

While Andrew was on the phone, I continued browsing beautiful waterfalls in Colombia. None of them looked like the one from the sketch. They were all too popular. Curious tourists or locals would have discovered the lost treasure by now.

"I was wrong." Andrew dropped next to me. "Cascada de Belleza Escondida is the place where they got married. Ángel Hermosa must be another location."

"And did other things." A teasing smile danced across my face.

"Right." Without meeting my eyes, he opened the maps app on the iPad, and without typing the name of the place swiped his finger across the Colombia map. "It's about a two-hour drive from here." He zoomed in on a blue dot. "Once we get there, it won't be a short jaunt."

"So far, this journey hasn't been for the faint of heart. How bad is it?"

"Four-mile hike through the jungle, mostly uphill."

"Of course." I rolled my eyes. "Round trip?"

He shook his head.

"Are you serious? Can we hire some horses or donkeys?"

Andrew's gaze perused down my body, his lips curved in a private smile. "You'll need to buy hiking-appropriate clothes and shoes. In the morning, you and William can take a car into town while I take care of a few things."

My lips curled at the thought. "If I see a Fedora, can I get it for you?"

It was Andrew's turn to roll his eyes. "If you must."

My phone buzzed with an incoming message.

WILLIAM

Would you be terribly upset if I go out with Brandon tonight? We want to do a sunset horse ride, and then have dinner at the top of the hill.

You're making me nervous. You know he works for the bad guys.

I do, but I think he's one of those good guys who is confused.

?

😊 I don't think he believes in what he's doing.

Fine. I don't care if you hang out with him just make sure he doesn't know who you are.

how did today go?

I didn't risk telling him. If William had a few drinks, he could get a loose tongue. If he accidentally shared with Brandon that we were searching for something it would be one thing, but if he were to announce what we found that was a total catastrophe.

Fine. I'll tell you later.

Did you and Dr. Johnny Rocket make out while you were hiding in a closet?

don't have too much fun with Brandon. Love you.

> btw, did he mention if Brie or Richard are here?

He says he's traveling alone

I looked up and caught Andrew watching me with an amused expression. "Is that William?"

"Yes. He is going to have dinner with Brandon."

Andrew glanced at his watch. "He's either really into playing a secret agent or he likes the guy."

"I think he likes him." I also checked the time. It has been four hours since we sent William on the spy mission. "It's after five. I think I'd like to go back to my room and take a shower. I'll leave you alone to do the rest of your work." I collected my shoes. Andrew got up before me and held out his hand. *Like I need him to touch me again.* I pressed my palm into his. At the contact, the sensation of being molded against his hard frame threatened to overwhelm me. But he would have to make the first move. He drew me to my feet and held on to my hand for a beat or maybe five before letting go.

His broad shoulders relaxed, his hands were now in his pockets, and an easy smile lifted the corners of his lips. "Thank you again for helping me." His sincere expression told me he actually meant it.

I didn't do much. I was not even sure what we agreed our next move should be because my mind was muddled by unforeseen lust.

"Anytime." I walked backward to the door. I had a date with the tub's showerhead.

"Meet me for dinner at seven?" he said in a warm, gravelly tone.

Halfway out the door, my shoes dangling on my fingers, I turned to look at Andrew over my shoulder with what I hoped was an enticing smile. "Tonight, I'll get you drunk, and you'll tell me the rest of Augustine's dirty letter."

Or better yet you could show me.

Chapter Fifteen

The showerhead water pressure didn't disappoint me. Twice.

I pulled my hair into a loose, low bun and added a splash more make-up. Well, more than a splash, but nothing over the top, just more dark eyeliner. I was going to a celebratory dinner after all. I wasn't trying to impress Andrew.

But I think I did.

When I arrived at the bar, Andrew—as always—was already there. He'd changed into a white button-up shirt, dark pants, and he'd brushed his hair. I personally preferred his earlier *post-roll-in-the-hay* style. The expression on his face told me everything I needed to know—he liked what he saw. And I would be lying if I said I didn't enjoy the moment our gaze connected. I loved the way it made me feel. Like I was his queen.

The hostess seated us outside on the patio at the candlelit table closest to the garden. A light breeze ruffled my hair, bringing out goosebumps on my shoulders. The sun hadn't fully set, and its low rays created a warm hue behind the green hills. Twinkling tealight candles in crystal bowls encircled a miniature magenta floral centerpiece. This was an unexpected dinner setting. The surrounding tables had flowers but no candles. Was this Andrew's touch?

A young, handsome server brought a wine binder and presented it to Andrew.

"She's the expert." Andrew handed me the heavy leather-bound folder.

"This is an excellent collection of wines." I perused the list, flipping pages. "Red or white?"

"Surprise me."

Andrew picked up his glass of water and sipped it, watching me with tense, dark eyes. I tried to act nonchalant, but underneath I was melting like a soy candle. His stare was like he was undressing me, and oh god, I wished he would. I bit my lip and continued looking over red wines, aware he was studying me. "You're staring at me. How do I stop it?" I glanced at him over the edge of the binder.

"You look ethereal tonight."

Good lord. Who used words like this? How would one reply to that?

"I know, right?" I rolled my eyes, but my cheeks burned, and other ladies' bits too.

"Why are you single?"

"Oh, here we go." I hid my face behind the list. "You've already asked me that."

"And I don't think you gave me a real answer."

That question had a loaded and super complicated answer, which I wasn't going to give. Not tonight. Perhaps, just like

William, I haven't found the right person. But I also wasn't looking. Or maybe, I was a realist about true love. It didn't exist. It didn't work for our parents. It didn't work for William. It didn't work for Greg and me. The best analogy was people who got bitten hard by a dog when they were young. The accident had lodged a seed of fear that was to stay put for the rest of their life. They understood that not all dogs were mean; they saw others owning a dog or even playing with a stranger's dog, yet they stayed cautious of the animal, not taking chances of getting bitten again.

Our server brought a generous basket of bread and a dish of butter and asked if we were ready for our wine order. I couldn't decide between two bottles, so we ordered both.

The best way to avoid answering a question was to respond with the same question.

"So, are you seeing anybody?" I reached for a bread roll.

I bit into the warm and sweet piece of heaven and let out a happy sigh.

"Don't think I'll let you ignore my question." The creases around his eyes deepened as he smiled.

With my mouth full, I gestured for him to continue.

"After Brie and I split, I didn't want to get involved, and then I got too busy with work."

"Is being a university professor busy work?" I finished the roll and went for another.

"Yes. No. But starting a relationship is hard when I leave for unexpected expeditions that can last weeks. The only time I stayed at home for over a year was when my parents died." The sadness crossed his face, and he looked away. "Charlotte needed me, and I needed her."

My pain—and bitterness—over not having a good family couldn't be worse than the insurmountable ache of losing loving parents. I grew up not knowing what I missed, whereas Andrew knew exactly what he'd lost.

"I'm sorry," I said quietly and reached out and touched his forearm.

"It happened a long time ago." His gaze fell on my hand, then he looked at me, his lips curling up. "Now, your turn to answer."

I retrieved my hand. "How did you and Miss Bleached Hair meet?"

His eyebrows pinched for a split second, and he scoffed. "Through a mutual friend. He set us up on a blind date."

It was hard to believe Andrew had to go on a blind date to find himself a girlfriend. You'd think that with his charisma and melt-your-panties façade women lined up to date him. And he had to pick a total bitch. One thing Andrew and I had in common, we both sucked at selecting the right partners.

The server returned with our wine, and I let Andrew pick which to open first.

After the server poured, I took a quick sniff—the scent of plums, strawberries, and vanilla veiled my mind—took a long sip and swallowed, feeling the burn of alcohol down my throat.

"Delicious." I smacked my lips. *I don't know why I did that.*

Andrew raised his glass, the tension line now relaxed between his brows. "May the hinges of our new-found friendship never grow rusty."

"Very poetic," I said before bringing my glass to my mouth.

"What would you toast to?"

"Here's to you and here's to me. Friends may we always be. But, if by chance we disagree. Up yours. Here's to me." I clicked my glass to his, suppressing my smile, and drained my entire glass. William and I have been using this toast forever. I couldn't even recall where we first heard it.

Andrew chuckled and took a long sip.

"So." He set his glass on the table. "You still owe me an answer."

"You should try this bread," I said, nodding at the basket. He shook his head. "Watching your figure?" I teased.

"Something like that."

I gave him an assessing look and reached for the next roll but then paused. I realized that, in all the times we had eaten together, Andrew only ate fruit, vegetables, and protein. Maybe he had a gluten allergy, and here I was making fun of him. Guilt rocketed inside of me.

"I'm being rude." I dropped my hand on my lap without taking bread. "I wasn't trying to body-shame you."

"I know," he said, with an easy smile and leaned back in his chair. "Now, you were going to answer my question…"

The sun had finally retired, leaving us with just a few last pink streaks lingering in the indigo skies, and already several glimmering stars. I poured more wine into my glass and drank half of it.

An irresistible attraction to Andrew set my defense wall around my heart on fire and made me want something more beyond this trip. But it was pointless for me to want it because people like me never ended up with people like Andrew. Life wasn't a Cinderella story. He came from a blue-blood family, bound together with posh education, nobility, and a solid household. Whereas I had no college education, was probably nth generation hillbilly, and I had a problematic relationship with the only alive—to my knowledge—parent. As painful as it was to accept my college ex was right, no matter what I'd become in my life, no matter how much money I had, I was a girl from a trailer park.

"Why is it so vital for you to know? After this trip, we'll go our separate ways," I said.

I was either totally taken with Andrew or too drunk because a lump developed in my throat, and I washed it down into the pit of my stomach with more wine.

"Don't forget that you're invited to the museum exhibition opening night when this treasure hunt is all over," he said, his voice quiet but pulling me out of my spiral before it dragged me deeper into a dark woe. He poured more wine into my glass and added some to his.

"Oh yes, we'll see each other again."

"Adriana," Andrew said, a shadow of hurt or perhaps disappointment clouding his expression. In this light, the colors in his eyes were indistinguishable. The shade of a tropical ocean at twilight. God, he was beautiful. "We'll stay in touch. I don't understand why you think we won't. I'd like us to continue our friendship."

As with everything—lovers or friends—when it came to a long distance, any relationship was doomed to die. Some sooner than others.

"Yes." I smiled, nodding. "We can WhatsApp each other. You can send me photos when you go on a new quest, and I can send you pictures of my store—if I have one—and then eventually we'll get busy and forget about each other." I was turning into a Debbie Downer. Andrew's eyebrows furrowed, and he leaned back in his chair. My chest cramped, and I blew out a long, slow breath. "I'm not negative by nature, but this is just reality. You meet someone new, have an exciting time with them, and then you go your separate ways swearing to stay in touch and be friends. At first, you text like crazy, but over time you stop. This is just business, Andrew."

His expression was unreadable. "Is it now?"

And the edge to his voice cut me through and through. I looked away.

Mellow Latin music echoed around us, and a warm breeze caressed my shoulders. The couple at the table next to us were whispering, the guy brushing his finger down his date's neck. She closed her eyes, obviously enjoying the moment. I envied her. I wanted that too, but with my attitude, I doubted I'd get it.

He changed the subject. "You never told me how you got into the wine business." Andrew turned the bottle by its neck and checked its label. I sent a small prayer for the welcome interruption to my negativity.

"It was pure fluke. My college degree was in biology … well … I didn't exactly graduate." I peered into the depth of my glass, the warmth of wine spreading inside my chest, but embarrassment turned my feet stone cold. My scholarship could have gone to someone else, and I'd wasted that money. "At the start of my last year, I took a trip to the Biltmore, and at a wine and chocolate class, I tried to impress an instructor with my wine production familiarity. I used all the knowledge I got out of the two-semester Botany 341 class. A gentleman from the neighboring table started chatting with me. He introduced himself as Robert Parker, the owner of Salzburg Distributing Company. He called me 'a diamond in the rough.' A sommelier in the making. And right then and there he offered me a job. I saw an opportunity to make more money than I would have as a biology teacher, so I jumped on it."

I peeked over the edge of the glass, catching Andrew watching me with an unreadable expression. "What?"

"Your green eyes turn a shade darker and twinkle when you talk about something you love or want."

In silence, we studied the menu until the server returned, uncorked the second bottle, and took our order. Smocked spare dibs with sugar cane sauce and potatoes for me, and Andrew asked for salmon with vizcaina sauce on a bed of slow-roasted vegetables.

"Are you a master sommelier?" Andrew asked.

"Oh gosh no. I'm certified. I love wine, know a lot about it, and am good at sales, but I can't be one of those talented people. They must give up so much. Food, perfume, drinks, soaps, smoking … not that I smoke. I want to own a boutique store where people can sip on their wine, take wine pairing classes, and so on."

The fourth glass of wine made me relaxed and fuzzy inside. *I should drink some water.* Working years in the wine business hadn't increased my tolerance.

"What made you want to open a store?"

"The idea came to me when I met an artisanal olive oil and balsamic vinegar importer at the woman-owned wineries symposium. Her successful life story of going from cleaning toilets in a restaurant to running her company inspired me to have my own business. I took some of her seminars teaching about oils, and," I said with a shrug, "I know a lot about wines, and the two sort of always go well together."

I left out that the main reason for this idea was a hope that, in people's eyes, I would look more noteworthy if I ran my own thriving business.

"How much money do you need to open your store?"

"A lot. Right now, the building is an empty shell. The person I purchased it from gutted it but then stopped their work. The building's location is perfect, and it has a second floor that I was planning on turning into a small apartment to live in. I know it will take more money to fix it up. And the city has byzantine stipulations when it comes to historical buildings. I'm not against preserving antiquity—I support that —but some rules are a real doozy." I drew in a deep breath of fresh air. Saying all of that out loud brought the old thrill of becoming a businesswoman, promoting and helping other women-owned companies.

The *conjunto* began to play a lovely melody and a few couples left their tables and started to dance. Andrew placed his linen napkin beside his water glass and rose to his feet.

"Dance with me?" He offered me his hand.

Nerves, excitement, and drunk adrenaline coursed through me. My body hummed with anticipation of Andrew's touch, his closeness.

We sauntered to the center of the patio. I had danced before, but I felt out of my depth. My nose twitched. Once. Twice. I glanced up at Andrew. He watched me with tenderness, and a lovely smile adorned his face. It took a lot of restraint not to reach out and trace his lips, running my fingertips over them.

He placed a hand on my mid-back, setting off a wave of goosebumps over my skin. His left hand clasped my right one, and he laced his fingers with mine. I rested my other hand on his shoulder, my fingers barely touching the exposed skin of his neck. It was pure torture not to be able to crush my entire body against his.

We slowly moved to the rhythm of the music. To maintain an even pulse, I tried to control my breathing. Inhale. Exhale. Repeat. It didn't work. My heart beat so fast and loud he probably could hear it. He focused straight ahead, his lips curved up into a relaxed smile. A faint scar I hadn't noticed before under the crease on his chin stood out among his stubble.

His smile stretched wider, and he dropped his eyes to mine. I averted mine, pretending to study the collar of his shirt. "You're staring."

"I wasn't." I mustered bravery and met his gaze. "How did you earn this?" I traced the zigzagged skin with my finger.

"Nekhen, Egypt. My grandfather took me for a two-week-long dig at an archaeological site. I tried to balance on two stacked rocks, and it didn't end well. I broke my wrist and busted my chin."

I winced. "Ouch."

"It didn't hurt as much as my pride. I was trying to impress a girl." He bent so his lips were near my ear. "By the way, I didn't see anything in the church." His breath caressed my skin. "But I did notice your underwear hanging in your bathroom."

My cheeks caught on fire. I'd forgotten I'd washed my

panties and hung them to air-dry. I rested my forehead into his chest and chuckled.

Andrew's palm pressed me closer, then he moved my right hand up, placing it on his shoulder. I loosely wrapped my arms around his neck, closing the space between us. The world disappeared, and it was only the two of us, swaying under starry skies, blanketed in balmy air. My skin pleasantly tingled where his palm pressed on my back. The warmth of his body penetrated mine, and he lit all my sensitive nerve endings on fire. His heartbeat was strong, and mixed with my own, creating a wonderful symphony in my soul. This moment was perfect. Andrew holding me felt right. Emotions were thick in my throat as I tried not to think about how much I'd miss him when this trip was over.

The song ended too soon. I wished it would go on until sunrise. Andrew and I stopped dancing and stood still, simply embracing each other. Against my own wish, I peeled away from his body and went to our table, our dinner waiting for us. I grabbed my glass of wine and finished it.

After our initial bites, we exchanged pleasantries, and then we lapsed into silence, only stealing a few *discreet* glances at each other as we ate.

Feeble light from oil lamps added an enchanting touch to a dimly lit hallway as we silently ambled. The air around us was full of crackling electricity—or maybe it was just me.

When we reached my room, I dug the iron key out of my purse. This time I gripped it tight so I wouldn't drop it. I turned to steal a last glimpse of Andrew. I swayed. *Oops, wine tide*. Andrew's hand moved to my elbow, steadying me. His eyes searched mine, his chest rising and falling with each breath. His grip tightened, and I wanted those fingers to press on the other aroused part of my body. I wanted this man in an undeniable way I'd never experienced. I was a sexually deprived—*drunk*—grown-ass, woman who could do whatever she wanted. And I wanted to throw myself at him, turning this evening into another deeply satisfying part of this trip. A perfect *la fin* to this adventure. A heartbreaking but mind-blowing fling.

He relaxed his grip, and his hand skated down, his fingers curling around my finger. I glanced down at our linked hands and then lifted my eyes to Andrew's. His pupils were wide, and his sultry gaze held mine firmly, pinning me in place, and for a moment I hoped he would lean in to kiss me. I bet he was a toe-curling kisser, which would get my heart into a lot of trouble—the heart that was already beating unsteadily at the sight of his smile.

Andrew swallowed. Stepped to me. The air got hot and thick. I tilted my head. He was so much closer, yet there was too much space between us. His lips curved slightly at their corners, and he smoothed my hair off my face, losing me in the gentle touch. His eyes slid toward my mouth. *If he doesn't kiss me now, I will die.* He lowered his head, and I closed my eyes, trying to keep breathing despite the lack of oxygen, waiting for Andrew to ravage my mouth, press me against the door, slide his hand around and under my dress, brush his fingers over my clit.

His soft, warm lips pressed against my cheek.

"Thank you for a lovely evening," Andrew said in a gravelly tone, his stubble grazing my skin. A simple sweep of a kiss on my skin, yet it set off an army of goosebumps over my body. I leaned into him, wanting more, but he stepped back, releasing my hand, and my stomach plummeted. "Goodnight, Adriana."

I'm in trouble

WILLIAM

What happened?

I like Andrew. Like REALLY like him.

YaY

It's not a Yay. I don't need this heartbreak

No heartbreak. Just enjoy the moment. Think of it as your sex therapy.

Who said I'm going to have sex with him?

aren't you?

No.

Yes. I want him like I never wanted anybody else.

BOWCHICKAWOWOW

😶 where are you? It's almost midnight

I'm still with Brandon. He is soooo hot. So much fun!

are you going to Andrew's room?

No

why not?????

I have to think about it

What's there to think? He wants you. You
want him. Go!

??? He wants me?

Are you dense? He undresses you with his
eyes every time he looks at you

Didn't notice

[Contact Shared] Eye Center of Atlanta

why did you send me that?

because you're clearly blind. Andrew looks at
you like you're the only woman he has
ever seen

whatever 😒

he watches you like he wants to pee all over
you to mark his territory

eeewww

he wants you

he didn't kiss me tonight

I'm done talking to you

Aren't you going to ask more?

Love ya

Did you read my txt above? He didn't kiss me!!!!

You probably did something stupid and scared him away

BTW what did you find tonight?

We found a twin bracelet, a working cipher, and a bundle of old letters.

Do we know our next move?

Yes some waterfall where the pirate went down on his lady.

Whoa. Details, please?

That's all I got

oops got to go. Chat tomorrow. YAY you going to get laid!

In the morning we need to go shopping for new clothes and boots. We are going on a hike.

Another YAY

Chapter Sixteen

The next morning, William and I were on our way to the nearest town to find a clothing store. As we recapped yesterday's events, we zoomed by a vast expanse of green hills and rows of vineyards. He had an amazing day—and night— with Brandon, and I told him about my evening with Andrew.

"I can't wrap my head around why Brandon told you he was scouting for an archaeologist and his wife," I said.

"Because I'm charming and can make people spill their secrets." William snuck a glance at me and then returned his focus to the road. His right hand rested on the steering wheel and his left propped on a door. Brandon must have done a number on him. William was beyond relaxed and cheerier than at any time I have seen him after a successful date.

"What else did he say?"

William shrugged one shoulder. "We talked about this and that, then about my practice, then about his job at the Ashmolean Museum." He grinned at me. "You'd really like him."

"What does he do again?"

"He's a curator. Anyway, I told Brandon I was on a spiritual vacation. Alone. Searching for new inspiration for my work, and when I asked him if he was on vacation too, he just blurted it out. Then, he quickly said 'ha-ha just kidding.' I feel like something was bothering him. You know how you can tell that people do their job, but they don't enjoy their job?"

It was my turn to shrug. I loved my job; quitting it was a hard decision.

"Or maybe he knew who you were but was bad at lying so he was nervous," I said.

"Nah, I think it was something else," William said. "But those are boring things that we already talked about. Explain to me again why you don't want to sleep with Dr. Mucho Grande?"

I chuckled at the new nickname, then sighed. "Because I like him."

And that was a huge problem. This idea of an affair with Andrew teetered dangerously on the edge of a massive heartbreak. My heartbreak. And I wasn't a masochist. I wasn't about to subject myself to more misery. Last night I decided I was playing with fire, and it was best to wait out the next couple of days and not cross any lines with Andrew. And what also bugged me was that he didn't kiss me or invite himself to my room. Was he playing a game of hard-to-get, or was he not interested and I'd totally misread the energy between us? My hand fidgeted with the bracelet, running it around my wrist, my fingers pressing on the stones.

"Even more confused now. It's good to like someone you want to sleep with. It makes sex so much better."

"I like to keep sex separate from emotions. I don't have sex with anybody for whom I could develop feelings. It's … like…" I struggled to explain my own stupidity. "Once you cross that line, it sort of seals the deal."

"What deal?" William squinted at me, the car drifting to the left. The truck that was going around us honked, and William swerved to the right.

"Watch the road, please." I pointed ahead as we approached an intersection. "If it's more than lust, the sex is no longer just physical; it's something special. And I don't do special. Special hurts."

We stopped at the traffic light and idled in silence for some time—a rare moment for us. William never usually stayed quiet about anything, especially on the subject of sex or relationships. I tapped my index finger on the top three stones on the bracelet—left, middle, right, left, middle, right, left.

"If you keep playing with the bracelet"—William jerked his head my way—"you'll unlock it by accident, and poof! Off we go back home."

My finger froze. I wasn't ready to part with Andrew, sex or no sex. I enjoyed his company. Too much.

"Look, the universe is telling you to date this perfect male specimen," he said, pressing the gas and jolting the car forward.

I yanked hair out of my mouth and readjusted my sunglasses. "How exactly is the universe telling me this?"

"By cuffing you to him with the bracelet. So please have fun right now and then don't stop once we get back home. Find a way to continue seeing him."

I wanted to remind William that the prospect of long-distance ended his relationship with Rai. But he was finally back to his happy self; there wasn't a need to ruin his mood.

I laughed dryly. "It wouldn't work out. We come from different backgrounds. Andrew is Harrods, and I'm Goodwill." I wished we weren't. I wished I was part of his upbringing and not mine.

"It won't work out because you don't even want to try," he said tensely.

Whoa. What's with the attitude?

He sighed. "Sorry, I didn't mean to say it like that. But you're so hung up on what that idiot Greg told you over a decade ago that it makes you stupid. Greg's a loser. And even after all these years you're still letting him have control over you. You exceeded him in everything, and he had to find a way to hurt you." William turned the steering wheel and soon parked on a street with a small grocery store, a few restaurants, and several shops painted with colorful murals. There was hardly a soul in sight. "I recently internet stalked him. Guess where he works?"

"I don't know." I shrugged. "He has a business management degree. So, he must be a CEO of some sort?"

William made an awful game buzzer sound. "Wrong. He's a manager at a car dealership."

I gawked at him. "He owns a dealership?"

"For a clever woman, sometimes you surprise me." He shut the engine off and turned in his seat. "He's a fraternity loser who sells cars. The only reason that dipshit graduated from UGA was that his daddy stuffed money into the university. He cheated his way through college. He said what he said because you were smarter than him, and he didn't know how else to put you down."

There was nothing wrong with Greg's job, and I shouldn't be gleeful. I didn't make it in my life either. Let's not forget my metric-ton of debt. I had no right to be gratified by someone's failure to reach their life goals.

"Don't you feel better now?" William asked.

"Sure." I rolled my eyes.

William took my hand and brought it to his chest. "Honey, I want you to be happy. I want you to be stupidly in love. You radiate when you're in love. I don't think there's an esthetician who could make skin glow like yours right now. Don't you want that soul-connecting feeling that will grow stronger each day?"

He sounded like a commercial. Yes, the feelings Andrew stirred inside me were amazing, but the pain of our inevitable ending would be much worse.

"I'm not in love. Stop saying it." I gave William a stern stare. My cheeks turned hot. "I just like Andrew."

"Oh, my god. You're so digging Dr. Jones," he said, with a huge grin. "Look at yourself. You're blushing." He cackled.

I crossed my arms and narrowed my eyes at him. "Reality check. He has a life in Cambridge, and I have mine in Atlanta." I didn't mean to say it in a harsh tone, but it came out that way. I was getting defensive. About what? Not sure, but tears prickled my eyes. "This was doomed from the start. So don't rent a tux just yet."

William stopped laughing, took his sunglasses off, and rubbed the bridge of his nose. "Yes. You're right," he said, shaking his head. "He has a fabulous, rich life in Cambridge, and you live in Atlanta with me."

I snorted sardonically. "I appreciate you pointing out that he has a *fabulous* life, and I just *exist*."

"Whatever." It was William's turn to roll his eyes. "Fine. Do whatever you want. I'm a selfish person anyway, and I need you to be near me, therefore I wouldn't let you go to live in some other country where people talk with a gorgeous accent and mingle with royalty."

"I'm glad you made it clear it's all about you." I smiled, unbuckling and throwing my seatbelt off.

"It's always about me." He winked.

I knew he was joking. When it came to me, William never made it about him. He was my rock and my best friend. I pulled on the door handle, ready to exit the car, but William placed his hand on my arm.

"Adriana, seriously, for once, don't think about what the future holds for you. Have fun. Have a fling with Dr. Ripped Spartan."

"You haven't seen him naked. How do you know he's ripped?" I teased.

William tapped his temple. "Laser vision."

I haven't seen Andrew naked either, but I've been pressed against him enough times to know that whatever was going on under his clothes was drool-worthy. Just thinking about Andrew's lips brushing my cheek made my body shiver and my nipples harden. *Exactly*. If a simple touch brought an explosive reaction, what would happen if he kissed me?

The store had a mix of traditional and everyday clothes in addition to cheap T-shirts meant for tourists.

"Get this one." William pressed a ruffled white blouse to my chest. "It's sexy."

"We aren't going to a Cumbia dance. I need something practical for hiking." I moved to the rack of shorts. The brown Fedora I'd nabbed the moment we stepped into this establishment slid lower over my eyes. I'd already selected a few shirts so all that was left to find was a couple of pairs of shorts, socks, and hiking boots.

"How about this one then?" He lifted a neon green crop top with long sleeves.

I threw two pairs of shorts over my arm and glanced at him. "Only if I want a satellite to spot me easily from space."

William tailed me to the shoe rack, and before I could even consider any of the boots, like a true shoe savant, he quickly picked a pair—in my size—and handed them to me.

"Ohhh-kay. I'm going to try these on." I strolled into a small changing room but before pulling a curtain closed, I said, "Could you please call the Costa Rica resort and ask them to remove our stuff from the room and store it in a secured holding area?"

William lifted his arm in a salute. "Yes, ma'am."

I slid my dress off and stepped into the brown shorts. They fitted me like a glove and were the right length, long enough not to be too sexy but also not to make me look like a middle-aged, tired, suburban mom. I checked my butt in the mirror. Not bad.

What was the definition of a fling, anyway? I had a boyfriend in college for three years until he destroyed my belief in true love and, with it, my self-esteem. A few years later, I met a guy from Seattle, who flew to Atlanta for work several times a year. For four years, Steve was my *get-it-out-of-my-system* guy. We didn't just have sex; we went to dinners, movies, and parks. I never invited him to my place, and I never spent an entire night in his hotel room. I was afraid that if I woke up next to him in the morning, it might change our friendship with benefits or whatever it was. What we had was a rule-based relationship between two consenting adults who liked each other but not enough to inspire an entire butterfly conservatory inside their bodies. And that was why it worked for me.

A fling with Andrew was something I could handle. I'd developed enough strength to allow my heart to feel something again while being able to pull on the emergency shut-off at any moment. I convinced myself that when Andrew's and my lives went separate ways, I wouldn't care.

I tugged a shirt over my head and tried on the next pair of shorts. They were identical to the first but with fewer pockets. Shopping completed.

"I'm done." I pushed the curtain out of the way and stepped out fully dressed in my new outfit: a pale brown button-up shirt with short sleeves, marsh green ponte pocket shorts, and hiking boots—a practical outfit for a stroll in a jungle.

"You didn't even let me see how the other things looked on you." William frowned.

"No time." I passed by him and headed toward the front of the store. William collected all the things he'd picked for himself. "These are comfortable, and that's all that matters."

"What if other shorts made your butt sexier?" William nodded, a gleam of malevolence in his eyes. "You know I'd tell you."

"I have no doubt you would."

At the register, we handed our items and the tags for everything I was already wearing to a doe-eyed beautiful woman.

"This too, please." I pointed at the hat.

William bent to my ear and whispered, "You just need a leg gun holster and a pistol, and you'd be Lara Croft."

———

Sitting near our piled bags, Andrew waited for us in the lobby, his eyes narrowed in concentration on the phone in his hand. I hid the hat behind my back and sauntered toward him, a huge grin plastered on my face. He tore his gaze from the screen, then did a double take. He gave me a once over, dragging his gaze over my legs, and then his jaw tightened, and the wrinkle between his brows drew deeper. Disapproval or revolt at how I looked? I hesitated, uncertain of his reaction. But then the tension in his face lessened and a reluctant smile lifted the corners of his mouth.

He stood, shaking his head. "I can't believe you're wearing shorts for a trek in the jungle."

"First my butt and now you don't like my legs?" I teased him.

"Christ, your legs are more than fine." He pocketed his iPhone. "What's going to bite them is not."

My insides melted and pooled between my thighs at the idea of Andrew's teeth sinking into my skin.

"It's too hot to wear pants, and we bought bug spray," I said. Andrew closed his eyes, took a deep breath, and shook his head again. I stepped to him. "I got you a gift."

His lips curled, and light danced in his eyes. "Should I worry?"

I plopped the hat on his head. It landed crooked, giving him a rakish air.

"Voila," I said, beaming at him like an idiot.

Andrew pushed the hat up off his eyebrows with his index finger. For a split second, our gazes collided, and there was longing in his bright eyes. Everything inside me fluttered.

"Now you're the real Indiana Jones."

"Only much sexier, right?" Andrew said with a quizzical smile.

He had no idea.

I nodded.

I was so fucked.

Chapter Seventeen

On the way, we explained to William why the Cascada de Belleza Escondida was the ideal next place to search for the clue. We knew where it was. It wasn't far, and there was a chance Pérez's treasure was still there because, after Maria's death, Augustine fell into a deep depression, and there wasn't any record of him relocating it from its original hiding place.

The first hour we sped on the highway, passing farms, rundown houses with horses tethered to the fence rails, and vendors on motorbikes. Then the old Jeep traversed rough terrain, climbing the road guarded by a rich forest on each side. In the last thirty minutes, we drove on switchback paths that seemed unused by cars, the contents of my stomach ping-ponging around.

The closer we got to our destination, the more enthusiastic Andrew spoke about how he couldn't wait to write a dissertation on Augustine Pérez. Andrew was like a child waiting for Santa Claus, dying to open his presents. Whereas for me, my stomach sunk lower with the notion that soon we would go our separate ways, and I would never know the feel of Andrew's strong arms wrapping tight around my body and bringing me against him. Preferably naked.

In a surprising turn of events—I loved the thrill of this trip.

Eventually, we arrived at the point where the car could no longer pass through the jungle. Andrew parked and turned the motor off. Giant trees dominated the skyline with their heavy tops reaching for the sun. Thick vines tangled from tree to tree, creating a complex network above our heads. No sunlight made its way through the leaves, but to my surprise, the grounds weren't as overgrown with invasive vegetation as I'd imagined. The humid air pulsated with insects buzzing and frogs yelping. Nearby a bird shrieked. At least, I hoped it was a bird.

Andrew compared the penciled-in markings on a paper map to his portable GPS.

"We'll walk the rest of the way." Andrew folded the map and slid it into his front pocket. He got out of the Jeep and stretched, making my pulse work harder, and then he put the hat on. An image of Andrew wearing *only* that hat and nothing else materialized in my head so quickly that I had to turn away, afraid William would read my mind and blurt something stupid to embarrass me.

We poured out of the car, each taking a machete and a backpack. We weren't planning to stay overnight in the jungle, but just in case, we had two days' worth of water and snacks. Andrew opened the rear door, unhatched its side, and removed a rifle stock and barrel with attached scope.

"Whoa," I said, frozen in place. "What's that for?"

"Wild animals. People that want to hurt you." He deadpanned and inserted the barrel into the wooden receiver.

He had a point. We were about to enter a territory governed by ferocious big cats.

"Wait." I paused, pulling the water bottle from the backpack's side pocket. "What people? Dr. Dickhead?"

"No. He might be a scumbag, but I can't imagine him getting violent, but it doesn't mean there aren't others who might hurt us. Just playing it safe." Andrew slid open the lever and loaded several rounds into the magazine, pushed the lever in its place, and slung the rifle over his shoulder.

"How long have you had it?" I nodded at the gun and took a swig of the water. Some missed my mouth and ran down my chin and neck.

Andrew's eyes followed the drop. "Since we borrowed the car."

"Do they teach you how to use it at Cambridge?"

"No. But my father did." Andrew checked his GPS and nodded straight ahead. "Just keep in mind," he said, pointing a finger first at William, who was taking pictures with his phone, then at me, "the jungle is not a playground. If you see anything cute or pretty, don't touch it. It most likely will kill you."

These words pulled William out of his selfie mode. "What do you mean by pretty and by kill us? Jaguars?"

"Jaguars, snakes, scorpions, frogs, spiders, ants."

I should have bought pants. A bug landed on my knee, and I smacked it.

William pointed his iPhone at Andrew and took a picture. "Princesses kiss frogs in fairy tales." I would need to ask him to airdrop it for me later. I hadn't taken any pictures of Andrew yet, and I wanted one.

"The poison dart frog has enough toxin coating its skin to kill twenty people. You wouldn't want to kiss that." Andrew's hand went over his shoulder to his backpack, and he removed a machete attached to it. "Give me a minute. And don't go anywhere."

He stalked in the opposite direction he'd said we would go. I stared at his fine ass before it disappeared in tangled green vegetation.

"Where do you think he's going?" I swatted at the bugs buzzing around my face. This was going to be annoying.

William shrugged. "Take a leak?"

I'd avoided coffee this morning for just that reason. There was no way I was going to pee in a jungle where apparently everything was lethal. William handed me a can of bug repellent, and I sprayed it around my legs and arms.

Andrew returned, and we started to tread through the striking rainforest, following the equally striking man leading our adventure.

"Do you know where you're going?" William scratched his neck behind the bandana.

"I'm making it up as I go," Andrew called over his shoulder, no humor in his voice. After a pause, he chuckled and chopped off a green waxy leaf, the muscles in his arm tensing against his shirt sleeves.

I thought Colombian jungles at higher elevations would be cooler, but I was wrong. Soon, sweat trickled down my forehead in a steady steam, and two hours later my shirt was sticking to my back as if someone had sprayed me with a garden hose.

By the time the roaring sound of the waterfall filtered through the lush greenery, my legs wanted to buckle, and I wanted to strangle William because his constant complaints about bugs didn't make our trek any easier.

"We're close." Andrew took the hat off and wiped his face with his forearm, then put it back on.

Meandering our way around tall bushes, we emerged at a site of pure grandeur. In the core of the untouched rainforest, there were a series of small tier-style waterfalls flowing around rocks and greenery, weaving their way down into a pool and toppling over an edge into a milky-blue lake with a kaleidoscope of white, pink, red, and yellow flowers all around it. A slender rainbow arched above it as if hinting at the path to the pot of gold. A thrill ran through me.

We wound down to the water and dropped our backpacks on the ground.

"What a fantastic view." I shielded my eyes from the sun with my hand and spied a flock of small white birds rushing from one tree to the other. "No wonder they picked this place to get married."

With his hands on his hips, Andrew surveyed our surroundings. William sauntered over to Andrew, his shoulders back, chest out like a royal penguin during mating season and took the same stance. "So, mate, what are we going to do next?"

"We go for a swim."

William looked mildly horrified, and I knew why. "You think the treasure is in the lake?"

"No. It's behind that." Andrew nodded at the broad body of water tumbling off the cliff about a hundred feet from us.

The aftershock of the stunning beauty vanished, and I realized that as alluring as this place was, it wasn't the same waterfall Augustine had sketched. The museum picture had a large, single waterfall, similar to Ruby Falls in northern Georgia.

"Andrew, this isn't the place," I said, stretching my back.

"You're right. But we know he hid things here. To get here wasn't difficult," Andrew said. "His crew could easily bring all the cargo and store it here."

"In his correspondence, the name of the location from where they brought the trunk is different than what they call this place." I pulled my ponytail off my sweaty neck and secured it into a bun.

"It's possible they called it by two names," Andrew said, turning to look at me. "We're here, and I'm going to see what's behind."

William raised his hands in the air in surrender. "I'm staying on the shore."

"What's the matter?" Andrew kneeled and began untying his shoes.

"My brother is only afraid of two things." I bent to undo my boots too. I wasn't going to stay here. I wanted to see what was behind the waterfall. "Muddy water and halitosis."

Andrew snorted and pulled his socks off.

"But I'll go," I said.

"And leave me here alone?" William whined. "With all the hungry animals?"

"Use the rifle," Andrew said. "It's already loaded."

"I don't know how."

"Take safety off. Point. Pull trigger."

Andrew unbuttoned his shirt and slid it off his shoulders. His arm and back muscles flexed and rippled as he neatly folded his shirt and placed it atop his backpack. And oh, my heart. We might not have found lost treasure, but I may have found the sole reason for global warming. Dr. Andrew Jones was *hot*. His torso resembled a chiseled marble masterpiece.

"So," William said to Andrew's back, mouthing *Oh My God* to me and fanning himself with his hand, "do you go to the gym regularly or does dusting off mummies keep you in such great shape? I'm a member of the gym in my office building."

I scoffed. Because that was all he was. A member, not a frequent visitor.

Andrew's hands went for his belt, and my jaw unhinged. Sweet mother of Jesus, he was going to take those off, too? He unbuckled his belt, unfastened his pants, unzipped his fly, and —I ceased to breathe by this point—stepped out of his pants. Holy mother of all round and hard places. I could bounce a quarter of that butt. It was like a giant, firm Georgia sweet peach. My favorite fruit. My mouth watered.

de·i·ty |ˈdēədē|

NOUN: The handsome, tender-hearted, intelligent, virile, living, and breathing god, Andrew Oliver Jones, with the body of an ancient Greek

statue, only with all body parts
attached.

ORIGIN: Probably in his early twenties
or right after he hit puberty.

"I run. I row," Andrew finally said. Wearing only the
Fedora and boxer briefs, Andrew rested his hands on his hips
again and looked straight ahead, his eyes assessing the lake in
front of him.

"Oh yeah, me too." William loosened the bandana around
his neck.

While Andrew stared at the water, I couldn't stop gawking
at him.

William offered the bandana to me. "Here you go."

"What's that for?" I asked, taking it.

"To wipe your drool."

"Oh, fuck off." I hurled the fabric at him.

Andrew dropped the hat on top of the pile of his discarded
clothes, grabbed a flashlight out of the pocket of his backpack,
and looked at me over his shoulder. "You coming?"

Wide-eyed, I nodded, and my fingers flew to my shirt.

"What are you doing?" William gaped. "Did you bring a
swimsuit?"

I didn't.

My hands stopped. What to do? Andrew needed me to go
with him. I wanted to go with him. Every fiber in my body
begged me to go with him. It never bothered me to parade in
front of strangers in a swimsuit, which was more revealing

than the beige panties and a bra I wore today. Damn it. I should have grabbed a lacier pair. My pulse raced but for the wrong reasons. What was I afraid of? My body was in good shape. Not great, but good. Constant traveling and eating out made it impossible to keep in tip-top form, but I ran several days a week.

What if Andrew didn't like how I looked naked?

No.

I didn't care. If he didn't like what he saw, then it was his problem.

"Ugh, what the hell," I muttered and began unbuttoning my shirt.

I glanced up and found Andrew staring at me. After a hesitation, I took off my shirt and tossed it on my backpack. He didn't look away, the smirk more prominent than usual. I hesitated before pulling down my shorts, my gaze interlocked with Andrew's. And I think he held his breath. Or was I holding my breath? Oh, whatever, who needed oxygen? Breathing was overrated.

I dropped my shorts on the ground and stepped out of them. Andrew's Adam's apple bobbed, and his eyes did a slow sweep of my body.

"I'll wait in the water." He quickly submerged himself into the lake until he was waist deep.

William brought a fist to his mouth and bit on it, rolling his eyes.

"Oh, get over yourself." I went past William, an impish smile plastered on my face.

"William," Andrew called out, "don't wander away. If we don't come back in an hour, come look for us."

"Make sure you come back here in an hour," William said, plopping on the ground near the rifle. "Are there any piranhas in there? Or water snakes?"

Turtles? I wanted to say, knowing it would get a rise out of William.

"We'll find out soon." Andrew flashed a cocky smile.

Leaving William on the shore, I carefully stepped onto the slippery stones at the edge, cool water engulfing my feet and bringing a refreshing feeling of relief after a hike in the jungle. I crept farther. Goosebumps rushed in quick waves over my skin, and for the first time this week, it wasn't Andrew who made my nipples hard.

I made the next step and the lakebed abruptly dropped, plunging me chest deep.

"Oh my god," I squealed from the shock.

"What?!" William yelped. "Is there something in the water?"

"No. It's just cold." I started laughing, remembering William's graduation party with his friends at someone's lake house. We had gotten a bit rowdy, and the guys, including my brother, had decided to skinny dip. I kept my bikini on and stayed on the dock, chatting with other girls. About five minutes later William screamed in pain. A turtle had bitten him. The good news was that most people in that group were in the medical field. They acted fast and saved his big toe.

"It's not funny," William shouted now. "It could have been another part of my body!"

"What is he talking about?" Andrew asked as I paddled to him.

"That's his story to tell."

We swam out as close as possible to the waterfall and then stopped. While treading water and fighting the strong current that kept pulling my legs under, I craned my neck and stared at the tall, gushing wall of water. The idea of swimming through it was much easier to imagine than to do, especially when I was near it.

"I can touch the bottom with my feet," Andrew yelled to me over the cascading water roar. "Give me your hand." He reached out and linked his fingers with mine. When he pulled me to him, my body bumped against his, and my heartbeat jumped into my throat.

I met his gaze, and I probably looked as shell-shocked as I felt. Andrew's face was so close to mine that the different hues in his eyes became clearer. Water droplets clung to his long, dark eyelashes, and he blinked them away. My brain short-circuited, over-processing what was going on below the surface. I pressed against Andrew's torso. My right hand wrapped around his neck, and his arm encircled my waist. My legs were halfway slung around his hips, and I was sure my left ankle was brushing against his John Thomas.

Should I do it again? Just to confirm?

"Take a few deep breaths," he said and took a deep breath himself, his chest expanding.

I followed suit but also pinched my nose with my free hand. Andrew tightened his grip on my body and stepped under the ice-cold force. The water pushed down on me, snatching my bra straps off my shoulders, and a blaring crash in my ears blocked off the outside world.

Chapter Eighteen

The pounding water turned into drizzle, and the waterfall's bellow echoed around us. I wiped the water off my eyes and took in the large cavern. At the end of the corridor, light filtered through the green hanging vines, illuminating water droplets that rained like an overhead shower into a sizeable pool below. Moss and small ferns blanketed the wall behind it.

The place was enchanting, but disappointment settled like a heavy lead in my stomach. I could only imagine how Andrew felt. There was no sign of the Asiento de Padua cargo. Andrew loosened his grip, and I let go of him. My feet found the bottom, and we walked to the waterhole's edge.

Andrew got out first, and I did my best not to stare too *much* at his wet boxer brief hugging his fine ass. Was it difficult? *You betcha*. He reached out with his hand and, with one yank, helped me out of the water. The cool air rushed around me and awoke goosebumps all over me. I wrapped my arms and stole a glance at Andrew. He was quick to drag his gaze from my body up to the ceiling as if he were studying it, but I was quicker.

Andrew cleared his throat. "All right. It might appear empty, but that's not always the case." He moved deeper into the cave and clicked the flashlight on. "Keep an eye on anything that looks out of place."

We went in different directions. Water dripped in random places from the ceiling, making the stone wet and slippery. I didn't have a flashlight, so I stayed mostly in the lit area, closer to the water and then to the back with the opening above. I concentrated on cracks in the rock wall looking for hidden passages and messages.

In silence, we searched high and low around the cave, passing each other many times. While I stole a few glances at him, I didn't notice him doing the same. Instead, Andrew was in archeologist mode, eyebrows pulled together, his focus dedicated to finding the next clue. He stopped near nature's overhead shower and shone the flashlight at the ceiling.

"Adriana," he said, "come here."

I hurried over. Tilting my head up, I peered at the crevice he was looking at.

"Does it look like something's inside there?" he asked.

I blinked a few times before noticing what appeared to be a brown cloth or maybe a leather bag stuffed deep inside the crack. "Yes. How can we get it out?" Inside the cave there were no rocks we could stack for Andrew to reach it. "We need to return to the shore and find a long stick to scrape it off."

"Or you could get on my shoulders and reach it," Andrew said.

"What?" My attention snapped on him. "No."

"Yes."

"I'm not sure I want your head between my thighs."

He held my gaze. His right eyebrow arched, and his smirk deepened. "You don't?"

My heart leaped. Goddamn it. Of course I wanted it.

I opened my mouth, but no words came out. I closed it. Then tried again, but I couldn't find a suitable reply. Dropping my shoulders in defeat, I shook my head. "Let's get this over with."

Andrew stepped behind me and squatted, my ass no doubt in his face. God, help me not to die from embarrassment.

"You need to spread your legs," Andrew commanded, his gravel voice vibrating in the right places and my inner parts clenched.

I did what he said, and he slid his head between my thighs, the brush of his wet hair on my skin sending a million emotions through me, and I tried—I think I succeeded, but I wouldn't know because blood was pounding in my ears—not to gasp or moan or make any other animal noises. Without leaning forward, he stood up, and I yelped from how fast it happened—*impressive*—my hand flew to his face and grabbed it. The warmth of his skin soaked into my cold legs, spreading fast through me.

"Take the flashlight," Andrew said, his fingers digging into the flesh above my knees.

Shining a light into the hole, I located the mysterious object, but before sticking my hand inside, I made sure nothing else was there, like a snake or tarantula. Did tarantulas live in Colombia? Or were they from Africa? I had no idea and I found myself cursing my lack of knowledge. Satisfied everything looked safe, I reached for the item. My hand a few inches away from touching it, I pressed my ankles tighter around his torso and lifted my butt off his shoulders, my groin rubbing the back of his head and—oh my Lord, I shouldn't have done it. The slight friction conjured up a dull pressure in my core. A weak moan turning into a hum escaped me, and I swayed, losing some of my balance. I jerked, releasing the flashlight straight into the pool of water, and grabbed Andrew's hair.

"Ouch," Andrew cried out.

"Sorry," I mumbled, my hands letting go. The flashlight quickly sunk, illuminating the bottom of a deep hole.

He turned to look at the flashlight. And my hands grabbed his hair again. "Andrew! Don't move like that. I'll fall."

"What were you trying to do?"

"The damn thing is about three to four inches out of my reach. I was trying to get a bit closer to it."

"Let's try it again." Without breaking contact with my skin, Andrew's hands glided from my knees to my ankles, and he pressed them hard into his torso, letting me use my entire leg muscles for leverage. I pushed my ass off his shoulders—this time focusing on my task—and my nails grazed the thing.

"God," I groaned. "I'm so close."

Thank goodness William wasn't with us; he would point out how it sounded.

Andrew's hands tightened, and he stood on his toes, closing the needed distance, and my fingers grabbed the leather object. "I got it." I yanked the dark brown pouch out of the stone's crack.

When I stepped off Andrew's shoulders, my legs tingled

where our skin had pressed together. A cocktail of being in contact with his body and the excitement of finding something rushed through my bloodstream. Andrew untightened the string around the leather bag and opened it. He angled it so light from above could reveal the inside. His eyebrows pinched. Frowning, he reached inside, and when his hand came out, clumps of wet yellow paper clung to his fingers.

"What is it?" I asked.

Andrew ferreted in the bag more, then finally said, "Something that is of no use to us anymore." He pulled the bag inside out and a decayed pale brown paper that looked like porridge landed between our feet.

"I'll get the flashlight, and we can leave." He handed me the bag and sat on the verge of the pool, lowering his legs into the water. Taking a deep breath, he pushed off and submerged, moving his arms to push himself to the bottom. I watched him reach for his torch, but instead of coming up for air, he stayed under as if he'd seen something.

He finally broke the surface and swept his wet hair off his eyes. "There's an underground passageway." He pushed to the edge and folded his forearms, breathing hard. "You stay here. I'll swim to see what's there."

The recent news flashed in my head about scuba divers who were lost in underground caves and ran out of air, their lifeless bodies found days later.

My stomach roiled. "Is it safe?"

"I'll be okay." Andrew began taking a series of deep breaths, filling his blood with oxygen. His eyes held mine before he took the last one and pushed off, diving deep into the water.

"If you aren't back in one minute, I'm coming after you," I yelled but doubted he heard me.

My fingers fumbled with my Apple watch as I started the timer. Andrew swam into the opening, and soon the light he carried vanished. I checked the time. Thirty-three seconds. How long can people hold their breath? One minute? Two minutes? Andrew was in great shape and obviously worked out, so he probably could stay without taking another breath for at least three minutes. I rechecked the time. One minute and four seconds. *What should I do if he didn't come up soon? Do I go after him?* I had no flashlight so I couldn't see there. Shoot. I should have thought about it and brought another one with me. I bit my nail, noticing my hands were shaking. Two minutes and forty-two seconds. I couldn't take it anymore. I dropped the leather bag and plunged into the cold water. I sank and peered in the direction Andrew had disappeared in, hoping to see a glimpse of light. I could barely make out the rock path, but it quickly turned into pitch-black, intimidating darkness. Pushing off the rocky bottom I went up and gulped in the air.

A frustrated groan left my mouth. I took another deep breath and submerged. I repeated it several times until my head felt dizzy, and I had to climb out before I went to Davy Jones's locker. I fell flat on my back near the pool, falling drops misting my skin, bringing waves of shivers. My chest rose and fell fast, and then it began to quiver, hot tears running down the sides of my face. I sucked in some more air and told myself that Andrew had found a different open cave and was now exploring it. Maybe he found the treasure and was rolling around in it, laughing like a mad person. If that were the case, I'd smack him when he returned for scaring the shit out of me.

I checked my watch. Seven minutes. Ice-cold fear coursed through my veins, and my lungs felt like they were collapsing under the weight of anxiety and horror. Andrew was either dead, or lost but alive, or alive and busy exploring.

After what felt like forever, the water in the pool gurgled and rippled, and I jumped to a sitting position. Relief washed over me when I saw Andrew emerging. He gasped for air when his head broke the surface.

"You are a fucking asshole!" I yelled at him.

Andrew wiped the water off his face and held onto the edge. "That's one way to say hello." His shoulders heaved as he panted.

"Goddammit. I thought you were dead." I squeezed my fists, holding myself back from smacking him hard. Tears swelled in my eyes. "What took you so long?" I croaked.

Andrew's face crumbled with remorse. "Adriana, I'm so sorry I scared you." He pushed out of the water and collapsed next to me, taking my hand. "I'm an idiot. I should have come back right away. Please forgive me."

I pulled my hand out and wiped my eyes. "You are an idiot, but it's okay." I sniffed. "Just don't do it again. Don't make me think I've lost you."

His heartfelt gaze searched mine. "You'll never lose me."

I took a shaky breath. "Did you find anything?"

Defeat took over Andrew's usual composed and confident posture. He sat with his head sagged, his elbows pressing into his knees, his hands clasped together. "There are two smaller caves. Both empty." He scoffed. "This was a colossal waste of time."

I wanted to say *I told you so* but my red anger subsided and I said, "I'm sorry."

"Fucking bollocks." He shook his head.

A deep sadness sank into my stomach. I scooted closer to him until our thighs touched, the heat of my body radiating against his cold one. I leaned in so I could catch his eyes.

He glanced at me. "I'm sorry I dragged you here."

My eyes searched his face, fighting the swell of ache in my chest.

"I'm not." I bumped into him with my shoulder. "I almost did a cheerleading stand." He huffed a silent laugh. "Do you think it was ever here?"

He shook his head. "I don't know."

"What should we do next?"

"The question of the hour." Andrew blew out another breath. He rubbed his forehead, his eyes closed. "Back to my notes and their letters. Back to figuring out the location of the palace." He scoffed. "If that even exists."

Andrew turned his face to mine, and the corners of his lips curved ever-so-slightly, but then his mouth relaxed, erasing laughing lines around it. "I'm tired of this."

"Of this trip?"

"No." He groaned. "Of this constant chase. It's always like this. You think you're getting closer, and in the end, it's an empty shell or another clue leading you somewhere else that leads you to another clue. My whole life is chasing clues."

"I thought you enjoyed discovering things. You and your team found parts of King John's treasure. That's pretty cool."

"Yes. But how many years have we wasted on that? I spend half of a year in constant motion. I'm turning thirty-five this year," he said. "I want what Charlotte has. A family. And what's worse, in two months, she's moving to Wales to live with her boyfriend. When I come home, it'll be empty."

He shifted forward and pressed his elbow hard into his knees again, burying his fingers in his hair. When a man was broken down and feeling weak, it wasn't a proper time to notice beautiful muscles rippling all over his body. But I did anyway. I had eyes after all.

"I'm sure they'll visit you often." I had no clue how long the drive was from Cambridge to Wales, but it couldn't be more than a few hours. My arm went up to his back, and I rubbed it—to comfort him. Despite the cold air around us, his skin was hot under my touch. I stroked his back, paying no—absolutely none whatsoever—attention to every contour of his muscles. "You could stop working for the *secret-saving-historical-crap-society* and only teach at the university. No more chasing things around the world. Just a regular nine-to-five job. If you sit for ten minutes in a pub or stroll in a museum, you'll find a line of women who want to have babies with you. You're a dream man."

A twinge of jealousy went through my gut at my own words. I wanted to be among those women. No, not among them. Just me.

He faced me, a brown curl of hair stuck on his forehead. "Even yours?" His brow puckered, and his eyes met mine and lingered.

A zing roared down my spine, and my smile dropped, but the corners of his mouth lifted. The cool air was heavy with our breaths. Something passed between us. I couldn't stop staring at his moist lips.

Andrew straightened. Shifting closer, his hand reached my face, and he smoothed away the wet hair that had stuck to my cheek. The brush of his fingertips over my skin took my breath away. His fingers traveled down my face and wrapped gently at the nape of my neck. I slowly gravitated toward him. His mismatched eyes glinted with a million questions in them. He cupped my cheek and leaned in, tilting his head. My heart thumped out of rhythm, and his chest's quick rise and fall suggested he felt the same way.

Andrew's lips parted, and his face was so close, his breath touched my mouth. I wanted to kiss Andrew so desperately that it hurt inside my chest. Or maybe I was having a heart attack. A fling was a bad idea because I wanted this man for more than one night—I was falling for him. No, not falling. I was plummeting headfirst into a maelstrom of forbidden feelings. And there was nothing for me to grab on to for safety. Andrew's mouth brushed over mine.

It was a soft kiss. Tender. Perfect. The featherlight touch of Andrew's lips was like a petal of a fresh rose. My hands moved to his chest, then quickly to his neck, threading my fingers into his hair. The low sound in his throat let me know he enjoyed it. The pressure of his mouth on mine triggered a hunger I hadn't been aware I felt. My mouth opened to him, and his tongue moved over mine. I moaned in pleasure. Andrew wrapped his arms around my body and brought me flush against him, his mouth devouring mine. My head whirled. I knew it would feel incredible to be kissed by Andrew, but I'd had no idea how drunk I would get on this.

Without breaking our kiss, I hauled myself on the top of him, his hard length pressed against me. I thrummed with need, and my greedy side took over. Arching into him, I ground my hips, my aching spot seeking friction and pulling another groan out of him. I shuddered at the image of his tongue on my body, of his cock inside me.

My heart was going to explode—

"Get a room, Jones." Richard's voice detonated like a bomb in the cave and Andrew and I broke apart as if lightning had struck us.

Chapter Nineteen

"Richard," Andrew snarled, his expression contorting into anger. He removed his hand from me, making me go cold all over, especially where he had just touched me. "What are you doing here?"

"I'd say the same thing to you. I'm here to find Augustine's treasure, but you're obviously"—Richard waved his hand at us —"getting busy with..."

I took a moment to scrutinize Dr. Dickhead. In contrast to us, Richard wore swim shorts and a white T-shirt and he held a snorkeling mask with a small oxygen tank—he was much more prepared. He was a foot shorter than Andrew, and a wet shirt that clung to his body revealed a teenager's narrow shoulders and slim arms. Such an ordinary asswipe. What exactly did Brie see in this man?

Andrew looked at me, and his eyes softened. "I'm so sorry." He pressed a gentle kiss to my forehead.

"It's okay," I whispered.

It wasn't okay.

I was making out with the sexiest man on this planet and maybe getting more than a mind-blowing kiss, and now the moment was ruined.

Andrew stood up, and I followed suit, feeling overexposed, naked, and unnerved. I hid behind his enormous frame, embarrassed that Richard had caught us barely dressed. Going for a swim in a bra and panties felt like a stupid idea now.

Richard dramatically shielded his eyes with his hand. "Not what I came to see."

"How did you know to come here?" Andrew asked.

"You aren't the only one who's clever. Don't forget, we used to work together. I know a thing or two." Richard angled his head and caught my stare. "Mrs. Jones, I apologize for ruining this private moment. If I knew what was going on here, I'd have waited outside. But since we're here, tell me, did you find anything?" He walked deeper into the cave, studying the same rock walls Andrew and I had examined earlier.

"It's empty, so you can leave," Andrew said.

"Why is it that every time we're in the same space, you want me to leave?" Like a shark, Richard made his way around us, his eyes grazing my body. I stepped closer to Andrew.

Richard glanced at the goo of old paper near the pool, his brows coming together. "What is that?"

"The next clue," I said, my eyes landing on the leather sack in the dark corner. It had no value, but I wanted Dickhead to think it did and that we were a step ahead of him. I bent and grabbed it. "Too bad it's ours."

Richard tilted his head up to nature's sky window, and then he peered at me. "Can I see the bracelet? The one that you found last night."

My stomach roiled. Goddamn it. William must have told Brandon. Of course, he did. But I was the idiot who shared the news with him in the first place.

Andrew drew in a deep breath, clenching and then unclenching his fists. "You can stay. We're leaving." He tugged my hand to go.

As I turned, Richard grasped my right arm, his fingers gripping tightly around my forearm.

"Let go!" I jerked my hand out of his grip.

In a flash, Andrew stepped to Richard. "You touch her again, and I'll break every bone in your body, starting with your skull."

Richard threw his hands up in surrender. "I just wanted to see the original one. I've only seen photos of it." He moved back, and his foot slipped on the wet rocks. At that moment, Andrew pushed on Richard's chest, and the jerk fell backward into the pool.

We turned and made our way to the cave's mouth.

"Oh, come on, Andrew," Richard called out. "Let's work on this together. It would be like the good old days. You need my help, my resources. I have more money at my disposal than you do."

Without looking back at Dr. Dickhead, Andrew wrapped his arms around my back. I looped my legs around his waist, my arms around his neck, and buried my face into his shoulder, pressing my chest into his. It was nice to be pressed into his body again.

"Take a breath," he said, slowly walking us into the rush of water.

Outside, a somber sky awaited us, and gusts of wind pushed on the tops of the trees. On the shore, William and Brandon sat on the ground next to our backpacks, and Brie was perched on a rock, talking on a satellite phone. She wore a khaki long-sleeve shirt, brown hiking pants with multiple pockets, and a high-braided ponytail. Two thickset men with shaved heads, dressed in desert camouflage uniforms, stood not far from her. As we swam closer to them, William leaped to his feet.

"I didn't say a word," William said as we slogged through the last ten feet of the water. "I swear."

My chest heaved from a long swim. I gave William a death stare as I marched to my pile of clothes and dropped the old leather bag. I could feel the leering eyes of the two hideous round-faced men on me, but my anger left no space for self-consciousness. I shouldn't have texted anything to William. He was a smart man, but I guess he had a big mouth when it came to pretty boys. I yanked my shorts off the ground.

"Andy," Brie said, a bit too breathless for my liking, her eyes perusing Andrew's body. "You are so … mmm. An extra six years looks great on you."

Jealousy gripped my throat. I wasn't too fond of the way she was inspecting him. *Argh.* She used to touch him too. I wasn't a violent person, but my hands itched to push her fucking face into the mud.

Andrew grabbed his pants and pulled them on without making eye contact with the bitch.

Brie pocketed her phone in a leather crossbody purse.

"Did you find anything?" William asked.

"Do you really think I'd tell you? In front of them?" I jerked my chin in Brandon's direction, stepped into my shorts and brought them up. "Maybe we did. Maybe we didn't." Frustration boiled my blood. Why did Richard always appear in the same place we were? Was it a coincidence? Did he know about the palace too?

I buttoned my shirt and grabbed my boots. I wrestled the left sock on, the fabric clinging to my skin. The feel of wet socks always hurled me back into my worst memories. So many times, as a kid, I had to wear damp shoes because they hadn't dried overnight. William and I owned only one pair of tennis shoes each, and we wore them until our neighbors passed down some of their kid's shoes. "Tell me, Brandon." I stared at the Dr. Dickhead minion. For some reason, I couldn't bring myself to look at Brie. "Do you guys follow us around because you have no clue how to find Augustine's treasure?"

"I... We don't..." Brandon said, his brown eyes round and eyebrows raised.

"Did you shove a tracking device up my brother's ass last night?" I pulled my other sock on.

Brandon's eyes widened more, his cheeks turning red, and his gaze locked on William. "You're related?"

"Isn't it obvious? Same features." William circled his face. "Of course, my skin tone is much better than hers. She's always outside, and I've told her it's harmful."

Andrew set his hat on his head and threw on his backpack. He marched over to Tweedledum and Tweedledee and reached for our hunting rifle at their feet. The left guy stepped on the barrel, holding the gun in place.

Andrew glanced up at the bonehead. "Let me have my gun."

"William," I snapped. "Why would you give them our gun?"

"I didn't," he said. "They took it."

The ogre spitted to one side, then sneered, baring his crooked teeth. He shook his head. Andrew straightened to his full height, his expression that of someone who was as calm as a bomb with a short fuse. He had a few inches on them, but I wasn't sure he could handle both at the same time if their staring contest escalated to something ugly. Andrew peered over his shoulder at Brie.

"Tell your guard dogs to let go of my gun," he said to her.

I quickly yanked my other shoe on and laced it up, stuffed the leather pouch into my backpack, and stood up. When I worked at Salzburg Wine Distributing, I often traveled alone, so I'd picked up a few self-defense moves just to be safe. If we were about to get into a fight, I was ready. *I think.* Of course, they not only had our rifle, but it was also hard not to miss the pistols on the ogres' belts. The events of this day hardly seemed real. First, the cave turned out to be a dud, then a scorching kiss with Andrew—*can't think about it right now*—and now we were on the verge of a tussle.

"Andy," Brie said, placing her hands on her hips, her ample cleavage very noticeable. Were her top buttons unbuttoned before and I hadn't noticed? I squared my shoulders. "Let's all work together."

"Not going to happen," he said with hostility.

"We'll split our share with you. Seventy/thirty. It will be

many times more than what you would get from the Octavian Global group."

"The gun," Andrew demanded.

"We can solve this puzzle in no time if we combine your knowledge with Richard's. Sixty/forty?"

Andrew's jaw tensed, as he clenched his teeth. William stepped to me, his backpack already on his shoulders. We exchanged glances.

Brie sighed. "Fine. Fifty-fifty."

"Brie. My gun."

She wrinkled her nose and crossed her arms. "No. If you want to leave without negotiating a deal. Then leave without it as well."

What the actual fuck? Had that cold-hearted bitch lost her mind? I was turning into a ball of pure anger.

"Seriously?" I muttered. "You want us to trek through the jungle without protection?"

She rolled her eyes and barked, "Igor, *otdai emu rujee.*"

Definitely not Spanish. Russian, maybe? The ogre released the gun, and Andrew picked it up. He slid open the lever and checked the rifle.

"And rounds." Andrew stuck his hand out, palm up.

The guy's hand went to his chest pocket, and he withdrew five bullets and dropped them into Andrew's hand. Andrew loaded the rifle and slung it over his shoulder.

"William, say goodbye to your pretty boy." I hoisted my backpack on my shoulders. "This is the last time you're going to see him."

Andrew pushed past us into the dark jungle, and we followed him.

"Text me later," William told Brandon and tailed after me.

For real, William? Even right now?

If the walk to the waterfalls was long, the walk back felt twice as long. The tension among us had gone wire taut. With no sun the jungle was blanketed in semidarkness. Strong gusts of wind harassed the rainforest canopy, making tree trunks groan and vines sway in an eerie dance.

"You are such an idiot," I said to William as I stepped over a log. "Why would you tell him what we've found?" I pushed a large waxy green leaf out of my way.

"I didn't," William yelled. "I didn't tell him anything. This morning we exchanged digits, and I left his room. He had no idea who I was. And then they just showed up here. And if someone is a fucking idiot, it's you. You're the one who texted me."

Touché.

"What exactly did your text last night say?" Andrew asked.

God, how could this day turn into such total shit? Guilt and fear punched me in my gut. Technically it was my fault I'd shared information with my brother. "Um, that we'd found a second bracelet." The words scraped my throat.

"For the love of god. I didn't show it to him," William cried out. "Why is it so hard to believe me?"

I stared ahead. Last night William was probably drunk and told Brandon everything.

"Brandon could have broken into your phone and read it," Andrew said, defending him for unexplained reasons.

"I'm telling you: he didn't know who I was until a few minutes ago."

"He was pretending." I shot him a mean glance. "Have you thought about it?"

"Well, he doesn't know my passcode to my phone. How would he read my stuff?"

"William." I stopped and turned to look at him. "How did you find out that Mason was double dipping?"

Two years ago, William thought he'd finally found The One until he got suspicious his boyfriend wasn't faithful. When Mason was asleep, William brought Mason's iPhone to his face and unlocked it. And with it he unlocked the Pandora's box of Mason's on-the-side dates.

"Shit." William pressed his hands to his mouth.

"Don't touch your face. Your hands are dirty." I couldn't help myself.

"At the lake, Brandon said—"

"Who cares what he said," I said.

"Let me speak," William snapped. "He said that Richard works with Dr. Garcia."

It was heartbreaking to quarrel with William. We rarely bickered, and when we disagreed, we never yelled hurtful things.

Andrew steered left from a gaping hole left by a fallen tree, its dark roots sticking out like crooked fingers. "Dr. Garcia is my father's old friend. He wouldn't work for Nicolai Kolesnikov."

"Then why would he say that?"

"To add disruption, slow us down. To ruin our trust."

"It doesn't feel right that they always show up at the same place where we are," I said.

"Richard is smart," Andrew said. "We shouldn't be surprised our paths cross."

"Maybe they bugged our car?" William chimed in.

We trod in dead silence for the remainder of the hike. Once in a while, birds or animals yawped and shrieked as if mocking us. William was annoyed with me for giving him shit about Brandon. I was pissed at William and myself. Rage rolled through me. I hated the way Brie had checked out Andrew. I hated her nauseating use of *Andy*. Why did she keep calling him that? He didn't look like an Andy at all. He was too handsome and too large for the cutesy nickname, especially when he was angry.

And boy, was he angry. The way he slashed vines and leaves with his machete to make a path for us was frightening. William and I were careful to keep our distance from him.

When we reached our destination, a stylish Land Rover Defender was parked next to our crappy, dirty Jeep.

"How come they got a nice ride, and we got this?" William folded his arms on his chest.

"Seriously?" Andrew gave him a look. He dropped the gun and his bag into the back and tossed his hat on the driver's seat. "I'll be back. Stay here."

I watched him march in the same direction he went after we arrived, my eyes glued to his broad shoulders and his *very* nice ass. The ass that I could have squeezed several hours ago before shit hit the fan. *Sorry not sorry.* Even in the current situation, I couldn't help myself.

"Dr. Sexy Hulk has a serious issue with his bladder," William said once the jungle had swallowed Andrew whole.

I threw my backpack next to Andrew's and slumped in

defeat on the car bumper. I was so mad I wanted to find a nearby rock and smash the windshield of their nice car. I glanced around but only found low shrubs and grass and vines hanging off trees. And I wasn't about to crawl into the bushes in search of something heavy since deadly creatures lived there.

Andrew emerged from the woods, holding the wrapped box we'd found last night.

"This isn't my first rodeo," he said, approaching us. "I couldn't leave it on the shore, and I couldn't leave it in the Jeep." He unzipped his bag and placed the box inside. "They searched it."

William and I both stared into the car. Nothing looked out of place. How in the world did Andrew know they'd rummaged around? I couldn't believe how dirty Richard played. More irritation pricked my skin.

"Screw it." I stepped to Andrew and yanked his pocketknife.

"Hey." Andrew caught my wrist, my hand gripping his knife. "What are you doing?"

"I'll give you one guess." I twisted my hand out of his grip and strode to the Land Rover.

Unfolding a blade, I squatted by the right tire and jabbed the blade into it. Well, I tried to jab it, but the knife bounced back, leaving a tiny poke.

Shit. That wasn't how it played out in my mind.

"It looks so easy in the movies." I glanced at my hand. "I want to slow them down, or to piss them off."

"Everything appears simple in the movies." Andrew crouched next to me and gently removed the knife from my fingers, then took my hand, turned it up, and pressed his lips against the inside of my wrist. The touch electrified my every nerve and fiber, setting my body on fire. I went still until he released my hand. My mind raced like a herd of wild horses, my fingers pressing onto the spot where Andrew's lips had brushed against my skin. His lips. Again. On my skin. I was about to combust from being unable to climb onto his lap and cover his mouth with mine.

"You shouldn't get your hands dirty," he said firmly, but a tiny flicker of amusement lit his eyes, "but I can."

With a quick move, he stabbed the knife against the rubber, then slapped the butt of the handle, driving the blade into the tire. Then he walked to the other side and did the same thing.

Chapter Twenty

"You don't really think I brought Richard's crew to the waterfall?" William threw open his luggage.

We were sharing a room again at the only B&B in the first village we had passed. Our room was plain, with two double beds, a large nightstand in between, a comfy, stain-free reading chair in a corner, and a possibly working TV. Nothing fancy, but it had a bathroom. It was a clean place, but so different from the Erizo at Las Loma resort. But frankly, I didn't care. I was glad we were away from Dr. Dickhead. What if we had found Augustine's loot in the cave? What would have happened? Richard and Brie had armed guards with them, and it didn't look like they'd brought them for protection from wild animals. I shuddered at that thought.

"I say and do stupid things when I'm drunk," William continued, "but for your information, I wasn't drunk yesterday. I only had one glass of rum."

"One glass too many," I said, pulling the cosmetics case out of my suitcase.

Thanks to all the Botox, William's expression was unreadable, but the hurt in his eyes was unmistakable. "You were the one who drank a bottle of wine last night," he retorted.

I slammed the door.

He was right.

I turned on the water, yanked my shirt over my head, and threw it next to my shorts on the floor. Arguing with William wore me out. I didn't like it. I also was exhausted from wondering how Dr. Dickhead knew where to find us. I was dirty and tired. And horny. A tornado of sexual confusion swirled inside me, destroying any functional thought my mind developed. What was I going to do about Andrew? Was he still interested in me? I shampooed my hair, my nails scratching my scalp.

"Are you mad at me?" William asked from the other side of the shower curtain.

"I have so many other things on my mind that there is simply no room for me to be angry with you. It was my fault for drunk texting you. Brandon just saw it on your phone. The end."

"You aren't going to like this," William said, "but I think you're wrong about Brandon. I believed him when he whispered that Dr. Garcia works with Richard. This is how they know what we know."

"I don't care anymore." I rinsed my hair. "Let's forget this."

He sighed. "What's wrong?"

"Nothing."

"Something is wrong. You didn't eat much at dinner."

While Andrew arranged the lodging, William and I had

walked to a food stand and bought beef empanadas and plantain fritters for the three of us. The food tasted great, but I wasn't particularly hungry. I turned the shower off, and William handed me a towel around the curtain. I dried and then wrapped it around my body.

"Andrew kissed me when we were behind the waterfall." I stepped out of the bathtub.

"I knew there was something between the two of you." He pointed his finger at me. "Details."

I twisted the water out of my long hair. A drop ran down the nape of my neck, and it reminded me of Andrew's fingers touching there. I took a deep breath and closed my eyes for a moment, relishing how his soft, warm lips had felt on mine, his hands sliding down my back, fingers pressing against the swell of my backside.

"It was better than I could have ever dreamed," I said.

"I can believe it." William dropped the cotton ball he'd used to clean his face into a garbage bin and waved his hand for me to follow him. "Come on. Spill the beans. What else did you guys do?"

In the bedroom, William plopped down on the bed and dropped his phone next to him. I tied a messy bun on top of my head and then out of my luggage I yanked a T-shirt with the words "I don't need a mood ring. I have a face", lacy panties, and my sleeping shorts. I dressed in the bathroom and returned to the bedroom, holding William's body cream with a hint of shimmer. "Nothing. Richard ruined the moment."

"I yelled to warn y'all that he was coming, but you probably didn't hear me. Wait…" William sat up straight in the bed. "Are you planning to go to his room dressed like that?"

"I'm not planning on going to his room at all," I lied and slathered a hefty amount of rich body butter on my hands and moisturized my legs, inhaling the soft powdery aroma. Of course, I was planning to see Andrew. But I wanted to look casual, like I didn't plan to go there, but something came up, and I had to stop by. I just had to come up with the *something*.

"Why not?"

I shrugged. "I think the moment passed. He barely said a word on the way here. And you saw how he was when we got our rooms." Andrew had grumbled good night and marched to his door.

"Riiiight." William cupped his chin between his thumb and forefinger. "Then what's up with the lotion?"

"Nothing." I didn't meet his eyes. "Just getting ready for bed."

"You never put on lotion."

"I do every night. I'm almost out of the one you gave me for Christmas."

"Exactly my point."

I rubbed lotion into my arms. "And what point is that?"

"It's the middle of February. You should have been out of it by the end of January."

I finished and threw the bottle into his open luggage.

Why was I putting on this show for William? He saw right through me. I was preparing to go to Andrew's room, but I wasn't one hundred percent convinced that tonight was a good idea. A small part of me tried to talk me out of it, and if I had known which part it was, I would have told it to back off.

William pushed off the bed, went to his suitcase, and rummaged in it. "Take these and go." He grabbed a line of condoms, tore some off, and pressed the silver packages into my hand, then his hands went to my bun. He pulled on the hair tie, fluffed my hair up and cocked his head. "You need lip gloss. And slap your cheeks to bring color to them." William was about to pinch my face, but I swatted his hands away.

"Stop it." I stepped back. "I don't need color in my face."

"Do some crunches to give your stomach more definition."

Seriously? Was that what he did before having sex? I mentally shook my head. I didn't need to know.

"It's flat enough. Why are you this way?" I was now hugging my midsection. "I wasn't sure about this whole thing from the start, and you're only making it worse."

"You know I'm teasing. You're in great shape and beautiful. But please change into a different shirt."

"No." I pulled my hair back into a messy bun.

"Why are *you* being so difficult? But fine! Fine. Just leave, please." He took me by my shoulders, turned me around, and pushed me toward the door. "And don't come back without details on how it went. I don't want to see you before breakfast." He opened the door and waited for me to exit. "Go."

"What do I say to him?" The self-assured-thirty-something-year-old me vanished, and more panic threaded through my veins.

"Say, 'I'm here to help you figure out the next clue.'" William leaned his head against the door. "But to be honest, hun, I don't think you need to say anything."

My heart hammered hard in my chest when I knocked on Andrew's door. Some part of me hoped he was asleep and wouldn't open it, so I could go back to my room and forget what had happened behind the waterfall. But the other part of me begged to break down the door and attack Andrew. I tugged down on my shorts. After a few more seconds, I admitted defeat. He either wasn't there or didn't want any visitors. Me in particular.

"Hello." Andrew's voice came from somewhere behind me. I turned.

He stood in the hallway holding a mug, dressed in a light green T-shirt and khaki pants. His hair was a tangled, wet mess, a five o'clock shadow covered his jawline, and the dark circles under his eyes were more noticeable than usual. He looked drained but sexy as hell. An electric current rippled through me. God, I wanted to fling my arms around his neck and press my lips to his smirk.

All I could do was stare at him, but eventually I said, "Hi." I linked my hands behind my back and rocked on my heels. "Did you eat your dinner?"

"Yes. Thank you." Andrew's eyes landed on my chest, and his lips curved at the corners. He lifted his right eyebrow, dragging his gaze to my face. "What mood are you in?"

Jesus Christ. Was I that obvious?

I searched my mind for a reply, but my brain packed its bags and said, *adios, amigo. You're on your own.*

I bit my bottom lip. I should have listened to William and used some lip gloss.

"Whaa-t do you mean?" I stammered. *Now I stammer. For real?*

254

"Your shirt." He nodded at it.

Ohhhhh.

"Yes. My shirt. It's my favorite. I like funny shirts. William got it for me. I don't remember if it was Christmas last year. Or maybe my birthday." First, I couldn't talk, and now I word-vomited. Andrew's eyebrow arched even higher, and his mouth stretched into a grin. "I was coming to check on you. To see if you … needed any help to … figure out clues and such."

"That's nice of you. Would you like some of my coffee? Or I can go downstairs and get another for you?"

I dropped my arms by my side, then crossed them over my chest. I had no idea what to do with myself. I shook my head. "If I have any coffee, I'll be up until sunrise. So, unless you're ready to be up with me all night…" My body went still and hot. Where was I going with that?

Andrew's eyes made a slow slide up and down my body, and when they met mine, a thousand questions swirled in them. A shred of panic rushed through me. Was this my cue to saunter over to him, put my hands on his chest, and finish what we'd started?

"Well, then…" He stepped to his door and pushed the key into the lock. Metal clicked a few times, and the door opened. "Come in."

Chapter Twenty-One

The room was the same size as ours, its ceiling sloped on one side, a fan lazily rotating above a double bed next to a surprisingly large desk. Andrew's journals, old books, and letters were scattered on the floor.

I gestured at the paper mess, carefully stepping around it. "You have a desk, but you seem determined not to use it." My voice came out too strained.

"Yes, I like to spread out my work. It helps me to think better."

Andrew kicked off his shoes and lowered himself onto the floor, crossing his legs. I sat close to him and picked up a pencil drawing of an outer design of swirls on the bracelet I wore. He pulled a sheet of paper from the stack of his notes and handed it to me.

"Is this the map from the second bracelet?"

"Yes." He sipped his coffee.

"You're great at sketching." I stole a glance at him, then my focus returned to the drawing. "Why do you draw these, anyway?"

"When something interests me and I can't take it back to a hotel or home, I make a copy and study it later. For example, this bracelet." He brushed his fingers over the metal on my wrist, and heat traveled over my skin. "It's on you, so you would always have to be next to me. When I thought of something and needed to check it, I would pick up your hand…" Andrew sat his coffee on the floor and did exactly what he'd just said. A slow pull turned his lips up. My pulse picked up at our contact. "I would look at it, then turn it over." He turned my hand, my wrist up. "And I'd study it for some time." His thumb drew gentle, slow circles in the center of my palm. I watched the movement, and possessive lust curled in me as if he wasn't just pressing there. I wanted him to put pressure in the place I needed him the most. I involuntarily shuddered and glanced up at him. And he gave me a smile that made my insides ripple with pure lust.

"You could take a photo with your phone," I said in a whisper.

"I do that, too, but I see certain details in my drawings. Something about paper and pencil reveals more to me than a picture."

Did I mention he was still holding my hand?

"I don't think it's the reason you like pencil drawings more than pictures."

"No?" he said in a low voice. "Then what is it?"

"I think," my fingers closed over this thumb, "you're old-fashioned … or don't know how to use technology." I didn't know what I was saying. I was blathering. Andrew bit his bottom lip, smiling. My nose twitched, and I jerked my hand out of his and covered it. Shoot. It was a big tic, and I was sure he'd noticed it.

Andrew reached for my hand and gently pulled it off my face. "It's cute."

"What is?"

"Your nervous tic."

"How do you know it's a nervous tic? Maybe you smell funny."

"I pay close attention to everything or anybody that interests me."

The lust and longing swelled where I was pulsing, wet and needy. "You're interested in me?"

"Very much." His smile dimmed. "You're like the loveliness of a summer sunrise, and the gentle elegance of a crescent moon," he said, serious but also endearingly nervous. His intense and hungry gaze moved to my lips and locked on my mouth. "I have traveled to almost every part of this world, and I thought I had seen every beauty it offered, but when I saw you I knew I'd been wrong." He looked into my eyes. "You're the most stunning allure this world can offer."

His words stopped my heart. If he had asked me to marry him right then, I would have agreed. I had known him only for a few days, but those words were so beautiful, my heart drowned in love. Many men had told me I was beautiful. Sometimes in a funny way, sometimes a perverted way, other times in a clumsy way, and sometimes in an honest, *from-the-bottom-of-their-heart* way, but no one had ever said it to me this way. It took all my willpower not to jump on Andrew's lap and smash my mouth against his.

Andrew dropped his head with a chuckle. "That sounded so cheesy. I'm sorry."

"Not at all," I croaked. "I think it was the most beautiful speech I've ever heard."

Andrew lifted his head, and his eyes burrowed deep inside my soul. His free hand cupped my face, then slid behind my neck. He leaned close—holding my gaze with his own—and I gravitated to him. The tips of our noses touched, and I could hear his rapid breathing. I closed my eyes.

Time ground to a halt.

Andrew's lips brushed mine. They were soft, wet, and warm. His tongue stroked along my bottom lip, and I opened my mouth to let him in. His tongue rolled against mine, and the electricity shot from my chest to my core. He tasted like coffee, and it awakened every fiber of my body. I pressed my hands on his chest, feeling his heart pounding under my palms. His seductive and masculine bergamot scent intoxicated me, imprinting itself in my mind. This was the moment I'd been craving for days now. If not my entire life.

Our kiss was slow and languorous, our tongues caressing each other. Andrew wrapped his arms around my body, his hands finding their way under my T-shirt, his palms pressing against my bare, hot skin. I fisted waves of his hair, and he made a quiet groan of appreciation, deepening our kiss.

Andrew trailed kisses along my jaw and down my neck, lighting my skin on fire everywhere his lips touched and his stubble scratched. His thumb circled over my stiffened nipple. I threw my head back, and a guttural sound escaped me, mingling with the low sound from his throat. His mouth moved down, and he took my hard bud into his mouth, grazing it with his teeth through the fabric of my shirt, and making my toes curl. He repeated the same with my other breast. Heat pooled at my center, and I needed his lips on every inch of my body.

The air around us turned searing hot, and I wanted him out of his clothes. I needed him to rip mine off. I wanted the weight of his body against mine so I shifted, slowly falling on my back, tugging him down with me until his body was firm on top of mine.

Andrew rose on his elbows. "I want you so much it hurts." His pupils were wide, hiding most of their blue and green color, his lips red and swollen.

My trembling hands clenched his shirt, and I pulled his mouth back to mine. We didn't have much time remaining on this trip. Why didn't we do this in the church when he told me he wasn't married?

"Just to clarify." I kissed the base of his neck. "In a normal situation…" Andrew pressed his mouth to the sensitive spot behind my ear, then sucked on my earlobe. My head spun. "If we were to date"—his hot breath was against my breasts—"we'd take it slow and have a few dates before we moved to third base."

His warm body hovered over me, and he stared at me. "I don't know what third base means, but I hope it means sex."

He crashed his mouth against mine, his thumb rubbing my hardening nipples over my shirt. We should really consider taking clothes off. I pulled my lips away from his.

"No." I took a breath. "It means touching everywhere you want to be touched." I swallowed. "Home run is when you have sex."

Andrew nuzzled my neck and dragged his teeth over my skin, his breath sending fireworks through my body. "Can we count our dinner at Erizo as one date?"

"I think so." I moved my hips, desperately seeking friction against his erection. A needy groan floated up from the back of his throat. He shifted down and dragged his mouth from my neck over my chest, stopping at my stomach. He bunched up my shirt, exposing my skin, and pressed his lips above my belly button.

"What about Iglesia San Antonio church?"

"Definitely." Dragging my fingers through his hair, I tried to pull him up to kiss him, but he resisted.

"And behind the waterfall?" His unapologetically demanding mouth slowly kissed its way down. "Can that be a date too?"

I arched my back. "Yes. Please."

"So that's three dates already. That means…" His lips reached the elastic band of my shorts. He stopped and looked up at me. "Third base. Or…?" He arched his eyebrow.

I let out a ragged breath. I sure hoped we'd do more than third base. "I think tonight is a home run." My hand went under my ass, and I fished the condoms out of my back pocket. I laid them next to us on the floor.

Andrew sat on his heels, and his lips pulled into a cocky smile. "You brought five condoms? You're not joking about keeping me up all night."

"That's too much?"

"Not at all." His fingers circled my shorts' band, and he tugged on them. I lifted my hips to help him to take them off. Andrew threw them to the side and took off his shirt. I took a moment to admire him. His Roman god's torso with its taut muscles took my breath away. And I could touch it now. I could press the entire length of my naked body against him. What was I waiting for?

I pulled off my shirt, and Andrew caught his bottom lip beneath his teeth. He dragged a lazy gaze over my breasts, and whispered, "You're perfect."

Andrew bent, his fingers sweeping the tender curve of my breasts, then he took my left bud between his teeth, teasing it with his tongue. I moaned and pushed my chest forward, feeling more wetness pooling between my thighs. He moved to my right breast. My hands fumbled with the zipper of his pants until I was able to unfasten them and push them down his hips. His mouth found mine, and I clung to Andrew for dear life, pressing my bare breast against his naked chest. I couldn't get close enough to him. As he kissed me deeply, he freed his body from his pants and lowered me back onto the floor. Now our bodies were pressed against each other, so much of his hot skin touching mine. My hands skated over his back, learning the curves and swells of his muscles.

I pushed him over, and we rolled. He was flat on his back, and I was straddling him, his large, bulging erection pressing into my aroused center. His hands seized and squeezed my thighs.

"I want to look at you." I pushed my hair off my face. Somewhere along the way, my bun had come undone.

He gave me a cheeky smile and crossed his arms behind his head. "Feast away."

"Oh, I like your smug attitude." And I liked his cock beneath me, too.

I let my eyes explore Andrew's body, noticing every detail I hadn't had a chance to see before. His broad chest had just enough hair. Three small moles were on the left side of his flat abdomen. I ran my finger around his nipple, making it hard, then down his stomach. His muscles flexed and goosebumps rose on his skin. I traced his well-defined abs until my finger came to a stopping point near the edge of his boxers. My finger curled inside, and he took in a sharp breath. Our eyes met.

"I want to kiss you more." He pushed up on one elbow, ran his other hand up my thigh, and cupped my bottom.

"You already did."

He sat up until our faces were close, my hand still between us, fingers curved into the fabric. The rich, seductive scent of coriander and ambrette enveloped me. I took in a deep breath like it was the last one for me. I needed to know the name of his cologne so I could bathe in it.

"Can I touch you first?" Andrew swept my hair to one side and traced his fingers over my bare neck. He tilted his head and his tongue dragged over my bottom lip. "I want to taste you."

Every muscle in my body tightened, and I captured his mouth. Andrew hoisted me up and rose to his feet. He carried me to his bed and lowered me carefully onto it, then he grabbed the condoms off the floor. When he laid on his side next to me, he leaned in, his mouth taking over mine. My fingers wove into his hair, gripping it. He dragged his warm palm over my breast, down my stomach, then over my soaking panties. My breath escaped in a whoosh. Without taking them off, he moved his fingers in a firm, circular motion, making me moan into his mouth and lifting my hip to chase this touch.

Slow circles.

Gentle but firm thrusts.

"Do you want me to stop?"

"Don't," I rasped, my lips moving against his. He pulled the fabric to the side and ran his fingers along my folds, squeezing my center between them with enough pressure to destroy my last rational thought and my soul with it.

Without breaking contact with me, Andrew shifted and with his free hand took my arms and pinned them above my head. He stroked his tongue over the edge of my mouth, then kissed me with urgency, setting my blood on fire. He made a possessive noise, and his long fingers eased inside of me, dragging a hiss out of me. He curved them and pushed at the right spot, making me cry out his name. With slow, deep thrusts, he moved his fingers in and out of my body, driving me closer to my release. He brushed his thumb over my clit and a deep rush of pleasure flooded me. I clenched around his fingers, and my orgasm came over me like a tsunami, drowning me in ecstasy.

"Andrew." I smiled against his mouth. "Can we hit a home run now?"

"You know why women are superior to men?" he asked, his fingers now lazily gliding in and out of me. There were many answers to his question, but I shook my head. "Because women can have multiple orgasms. One. After. Another." He kept moving his hand, fingers inside my soaking sex, his thumb grazing my pulsating nub. "I want you to come again," he said, teasing my breasts, stroking my skin with his tongue.

"Please." It came out as a moan. Might as well take as much as I could.

Andrew's fingers circled the waistband of my panties, then dragged them over my legs until they were off my body. His eyes pinned me down and he lowered himself.

"Your body is a treasure map," he said, his hot breath leaving a trail of goosebumps on my stomach, my pelvis, and beyond—avoiding the most sensitive spot—until his face was between my parted knees. Slowly he pushed my legs farther apart and I was completely open to him. His lips skimmed over my inner left thigh, the rasp of his stubble sending a lightning bolt to my core. I was so fucking wet and ready for him. He kissed the right thigh, then returned to the other, but his mouth landed closer and closer to my pussy. I bit my lip, shivering with pleasure and struggling to keep still. My chest fell and rose and—

In a long, slow stroke, Andrew ran his tongue along my slit.

I sucked in air.

His mouth found my center, and his tongue swirled over my clit, then gently tugged on it. My eyes rolled back as he licked and sucked, fast, slow, simultaneously pushing fingers inside of me, and I lost myself in pure pleasure. He did it over, and over again, until I shut my eyes, and my climax came out of nowhere, my hips jerked up, and my body quivered. Andrew's mouth rode out the orgasm with me, licking me softly, until I came apart and landed on the mattress.

Mustering the energy to raise my head, I looked at Andrew. I was in love. "Oh. My. Lord. You're so good."

Andrew grinned ear to ear, his face damp with my wetness. He rolled on his back and took his boxers off, then reached over for a condom, broke the foil open, and rolled it down his length. And then I was again underneath his body, his hard cock dragging against my thigh. I opened my legs wide to welcome him. He looped his hand under one of my knees and lifted my leg, letting me hook it around his hip, and then he buried himself inside me. I gasped, and he grunted. The sexiest combination of sounds I had ever heard. I tightened around him, and he growled like an animal. His eyes held mine, and he began to move.

We found the rhythm, our bodies moving together as if we had done this many times before. It was all new yet felt like we'd been this close for ages. He left a trail of tender kisses along the side my face, along my neck. When his thrusts got faster, I wrapped my legs around his waist, letting him enter even deeper.

"Please keep going," I managed to say, pressing my head into his pillow, and arching my body into his. My hands clutched at his sweaty shoulders, sinking my fingers into his flesh. An overwhelming hunger for Andrew, for another—if it was possible—climax roared inside me. "Please," I pleaded. I never thought I was a beggar, but my god I would explode if he didn't give me what I needed. Andrew's thrusts became more certain and rapid. Greedily, I wanted this moment to last forever, but at the same time, I needed to come undone. With each stroke, the slippery sounds got louder, and the pressure built higher until I shattered, once again, just as he buried his face in the crook of my neck, groaning against my skin.

Once our breathing returned to somewhat normal, Andrew fell on his back beside me, his hand found mine and he intertwined our fingers. Sweat glistened over his muscular body.

"I've never been to a baseball game," he said, still panting, "but if this is how it feels to score a home run, I'm a huge fan now."

I chuckled. "Don't tell anybody, but I have been to only a few games myself."

Andrew let go of my hand and got up, disappearing into the bathroom. A few seconds later he returned to the bed. "I'm confused. Are you talking about a literal game or sex?"

I laughed harder now, and a tear slid out of the corner of my eye. I wiped it. "I have only been to a handful of games. I have enough knowledge to carry some sort of conversation, but I have no clue what's going on or why people shout when something happens."

Andrew rolled on his side, propping his head on his elbow, and resting his leg over mine. His fingers gently glide over my breast, making my nipple harden at his touch.

"I thought," he said, "all beautiful American high-school girls dated athletes."

I rolled on my side, mimicking his head prop, and slid my leg between his so now our legs were entangled. "I guess I'm not all that pretty or not that much of an American."

"You're certainly both." He leaned in and kissed me.

"In school, I didn't have time to date," I said. "I was busy studying and working. I had to make sure I'd get multiple scholarships and grants."

And then I never finished college.

"Tell me more about yourself," he said.

"What do you want to know?"

"Everything." He smoothed my fallen hair away from my face, tucking strands behind my ear.

"That's thirty-plus years of things."

"Then tell me five things that nobody knows about you."

"Hmm." I bit my bottom lip, thinking. What did I want to share with this man who no longer felt like a stranger but someone I had known all my life? Once this trip was over, Andrew's and my paths would never cross again. I could share with him anything I wanted, and I sensed he wouldn't judge me for any of it. The familiar ache of loneliness uncoiled in the pit of my stomach. We were covered in sex and sweat, and I already missed Andrew. I already hated the thought of going back to my old life, where he wasn't part of it.

"The reason I don't like when people start explaining with the word 'well'…" A prickling sensation ran at the back of my neck. Over twenty years have passed. This shouldn't have bothered me anymore, but my gaze dropped to Andrew's chest, and I focused on its dark hairs. "When our father left us, his last lie was 'Well, I'll just run out to get some smokes.' It stuck with me. Even William doesn't know it. He keeps poking fun at me, and I let him. I do the same to him about his fear of dark water." Andrew laced his fingers with mine, and my gaze met his. And, of course, my heart tripped over its beat because a thought crossed my mind. The thought of how it would feel to wake up next to Andrew every day. The only probable answer to that question was: great. Wonderful. Spectacular. Supercalifragilisticexpialidocious.

Yep. That was a word in the English dictionary:

**su·per·ca·li·fra·gil·is·tic·ex·pi·a
·li·do·cious**
**| ˌso͞opərˌkaləˌfrajəˌlistikˌekspēˌalə
ˈdōSHəs |**

ADJECTIVE: Waking up next to Dr. Andrew
Jones; being next to Dr. Andrew Jones;
Dr. Andrew Jones.

ORIGIN: The day Dr. Andrew Jones turned
into a man.

I cleared my throat. "I'm sorry. I should come up with something fun to share."

"You don't have to." His thumb gently made circles on my hand. "You can share whatever you want."

"I rarely talk about my parents." Or ever.

Andrew nodded.

"Okay, so that was one. Next is ... I'm afraid of Gremlins toys or anything related to that movie. When I was about eight, William watched it on TV, and when the gremlins turned into horrifying monsters, it scared the living crap out of me. I had nightmares for years." I still sometimes did. Andrew's eyes sparked with amusement. "What?" I made a pouting face as if I was offended. "They're creepy."

He chuckled. "Yes. I agree." His hands slid down to my waist, his fingers trailing over my skin, leaving an arousing sensation and jumbling up my thoughts. My breath hitched at the thought of where his fingers had been and what they had done to me earlier.

I clear my throat. "Okay, so I'm done with two. Let's see, three is … when I was eighteen, I got a fake ID but was too chickenshit to use it, so it ended up being a waste of my money. Wait. No. I used it once at the Biltmore Estate to get into the wine-tasting class."

"And there you met the guy who gave you a job." Andrew's fingers made leisurely circles over my hip. I nodded. "So it wasn't a waste of money at all. What was your name on the ID?"

I racked my brain, trying to remember what it was. "Tiffany Rose Smith."

He peered curiously at me. "You don't look like a Tiffany."

"I didn't feel like a Tiffany." I hummed, turned my stare skyward, and tapped my finger on my chin. "Four is … after a long week at work, I often make a large batch of the unhealthiest, buttery, fluffy mashed potatoes, and eat the whole pot, while watching romcoms and drinking expensive wine. Butt-naked."

At that one, both of Andrew's eyebrows arched. "I like wine, mashed potatoes, and romantic movies," he said. "Can I join you sometime?"

"Only if you wear your birthday suit."

"Fine by me."

I laughed again. It was cute how he was joking about staying in my life. My heart cracked at the thought. I didn't point out that after this trip we'd never see each other again, and instead I said, "Five is I've never had a one-night stand. At least not until tonight."

He leaned in and kissed me on my lips slowly, gently. "You need to come up with a different fifth item because this isn't a one-night stand."

A silty warmth spread through my body at the thought that for the next few days I could swathe my soul in a fleeting romance with Andrew. It would hurt like hell when it was over, and I had hard work ahead of me to pick up all the shattered pieces of my heart, but that would come later. Right now I wanted to lose myself in the oblivion of being with him.

"Now it's your turn to tell me five things about yourself that no one knows."

Andrew blew a slow breath, running his fingers through his hair. "I saw this coming the second I asked you the question."

"Of course, it's the only fair way to play this game."

He gave me a coy smile. "One. For a brief time, I wanted to become a vet. But when I took a biology lab at uni, I couldn't stomach dissecting rat specimens. After a minute of staring at a dead animal, I excused myself and stumbled into a loo where I passed out in a stall."

I pressed my lips together, trying not to laugh.

"Go ahead." He rolled his eyes. "Laugh."

"I'm sorry." I chuckled. "You're such a large man, I can't picture you passing out from seeing a dead rat."

Growing up, William and I had mice traps around our trailer because we couldn't afford pest control services. We rotated whose turn it was to get rid of any new victims each week. Eventually, we got the situation under control—with Ms. Rudy's help—but ever since, a dead rodent had always been the least scary thing in my life.

"I'm sorry, I'm being insensitive." I got my giggles under control. "Please tell me your next four. I promise not to laugh."

"Two. I can't stand wearing socks. As soon as I have a chance to take them off, I do."

I glanced at his bare feet, with their nice-looking toes and clean and neatly trimmed nails.

"Three. I lost my virginity when I was twenty-three."

My jaw went slack, and my eyes widened. This was a doozy. How in the world had this Roman deity stayed a virgin that long? But then my eyebrows shifted together because I was sure his ex-fiancé knew about that. "Hey, we agreed on things that no one knows about you, and this—"

"Brie doesn't know." He ran his hand over my arm and his eyes followed the movement. "I was embarrassed to admit it, and then it didn't matter."

"Nothing is embarrassing about that." My fingers caught his, and I linked them. "It's sweet."

"Four." His gaze swept over my face, and then he smiled. A sugary, timid smile. "I wanted to kiss you on the plane when you took my mind off the flight, and also, it was so hard to lie to you that I didn't fancy your backside. You have the nicest one I've ever seen."

My heart stuttered like it had then during our flight. What was he doing to me?

"That's two things in one confession," I said. "But thank you."

"And five is," his deep voice rumbled, "tonight was the most out-of-this-world, mind-blowing sex I've ever had in my life."

I dropped my head on a pillow and covered my eyes with

my hand. "Liar. It couldn't have been your best sex. You did all the work. I just laid there."

Andrew rolled me on my back, pinning my hands above my head, and letting his heavy, hard cock drag across my body, his weight deliciously pressing on me. His eyes were full of unexpected earnestness. I wished he would stop looking at me like that because it stirred up feelings inside me I wanted never to have again. "Just being with you made it that much better." And he needed to stop saying things like that, too. He lowered his lips near my ear. "But you're right. I'm a liar." His breath on my skin drew moist from inside of me. "What's about to happen next will be the most mind-blowing sex I've ever had."

Chapter Twenty-Two

We snuggled in his bed and talked for hours. We had sex again, and then, with my head in the crook of Andrew's shoulder, his arms around me, we fell asleep. Sometime in the middle of the night, with the moonlight flooding the room with a bewitching light, we silently made slow, tender love. I wasn't sure if either of us climaxed, but it was like a promise. The way Andrew held my gaze. The way he kissed me. It had a deeper purpose, much more meaningful than any previous time.

A crisp and clear dawn seeped softly through the window into the room. Andrew's hand ran over my bare body as if he was memorizing every curve and nook. We laid sideways, my body molded into his, his hard length pressing against the small of my back.

"I should probably find William. Let him know I'm alive," I whispered.

"I'm sure he knows you're with me." Andrew cupped one of my breasts and landed a light kiss on my shoulder. "I imagine the entire town knows," he said, a smile in his voice. He pressed his warm lips against the side of my neck.

I snorted and buried my face into the pillow. "I'm sorry. I tried to control myself."

"Don't apologize. I loved it. And who cares what others think?"

"I know exactly what Williams thinks."

"And what is he thinking?" Andrew's hand found its way around my hip, and now his fingers were moving to my center. On instinct, I parted my legs, welcoming him in.

"His first question would be"—I inhaled a deep breath when he found it—"if we used all the condoms."

Andrew hummed near my ear, his fingers sailing in my slick wetness. My back arched into him, and a short moan escaped my lips.

"What would his second question be?" He dove his index and middle fingers inside me.

"How many more condoms do I need?" I managed to say.

He whirled his fingers, and my hips undulated ever so slowly. "Christ, you're so wet." Andrew leaned his forehead to the back of my head. "I want you again."

"Then have me."

Andrew's hand left my body, and he reached out somewhere behind him and fumbled for the last condom. He ripped the foil, and several seconds later, his chest was against my back. I shifted my hips, and he glided inside me, making me gasp, my hands bunching the sheets. His fingers returned to my center, making me take another swift breath.

When I awoke again, Andrew was shirtless and sitting on the floor, holding a large mug in one hand and some of his notes in the other. He wore black-rimmed reading glasses, making him a doppelgänger for Clark Kent. No. Better. It made my heart swell.

I should have left hours ago, but I couldn't bring myself to vacate his bed. My body ached, but in a good way, like after a great workout. I wanted to wake up each morning feeling like this. Worn out and happy. Was it because of multiple orgasms? Or was it Andrew—a fascinating man with a face so handsome it was trouble, and hands so skilled that everything inside me got tight at the thought of them. And then another thought snaked like a python around my heart, strangling it. This was only temporary. This fling was only for the next few days.

A breeze from an open window moved the sheer white curtains and lazily played with the corners of some papers scattered on the floor. The street hubbub was cacophonous. A nightstand had a lamp but no clock, but my eyes landed on a coffee cup covered with a small saucer plate, a plate with a bright purple flower and a baked roll, slices of butter and cheese. Breakfast? For me?

Andrew hadn't glanced my way. He sipped from his mug, then set it on the stool. He bent and picked up a folder, the lean muscles on his back and arms dancing beautifully with each move. His shoulder had a few scratch marks on it. I did that to him. How many other women had woken up tired but satisfied like this in his company? A mean, covetous wave rushed over me. It was wrong to be jealous of something that wasn't mine. Yet, I couldn't stop myself from feeling that way.

What had Andrew done to me? I couldn't recall any man in

my past who had brought on these sensations. Only disappointment and heartaches. This was going to be a heartbreak, but that had been obvious from the beginning.

A car honked outside and broke my reverie. I rubbed my eyes with the heel of my palm. "Good morning."

Andrew's full lips pulled into a lazy smile. "Good afternoon, beautiful."

I hugged his pillow. "What time is it?"

He glanced at his watch. "Quarter past noon."

"Really?" I sat up, pulling up the flat sheet to my chest. "Why didn't you wake me up?"

"I couldn't ruin whatever you were dreaming about. You were smiling."

"I was?"

He nodded. "What was your dream?"

I couldn't remember anything. "Probably you." He smiled wider. "Is that my breakfast?" I nodded at the nightstand.

"Yes. Coffee is probably cold now though."

I removed the small saucer and picked up the cup. It was barely warm. I took a long sip anyway, enjoying its strong aromatic taste. "Mmm, this is good."

"They didn't have cream, so I added milk and one spoonful of sugar."

My heart expanded, a few more days with him, and there wouldn't be enough space inside my ribcage. "Can I ask you a personal question?"

"Sure, as long as I'm allowed to ask one, too," he said and shifted his glorious body closer to me.

I cleared my throat. "Do you often... I mean... How many..." Why was it so hard to get the words out? "Forget it. I shouldn't ask you, anyway." I drank my coffee, averting my eyes.

"No, go ahead and ask," he said in a low, heartfelt tone.

I closed my eyes as if that meant I became invisible, and it could help me ask my stupid question. "How many women have found themselves waking up like this, in your room?"

He smiled softly, a glint in his eyes. "Not many. Brie and now you."

Get out of here. I scrunched my face and squinted at him with one eye. "Really? You're thirty-four and you've only had sex with two women?"

"No. I meant…" He chuckled. "I don't bring women to my house, mostly because it's Charlotte and Lulu's home too. And I haven't met a woman I wanted something more besides just to…" His eyebrows quickly jumped up and dropped down.

"Make love?"

"I wouldn't call it that." He reached for his coffee and took a long sip. "You must be in love with someone to make love to them. I'd call it casual sex."

A sharp icicle of disappointment dropped into my gut. Whatever we had last night, it was more than sex to me. I needed to slap some sense into myself. What was I thinking? Of course he saw it as nothing more than remarkably great casual sex.

"Did you make them breakfast?" I glanced at the flower near the bread roll, then took another sip of my coffee. I didn't have my toothbrush, and on the off-chance Andrew decided to kiss me, I needed to mask my morning breath. But he wouldn't kiss me. Nobody kissed after *casual* sex. The words had started to rub me the wrong way.

"No. We were in her hotel room or her place."

"We're in a hotel room." I waved my hand as if to prove my point. What was my point? Where was I going with this? "And yet there is food next to the bed."

His eyes twinkled, and a devastating smile spread across his face. "It's a different circumstance."

And dammit if my heart didn't skip a beat at that. "How?"

"I think that's more than one question. It's my turn now."

I finished my coffee and set it on the nightstand, then vigorously ran my fingers over my scalp and hair to make it look like sexy morning hair and not a mop. "Ask away."

"Earlier you said you don't date. Why?"

"Pff." I rolled my eyes and settled against the wall, pulling the sheets higher. He leaned back on his hands and stretched his long legs out. "I can ask you the same question. You're kind and smart. I think you have a good job—however, I haven't reached a verdict on that one. You're good-looking, and I must say," I fanned myself, "You are a *god* in bed. So, what is wrong with you?"

"Enough with compliments." He stared at me, the corners of his eyes crinkling. "Answer my question."

I shrugged and pinned my gaze to the window. "It's easier to be single. I was busy with work. I traveled nonstop. I didn't even get a cat because it would be alone in my apartment for days, sometimes the entire week. And now *if* I'm going to start my business, it'll suck up all my free time." Yes, I didn't give him a real answer, but what I said was also true. I sighed. "And I guess I just haven't met Mr. Right." Someone who would think I was good enough. And there was my real reason. The fear I'd never be good enough held me back. I couldn't change where I came from no matter how far I went in life. No matter what higher circle of class I reached, I was always going to be a girl from a trailer park. Greg's words struck me again, and a string behind my eyes burned. I could have tried to find a guy from the same background as me, but it was not like there was a box *"must come from a trash family"* to tick in the dating app. Good lord, I could only imagine what suggestion I would have gotten.

I cleared my throat and rubbed my nose with the back of my hand. "I should find William. He's probably wondering if you murdered me." I pulled the sheet around my body like a toga and planted my feet on the cold floor. Where did we throw all my clothes last night?

"He knows you're alive. I saw him when I went to get breakfast. He slid these under the door about an hour ago." Andrew tilted his head to the stool where several foiled condoms laid near his coffee mug.

Heat crept up my neck and up to my cheeks. "So thoughtful of him. But I should go. You need to work." And I needed to pee badly. "Do you know where my clothes are?" I twisted left, then right, searching the room. Andrew rose to his feet, stepped around the bed, and from the chair, he picked up my neatly folded t-shirt, PJ shorts, and lacy underwear.

"Thanks. Um … do you mind turning around?" I clutched the sheet to my body with one hand and reached out with the other one for my clothes.

His eyebrows shut up. "I already saw you naked. And I wouldn't mind seeing your gorgeous body again."

"I know but…" I took a deep breath. "That was in dim light, and now it's bright, and you might see my imperfections, not that I care if you think I'm not perfect. Because this was a one-time casual sex thing"—*with multiple orgasms*—"but I want you to have a flawless image of—"

Andrew stepped to me, laced his hands behind my neck, and his sultry mouth took over mine. It was a tender, lingering, knee-buckling kiss. Then he drew his face a few inches away and his beautiful eyes searched mine. "Adriana, you're perfect. And this isn't a one-time casual sex thing."

Then he kissed me again.

While his lips moved from my mouth to the side of my neck, he took my clothes and tugged on my hand clutching the sheet. I relaxed my grip, and it pooled at our feet. Still kissing me, Andrew ran his free hand down my side and cupped my bottom. A low growl sounded deep in his chest. He left a trail of kisses on my breasts, taking in each nipple and drawing gasps out of me. Maybe because I needed to steady myself or maybe because I wanted to, my fingers laced through his hair, gripping it lightly. Andrew kneeled in front of me and kissed my stomach. When he reached my pubic bone, he stilled and looked up at me, a feral glint in his gaze. A bolt of lightning shot through me, and I wished I could stay longer. Forever. He kissed near my center as his hand that grasped my bottom glided down my thigh to my ankle. Everything inside me burst into color. I was transfixed, my heart hammering, and I was on the verge of tipping over into a climax if he didn't stop there. *Please don't stop.* But, alas, his lips left my skin, and he picked up my panties and held them low at my feet. Reluctantly, I stepped into them, and he slowly dragged them up my legs, his fingers caressing my skin, his lips tracking after them. Next, he picked up my shorts and held them for me to step in. Once they were on me, he pressed a lingering kiss over the fabric exactly where his lips had been a few moments ago, his hands gripping my butt.

With my T-shirt in his hands, Andrew unhurriedly stood, dropping a pathway of kisses over my body. He fondled my breasts, his tongue teasing and stroking my buds. I struggled to keep still, loving the feel of the wet desire pooling at my core.

"Andrew," I whispered, and my body vibrated. The throbbing between my legs reached its highest point, and it felt like a caged wild animal searching for an escape. A reaction I'd never had around other men. "Please."

His mouth brushed my neck, my jawline and it found mine. I was waiting for a hungry kiss, but Andrew kissed me with so much tenderness it brought my climax closer to the surface. As his lips gently moved over my smile, he lifted my hands above my head. He drew away and leisurely tugged my shirt down over my head. With my shirt on, he took one step back, his enormous erection pushing against his pants. *Oh, come now.* He couldn't possibly be this mean. It would take him less than two thrusts to help us both.

"You are such a tease," I said, my voice husky. This was the sexist dressing-up game I'd ever played. I wanted to rip my clothes off and ask him to do it again. "Would you move in with me so I can get ready like this every morning?"

Andrew's smirk deepened into a lopsided smile. "You'd better leave before I lose my willpower not to bend you over and have my way with you."

His eyes burned into mine. Did I have the willpower to leave? Did I have to go? I had no plans. Andrew's phone rang, spoiling our heated stare. I glanced at it. It was Lulu, and he never missed her calls. He pressed a gentle kiss to my forehead, then reached for his phone.

"I'll see you later?" I whispered, not sure why it came out as a question. I knew I'd see him later. If not to have *casual sex*, then to open the bracelet.

Chapter Twenty-Three

"So, you're telling me you almost orgasmed when Dr. Super Soaker put clothes back *on* you?" William said and took the last bite of his cheesy *enyucado*. We sat on a bench at a small park we'd found in town, looking into the distance where the afternoon sun glinted off the ocean. I went over my night with Andrew, listing out all my confusing emotions and, of course, giving him the most precise body part measurements and all the sex tricks.

"Yep." I set my half-eaten dessert between us and raised my phone to snap a picture of our view. "I have to say I never thought I would enjoy visiting Colombia as much as I am. It's a beautiful country with friendly people."

"You're riding high on an orgasm overdose," William said around a straw in his mouth, as he slurped on *limonada de coco*. He bumped his shoulder into mine. "So, is this a one-time thing between you and Dr. Indiana Bones or…"

I sighed. "I don't think so." The way Andrew's lips had pressed to my head as a goodbye was a promise of something to come. "But it's definitely a one-trip deal. A memorializing fling."

A hollow feeling grew inside me. It wasn't just about sex now. Jesus, my heart would have a difficult time getting over Andrew. We were two lonely people connecting, and this connection would never progress to anything else because we had no future. Too many factors pulled us in opposite directions. And I had my entire life waiting for me in Atlanta. I had a business to run. This was the fifth day of our trip and— per wire transfer notification emails I received each night— Andrew had kept his word. I already earned enough money to renovate my store. It felt wrong to ask for more.

"I'll tell Andrew to stop paying me." I blurted out before my brain could process the thought. Damn those wonderful commotions Andrew's voice or touch created in my soul.

"What about your store? Are you giving up?"

A few more days and I could have ordered inventory without the need to look for an investor. I could be the sole owner of my dream. Stupid conscience.

I shook my head. "I'll figure something out."

William poked me in the thigh. "You're totally smitten with him."

"I'm not smitten with anybody." I peered at him over my sunglasses.

William laughed. "Oh my god, you so are!" Then his mouth dropped into a flat line. He squeezed my hand. "I think you're in love. I want to see you like this all the time. When we go back home, you and Andrew need to date."

"Are you stoned?" I stared at him with a mildly horrified expression. "It's not possible. With all the work waiting for me, I doubt I'd have time, and Andrew never said he wanted this to be something more." Did he? "And I'm perfectly okay on my own."

"Again, my dear, you're wrong. We already went over this. It is possible if you give it a chance. And you think you're okay, but all these years I've done nothing but worry about how lonely you are."

"I'm not lonely. I have you, and I can get a cat."

"No. There's a difference." He frowned. "There is alone, and there's *lonely*. You, my dear, are lonely. You think your monthly prime delivery of double AA batteries for your Captain America and unlimited Kindle pile of romcoms would keep your soul fulfilled, but you're wrong."

My mouth dropped open. "I don't read rom—"

"Stop it." William put his hand on my mouth. "I saw the smut you read. You can't hide that from me."

"But my Kindle is password protected."

"Please." He rolled his eyes, brushing out the crumbs off his shirt. "You use the same numbers. My birthday. Sometimes with a year, sometimes without it. It takes me one to four tries." He placed his hand on his heart. "I'm so glad I got it off my chest. I discovered it the first day you moved in with me. Let me tell you, I was so relieved you're a human being who believes in love. So, you and Andrew are going to long-distance date until we all figure something out."

"It would not work."

He gave me a stern expression. "It will."

I let out strident laughter. "Like it worked with you and Rai when he moved away? You guys were together for four years. Planning to get married. And you still called it quits. How do you think it will work for Andrew and me only after maybe another week?"

"You're wrong," William said calmly, but I could hear something—maybe hurt or maybe controlled anger—in his voice.

"I'm not wrong."

"Oh my god! You're so fucking stubborn," William yelled.

WTF? Were we actually arguing about this?

"You're yelling at me again," I whispered—my brain was in shock at his behavior.

"I'm sorry. But you've started pissing me off. You have something good here. You guys have this great chemistry. Why push it away?"

"Because we're too different!" I shouted. Twisting, I checked that nobody had heard us. Thankfully, most people had their noses in their phones, minding their own business. "I'm a girl from a trailer park," I hissed. "His family will never accept me. You know what? I'm done talking to you about this." I jumped to my feet ready to leave, but William grabbed my hand, reeling my ass back down on the bench.

"Adriana, I don't want you to make the same mistake I did."

I turned. "What mistake?"

"It was me. I broke Rai's heart." William glanced up at the blue sky. "He begged me to go with him, but I said no. I was afraid. When he told his parents he was gay, it didn't go well. They were hoping for a nice Japanese girl and not a white boy."

"I remember that, but it happened in like the first few

287

months of your dating," I said in a low voice. "And they were fine afterward."

"Yes, they were, but they wanted him to have a partner from the same culture. When he moved, I let him go because I was too chickenshit, worrying his family wouldn't accept me. And guess what? Rai is now married to a Turkish swim instructor. Very much not Japanese." William sighed. "I came across his Instagram account several weeks ago. Rai's mom and dad were on either side of them, smiling and hugging. That could have been me."

My heart was breaking all over again over what William had gone through. I looped my arms around his frame. "I'm sorry, handsome."

He leaned his head to mine. "It's water under the bridge. Please don't let your fears get in the way of something that could be wonderful. If it doesn't work out, it doesn't work out, but you shouldn't give up without a fight. You want Dr. Thor Hammer, don't you?"

Of course, I did. Who wouldn't?

"Yes. He's like nobody I've ever met." The last part came out with a dreamy sigh.

Could it work out between Andrew and me? Him living in Cambridge and me in Atlanta? Could we find a way to be together? The first year would be challenging since I would be busy with my store, but it would get easier once I got a grip on things. We could spend the holidays together. He could visit me, and from time to time I could get away to visit him. Money would be tight for a while, but I was trained to save. Each month I could put cash aside for an airplane ticket. A small hope slowly rose in my chest, the same sensation I'd felt when

I received the UGA acceptance letter, got an offer at Salzburg Wine Distributing, bought a building in Roswell downtown, and when Andrew kissed me for the first time. The hope that something great was about to happen in my life.

It was hard to believe that two weeks ago, I had sworn off all men, and now I was falling in love like a complete fool with a man after just a few days.

"I must be seriously deranged to say this, but fine, I'll give it a try."

William kissed my temple. "I shall thank Andrew for finally breaking your dry spell and reminding you how nice it is to be in love. Now, are you going to finish your cake?"

I pushed my sunglasses further up on my nose and passed my cheese and coconut dessert to him. "It's all yours."

———

Andrew was in the center of a paper mess on the floor when I returned to his room.

"I brought you food," I said, closing the door behind me. I wore a floral cyan blue sleeveless dress I'd bought earlier that day while strolling the streets with William. It had a deep V halter neck and was smocked snuggly through the bodice, with a wide circular skirt.

Andrew smiled, and my heart felt as though it might burst from my chest. I put the food on the desk and walked over to him. He reached his hand out to me. In one motion, he caught my wrist and pulled me down into his lap. His soft yet firm lips found mine and warmth ran down my spine at the contact.

"I missed you," he said, his mouth against mine.

I smiled and drew back. "You did?"

His eyes skimmed over my face, and he scooped a lock of hair off my cheek and looped it behind my ear. "Yes."

"After dinner," I said, trailing kisses down his neck, "will you show me how much you missed me?"

His hands squeezed my ass, his erection growing beneath me. "Gladly."

I climbed off him and went to the desk. Out of the bag, I withdrew a bottle of water, a brown paper box with rice and grilled vegetables, and a fire-grilled beef tenderloin.

Andrew took a seat on a chair. "Thank you."

"I need to make sure you have a lot of energy." I kicked off my shoes, nestled on the bed, and crossed my legs at the ankles. My heart racing, I waited a few seconds before I said, "Andrew, I need you to stop sending me money. Starting today."

He glanced at me with a question in his eyes. "But we agreed on—"

I raised my hand to stop him. "I know, but I have enough now, and I'm grateful for what you already sent. From now on, I just want to be a part of this search. No more payments."

"Are you sure?" His eyebrows grew together.

I nodded. "Now tell me, any progress on the location of the palace?"

He watched me for a moment longer, a smile growing. "I have several likely locations." He cut into the steak. "But I need to narrow it down to maybe two."

"Can't you cross-reference it with the records of the properties Augustine owned?"

Andrew shook his head, mouth full of food. I studied the

bracelet, my fingers rotating it. Augustine cared about his wife. He poured his love into his letters, brought her things from every place he visited. He wanted to build her the palace of her dreams, and he died heartbroken after her death.

"You stated that after Maria had her first son, she developed severe motion sickness," I said, and Andrew nodded, chewing. "I was thinking, if she couldn't ride even a short distance before she had to throw up, as a loving husband, Augustine wouldn't build a palace somewhere too far away from where they lived. He wouldn't make her walk across the country, and he wouldn't put her through the torturing misery of a long ride."

Andrew's eyebrows pulled together as he took a sip of water. After he swallowed, he said, "Go on."

"You mentioned those who worked on the second villa were brought in carriages blindfolded to the location and were not allowed to leave. When construction stopped, they were taken back again blindfolded. Your notes suggested that rumor had it that Augustine started a palace in Brazil with a large cellar and an elaborate security system. What if drivers rode for days in circles over the mountains and through jungles making men believe they were in another country? Jungle here and jungle there most likely looked the same." Andrew stopped eating, and I knew I had his undivided attention. "I think if we were to look for possible places, our center point should be where they lived, and from there we should draw a short radius, and increase little by little as we exhaust our options. We'll avoid any overpopulated or popular hiking areas because obviously by now the unfinished large building would have been discovered. Can't the Octavian Global group contact NASA or somebody and request mega-clear satellite photos of Colombia? I understand that after three hundred years the jungle might have swallowed it whole, but we could analyze images, search for the outline of a structure."

"They're not the United Kingdom's foreign intelligence agency." Andrew chuckled, scooping rice with the fork, but then he paused and looked at me. "Your brilliance is limitless." The corners of his mouth turned upward, and then he was full-on smiling. "I love working with you."

Undeniable happiness twined in my heart. The feeling was so real that I could reach in and touch it. As I watched Andrew eat, the most delicious images materialized in my mind: me parking in a secluded spot in the Atlanta airport on the day I picked up Andrew; me wearing a dress no matter the weather; us loading into my car, and me climbing on his lap and hungrily welcoming him inside me; us having late dinners that we made together in my home; us making love in the shower, on the couch, on the kitchen countertop; me falling asleep on his chest, in my bedroom with window curtains wide open and a bright moon in the velvet skies. Something dominant—and alarming—swelled in my chest. And I couldn't ignore it anymore. My entire body vibrated with the desire I felt for those images to become reality.

Collecting the empty container, Andrew got up, dropped it into the paper bag, walked to the door, and set it on the floor. When he turned, his hand went over his shoulders, and he pulled his shirt over his head. I had seen him naked already, but my breath caught anew. He was devastating. My eyes roamed down his broad chest, a well-defined six-pack, and a distinct V disappearing into his pants. I had a strong feeling we were done talking about his work, and a filthy smile pulled at my lips.

"Come here," Andrew said, his voice husky and deep, his eyes dark, holding mine and warming my blood.

No need to ask me twice.

I sauntered to him, wetness pooling and excitement already moving over me. Looking up at Andrew, I ran my hands up his torso, his abs flexing under my touch, over his chest, over the wide planes of his shoulders, coming to his neck and finally looping them around it. He framed my face with his large hands and dipped his head to mine.

Andrew kissed me deep and hard, just like he would fuck me soon. His mouth tasted of the salt and sweetness of his meal. My body ached, wanting him to repeat the things he had done last night. He was like heroin, and I was addicted to him.

His hand slid down my back, down to my ass. He cupped it, pressing his dick into my stomach. Then his hands traveled lower, and he bunched up my skirt, exposing my bare bottom. A surprise groan rumbled deep in his throat, and he squeezed harder.

Andrew walked me backward to the desk. Pressing his large palms on each side of my waist, he lifted me and set my ass on it.

"This dress is beautiful on you," he said, his lips against my mouth, "but it will look better on the floor." His fingers pulled on the bow at the back of my neck, undoing the knot and letting the halter-top drop. Andrew trailed kisses on my jaw, down to my collarbone, his hand gently massaging my breasts, simultaneously squeezing my nipples between his thumb and index finger. He caught one with his mouth and sucked it, before biting. I moaned, sifting my fingers through his hair.

Switching his attention to the other nipple, his hands gripped my ass, and he brought me closer to the edge of the table, my wet center soaking the fabric of his pants where his rock-hard cock pressed. My finger fumbled with the zipper.

"Not yet." Andrew snatched my wrists and sat my palms flat on the table on each side of me.

His teeth sank gently into my shoulder, and I shifted my hips, desperate to find more friction against him. Andrew's lips found mine, and his tongue swiped across, his hand clenching my throat with just the right amount of pressure. He broke our kiss, his lips swollen and red. We were both silent, breathing as if we'd just come up from a deep dive. His gaze coasted over my face, his expression unreadable. There was lust and hunger, but there was also something else tender and timid, and he looked like he wanted to speak but couldn't form words.

"What?" I murmured.

A playful smile tugged on his lips, but his gaze was earnest and direct. "Just you," he said, leaning in again to kiss me.

His hands brushed over my breasts, over the bunched fabric on my stomach, until they reached my sleek sex. A satisfied hum resounded in his throat when he slid two fingers inside me and dragged a whimper out of me. He broke our kiss again and pulled his fingers out, this time my moan was because of raw disappointment.

"Why … stop?" I found words, exasperated.

Kneeling, Andrew widened my thighs. He lowered his face to my center and dragged the flat of his thick tongue from the base to the most sensitive point. My eyes rolled, and my head fell backward.

"Christ, you taste like honey," he drawled before repeating the slow lick.

"Do I?" I whispered.

The two wet fingers he'd had inside me nudged my lips to open. He engulfed them in my mouth, letting me taste my sweetness. I sucked them. He licked me harder. My body convulsed, and he pulled his hand away from my face and pressed it onto my lower stomach to keep me steady. My orgasm rushed towards me like a freight train. So sudden. So powerful. Andrew's tongue circled my sensitive clit again, making my hips jerk, sending a blend of pain and pleasure through me.

"Andrew." His name was a needy sound on my lips. "Get insi—"

He licked my sex again, and a hot white agony shot through me. I gasped, gripping his hair and yanking his face away. "You're a fucking menace." He grinned like he was drunk. "You've had enough of tasting, now fuck me like a gentleman."

He wiped his mouth on his shoulder and got to his feet. "I don't want to be a gentleman tonight."

Andrew withdrew a condom from his side pocket and unzipped his pants. As he removed his last clothing item, I pulled my dress over my head and tossed it on the floor. It did look better there. Instead of leaving his pants near his feet, Andrew folded them and tucked them under my lower back and ass.

Clenching a silver packet corner between his teeth, he ripped it open and offered it to me. "You do it."

Before rolling it on his length, I wrapped my fingers at its base and dragged my hand up to its head, drawing hasty breaths out of Andrew. My thumb circled the tip of his cock, smearing silky precum. My mouth salivated, and I played with the idea of letting him stand while I sucked on his glorious dick. I arched an eyebrow and bit my lip.

Placing the condom on the table, I moved to get off. "I have a better idea."

"No." Andrew pinned my hips back. "I appreciate your intentions, but I've thought about you on this desk over a million times…" He picked up the condom and rolled it on. "You need to lay back."

I obliged, the cold surface of the table a refreshing touch on my overheated skin. Holding my gaze, Andrew glided into me with one thrust, stretching me and making me cry out his name. He gripped my hips, his fingers digging into my flesh as he buried his cock even deeper. Without breaking our gaze, he moved in and out with a steady, deliberate rhythm, telling me I was beautiful, telling me he was grateful I put on the bracelet, telling me he didn't want this to end. I couldn't get enough of him. My hand found a wall behind me, and I pressed on it, pushing my pelvis more into Andrew, my inner muscles tightening, seeking a release.

"More," I commanded and took a deep breath.

He let go of my hips and brought my legs up, resting my ankles on his shoulders. Locking his muscular arms over my legs, veins in his forearms bulging, he lifted me and began driving his cock fast, thrust after thrust, hitting me in just the right spot. The wooden desk's creak, our mingled groans, and the sound of his body slapping into my wetness pulsated through the air. Every muscle inside me coiled around him, and a colossal star explosion set off inside me, unhinging me and making me come hard.

"Fuck," Andrew grunted and plunged one more time before surrendering to his orgasm. His movement slowed down, and he let go of my legs, allowing me to embrace his waist with them. He leaned forward until his chest pressed into my hot sweaty breasts, and he rested his face on my shoulder, his fast breathing matching mine.

I wanted to laugh or maybe cry, I was that giddy with happiness. When I got home, I'd need to buy William a huge thank-you gift for bringing a semi-truck load of condoms. And for convincing me to put my guard down and allow myself to fall stupid in love.

"Was this everything you hoped for?" I asked, my fingers gliding over Andrew's damp back.

"No." Andrew perched on his forearms and grinned. "It was much better."

The next morning, the early sun hues were blooming in the sky when I tiptoed across the creaky wooden floors out of the room, leaving Andrew asleep, mansprawled in the bed, sage cotton sheets partially covering his glorious naked body. It was my turn to serve breakfast in bed. It took me longer than I'd expected to pick us food because I wanted to find a vendor cart or a shop that sold flowers, but alas it was too early.

When I returned with a greasy bag and two coffees in my hands, Andrew was dressed and clean-shaven, talking in Spanish on the phone by the window. I loved his voice even when I couldn't understand a word he was saying. He stood tall, his shoulders square, with his right hand on his hip. Confident and so impossibly sexy. Something powerful inside me expanded. Only god knew how much therapy I'd need if he didn't want to continue whatever *this* was between us.

He glanced over this shoulder and then held his finger in *just a minute* gesture.

"Yes, that would be helpful," Andrew switched to English. "Not right now. Today we're going to Árbol Hueco Isla. It's an island about a thirty-minute boat ride from the local marina." He went quiet, listening to … Dr. Garcia, I assumed? He laughed, nodding as if in agreement. "Yes, I believe we're getting close. Yes. Will do. Thanks." He hung up and walked to me. He cupped my face with his hands and kissed me, the taste of his minty breath mingling with the sips of coffee I'd had earlier. My knees went weak, and I had to lean into him. He broke the kiss and gave me the most devastating smile. "Ready to go on a short trip with me?"

I would travel to the moon with him if he asked.

Chapter Twenty-Four

The marina was nearly deserted, with a few vessels bobbing in the sapphire water by the pier, wavelets calmly lapping against their hulls. The sea shimmered in the morning sun, the teasing breeze carried salt and warmth that coursed through my chestnut hair. In the distance, the squabble of seagulls chased fishing ships dragging heavy nets. On the horizon, the Árbol Hueco Isla appeared as a small brown spot, barely visible from the shore.

"I hope the boat you rented is better than the plane that brought us to Colombia," I teased Andrew as we exited the car. It was just the two of us as Andrew had asked William to stay at the hotel and sign for a package delivery.

Andrew retrieved his backpack, a picnic basket, and a blue blanket that I hadn't noticed before from the car's trunk.

"What's with the basket?" I followed him down the steps to the marina office building. Two men exited the building, chatting in Spanish, and strode toward the parking lot.

"Just in case we get hungry."

I suspected that there was something more to the reason William had to stay behind. My stomach fluttered at the thought that it may also be a date.

Andrew stopped at the door and set the basket on the ground. "Wait here. I'll get our boat keys." He pointed the finger at me. "Don't peek inside the basket."

"Hmm, now I want to see what's there."

"Please don't."

Since the first kiss we'd shared two days ago, Andrew had found every opportunity to brush his lips against mine, or my temple, my shoulder, any part of my body he could reach. I'd seen couples like that who constantly touched and kissed one another, and I was sure they were faking it, making a show for the outside world. Now, we *were* that couple. And I loved every part of it and would never get tired of this.

In the building, Andrew talked to a plump, friendly-looking woman. He waved his hand in the ocean's direction, and she laughed, shaking her head. He signed some papers and turned to face me, a mischievous smile tugging on his lips. And then he winked. The man winked at me. Not sure why, but that made me giggle, and the heat rushed to my cheeks. For the love of God, William was right. I was smitten with Andrew.

After a few minutes, Andrew glided towards me, dangling a boat key on his finger. "Call me your captain." He snatched the basket off the ground and laced his fingers with mine. He had so much joyous energy in him, he practically bounced on his feet. "Let's find our ride."

The small motorboat wasn't anything fancy; it needed new paint and maybe new seat covers, but other than that, it was in decent shape. And thankfully it appeared to have no issue staying afloat.

Andrew jumped in first, then helped me. As soon as I was in, he wrapped his arms around me, and my body instantly melted into his. I rested my chin against his chest and gazed helplessly into his eyes, wanting the comforting touch of his lips on mine. A question danced on the tip of my tongue. *Would you like to continue us?*

The breeze played with his wavy brown hair, and waves gently swayed the boat. His eyes searched mine. "You look like you have something on your mind."

I smiled and buried my face into his chest, inhaling his cologne. Andrew tightened his arms and kissed the top of my head. The warmth I felt in the center of my chest wasn't from the sun or Andrew's embrace. How long could we stay like that? As if summoned, a mean wave hit our boat and we staggered sideways, breaking apart—the universe's way of answering my question. It was time to get back to our search. Andrew started the boat, and I took a seat up front.

Waves calmly rolled in on the sandy beach that wrapped around the perimeter of giant rock rising out of the sea. Besides a small line of palm trees guarding the foot of the hill, the shoreline had sparse greenery. A stone stairway in the cleft steeply climbed up and rounded the corner.

Andrew tied the boat to a frail wooden dock which was missing quite a few planks and looked as if it could collapse at any moment. Leaving the basket behind, we gingerly stepped onto the structure. The end near the shore was in an even worse condition, so Andrew threw his and my shoes on the beach, then tossed his backpack, too. With his pants rolled to his knees, he jumped into the water and held his hands to me.

"I guess not many tourists come here." I gripped his hands. Andrew's free arm went around my thighs, and he hoisted me up. A squeak escaped me. "What are you doing?" I plastered myself to him for stability.

"I don't want your feet to get wet," he said. His thoughtfulness accelerated the flutter in my chest into full throttle. With my butt parked in Andrew's grasp, he navigated to a dry spot near the staircase.

At the top, against a blue sky dappled with white clouds, a forlorn Árbol Hueco church—a four-wall building with no roof —stood in the middle of the field blanketed with green grass. An enormous mahogany tree to the left of the ruins overshadowed a fenced-in area with seven gravestones.

Holding hands, Andrew and I walked toward the graveyard, tall grass blades tickling my legs.

"Who are these people?" I asked, studying partially illegible words carved into weather-beaten stones.

"A man named Father Rodrigos and some of his family. I don't know much about him except that he and his wife had five children. When she passed away, he remarried and had six more kids." Andrew crouched near a stone and ran his hand over letters covered in moss. "Rodrigos was the last one to be buried here. After his passing, the remaining children moved to the mainland to live with their older siblings."

"I don't blame them. What a boring life to live on this island, with one tree and nothing else to do."

"At some point, there were more fruit trees and a garden, sheep, and goats. I'm sure they kept themselves busy."

A lustful smile pulled my lips up. "Are we going to get busy, too?"

Andrew gave me a cheeky grin. "I didn't mean it in that way, but I like the way your mind works. I'm sure they had plenty of sex, but most of their days were spent working in the garden, taking care of the few animals they had, and doing other things to ensure their survival."

I weaved my fingers into his. "Come on, let's look for Pérez's long-lost treasure."

Like its roof, the church doors were missing, and we passed over the threshold into an empty and ghostly room. Only the remnants of an old fireplace remained visible. On the left side, toward the end, a narrow staircase led down to the underground level. Andrew stopped near the opening in the floor, turned on two flashlights, and offered me one. "Fancy going into the church cellar?"

"It wouldn't be the first time."

As we descended, the damp air blanketed us along with endless cobwebs. This basement was much less exciting than the Iglesia San Antonio. Why would a pirate hide something here? They would have to haul chests up the hill and then carefully store them using the puny steps. I removed a dusty web from my face, making the flashlight beam dance all over the room.

"I thought Pérez stole lots of treasure. This seems too small to hold it."

"We're searching for anything that resembles an opening

big enough for you to slide your hand with the bracelet in," Andrew said.

"If this is a church. Where did the family live?" I turned on the spot, searching for evidence of *anything* treasure related on the stone walls.

"The main house burned down about two hundred years ago. We can check out the outline of their house after we explore this place." Andrew inspected the perimeter of the space.

I continued on, pausing at certain places and running my hand over moss-covered stones and ferns that clung to stairs where the sunlight had reached inside. After a while, I was ready to give up. I turned to ask if we should search elsewhere, but Andrew gazed at me the same way he often did, with a gentle smile.

"What?" I asked.

Andrew approached me, and his fingers found their way to the back of my neck. He angled my head and pressed the softest of kisses to my lips. Warm and tender. His touch muddled my senses, time losing its meaning, and a hot shiver roared down my spine. I reached up, threading my fingers through his hair, and yanked his mouth harder to mine. I wanted to lose myself in Andrew.

He pinned me to the stone wall and pushed his body against mine. The air buzzed with electricity as if lightning had struck near us.

I broke our kiss. "Isn't it a sin to dry hump in a church?"

His gaze glowed with desire, no doubt matching mine.

"Then call me a sinner." Andrew hitched up my leg, nuzzling his face at the side of my neck, scorching my skin with wet, hungry kisses. Every nerve hummed in me. "Adriana," he said in a husky voice, "what I want to do to you is hard to express in words." His mouth took control of mine again. My body burned for the man whose hardness throbbed between my thighs.

"Show me," I said, breathless, my hands tugging on his shirt, needing to feel his skin.

Andrew pulled my hands away and trapped my arms above my head with one hand, his mouth never leaving mine. His other hand brushed gently down my side until it reached my shorts. He kissed me harder, his tongue dipping inside and stroking, and his hand slid between my skin and the rough fabric of my cutoff jeans. His palm traveled over my soaked panties.

"I made you this wet." He groaned, his fingers working my center, moving with perfect rhythm up and down, and fueling my blood with more need. I rocked my hips against his hand, increasing the friction. I wanted the damn thong to be gone. I wanted skin on skin.

He trailed kisses down my neck and my collarbone. His hand released my arms, and he dragged my shirt and bra straps down, exposing my left breast. He cupped it, and his mouth sucked on my hard bud, then nipped with a tease. I untangled my arms from my shirt, and arched my back, drawing him closer. His fingers finally pulled the wet fabric to one side and massaged my clit. A moan escaped me. Swirling his finger over my pulsating center, he made me thrash and whimper. The heated pleasure inside of me threatened to explode any second.

"Don't stop." My words came out as a breathy plea.

Andrew's mouth found my other nipple, and he pinched it with his teeth. He gently caressed my clit between his thumb and index finger, then pressed his fingers flat and swiveled, encouraging me to come, propelling me over the edge. I cried out, my entire body jerking forward with powerful spasms. Without once pushing into my entrance, Andrew had made me come undone. My legs went weak, and he held me upright, his arm wrapped my waist, his forehead pressing to the top of my head. Both of us panted as if we'd just finished a marathon.

I rubbed his erection with one hand and snatched a condom out of the back pocket of my shorts. I slapped it against Andrew's chest. "We aren't done."

Andrew's lips pulled into a lustful grin. "Not at all."

If taking off clothes had been an Olympic sport, we would've won two gold medals. In no time we took off our shoes and threw every piece of fabric from our bodies to the floor. Andrew pinned my back to the cold stone wall again.

"Oh my God." I squealed with laughter. "It's so—"

Andrew's hot mouth covered mine while his fingers worked quickly on the condom, rolling it down his cock. Then he slid his finger inside me, and I gasped.

"Just making sure you're still ready for me," he rasped. I was ready for him the moment I saw him this morning. I wanted him more now. Raw and fast.

He cupped my ass with both hands and lifted me. I encased his waist with my legs, and my arms circled his neck. He guided his cock into me, stretching me wide. I inhaled with equal amounts of pleasure and pain. A satisfying groan rumbled deep in his throat, the most arousing noise I've ever heard, and it made me wetter. He moved his hips, spinning pleasure out of me with every movement. My breath caught, and I clung to him. The hot sweat of desire covered our bodies.

Andrew's jaw tensed, and his breathing became labored. I grabbed a fistful of his hair and kissed him with so much intensity I could taste blood. Needing him deeper and craving another climax, I released my grip. "I want you behind me."

He withdrew, his hand holding me, letting me plant my trembling legs on the floor. I turned, placed my palms on the wall, and spread my legs apart. He bent forward, his chest pressing against my back, and his hard dick toyed with my opening. He kissed my neck, then sucked on my earlobe as he reached under, and his fingers slowly circled my clit, then slid deep into me, manipulating me to my next orgasm.

"You're so sexy." His words rumbled over my skin, then his hands gripped my hips, and he rocked back in. He thrust in and out, going deeper each time, making me cry out. He felt so fucking good. Heat coursed down me, and my spine arched, inviting more of him. He picked up a driving rhythm, his firm grasp on my body steadying me. I shut my eyes when another orgasm ripped through my body, and a hoarse scream erupted from me. Andrew's breaths became hard and fast. He groaned, low and deep, his fingers tightening on my hips, and then his movement slowed until he was still. We remained there, winded, his head resting on my shoulder and his palms braced against the wall.

Andrew kissed my shoulder. "If any ghosts lived here," he said, still catching up his breath, "I think you did a good job scaring them away with your screams."

I laughed. "I'll try to be quieter next time."

"Don't. I love it." He kissed the side of my face.

Dressed, we walked—holding hands—to the outline of the old building. Small piles of debris had been taken over by moss and overgrown grass. Andrew gave me a brief story of the family that had lived here, and with nothing else left for us to do or explore, he left me standing on the hill while he dashed to the boat.

Andrew returned with the picnic basket and a blue blanket. He spread the blanket on the shaded spot beneath the tree and invited me to join him there. The obscure Colombian coast was behind us, and a vast shimmering ocean was in front of us, seagulls flying in the distance.

I kicked off my boots and let the sun warm my feet. Andrew uncorked a bottle of red wine, poured it into glasses, and offered me one.

"Wow, actual glass stemware? At a picnic?" I sipped my wine. "Are you that environmentally cautious or too posh? Usually, people bring plastic cups."

"I don't mind helping our planet, but you also commented the other night that drinking wine out of plastic ruins its taste."

"Oh, god." I laughed and covered my eyes with a free hand. "You're making me sound like such a wine snob. I don't care. I was just pointing out that when you're trying a new wine for the first time, it's best to do it out of a glass, not plastic. But thank you. This is a lovely Malbec."

Out of the basket, Andrew took out two plates covered with brown paper. He unwrapped them, revealing pre-cut cheese and fresh bread, red grapes, and gooseberries. Aw, he remembered golden berries too. He gave me a sweet smile and withdrew a tiny glass bottle with clear liquid stopped with a cork. Andrew uncorked it and added a white and purple Cattleya Trianae orchid. A warm glow shifted through me at his thoughtfulness and romantic nature.

"Come now," I said in an awed whisper. "What else do you have in there?" I peeked in. The basket was mostly empty, except for one silver condom packet at the bottom. I glanced at Andrew without suppressing my smile. "You were serious about your plan, weren't you?"

"Of course." He kissed the tip of my nose.

We lapsed into a comfortable silence while nibbling at our food, stealing glimpses of each other now and then. I munched on everything, whereas Andrew only ate cheese and fruit.

"Why aren't you eating bread?" I said, smoothing away loose strands that the wind liked to play with. He shook his head and held up a finger while he chewed.

"I was always a chubby kid," he said once he'd swallowed. "And all the shite I had to take from other kids could top this mountain. I was fifteen when I joined a cricket team. Later I tried rugby but didn't enjoy it much." His gaze focused on something in the ocean. "Maybe it was that, or maybe I finally hit my growth spurt, but in the next two years I grew two feet more, and muscles replaced my baby fat. I got different attention from everyone, especially from girls, but the fat, insecure kid stuck with me for years. Of course, I enjoyed the attention and didn't want to lose it, so I lived on a strict diet and worked out like a maniac." He shrugged. "The diet became a habit. I can have whatever; I just don't crave it."

"I bet you were a Casanova." I crinkled my nose and bit into a large, red grape.

"The kid inside me pushed me to stay fit, but also kept me on a short leash of insecurity."

It was hard to imagine the stunning and confident Andrew as a chubby kid or a timid young man. He for sure wasn't shy anymore, at least not with me, and I loved his pure animal magnetism. And what baffled me the most was why in the world Brie let Andrew go.

"How long were you and Brie together?"

"Three years."

I raised an eyebrow. That many years meant a serious relationship. I was having a hard time picturing them together.

"I thought she was special with her being my first and such, but we got too busy with school and drifted apart. We reconnected several years later. Things were going well, but then my parents died and…" Andrew looked away.

"And what?"

"I found her with Richard." Andrew scrubbed a hand down his face as he blew out a slow breath. "While I was grieving and helping pregnant Charlotte, they were making a fool out of me."

What a bitch.

"I think she's an idiot." I took his hand and laced my fingers with his. Andrew smiled, rubbing his thumb over my knuckles, his eyes running over our linked hands. "I fell head over heels for Greg on the first day of our economy class when he had this long debate with the professor. For three years I was so blind I didn't see any red flags … like how he never introduced me to his family. He always had great excuses why, and I believed him. They lived somewhere in North Carolina and often traveled, so he always went to visit them. Alone. I couldn't pay for a trip, and he didn't offer to pay, but anyway…" I exhaled a heavy breath, the weight of how stupid and naïve I'd been pushed hard on my chest. "When they came to his graduation, he introduced me as his friend, and acted cold and fidgety." Andrew listened with a tense expression, his brows pulled together, creating a deep cleft in between. "Long story short, he broke it off outside the football stadium after the graduation. He said I'd been stupid to think there was a future for us. He couldn't muddy his family blood with someone like me—trailer park trash." The same gut-punching sensation I'd felt that day crashed into me again. I looked up at the sky through the tree branches, blinking away the tears forming in my eyes. I wasn't going to cry over that shithead. "His exact words were, 'You can take a girl out of a trailer park, but you can't take the trailer park out of a girl.'"

"Adriana, Greg is a brainless numbskull fucking imbecile."

I chuckled, shaking my head. "Oh gosh, I was so infuriated. One drunken night, William and I set a goal for me to marry into a royal family. We wasted hours researching and planning a scheme for how I could insert myself into their circle. Obviously, the next day while enduring a major hangover, I came up with a better plan: to work hard and move up in my career. I understand that I can't rid myself of the past, especially one I had no control over, but the idiot's words convinced me that I wasn't good enough."

Andrew grasped my hand. "You're more than enough. The most important things in life are how pure your heart is, who you become, and how you treat others. Not how blue your blood is, or where you grew up, or how posh of a school you went to. You're so astute, smart, and beautiful that you leave even the most confident man speechless and wonderstruck."

"That's kind of you to say," I whispered. I set the empty wineglass next to the basket and laid back on the blanket. A lazy cloud drifted in the infinite blue sky before us, and a gentle breeze played with leaves on the tree. Andrew moved plates out of the way and lay next to me, one hand under his head and the other finding mine once again.

"Which royal family?" he said.

I laughed. "I think we primarily focused on any bachelor with straight teeth."

Andrew rolled on his side and leaned into me. "I'm a bachelor. And I have straight teeth." He grinned like a mad man, making me laugh harder.

"But you aren't related to the King." I looped my arms around his neck and pulled him on top of me.

"I'm not, but I plan on giving you the royal treatment…" He pressed his lips to the corner of my mouth. "Right." He kissed my jawline. "Now."

It was close to five in the evening when Andrew and I returned to the marina. His picnic had worked out just like he had planned, and nothing he'd brought in the basket was wasted. Despite our next clue hunt turning out to be a dud, Andrew hadn't stopped beaming since we'd left the island. We walked from the boat to the marina's main office holding hands. I loved the feel of my palm in his large one. He went to return the keys and get his deposit back, and I took the empty basket to our car.

I was securing my backpack in the back of the Jeep when Andrew ran up the stairs to the parking lot three steps at a time. He stopped dead in his tracks, his face streaked with confusion then shifting into obsidian anger, muscles in his jaw spasming as he clenched his teeth. His eyes were glued to someone or something behind me, the crease between his eyebrows deepening. A sense of unease coursed through me, and I turned.

Richard leaned against a green Land Rover's hood, his hands folded on his chest, a sickening smile pasted on his face. Tweedledum stayed in the driver seat inside, his sunglasses too small on this stupid flat face. Tweedledee stepped from behind the car, swinging a gray Yeti duffle over his shoulder, his shirt rising and exhibiting a black gun in a holster.

What the heck? My thoughts whirled with possibilities. Had they been here all this time, waiting for us to return with a new clue or actual treasure, or did they just show up? Was someone spying on us, or did Richard track our phones? Or had someone told him we were here? My mind reeled through every instance William had hidden his phone as soon as he'd noticed me watching him texting. Was he talking to Brandon? Was William that stupid to leak our location? Or did Brandon track William's phone? No, that couldn't be it because William didn't come with us to the island, so he must have just shared it in conversation.

Andrew stopped at my side. "Fucking hell."

"Mrs. Jones, it's a pleasure to see you again." Richard gave me a curt nod.

I won't deny that it gave me great pleasure to be mistaken for Andrew's wife. I threw Dickhead a dirty look. "I can't say the same."

"We just arrived." Richard nodded in the direction of the ocean. "Do you care to share with me what you found on Árbol Hueco Isla? Remember, we could always split the share."

"We should go." Andrew opened the passenger door for me, and I slid into the Jeep. He pushed past Richard, rounded the car, and jumped into his seat. Without buckling up, he started the car and backed out of the parking spot, making Richard jump back to avoid being hit.

Andrew navigated us out of the marina, buckling up as he turned onto the main road, heading back to the town where we were staying.

Andrew's grip on the steering wheel was tight, his knuckles white, as if at any second he would rip the wheel off the dashboard.

"I must apologize to William," Andrew said.

I shifted in my seat and smoothed away the hair whipping my face, "Why?"

"I was wrong not to believe him." Andrew looked at his side mirror and steered the car around a slow truck going up the hill with livestock. "Dr. Garcia *is* collaborating with Richard."

Chapter Twenty-Five

"Don't jump to conclusions," I said over the roar of the engine. "You yourself said Richard was good at his job. He could have figured this location out on his own."

Andrew glanced at me with an apologetic smile. "Our visit to the Árbol Hueco Isla had nothing to do with Augustine Pérez."

A mix of confusion, nerves, and excitement churned in my stomach. "I don't understand."

"Richard wouldn't have known about the island unless Carlos told him. I made up the location of the clue. I just wanted an excuse to take you on a date, spend time alone with you, and woo you with my cheesy lines." His mouth twitched. "Are you mad I lied?"

Joy exploded inside of me. If he weren't driving, I would have grabbed his shirt by its collar and pulled his face to mine. "I'm devastated." I laughed at his reaction. "Why would I be mad? Today was the most romantic date anybody has ever planned for me."

"Once we're done with this trip, I'm taking you on a proper date." He brought my hand to his mouth and kissed my knuckles. "On many dates."

Andrew's words made my heart soar. He didn't care about our different social backgrounds, and the ocean that separated our lives. He wanted more dates with me. He wanted more of me.

"You were right!" I barged into our hotel room, my mind and heart full of all sorts of feelings. William was on his bed, his legs crossed at the ankles. He dropped his iPhone on his chest.

"Jesus, you scared me," he said. "Of course I'm right. Just tell me about what."

"Dr. Garcia is a traitor." I walked to the bed and dropped next to him. "Dickhead was waiting for us at the marina parking lot. The island wasn't part of the job. It was just a date," I said dreamily, a smile working up my lips at the memory of my time with Andrew. Except for the unfortunate news, it was a really, really good date.

"Brandon said that old rat sold out Andrew for half a million dollars. They had him before we arrived in Colombia," William said, shaking his head. "I can't believe we were leading that asswipe to your treasure all this time."

I raised an eyebrow. "It's not mine."

"Given the time and energy you've put into searching for this damn thing, I think you have all the right to call it yours." William prodded my shoulder with a finger. "BTW, you're glowing. Tell me about your day with Dr. Long Dong Silver.

Did he tell you I helped him with the basket? Did you two have fun?"

A stupid grin grew on my face so wide it hurt. "We sure did. Twice."

William's eyes went round—good thing the FDA didn't approve Botox into eyelids. "He only asked for one condom."

I sheepishly smiled. "I took one before I left the room."

"Thief."

I rolled my eyes. "You stole a good bottle of wine from my apartment." I pointed my finger at him. "Don't think I didn't notice that. And that bottle cost five times more than the box of condoms you bought at Costco."

"Hey, condoms cost a lot. And there'll be none left at the rate you and Dr. Hot Ass are going."

"Are you serious?" I gawked at him. "You brought a box of forty. Were you actually thinking you'd need that many on our vacation?"

He shrugged nonchalantly. "You never know who you'll meet. And I was thinking of both of us. Only, so far, you're the only one taking advantage of it."

Wait. What?

"What about the night you spent with Brandon?" I said, puzzled. "Didn't you guys...?"

"Nope, we just talked," William said with a sigh, his face relaxing into a dreamy expression, probably matching my earlier one. "We fooled around a bit but that was it. It was a magical night. I've never experienced anything like this before."

Five days ago, I would have rolled my eyes hard because William had *never-before-like-this* affairs with pretty much every new guy he temporarily fell in love with. But now I understood how he felt because I was in the same *never-before-like-this* boat with Andrew. And it felt wonderful.

"I assume you've been keeping in touch all this time?"

William grinned, showing most of his beautiful white teeth. "Are you going to be mad if I say yes?"

"Only if you share our research with him."

"We mutually agreed not to bring up Augustine Pérez." He lifted his left hand, holding up three fingers. "I swear."

"Put your hand down. You aren't a Boy Scout. And it's the right hand, not the left." I picked up his phone and handed it to him. "Please unlock it."

"What for?" He did as I asked and gave it back to me.

"I want to see if Brandon has been totally honest with you and didn't install some spy tracking app." I flipped through his screens with millions of colorful icons unsure what I was looking for. "Good grief, why do you need so many apps? There is no way I could know if any of—"

A message appeared on the screen from none other than the man himself.

BRANDON

I found the cutest B&B in the Cotswolds. I'll send you a link. Want to go in April? It's the best time to visit.

I glanced at William. "Why is he talking about the Cotswolds in the Spring?"

His phone dinged with another incoming text, but I didn't look at it.

"I'm planning to visit him in the UK," William said, the corners of his mouth tugging up.

"Oh." My lips turned up in a weak smile. A pang of fear hit me. What if William migrated to England? "Just promise you won't move away," I joked, but then a shiver ran over my body.

William stared at me, frowning. "I'm sorry, but I can't promise you that."

"Really?" I croaked, feeling betrayed. It was stupid to feel that way because I was a grown-ass woman who didn't and shouldn't ask her brother to stay where she was, but I was scared. If William moved, then I had nobody. My mother lived two hours away, but she didn't count. My friends were just acquaintances, fun to hang out with, and often left my life without a trace. An overwhelming ache went through my chest. What would my weekends be if William didn't live in the same city? My face scrunched up, and my nose tingled.

"Hey, hey." William sat up and rested his hand on my shoulder. "What's up with that face? I'm not moving anywhere … yet."

I stared helplessly at him, and stupid, fat tears rolled down my face. And then I was full-on sobbing, though I wasn't sure why. Fear of William moving to another country? Fear of the unavoidable massive heartbreak if it didn't work out with Andrew? Too much sex in a short period of time?

"If I move, you move with me."

"No, I can't," I whined. "My home is in Atlanta, and I have a business to run." I bawled harder, my whole body shaking. "I'll be alooooneeee." It came out as a wail. Okay, I didn't recognize myself. My mind was overheating with way too many things to process: Andrew wanted to date me; Dr. Garcia was a mole; my brother wanted to move to a different country.

"Oh, goofy." He wrapped his arms around me and pulled me to his chest. "You won't be alone. Dr. Darcy Andrew Jones will be with you."

"Not all the time, only when he can visit me." I shook my head, wiping my nose—not intentionally—on his shirt.

"Stop crying. It's bad for your skin."

I took a deep breath, tightened my arms around William's waist, and enjoyed his big brotherly warmth. God, what would I be without him? For thirty-three years, the furthest we lived apart was an hour. After a moment, I extracted myself from his hug and wiped my face with the hem of my shirt. "I'll miss you if you move, but I'll be okay."

William glanced at his chest and cringed. "I know you'll be okay. It's not like I've moved already. Don't forget I also have a clinic."

He got up, unbuttoned his shirt, and limped to his suitcase.

"William," I said. "What's wrong with your leg?" And only then did I notice that there was a pillow under his feet. His feet weren't crossed at the ankle as I'd initially thought, he was elevating one of them.

He took his shirt off, grimaced at the wet spot my face had left, and then folded it neatly and placed it in his dirty pile. His left side and part of his back had red marks and bluish-purple bruises. I jumped to my feet and rushed to him.

"What happened?"

"It's not so bad." He stepped away and shrugged on the shirt.

"Not so bad?" My mouth dropped open. "William, let me see your leg. Is it broken?"

"No. Just a sprained ankle."

"Who did this?"

"OMG, Adriana. What's with all the questions? I did. Okay?"

"What? How?" I stared at him.

William wobbled back to the bed, doubled over the pillow and rested his right leg on it. He leaned against the headboard, checked his watch, and *finally* met my eyes. "I wanted to see Brandon. He said he wasn't far, just in the next town. So I rented a scooter."

I was thunderstruck. "You rented a scooter?" He nodded. I hadn't seen any rental places around here. "Where did you find it?"

He shrugged. "A guy at the shop next door let me use his."

"William," I said, but I wanted to yell. "You don't know how to ride a regular bike, why would you think you can handle a scooter?"

"I handled it just fine."

"Yeah. Clearly." I waved my hands at him. "Did you at least wear a helmet?"

"Please." He rolled his eyes.

"Please what?"

"Of course I did. It was the grossest, but I'm not an idiot."

That was debatable.

"Wow. Yeah. You must *really* like Brandon if you were willing not only to drive half an hour on a vehicle you've never used before, but also," I said with a snort, "to put on someone else's greasy, nasty, dirty, filthy, infested with dead skin and maybe even,"—I gasped—"lice helmet. It touched and rubbed against your skin and—"

"Okay! Enough." He shuddered. "I get your point."

I laughed. "So, your leg. Is it mostly okay?"

"Yes. I just twisted it when I fell trying to make a sharp turn."

"Did you at least make it to Brandon?"

William's smile dropped. "No. The accident happened two streets from here."

"I'm sorry." I felt terrible for him. *Truly*. I did. "Why didn't Brandon come to visit you?"

"He couldn't. He was working with Brie. He was going to excuse himself and run out to say hi. I have a feeling Brandon keeps it a secret from them that we talk."

Someone knocked and I opened the door to find Andrew standing on the other side. In an instant, my heart started a happy dance to a song called *He Wants to Date Me*.

"Hey, stranger," I said, stepping aside. "Come in."

Andrew's eyes narrowed on me. "Were you crying?"

"No," I lied.

"Honey, he knows you are lying. You have some…" William tapped under his eye.

Oh shoot, my mascara.

"Do we need to talk about it?" Andrew arched an eyebrow.

I shook my head, backing away in the direction of the bathroom. "I'll be just one second."

The reflection in the mirror was something I hoped was a lie. My hair stuck out in different directions, my messy bun resembling a tumbleweed, and my mascara was smeared under both eyes, with black streaks running down my cheeks. I got to work.

Several minutes later, I emerged from the bathroom. My hair was brushed and neatly braided, and my washed face had freshly applied mascara and lip gloss.

My heart sank a little. Andrew was gone.

"Where did he go?"

"He came to apologize to me and asked if we wanted to eat dinner in his room while brainstorming where to go next. I said to text us when he's back." William patted a spot next to him. "Now, while we're alone, tell me *everything* about your date."

The empty containers with traces of *sancocho* and *pandebono* we'd had for dinner littered the desk in Andrew's room. For an hour, we'd scoured the possible location of the palace, joining the maps Andrew had sketched from the bracelets and trying to compare them to a real map.

William perched on the bed with his right leg elevated, searching the historical maps archive website. Andrew and I were on the floor in a mess of papers. Andrew sat with his left elbow balanced on a bent knee, his hand supporting his head. The other hand held his iPad, on which he was using the Library of Congress website to study maps of Colombia. Google Maps had worked for a while but each time he zoomed out, a river or road would disappear, and it'd become annoying, so he'd switched to the old-fashioned atlases.

I was lying on my stomach, feet kicking in the air while poring over two pages with faded lines that looked like an unfinished floor design. Augustine had many strange sketches of flora, and animals, half-finished portolans with seaport names, and numerous designs of devices that resembled works of Leonardo da Vinci I had seen on display in museums. But these two sheets were nothing like the other. They could have been early architectural plans for Maria's palace. And I wasn't an architect by any means, and yes, with time the pencil marks had faded in many parts of the sketch, but my gut feeling was that something about them was off.

I sat up, my back screaming bloody murder after laying on a hard surface for too long. Placing one of the sheets on the floor at my feet, I opened my camera app. Trying to avoid the light reflection of the plastic, I maneuvered my phone above it.

"What are you doing?" William asked.

"I want to try a trick in the Photoshop Express app. There's a way to mess with brightness levels or whatever it's called. I used it another time and"—I snapped a picture, replaced the first sheet with the other, and hovered my phone over it—"some of the barely visible lines became more noticeable." I took the second picture. "Anyway, I want to try it on these to see if anything pops up."

William threw his head backward, dropping his phone on his lap. "This is so taxing. My head hurts." He groaned. "How can you do it for hours? I close my eyes, and all I see are rivers and outlines of mountains. What if you're wrong and Augustine didn't build it near their old ranch? Maybe he thought he could drug Maria and transfer her passed out from one place to another."

Andrew looked up, and I could clearly see gears turning in his head, thinking about it. Then he shook his head. "No. I don't think he would do that."

"Okay, fine, so he was this super *nice* pirate," William said, making air quotes with his fingers, "who robbed others and killed anyone who got in his way, and who loved ciphers and made everything super secretive and complicated for subsequent generations of venturesome treasure hunters who tried to lay claim to it."

I sighed. "Where are you going with this?"

He held one finger out. "What if, to make it more pain in the ass for people like us, the bracelet map is a reversed image of a real map? Hm?"

Andrew and I exchanged glances.

"We need a mirror," I said, looking around. "I have a small one in my bag."

"We could use the one in the bathroom," Andrew suggested.

"But it's mounted," I said, rising to my feet.

"I can hold it next to it, and you can take a photo." Andrew also got up.

"Or," William chimed in, "you can take a photo and flip the image using your fancy Photoshop app." He dropped an imaginary microphone, making me chuckle.

We took a picture of the sketched map and then I flipped it in the app and airdropped it to Andrew's and William's phones.

"Oh, look at the time." William shook his head, sitting up and slowly moving his legs to the edge of the bed. "You love birds can continue with the chase, but I'm going to my room."

William shuffled to the door, but before he left, he paused. "Also, if I'm not mistaken, you can make the image translucent, overlay it on the Colombia map, and see if you can line up rivers and such."

Once William left, Andrew's gaze met mine, and the corners of his eyes crinkled. "Will you spend the night here with me?"

Elation soared through me and landed straight in my core.

"I'd love to," I said, trying and failing not to grin too wide. "I promise not to be distracting."

Andrew's eyebrow went up, and his lips pulled into a sexy smirk. "That's impossible. You can be in the building next door, and my concentration will still be on you."

My skin lit on fire, and it took all the willpower I had not to set my phone aside and straddle Andrew. "So, want to work for an hour or two and then go to bed?" I bit my bottom lip.

"Sounds like a good plan."

I scooted towards him. "Why don't you download the app on your iPad and we could use my login? It would be easier to do what William suggested on a larger screen."

Andrew tapped on the App Store icon and typed in Photoshop.

"What are you going to do about Dr. Garcia?"

"I can't forgive him for betraying me and sabotaging my work. Professionally, there isn't enough evidence he's done anything wrong, so he goes unpunished, but after this trip, I won't be staying in touch with him." He stared at the screen, focusing on a blue line slowly drawing a circle. "Whether or not we find a possible location of the ruins tonight, tomorrow morning I'll leave him a message to say that we're going to the history museum in Nava de Luenga. It's seven hours from here, which should send Richard on a nice wild goose chase. The further they are from us, the better off we are."

Several minutes went by while we familiarized ourselves with the app functions, and then we uploaded the images and got to work. At first, the modern map we were using was too dark, so we searched for a better one to use as a base layer, eventually downloading the 1997 map from The Library of Congress website. We played with the sketched map, changing its saturation and sharpness. Then we dropped translucence to fifty percent and began slowly moving the sketch over the base layer in search of the perfect alignment between the two.

My heart skipped a bit when a line from both layers merged into one. "Stop."

Andrew's finger paused.

"There." I pointed to the top right corner where the zigzag of the rivers in both images had consolidated. Andrew carefully scrolled until the rivers and mountains with the old ranch and hallmark representing the alleged location of the palace were in the center of the screen.

"Oh wow," I breathed out and gaped at Andrew. "We found it."

Andrew lowered his mouth to mine, his nose gently rubbing my nose, his lips caressing my lips. "Thank you," he said, and then he gave me the most toe-curling kiss ever. I never wanted it to end.

His tongue explored my mouth, making me whimper and turn into melting goo. His free hand cupped my neck, and he groaned when his teeth made the slightest bite on my lower lip. Andrew's hand drifted lower, he lifted my shirt, and his hot palm smoothed up my skin until it found the curve of my breast, and his fingers generously massaged it. He deepened the kiss, rolling a hard nipple between his thumb and index finger.

"Should we finish pinpointing the location first?" I said, breaking our kiss, breathless, soaking wet, and irritated at my own words.

Pressing his forehead to mine, Andrew closed his eyes and exhaled. "Yes. We should." He squeezed my nipple again, withdrawing a moan from me. "I need maybe an hour to map our route. And then I'll thank you properly."

While Andrew began working on GPS coordinates, I used Photoshop to alter the two photos I had taken earlier of Augustine's sketches, first making lines bolder and more defined, and then stacking them and making the top layer sixty percent translucent. For the second time that day, my heart skipped a beat. It wasn't a layout of a floor plan as we'd originally assumed. On the screen, I had a rectangle made out of an irregular network of paths. A labyrinth of some sort. It wasn't as uniform or complicated as a maze—it didn't have concentric repeating patterns—but it did have a continuous path with few smaller paths that branched out with a squiggle or a letter at the end. It was hard to understand what these symbols meant, even after I'd adjusted the brightness of the picture.

"Andrew, look at this," I said, stretching my arm out with my iPhone. "Do you know what this could be?"

Andrew took my phone and examined it, his eyebrows

pulled together. "I don't..." He made a surprised sound. "It's a passage... But the image looks incomplete." He handed it back to me.

I rubbed my eyes, exhaustion having slowly distorted my vision, and looked at the image again, noticing that in some places the lines had gaps. "You might be right. Where did you get these outlines?"

"Carlos."

"Damn. It would be foolish of us to ask him if he knows anything about them or if he could locate the other piece of the image."

Andrew nodded. "No need to bring Richards's attention to whatever this is. For all we know, it could be the path to the Asiento de Padua cargo in the palace's basement."

I gave myself another ten minutes to study the image before I left Andrew on the floor to figure out tomorrow's journey, and went to the bathroom to wash my face and brush my teeth before climbing into his bed, wearing absolutely nothing—not being distracting at all. Closer to ten, someone—William—slid condoms under the door. Andrew took it as a clue he was done working. He closed his journal, plugged in the iPad to charge, went to the bathroom, took out his contacts, and brushed his teeth. He stripped off his clothes, plucked the long row of silver packets off the floor, and before I knew it, he was lording over me, the hardness of his erection pressing between my thighs.

"Do we know our next chess move?" I asked.

"Yes." His mouth was next to my ear, his hot breaths sending ripples of lust down my skin.

"And you're not tired?" I wholeheartedly hoped he would

say no. I was spent but didn't want to pass on another treat of Andrew's body.

"No." He nuzzled my neck, then his lips traveled from my jaw to my neck. "But you will be in the morning." And then he pressed his entire length into me.

Chapter Twenty-Six

Speculating that we would be spending possibly two nights—but hopefully just one—in the jungle, Andrew and I had bought extra supplies, and I took the opportunity to pick up trousers and a long-sleeved shirt. That morning, before the sun bloomed on the horizon while the last dying stars held to the sky, we loaded our car and left the hotel, driving north. We drove two hours past the Erizo at Las Loma retreat and the opposite way from the waterfall until we found a good place to abandon our Jeep and start our hike.

We were on our fifth hour prowling through the dense rainforest and still had another to go. The jungle's complicated depth seemed more impenetrable the deeper we immersed ourselves. My heavy breathing mixed with the constant bird calls and hoots and monkey screeching and thrashing above our heads. Sweat ran down my temples, my neck, and between my boobs. My leg muscles ached, and the backpack somehow felt as though it weighed ten times more than it had when we'd started. Even if I wanted to whine and ask to take a short break, I didn't. Thank goodness William was back at the hotel resting his ankle. He'd been desperate to come with us to find the treasure but in his state he wouldn't have made it the first fifteen minutes. To make William feel he was still part of the treasure hunt, Andrew had entrusted him with the safety of the book we'd located in the San Antonio church and the box with all its contents we'd found at Erizo.

"We should be able to reach the ruins before dusk." Andrew held my hand and helped me across a fallen tree. My right foot slipped off the trunk, and I stumbled. A thorny branch caught my sleeve, ripping the fabric and biting through my skin.

"Shit." A wave of pain coursed through my left arm, and my body slammed forward into Andrew's.

Losing his footing, he staggered backward and fell. His hat flew off his head, and I landed on top of him, my forehead crashing into his. Stars flew out from the corner of my eyes, and temporary light-headedness threw me into a fog of confusion.

Andrew grunted and cursed under his breath.

"Son of a gun, that hurt," I mumbled, rising on my elbows and blinking at him.

"You okay?" he asked, smoothing hairs off my sticky forehead. "We might both have concussions now." He chuckled.

I rubbed my thumb over a red spot above his right eyebrow. "Good thing I didn't knock out any of your pretty teeth."

"Will you still love me if I was missing a few teeth?" he

asked, now running his fingers over the probably red bump on my forehead.

My heart gave an aching jab against my breastbone at his words *will you still love me*, and that caught me off guard. Fucking hell. This was maddening. This feeling. This thing that Andrew did to me. I knew he meant it as a joke—of course, he did, and I needed to joke back *yes, I will*. But would it be a joke?

This was silly. This wasn't love at first sight. I didn't believe in that.

Or maybe it was.

Well, not exactly at first sight. It was love from the third day. Or was it on the fourth day? Shoot, I couldn't remember when I'd fallen for Andrew. Without a parachute.

Andrew's smile dropped, and his eyebrows pulled together in deep concern. "What's wrong? Are you going to throw up?"

Nice. Apparently I looked nauseated when I was thinking about being in love with him.

"Hollywood likes this head-hitting move in the movies," I said, pushing off his chest and straddling him. I rubbed the sore spot on my face. "It hurt like a motherfu—"

"Adriana, you're bleeding." Andrew gently caught my left wrist.

"What?" I peered at my arm, and oh wow, I had a nasty gash in my forearm and blood had soaked into the torn fabric. My Apple watch was also missing. "Oh," I whined. "The stupid branch ruined my shirt. And where is my watch?" I scanned the ground, looking for the light blue band.

Andrew crouched next to me and took off his backpack.

"You have a deep cut, and you're worrying about your shirt

and watch?" Feeling around inside his bag, he found a first-aid kit. "Let me see it." Andrew unfastened the button at my wrist and carefully rolled the sleeve up. He applied a dressing to stop the bleeding.

A monkey screeched above our head, probably laughing at my clumsiness.

"Do you think blood will attract wild animals to us?" I joked, and then it hit me. What if it was true? Bears can smell blood for miles. My panic hiked up. "Andrew, are we in trouble?"

"No. We'll be okay." He removed the soiled dressing and examined the cut. The bleeding had stopped.

"It's not so bad," I said. "I wouldn't run to urgent care with it."

"Let's just hope it doesn't get infected." Andrew opened a new water bottle, angled my hand away from us, and cautiously poured water on the cut.

I sucked in a breath.

Andrew did the same and glanced at me, his eyes full of apology. "I'm sorry it hurts."

"It doesn't."

It did.

He peered closely at the raw flesh. "Doesn't look like it has any splinters." Andrew took a pen and drew a circle at the perimeter of the redness.

"What are you doing?"

"Marking it."

"I see that. What for?"

"If the redness spreads past the line, it means the infection has worsened."

He applied antibiotic ointment on the sterile bandage and taped it around my wound.

"You seem like you know what you're doing," I said, watching his skilled fingers orbit my wrist as he firmly wrapped a dressing. "Have you done much booboo fixing?"

"I make it up as I go." He smiled. "My medical expertise doesn't extend beyond putting Peppa Pig plasters on Lulu's scraped knees."

My heart overflowed with warmth at the image of Andrew lovingly talking to his tiny niece, saying sweet and kind words to make her stop crying and gently wiping tears from her cheeks. He probably stuck a Band-Aid on his nose to make her giggle.

"What did the doctor give to a sick penny?" Andrew said as he secured the wrap and pulled me out of this other world.

I shook my head. "I don't know."

"Penny-cillin." He grinned.

The joke was so unexpected I barked a laugh. He was utterly adorable. And I wanted Andrew to always be the one to take care of my scrapes.

His eyes glinted, and he leaned forward and nudged my nose with his. "Think you can continue our walk?"

"Yes."

Andrew stuffed all the things back into his bag, and he helped me back to my feet. He snatched the hat off the ground and wiped his forehead with his sleeve before putting it back on. With a final (and failed) attempt to locate my watch, we continued our quest.

After walking a mile, we came out of the wild darkness to a spectacular, colorful vista. The sun barely touched the mountain edge, casting the warm light over a valley below that featured a river weaving its way through a green grassland and disappearing into a rainforest. Andrew navigated us down the hill, and we slipped into the jungle's shadows again, the green canopy shielding the afternoon sun as we went deeper. Soon, like a dark, hunched animal, the palace remains loomed in the distance.

The construction had stopped when the first-floor walls were erected, but even at this early stage, the imposing size of the structure's footprint grew ever more impressive as we moved closer. The eerie tranquility struck me. Ten thirty-foot-high pillars stood like guards clothed in dark green and tethered together by beefy ropes of vines. Dense moss smothered the structure's walls, tree roots pushed up the front steps of the staircase, and thick vines like snakes looped around standing columns. Maybe some of them were snakes—yuck! The hairs on my back stood up, and I shifted closer to Andrew, my arm bumping into his. I wrapped my fingers around his wrist.

"This is a good stopping point," Andrew said. "With the first morning light, we explore."

Wet wood logs popped and crackled, sending wisps of smoke and flickers of light toward a full moon amid the starlit graphite canvas. The canopy of treetops blocked most of the skies, but I could see stars in some places. Andrew rested his back on a column, his legs outstretched toward the fire, his right hand on the hunting rifle, his left one entwined with mine. I used his shoulder as my pillow, enjoying the warmth of his body beside mine. He smelled of sweat, smoke, and bug spray, and somehow, I found it sexier than his usual bergamot and powdery coumarin cologne.

I tried hard not to focus on how petrifying the jungle became once night blanketed it in darkness, so I thought about what Andrew and I would do when this was over, when we returned to our everyday life.

"After this trip," I said, "where would you want our first date to—"

"Gordon's Wine Bar," he said, before I'd even finished my sentence.

"I was afraid you'd say The Museum of London Archaeological Archive or something boring like that." I lifted my head and looked at him. His eyes were closed. The golden glow danced on his firelit face. "And hey, you didn't even have to think about it. Is it like your go-to place for all of your first dates?"

"I've never been there, but I thought you might like it."

His exceptionally kind and romantic heart stirred a flutter inside my chest. He needed to stop saying and doing all the nice things because I wasn't sure if my ribcage could expand to fit all the feelings I had for him. I kissed his stubbled cheek, then rested my head back on his shoulder.

"When you visit me in Atlanta," I said, squeezing my fingers tighter around his, "I'll take you to my two favorite places. First, Savannah, and then the Biltmore Estate. I know you're spoiled with beautiful European palaces, but I promise you'll fall in love with the US's largest privately owned house."

"I also want to take you to Dorset's Jurassic Coast. Lulworth Cove is where my parents met," he said. "At the end of May, before it gets busy with tourists, you and I will go there for a holiday. We'll stay in a fishing village, at a quaint B&B, or a small cottage. We could rent a boat and sail. Go for a walk after breakfast and watch the sunset on the beach."

I loved that Andrew had already put so much thought into our future dates, but how expensive it would be to fly to visit each other. And when would we find time? Anxiety and doubt oozed into my thoughts. Where would we be in five or ten years? He'd stated that he wanted a family. There was no way for him to have it if we lived apart.

"Andrew?" I said, closing my eyes too, it was hard to fight off the looming exhaustion. "Do you think it would work between us? You in England and me in the States."

"Sure. Or you could move with me to Cambridge."

I sat up and stared at him. "And do what?"

"I don't know." He faced me. "Do the same thing you would do in Atlanta."

"Why should I be the one to move?" I said, with bitterness in my voice. "Why don't you move in with me?"

"My job keeps me in Cambridge."

Hot irritation boiled my blood.

I scoffed. "You want me to drop everything in my life so I can fit into yours?"

"You're not dropping everything. You can still open your store, just in a different country."

"With what money? I can barely afford to do it in my hometown. And Georgia real estate is cheap compared to other places."

"I can loan you some money."

No, thank you. I went through that bullshit of *I'll-loan-you-money* with someone else, and that *really* worked out well for me.

"I don't need your money," I bit off.

"That's fine. My cousin is a senior financial manager at a bank; she can help you figure out how to get a business credit line."

I rolled my eyes. Everyone who had never tried to open a business thought I could just waltz into a bank and they'd hand me everything on a silver platter. It wasn't that simple.

My pulse hammered in my ears, and out of nowhere, my old insecurity snaked inside my head. I couldn't see myself living among his sophisticated, educated relatives, friends, and colleagues. Just like Greg, they would be polite and friendly to my face, but behind my back, they would laugh at me and my upbringing.

I wanted to put space between us, but there was nowhere to go in the dark jungle. I scooted a foot from him so our bodies were not touching. Andrew tossed a log onto the fire, and hundreds of red sparks jumped into the night air.

"This was fun, but it won't work out between us," I said, my voice breaking on the last word.

Andrew turned to me, propping his shoulder on the wall. "I'm sorry. I shouldn't have assumed you would move. Why don't we take things slow, visit each other when we can, meet in different places, and spend vacations together? We can decide later how to close the distance."

I shook my head, swallowing a lump in my throat. Why couldn't he understand?

"Why are you shaking your head?" he said, reaching for my hand.

I shifted out of his reach. "Because you're some fucking national hero of history who goes to museum openings and fist bumps with royalty and—"

"Are you kidding me?" Andrew's palms went up, and he let out a bitter laugh. "Have I ever mentioned mingling with royalty?"

I blinked at him. No, he hadn't.

"Well, your family have been professors at Cambridge for generations. You're all educated and fancy ... and I don't even have a college degree. I make stupid financial decisions. And I was born into a white trash family. Your people would laugh at me."

"Christ, you're back to this." Andrew laughed harder now.

"This isn't funny." I was on the verge of crying.

"Yes, it is," Andrew said with a firm tone. "My *people*." He returned to leaning his back to the wall, legs crossed at the ankles. He stared straight ahead. "You shouldn't care if some twat thinks less of you because you didn't finish college or grew up in a trailer."

"It's easy for you to say!" I said louder than I should have, but my old hurt was reaching its peak. "You were born into a highly respected family. Your blood and my blood don't mix."

Andrew glanced skyward and released a heavy breath. "I never knew my biological parents. Mum and Dad adopted me when I was a few months old. A year later they adopted Charlotte." He looked at me, and the ever-present warmth was back in his gaze. "Now please, Adriana, stop using the excuse that we can't be together because you don't have blue blood. I don't care about any of it. I want you for who you are." His eyes crinkled at the corners. "For all you know, I might have green blood."

I hadn't known any of this, and for unexplained reasons, I felt like a jerk. Andrew was right. I shouldn't care what others thought, but I wasn't sure how to convince myself I wasn't damaged goods.

"Why didn't you tell me you're adopted?"

"Because I never think of it. I'm simply grateful I had loving parents."

Leaves rustled and the snap of a branch somewhere in the distance pushed adrenaline through my body as my blood went cold. I shifted back to Andrew as he straightened, grabbing the hunting rifle.

"What was that?" I asked, barely hearing my words over the rushing blood in my ears.

A wild animal? Richard and his gang? Or someone else? A chill crept up my spine one vertebra at a time. Whoever or whatever was roaming in the jungle was probably watching us. I peered into the darkness, hoping not to catch the reflection of our fire in glowing eyes.

For many long minutes we sat motionless, scrutinizing the dark forest encircling us. My throat went dry, but the water bottle was in the backpack which was beyond arm's reach.

"Probably an animal," Andrew said, easing up his posture.

Shit, did it smell my dry blood? I'd forgotten about my forearm, and now it started to ache again. I had never been more terrified in my life.

A log in the fire popped, and I flinched. "Should we wave

our hands like crazy and yell? Make as much of a racket as we can."

"If it's an animal, it will go away." His fingers brushed off a small twig that had stuck to my face.

"Maybe it's Richard."

"I'd rather it was a jaguar," Andrew said, his voice devoid of humor.

"I'm afraid I'd have to disagree with you," I said.

Andrew chuckled. "Do you want to make a huge fight out of this so that we can have make-up sex?"

I huffed. "Not really."

But my smile meant that Andrew's comment had done what it needed to. Looking pleased with himself, he added another stick to the burning pile, sending yellow embers into the dark sky. My heartrate slowly returned to normal as we fell into silence, staring into the darkness and listening to the night creatures' uninterrupted pulsating chirp. Perhaps whatever had made noise earlier had already left or had never been there in the first place.

"Once we're back at the hotel and rested, let's return to our earlier conversation." Andrew leaned back against the wall and extended his arm, inviting me to snuggle into him. "We can work it out. I like you too much, Adriana Jones, to give up so easily."

I eased into Andrew's embrace, and he kissed my temple.

"I like you too," I said with a yawn. "And if we aren't eaten tonight by some large animal, we can figure *us* out later."

Chapter Twenty-Seven

I t was eight in the morning, and the air was humid and quaked with a racket of daytime creatures. There wasn't a single muscle in my body that wasn't sore. After Andrew redressed my wound—thankfully, the redness hadn't passed the blue-inked border—we snuffed out the fire and combatted overgrown vines. Well, he was battling with nature. I was supervising while wearing Andrew's hat and holding his gun, his backpack at my feet. My lustful eyes devoured Andrew's broad back and flexing shoulders, every muscle visible under the sweat-drenched fabric as he swung his strong arm, his pleasure-eliciting hands gripping the machete, slicing and severing and tearing through the web of vines and roots.

After Andrew finally carved us a portal into the palace, we turned on our flashlights and climbed over the collapsed archway, its cracked and faceless keystone in the center. Passing through a moss-covered passageway, we entered the inner sanctum that was as much jungle as outside. The structure had no roof, and nature's canopy above shielded us from the sun and blanketed us with a damp coolness. Giant trees grew out of the floor, their roots crawling across vast blocks of leftover marble slabs. Vines wound over walls and columns, and ferns covered the ground. Dark shadows slithered over every surface, playing tricks with my mind. Snakes, lizards, spiders, and maybe larger animals were clearly long-time tenants of this unfinished alcazar.

My neck hair raised, and I shivered. The damn treasure better be here somewhere.

"Over there is the beginning of the grand staircase." Andrew pointed at the crumbling stone stairs that twisted and rose across the ascending arch. Twigs and dead layers of leaves crunched under our weight as our feet gingerly tread on the spongy ground. We meandered between rocks, navigated past the stairs, and didn't stop until we reached an overgrown gateway.

"Do you know where you're going?" I asked, looking over my shoulder to ensure nothing followed and was about to pounce on us.

"I'm hunting for a way to the basement." Andrew shone the flashlight into the network of plants. "And this might just be it. Step back." He swung the machete and severed the hanging roots.

Andrew and I edged around vegetation and trailed through a vaulted passageway with pastiche Romanesque arches. A net of ancient spiderwebs clung to the metal but Andrew waved it away with the machete.

Soon, we approached an opening with narrow stairs leading down. My pulse pounded painfully against my skin, and my brain screamed that climbing above a long-dead skeleton was one thing—it was dead and couldn't hurt me—but going into a dark basement potentially filled with very much alive killer animals was something else entirely.

"Maybe it's not there." I pulled on Andrew's arm, silently pleading for him to stop. "We should go back."

The side of Andrew's mouth curled up. "You slept in a jungle, and now you're afraid?"

"It would be tough for anybody to carry a chest full of gold down this way." My fingers dug into Andrew's skin.

"We're already here; we can't leave without checking it out." He offered the rifle to me. "If you want, stay here. I'll go and call you if I need you."

I scoffed. *Nope.*

He pushed aside a dangling vine, and we descended a circular staircase, inhaling earthy wet soil tang.

We came to a tapered room the size of a sixteen-foot storage container enclosed with granite walls. The floor was strewn with leaves and twigs and as I cast my flashlight over the walls, my heart lurched to my throat. A human skeleton reclined on the ground in the corner next to us, its skull angled, jaw slack.

"Fuck!" I yelped and jumped aside, yanking Andrew with me.

"Christ, Adriana," Andrew breathed out. "You scared me."

I clutched my injured hand to my chest. "I scared you? That scared me." I pointed my flashlight at the sad remains still dressed in blue breeches and a brown vest.

"It's just a skeleton." Andrew squatted near the poor fellow and picked up the remains of a black hat with a red band.

"How old is it?"

"Based on what's left of his uniform, I believe he was a soldados de cuera. A leather-jacket soldier who served in the northern Viceroyalty of New Spain." Andrew leaned over to examine a musket the skeleton still held. "And this soldier has been here over two centuries. I'm unsure if he was lost or had a reason to come here but…" Andrew placed the hat on the soldier's lap and stood up. He wrapped his arms around me, pulling me into the heat of his chest. "He isn't harmful," he said into my hair, before kissing the top of my head.

I didn't understand how he could be so collected and calm. Maybe it was years of digging where skeletons were buried, or perhaps it was just him. I let out a shuddering breath and slumped into him.

After several minutes, Andrew withdrew and looked at me with a coy smile. "Are you good now?"

Not in the least.

I nodded.

Andrew took off his backpack, rummaged in it, and then pulled out a handful of glow sticks and his notebook. He cracked them and dropped them around the perimeter on the floor. The room lit up with a neon white glow that cast a ghostly light around us, revealing carvings like those under the Iglesia San Antonio.

To the left, the wall revealed a tale of rural life. The opposite one exhibited a world atlas with ships crossing the ocean and sea monsters lurking beneath them. The wall behind us, which our new friend was leaning against, showed a jungle crowded with animals, snakes, and hunters. The wall in front of us replicated the same structure we saw in the church, only no angels floated above it. Instead, two figures rested side by side in the dead center, their eyes closed, hands folded over their chest.

But most startling was the distinct outline of a hidden door with a hollow round slot to its right side. Excitement rushed from my toes to the top of my head like bubbles in a glass of freshly poured champagne. *We finally found it.* At the realization, relief flooded my limbs. We'd discovered it first. We'd won the race and beaten the Russian oligarch's minions.

"Augustine's final resting place must be on the other side." Andrew stepped forward and ran his palm over the stone, studying it. He hummed at first as if he wasn't sure what he was looking at, and then he made one positive scoff. He dug the dirt out of the opening and shone his flashlight inside. Then he crouched and opened his journal.

I dropped my own backpack on the ground and moved away, pulling my phone out of my pocket.

"Moments like this make me thankful I picked this job because sharing history with the world is one of the greatest feelings." Andrew flipped the pages. "You might finally meet the Royal Family at the opening night." He looked at me. "Just don't swap me for an eligible monarch."

"No promises." I grinned and snapped a picture of him. The light of his flashlight illuminated his handsome face and it looked like a still from a new Indiana Jones movie. I chuckled. This would be my favorite picture: Andrew knelt at the wall, wearing a Fedora and a dazzling smile, holding his journal in his left hand.

"Okay," Andrew said, rising to his full height. "If I'm correct in solving Augustine's encrypted notations, you need to place your arm with the bracelet inside here. You'll feel a bar that you'll need to turn."

This was it. This moment was the reason I had agreed to go on this mad caper. I examined the bracelet. After so many days of wearing it, it felt like a part of my body.

Pulling my sleeve to my elbow, I looked at the dingy hole. *Righty tighty, lefty loosey, right?* Augustine was famous for hiding valuables in places with elaborate locking systems. He could have made unlocking this door extra tricky. Barbed wire fear swirled and burned in my gut, and my heart hammered hard in my chest.

"Clockwise?" I swallowed. "Or counterclockwise?"

The crease between Andrew's eyebrows deepened as he chewed on this answer. "Well…"

That word.

I grunted, dropping fists on my hip. "Seriously?"

"Sorry." He shook his head. "Clockwise. Turn it clockwise."

"Are you sure?" I said dryly.

"Yes."

I shone my flashlight into the hole, and I went rigid. An army of bugs kept running in and out of the light, some small and some sort of big. They didn't look like scary bugs, but…

I glanced at Andrew. "What if there's a bloodsucking spider that bites me?"

"Here … I'll do it first." Andrew's chest pressed to my back, the warmth of his body instantly seeping into me, and I wanted to relax into him. He pushed his hand into the orifice, and moved it side to side, up and down as far as space allowed, then he pulled his arm out with a few spiders and other bugs taking a free ride on his sleeve. "See, nothing besides these little guys."

I closed my eyes and rolled my shoulders. Keeping my back straight, I took deep breaths in and out, feeling the air passing through my windpipe. I could do this. I could insert my hand inside the insect-infested opening. I had often crawled under our old trailer dominated by disgusting spider crickets to fix a busted water pipe or drag out a rotting rodent. This was not so bad.

Just bugs. Little, yucky creepy-crawlies.

A quiver shot down my spine.

I *so* didn't want to do this.

"Okay." I cringed, turned away, and guided my right wrist inside, palm facing down. My skin prickled as creatures started using my arm as their unfamiliar territory to explore. A cold sweat broke over me. "Oh, my Lord. This is disgusting." My left hand curled into a fist, nails digging into my palm.

I was shoulder-deep when my fingers grazed the outline of a rock or metal bar in the dead center of this hellhole. "I found it," I said through my clenched teeth. A bug ran up my neck. "Now what?" I said, impatiently.

"Now imagine a split bearing. There are two halves—one at the bottom and the second at the top—with a diameter big enough to fit the bracelet. Try to move your hand from side to side until you feel the bracelet setting into the bottom one."

I did what Andrew said until the bracelet caught on something, and I lowered my wrist into it. "I think I got it."

"Good. Can you reach the handle?" Sweat glistened on Andrew's face and neck. I wasn't sure if he was nervous, worried, or both.

I nodded, my fingers wrapping around the cold bar.

"Ready?" he asked, our gazes locking.

Not really.

My thoughts raced. The dildo of consequences rarely arrived lubed, and if I had wronged someone badly in the past, this was surely where I'd get my payback. What if Andrew was mistaken and it was booby-trapped? My hand was inside. Could I lose it? Beats of sweat covered my face, too. And bugs now ran down my sides, and under my shirt.

Fuckity fuck.

"Wait." My mouth was dry. "What if it crushes my hand? What if it's not how to open it?"

"I'm certain this is the correct way to unlock the door."

I raised one eyebrow. "You were also certain Dr. Garcia was a decent man."

"Yes, and I was wrong about that." Andrew hung his head and took a deep breath, then looked up at me. "But I'm not wrong about how to open this door. In a letter, Augustine encoded a series of specific instructions. I have no doubt it's for this room, and I'm sure I interpreted them precisely."

"If *this* situation goes south, Dr. Andrew Oliver Jones, you'll owe me for the rest of your life."

He smiled. "Even if nothing happens to you, I'll owe you for the rest of my life."

My fingers tightened, and I struggled to rotate the handle clockwise. I gritted my teeth and tried harder. Again.

Nope.

It didn't budge.

"It doesn't want to turn," I hissed.

"Try the other way."

WTF.

I shot Andrew a *what-the-hell* look. "I thought you knew how to open this!"

"I don't have the *exact* step-by-step instructions. There was a fifty-fifty chance which way to turn."

I took a deep breath and tried to twist it counterclockwise. It still didn't budge. Perhaps the locking mechanism had rusted after so many years. "It's stuck. Or it's broken." I relaxed my grip.

"Let me think."

Andrew took off his hat and wiped the sweat off his forehead. Then he replaced it and closed his eyes. I didn't want to be an asshole and break his concentration, but there was a highway of bugs going over, in and out of my bra, and quickly migrating south on my stomach.

Hurry up, Andrew. Hurry the fuck up.

Andrew opened his eyes. "Pull on the bar, then turn it clockwise."

I wrapped my fingers again around the bar, squishing bugs by accident. Yuck. I tugged. Then tugged harder.

A movement.

Stone grinding on stone.

My eyes met Andrew's, and we both gasped.

"It's working," I squalled, my heart lurching, hard.

I twisted the bar clockwise. The enclosure around my wrist shifted, and light pressure surrounded my hand, pressing on the bracelet. I envisioned huge pliers or crab cracker clamping my wrist. "Oh, my god."

"What?" Andrew stepped closer to me. "If you feel something isn't right, pull your hand out."

Now he tells me that.

A gear-shifting sound reverberated through the chamber and my bones. A loud clack sent my pulse and mind into total panic. If the floors started shaking, I was out of there. With or without Andrew.

The compression around my wrist lessened, and I yanked my arm out. The bracelet loosely dangled, no longer locked. I was free at last. I viciously shook my body, hitting my clothes everywhere, trying to get rid of the nasty bugs.

More mechanical racket erupted, the clink clank of gears moving like a phantom behind the walls. My eyes darted around the dim space, trying to follow it. Blood rushed to my ears and I had to swallow a lump of fear to clear my hearing. I inched back until I was flattened against Andrew. His hand gripped mine, and he veered me to stand behind him.

The air changed, and the stone door moved, rupturing the interconnecting fine vines.

We staggered back, Andrew's body blocking mine, our boots crushing the skeleton's bones.

The door opened more, then stopped, leaving enough space for one body to pass at a time. Everything became deadly silent. Andrew's heavy breathing and my drumming heart were the only sounds.

And just for shits and giggles, my brain had to hurl in the image of Hodor blocking the door with crazed white walkers on the other side. The same shudder that had swept through my body at the realization of the root of his name *hold the door* now washed over me again.

What if we were not supposed to open this door?

Chapter Twenty-Eight

My blood had circulated what felt like over a million times in the last minute. No white walkers. No zombies. No animals. Not even a sound rounded the corner. *So far, so good.* The next step was to peer into the darkness behind the half-open door.

My hands clasped Andrew's forearm as he shone his flashlight inside the new path, but it was impossible to see anything from where I stood.

Andrew ran light over the foot-thick edge of the door. "You stay here."

"Why?"

"Just in case."

"Of *what*?" I barked. I didn't mean it to come out as an accusation, but my nerves were jagged. And then it hit me. "In case the door closes. So instead of both of us getting stuck inside, it will be just you. But then what?" I pointed to the stairwell. "I go look for help?"

Andrew's throat worked as he swallowed hard and pushed

the rifle into my hands. Anxiety stabbed at the base of my ribs. I didn't want to stay alone here with the remains of a Spanish soldier. Actually, he didn't bother me as much anymore, but the vast jungle above us did. "You realize there's a good chance I'll get lost in the jungle? And end up like him."

"Yes, but there's a chance you won't, and you can call for help." He tilted his head. "Or you could reopen the door."

Oh. Right.

I let go of his arm and pulled a water bottle out of my bag. I gulped some of it, then handed it to him. "Might as well take this one. Just in case."

Andrew shook his head. "Keep it." He threw his backpack on his shoulders and then winked. "Don't go anywhere."

"Don't you want a kiss? In case it might be your last one?" I joked with a timid smile.

He adjusted his hat. "I'll get it once I'm back."

And he stepped inside.

"Please keep talking to me while you're in there," I called after him, a fear tightening my gut into a firm knot. "Andrew, tell me what you see?"

Footsteps accompanied by flashes of light echoed from the gap.

"I'm in a fifteen-by-fifteen space with large cobwebs," Andrew finally said, "and one huge open-face sarcophagus." There was a pause, and the soft footfall stopped. "And two very dead skeletons ... and ... that would be it."

Defeat popped my bubble of excitement, and I deflated like an old balloon. "No trunks?"

"No."

"Any other secret passages?"

"No." His voice dropped off. The sound of metal hitting a stone pierced the stillness. The light in the room went out, and Andrew swore. Then there was a moment of struggle, grunting, heavy breathing, and whispers of strangled cursing. My pulse picked up.

"You okay?" I stood up and crept to the door. "Andrew?"

I didn't want to chance sticking my head through the opening—with my luck, the door would shut at that moment. "Andrew?" I repeated louder. More grunting.

Screw it. I slipped into the crypt. The light of my flashlight fell on Andrew's feet dangling off the ground, his body bending over the edge of a big-ass white marble sarcophagus as if something was pulling him in.

"Andrew!" I scurried down a short staircase, missing the last step and coming down so hard with my right boot on the floor that my joints painfully popped.

"Stop!" Andrew pushed off the edge, looking up at me wide-eyed. A thick layer of cobwebs decorated his hat and clung to his face.

I froze.

Under my boot, the ground sank an inch, and a metal bang went out like a shotgun. A mechanical racket erupted, gears turning and working, the scrape of a stone on stone.

This didn't sound right.

Andrew lunged in my direction, his hat flying off. He took all three steps in one jump and threw his body into the closing door. His boots scraped the floor as the door overpowered him and sealed shut. Dead silence fell upon us.

fucked | fək-əd |

VERB: [w/ object] have sex with
someone. Nope, not at the moment.
[w/t object] Dr. Andrew Jones and
Adriana Jones's current circumstances.

ORIGIN: Possibly Germanic (Swedish
dialect focka and Dutch dialect
fokkelen) early 16th century.
Certainly Colombia, present day, ten
thirty a.m.

I was half expecting the floor to shake, rocks to fall on our heads, and water to rush in like it did in movies about tomb explorers. But it didn't happen.

Andrew pressed his forehead into the wall. "I thought I told you to stay put," he said through what sounded like gritted teeth.

"I'm sorry," I mumbled, my muscles so tense they hurt. Was it safe for me to move? The way Andrew had hurried, he didn't care where his feet landed. "I thought you were in trouble."

"I wasn't." He hit his forehead again and exhaled sharply. "Jesus Christ."

Andrew snatched my flashlight out of my hand and marched to the side of the sarcophagus. He pulled himself up, bent over the edge, and a moment later jumped back, gripping his torch. He returned and handed me mine.

I dropped my chin, my gaze on the floor, unable to meet his eyes. I lifted my foot, and an outline of a square came into view. *Shit*. How could I have known there was a trap button? He could have warned me.

I mustered my courage and looked up. I wished I could say Andrew's expression was unreadable. But it was quite the opposite. It was very comprehensible. His jaw was so taut, I'd likely hear his teeth cracking any second, and his usually kind eyes were ablaze with irritation.

"There's probably a release shaft or something," I whispered. He stared at me.

Andrew's gaze went to my shoulder. His eyebrows pulled together. "Where is your backpack?"

I tilted my head in the door's direction, a cocktail of guilt and stupidity slashing in my brain. "Out there."

Half of our food and water supplies.

The rifle too.

Not that we'd need it in a closed-in stone box with two dead bodies.

Andrew dropped his head. "Bloody great." He took a deep breath. I winced, getting ready to be on the receiving end of a shit storm of unpleasantries that was coming my way. "I placed the satellite phone into your bag," he said in a low voice.

I needed a second to process that. He did what?

"Why would you do that?" I barked and stepped back. I didn't care if I pressed another button and the entire floor collapsed.

"In case something happened to me," he said, still not raising his voice. "In case we got separated." He groaned.

"God, you have proved to have a talent for creating difficulties. First, you put on the bracelet, and now you've locked us in the bloody tomb."

That stung. Earlier, he was glad I'd tagged along with him on this trip.

"You should warn me when you do things like that," I yelled, throwing my hands up.

"I thought you saw me doing it last night, and I also didn't think you'd follow me in here." He looked somewhere past my shoulder, shaking his head.

"You didn't answer when I called your name, and you were struggling."

Andrew's eyes locked with mine, and his nostrils flared. "If I'd heard you," he said in a controlled tone, "I'd have answered."

Shouldn't he be in a frenzy of furious rage? Tearing me apart? Shouting at me? I could *clearly* see he was annoyed with me, but why was he trying to be composed? I was the one who had made a mistake, and I wanted to pound on his chest as if it was his fault.

"Why aren't you yelling at me?"

Andrew lowered to the ground and planted his elbows on his knees. "I'm saving my strength."

With his eyes closed, Andrew rested his chin on his linked fingers, grasping the flashlight, the beam pointing at the front wall of the coffin. It had a design of steps leading up to a door with a double-sloped roof in Roman or Greek style with a decorative pedestal placed on the pediment. There were inscriptions at the bottom and at the top. I wanted to ask what they said, but it was probably best to let Andrew stew for a while.

Fear and guilt bottled up in my chest as I padded in the opposite direction and slid to the floor with my back to the wall. I fought the sob wedged in my throat, and then my chin quivered. I should have hugged William before leaving instead of kissing his forehead. The thought of him was like a blow to my gut, and the sob burst from my mouth. With trembling fingers, I fished out my phone from a pocket, and the home screen came to life with a photo of William and me, laughing our asses off at his last birthday celebration in Savannah. Hot tears spilled down my cheeks. I wiped them with my grungy dressing on my forearm. I'd miss seeing his face and hearing his jabbing remarks. Because of my stupidity, we would never go on another spontaneous trip or watch a cheesy movie while talking over each other. But at least he was safe. God, I never thought I would be glad he'd hurt his ankle.

I hit the back of my head on the cold granite. My karma had a wicked sense of humor, and she'd outdone herself this time. I drew in a shuddering breath and put my forehead to my knees.

An hour passed, or maybe even more, before the shock of the situation started wearing off. The entire time, Andrew and I sat in stale silence, the dust particles flowing in the beam of our flashlights.

What would come first: death from thirst or a burst bladder because there was no way in hell I'd pee locked in a room with Andrew? I shook my head. I shouldn't think about that. I should channel my energy into something else instead, like chiseling our way out of here. Sitting and sobbing was unproductive. If I were to die here, I would die trying to find the way out. My hand twisted the bracelet, loosely dangling on my wrist. I didn't need it anymore.

Taking it off, I shuffled to Andrew's backpack, unzipped its front pocket, and carefully lowered it in. Then I circled the white marble casket, not daring to climb it and check what was inside.

All four sides were decorated with magnificent works of art. The right side had a garden with fruits and blooming bushes, a man and a woman with two small children on either side. Augustine and Maria with their sons. And everywhere there were birds. In the skies. On trees. On the ground. In the hand of each boy.

The back side had a design of the same birds facing each other that we had found on the tile at Erizo at Las Loma. The left side had the carving of the palace from the sketch: the building that we were in. I traced my fingers over the curves and valleys of its roof and turrets. The details were unbelievably vivid. It would have been a beautiful place to live.

When I'd made a full circle, Andrew crouched by the front of the sarcophagus. His eyebrows furrowed, and his eyes narrowed as he concentrated on the design. At least my last days would be in the company of a handsome man who probably regretted his earlier words that he was glad I'd come on this trip.

"You're staring at me," Andrew said without lifting his eyes to mine.

"Yes, I am, because there's nothing else pretty to look at." I bent and picked up his hat and dusted off the cobwebs.

"Again, I'm very sorry for … messing up." Andrew hummed, thinking, his teeth grazing his bottom lip.

I placed the hat on my head and returned to the locked door. The bracelet was the key to unlocking this vault. From outside. Inside there were no holes in the wall for me to push my hand through. Why would Augustine need to shut the door from the inside if only the dead were here? To keep zombies from leaving? I scoffed. This space was designed to be a safe. And only later must have been converted into a crypt. The trap must have been original to the design. What was the purpose of it?

What if it was also a panic room?

"There must be a way out of here." I spun around to look at Andrew. "Maybe one of these blocks is a button of some sort?" Of course, one of them could also be a "release the booby traps" button. Crap. I wasn't sure I liked Andrew's job. He should stick to teaching if we get out of here.

He hummed again. "All right." He rose to his full height.

"All right, what?" I peered at him.

Andrew took a step toward me, removed his hat from my head, and placed it on his. "You promised me a kiss." He palmed the back of my neck and took over my mouth with his. It both surprised and electrified me. But as much as I loved the feel of his soft lips, I was also very much confused. I broke our kiss.

"I'm lost. First, shouldn't you be outraged and not make out with me? And second, is this a goodbye kiss?"

"I was mad. Yes, you should have listened to me, but you didn't lock us in intentionally." Andrew's breath ghosted over my lips. "I believe I know the way out."

A new energy and relief surged within me. I arched backward. "Where?"

Andrew pointed the flashlight at the design with the door and the stairs. "Through that."

I narrowed my eyes at the inscription. "Is that what it says?"

"It says, 'Everything I lived for is here with me. My only love, my most treasured.'"

"That's sweet Augustine called Maria his most treasured, but I hoped it said something like 'push the second stone down to the left and the door opens.'"

"Don't worry, there will be pushing."

Andrew ran his hand over the groove where the sarcophagus's front-facing wall met its side ones. He handed me his flashlight, then propped his shoulder into the corner of the marble crate. I had no doubt Andrew could lift or move many heavy objects, but there was no way he could shift this massive box. Even if we tried together, we couldn't do it.

"What are you doing?" I asked.

"Trying to slide this panel." Andrew pushed with his legs, his thigh muscles straining against the fabric of his pants. His boots skidded on the floor. He braced his right leg against the wall and pushed harder.

The sound of stone scraping against stone mixed with Andrew's deep growl, and air wheezed through a one-inch opening.

"It's working." I wanted to clap with joy.

"Christ." Andrew slumped to the ground, his chest rising and dropping fast. "This is not easy."

He took several breaths and twisted on his butt. Leaning

his back to the wall, he planted his feet on the side of the panel. He clenched his teeth and tried to straighten his legs. Dropping the flashlights, I reeled to the other side and gripped the panel's edge, my nails painfully digging into the stone. Pushing with my foot on the coffin I used every bit of my strength to tug. We struggled until the heavy panel gave in and, with a harsh grating groan, slid open.

My pulse drummed in my neck as I picked up my flashlight and sidled to assess the portal—most likely to hell—we'd just uncovered. A cool, clammy draft ruffled the ghostly cobwebs in a dark passage with straight stairs leading deeper down into the bowels of the building. Andrew grabbed his backpack off the ground and stepped to me.

"The machete or the rifle would be nice to have," Andrew muttered and waved his hand. "Ladies first." *Yeah.* I shook my head. "Just kidding." He ducked into the opening.

Andrew and I had to bend our heads as we descended the staircase sidled by bare granite walls, the never-ending spiderwebs piling up on Andrew's hat like a dirty bridal veil.

"How exactly did you figure out there was a passage?" I peeled a grim mesh off my face.

"The inside of the sarcophagus is sloped and about half a meter deeper on the front side." Andrew straightened as he stopped on the last step. "And the door design with inscriptions was a giveaway."

At that moment a loud bang like a bomb went off behind me, jolting my body. My heart slammed against my chest as the debris of rocks hit my back and head, and a dust cloud ceased my breathing.

Chapter Twenty-Nine

ndrew struggled to his feet and then hauled me up. He cradled my face. Over the ringing in my ears, I could barely make out what he said. An inch-sized cut bled above his left eyebrow.

"You hurt?" I peered up at his face cast in shadows. Our flashlights were somewhere on the ground behind us.

"I'm okay. Are you?"

"Did we set off a trap?" My words scraped my throat. Andrew blinked slowly and swayed. His hands slid to my arms, his fingers tightening around them. My hand went to his hips to stabilize him. He must have banged his head hard when we'd tumbled. "You need to sit down."

"I'm fine." Andrew turned to look up the staircase.

Through the settling dust, bright lights flickered, and silhouettes shifted. I swallowed, and my ears popped. The noise of gravel crunching under multiple boots grated on my nerves. Hairs rippled down my back, when I realized we hadn't triggered a trap. A blast had taken out the door in the room above.

"Anybody alive?" Richard's flashlight blinded me, and I raised my hand to block it.

"Are you out of your goddamn mind?" Andrew shouted. "You could have killed us."

Richard stepped off the last step. "But I didn't."

Rage churned inside of me at the sight of the scoundrel.

Tweedledee shadowed Dickhead, his bald noggin reflecting a light coming from behind them. My heart dropped into the pit of my stomach. William slowly limped down into the cave. Brandon, Brie, and Tweedledum trailed after him, a headlamp strapped to his shaved head.

When William entered the space, tears blurred my vision. I dashed to him and threw my arms around his neck. "I thought I'd never see you again." He staggered, embracing me. I drew back for an instant to confirm that I was looking at his handsome face. I hugged William tight again. He shouldn't be here, but damn it if I wasn't happy to see him.

"Why are you here?" I leaned away to peer at him, not ready to let go of him.

"It was *my* idea to join Andrew on a treasure hunt, right? I'm sorry I told them the location coordinates." He smiled, but it was a weak attempt. He winced. "You might not want to put too much pressure on me. My foot is killing me."

A fresh swell of rage rose in me, and I faced Dickhead. "My brother is hurt. Why did you make him hike?"

The abundance of light chased the blackness, and the area came into full view. It resembled an old underground mine with two wood-framed passages about ten yards away. Four hefty beams with symbols carved into the wood propped a timbered ceiling. The bare stone walls had clusters of shimmering quartz and garnets.

Richard looked over his shoulder and then shrugged. "Extra collateral."

"It was you last night in the jungle," Andrew said in a terse tone.

Richard strolled to the closest post and studied a ship carving.

"No. It was Igor and Vitali." He pointed at the pole. "Have you already figured out the meanings of these marks?"

Andrew bent and reached for his hat. "For once, you can do your own work instead of taking advantage of mine."

"It's easier this way."

Andrew stepped in Dickhead's direction, but the neckless Tweedledee directed a gun at him. A fear pushed through me. I had no doubt the dumbass wouldn't hesitate to pull the trigger.

"No need for a confrontation." Brie placed her hand on the gun, lowering it. "Andy, we tried to be nice. We offered a cut of our share. But you didn't want it." She sashayed to Andrew and placed her palm on his abdomen, then it slid down, her finger hooking over his belt buckle. His forehead furrowed. My stomach hardened with jealousy. "How about we make a different deal? You help us find Augustine's loot, and we divide it. Your precious museum can have some; our client will have the rest. Simple."

Andrew breathed heavily, his nostrils flared, as he gripped Brie's wrist and pushed her hand away from him. "How about a hard no?"

Brie tilted her head, her lips pulling into a pout. "Oh, Andy, don't be that way."

"Stop fucking calling him Andy," I bit off and snatched the flashlight off the ground.

She gawked at me first, then snorted a dry laugh, showing off a row of pearl-white teeth. "I can call him whatever I want. Don't forget, he was mine before he was yours." Her chin thrust forward, and she pushed her enormous boobs out. The haughtiest expression took over her face. "I told Andy 'I love you' in six different languages. Can you do that?"

Earlier anger at them being here and having taken William hostage turned into red fury. My face flooded with heat, and my fingers tightened over the metal in my hand. I had never been in a fight, but there was always a first time for everything. Yet the better half of me understood that Brie's flirtatious behavior was primarily her trying to provoke me, pushing my buttons, wanting me to show my ugly side. I wouldn't give her the satisfaction.

"It doesn't matter how you said it because you didn't show it," I said, trying to sound irate and not wounded.

"That's enough, Brie," Richard snapped. "Let's focus on the important things."

"Fine." Andrew pointed at the two passages. The light reflected off a small golden statuette on the wall at each entrance. "We divide and conquer. Whoever finds it first keeps the most. Which way do you pick? Left or right?"

What was he doing? I approached him and arched an eyebrow, silently asking what the actual hell. Andrew's eyes searched mine, his lips curling up. Had he figured out something but couldn't share?

"Andy, what game are you playing?" Brie crossed her arms.

"I'm being fair. There are two ways to get out of here." He walked to the second torch on the ground and picked it up. He cleaned the grit of the glass lens. "And Brie, it's Dr. Jones to you, not Andy."

She rolled her eyes.

I looked at Brandon. "Will you stay here with my brother, please?"

"No," Brie snapped. "He's coming with us."

I swirled around. "He's hurt. He shouldn't be here in the first place."

"He made it this far just fine. He can continue for a while more."

"Briana," Brandon spoke, and I noticed a few days-old purple bruises under his right eye. "With all due respect, this is not the best idea. He'll slow you down. We'll wait for you here."

"What happened to you?" I asked.

Brandon's hand went to his face. "Igor's farewell gift."

"Huh?"

"He quit working for these assholes, and they didn't like it." William leaned against the wall, balancing on his good foot.

"We all go. Andrew, lead the way, or I'll shoot her." Richard withdrew a gun and pointed it at me. For fuck's sake, were they all armed? The muscles in my throat tightened, and I stepped back.

"Don't be an idiot," Andrew said.

"Now!" Richard yelled, his arm went up, and the gun fired

with a deafening bang. I clenched my head and ducked, expecting the bullet to ricochet.

One of the ugly twins snorted and said something in Russian. The pungent smell of burnt sulfur tainted my scent. My heart pounded in my ribcage as I straightened and surveyed William, then Andrew. They didn't seem to be hurt.

"You bloody imbecile!" Andrew shouted, his nostrils flaring.

"You need to take me seriously." Dickhead motioned with the gun. "Which way?"

Muscles in Andrew's jaw ticked, and he squared his shoulders. "I don't know. Adriana is the only one who knows it."

My mouth dropped open. "No. I don't."

"Yes, love, you do." He inclined his head. "The path. You remember it, don't you?"

Different thoughts sped like race cars: the Pérez family letters, Andrew's journals, carvings in the Iglesia San Antonio undercroft, outside the vault, Augustine's sketches. And then, at last, the file I made in Photoshop in which I'd combined the two strange drawings.

Sweat developed under my breasts. I could see it almost clearly, but it would be nice to look at it again. The phone was in my back pocket and my fingers itched to check it, but I resisted. These jackasses shouldn't be made aware that we had a map. Well, sort of. We didn't know the meaning of all the squiggly lines and markings. Those indications could mean anything. Right way. Wrong way. Dead end. Danger.

"Richard, I don't trust whatever they're doing." Brie scowled at me.

My eyes cut to her. "Unlike you, not everything I do has an agenda."

I went up to the passages. A cool breeze tugged on my loose strands of hair as I examined each gold statuette. The left one was a round-faced boy, sitting on his knees and cradling two birds in his hands. The other one looked like a kiwi bird picking grass at its feet. The Pérez family for sure was cuckoo for feathered creatures. Was this bird statue a symbol for anything? Upon closer examination, I noticed the bird's beak pierced a snake.

If I had to make a wild guess, I'd say the kid was a safer choice. But what if their meanings were purposely counterintuitive? Seconds stretched as my eyes darted between the figurines. I took a shaky breath through my mouth.

"We go this way," I said, gingerly stepping into the left tunnel, the flashlight beam quickly disappearing into the eerie darkness.

Everyone shadowed me: Andrew, Richard, and Brie, William wobbling after them, and Brandon following him. Tweedledee and Tweedledum trooped last. Gratitude that Brandon had decided to work against Dr. Dickhead, mixed with guilt at my failure to believe William about Brandon, twisted my stomach like it housed snakes. Or maybe it was anxiety about what would happen when we found the treasure. Would they let us go? Hurt us? Kill us? Cold sweat covered my forehead at that thought.

The path veered to the right and then went straight and appeared not to hold any danger, just an occasional cobweb. Nevertheless, I had seen enough movies to know negligence could kill me, so I watched where I stepped and paid attention to my surroundings for suspicious cracks or outlines with hidden traps.

A minute later, we piled into an ample circular space, its walls and ceiling lined with square stone blocks, a granite pedestal in the center, and four passages. On top of the stand was a golden statue of an anaconda twisted around a bearded man. His massive hands gripped its head as if he was choking it. Two red gemstones were in place of the snake's eyes. By the expression on the man's face, one could guess he was losing the battle. Was this a warning? A sign of a giant snake slithering in these caves? A shiver ran over me. I liked the bird statues much better.

I spun around the room, unable to remember a ring with four paths on the image. Needing to refresh my memory, I slowly skirted the pedestal and fished out my phone.

"What are you doing?" Brie asked, pushing her way to me.

I tilted the iPhone to my chest. "I want to take a photo of this. Isn't it breathtaking?"

She narrowed her eyes. "You didn't take photos of the first statues."

"They weren't that interesting." I shrugged while my fingers glided over my screen, searching for the correct image. I found it and soaked up the details. There weren't any circles. But there was a narrow passage—presumably the one we took—followed by a gap with a strikeout square in the center—the pedestal. Several millimeters above it were four routes.

Brie's thin fingers latched onto my phone, and she yanked on it. My grip strengthened, lurching my hand out of her hold. She might have had bigger boobs and a toned body, but I was much stronger than she was, and our height difference benefitted me.

"Give it to me," she commanded.

"Come and get it."

Richard advanced on me.

Andrew went after him.

Vitali caught Andrew's backpack and dead-legged him, knocking Andrew to the ground.

I smashed the iPhone screen on the pedestal edge.

Everyone stilled, their wide eyes on me.

"Why would you do that?" William howled.

The action shocked my system.

Blood hammered in my ears. I wiped sweat off my forehead, dirt scraping my skin. "Because now I'm the only one who knows the way around this hellhole." Did this put me in more or less danger?

"You stupid bitch!" Brie barked.

My palms closed into fists, and I fought the urge to boob-punch her.

Andrew got up and fixed the bag straps on his shoulders. He stepped up to Tweedledee. "Do something like that again, and you won't leave here alive."

"Save your threats. Vitali doesn't understand English." Brie ambled to Richard. Taking him by his forearm, she steered him towards one passage, stopping shy of its entrance. They colluded in hush tones, him casting a sideways glance at me. My stomach twisted into a knot. Whatever they were talking about wouldn't play out well for us.

Andrew gently guided me aside. He lowered his mouth to my ear. "You all right?"

"Yes," I whispered, pressing my damped face to his stubbed cheek. "The paths lead to the same place. Some just—"

Brie said something in Russian. Igor and Vitali nodded, their eyes cutting to Andrew and then me.

"Okay." Richard pushed his crusty blond hair back off his forehead. "Which way?"

I eyed each entryway. The image showed all routes feeding into one location. The left one had too many markings, which could mean nothing good. The right one had a break in the line. That could signify anything from a not easily crossed ravine, to an impenetrable obstruction, to something as simple as the graphite had rubbed off over the years and the passage was safe. The two in the middle, which had much larger gateways, had shorter paths with fewer symbols.

More sweat beaded over my skin. The air in the cave was surprisingly warm, or maybe it was the stress of working under the threat of death by gunshot, of an enormous snake that might or might not live here, or of being lost in the cavern labyrinth forever.

"This one." I pointed with my flashlight at the second opening to the right.

"And why is that?" Richard asked.

I looked over my shoulder. "Because I want to live and the others present challenges."

Andrew leaned in and kissed my temple. "Do you want me to go first?"

I might know the way, but it didn't mean I was brave enough to be the leader. I nodded, taking his hand into mine.

He took cautious steps, and I followed him.

Brie appeared at my side, her shoulder grazing my arm. "I don't trust you," she hissed.

"The feeling is mutual," I retorted.

We were ten feet into the passage when Brandon screamed, "Igor, no!"

A breath lodged in my throat, and I turned, my fingers slipping out of Andrew's. Richard, William, and Tweedledum were with us but Brandon and Tweedledee were somewhere back in the room.

There was a loud creak, then a bam. The floor dropped out from beneath me.

Chapter Thirty

I skidded on a jagged surface, then fell several feet to the ground. Excruciating pain shot through my shoulder, and I cried out. Another body slammed hard into me, knocking the wind out of me.

Brie moaned.

I groaned.

Out of everyone, why did it have to be her?

With a grunt, I rolled, pushing her sack-of-potatoes body off me. My breath rushed back in. "Shiiiiittt."

My first thought was that I had dislocated or possibly broken my shoulder. The right sleeve of my shirt was wet. Please don't be an open break. I reached for it with my other hand and touched my skin—the sleeve was gone—then brought my finger up to my nose. It wasn't blood, just wet dirt. If I found the way out of here alive, I never wanted to go into or think about another cave.

Blinking into the almost pitch-black space, I took in the hell basement we'd just landed in. Next to me, a colossal stalagmite stretched upwards. I cursed again. If I'd landed a yard to my right, I'd have died.

I turned my head the other way. Brie was curled into the fetal position and quietly sobbing.

"Are you hurt?" I asked. It was a stupid question. We were thrown like rag dolls down the jagged surface. Of course, she was hurt. Her response was a squeak.

"Anything broken?" I asked.

She whimpered. "I think I broke my back."

Excellent. The last thing I needed was to take care of her.

"Can you move?" I lifted on my elbows, ignoring the agonizing pain in my shoulder.

She slowly shifted, letting out a few sobs. "Yes, I can."

"Then you're probably fine."

"Are you a bloody doctor?"

Before collecting our flashlights, which were several feet away from us, I took a moment to check my body for injuries: scuffed knees visible through torn pants, scraped arm, and hurt shoulder. Everything else seemed to be okay.

With a great effort, I stood up, staggered and nearly fell. My hands shot for the stalagmite, and I managed to stay upright. I stumbled to our flashlights and picked them up. Mine had a cracked lens, but it worked. Leaning against a timber pillar that supported the mountain overhead, I surveyed the space.

The damp cavern held no skeletons. We must have been the first ones who'd fallen through the floor trap, or maybe the others had made it out of here alive. Or didn't and their remains were somewhere lost in the tunnels.

All I saw was more rock, stalactites, stalagmites, limestone columns, and passages. And a door. The misshapen wood frame door with an iron ring handle looked like something I had seen on a tour of the gold mines out west. I stilled. It made little sense why someone would build a trap just to let their victim leave. My scalp tingled with discomfort. Maybe it was another ha-ha-gotcha trap, or maybe we weren't meant to have survived the fall. I strained my neck to look up, and then my eye landed on the sharp stone sticking out of the ground, Brie flat on her back close to it. Were we lucky, or was it a design miscalculation? I shook my head. It didn't matter. We'd survived.

The beam I was leaning against groaned and creaked faintly. Perhaps putting pressure on a few centuries-old structures was a bad idea. Giving myself several seconds until the pain subdued, I carefully pushed off it and wobbled to the door, dropping Brie's flashlight near her as I passed.

The door bulged outward as if something was pressing on it from the inside. Wood could bow, but I was sure this wasn't an unbalanced drying problem. Better leave it alone. We'd return to it as our last option.

Brie was lying on the floor, eyes closed.

"Can you walk?" I asked. "We have to find the way out of here."

Her chin wobbled, and she turned her face away. "How did this happen?"

I peered up, my flashlight revealing the outlines of the trap. "I'd guess Igor picked up that statue and set this off."

Did others also fall into other traps, or had they been lucky? My heart squeezed at the thought of William having to deal with more troubles. Taking a deep breath, I expanded my lungs and yelled. "Andrew! William! Can you hear me?" My words echoed before fading into the void, but no one called back. I tried again and again.

"Oh my God," Brie said. "Stop yelling. You're hurting my head."

"Maybe they can hear us," I rasped.

"Obviously they can't. Otherwise, they would have answered." She moaned. "So shut up."

"You shut up!" I glared down at the skinny asshole on the floor, and rage rose in me. Would it be wrong for me to kick her? Just lightly? "Get up and let's explore," I said with anger.

She rolled on her side, stuffing her arm under her head. "Can't we wait for them to find us? Or maybe you can climb and try to open it back up?"

I scoffed. I liked how *I* had to climb, not us or her. "I'm not Spiderman. Without a ladder, there's no way for us to reach that wall." I pointed with the flashlight to the edge of the suspended sloping wall we'd slid down before dropping about twenty feet.

"Can't you at least try?"

I rolled my eyes. "Do I have to tell you in six different languages that there is no fucking way to get up there?" I stepped over her. "You stay here, and I'll go."

I walked to the enlarged tunnel, which had man-made chisel marks. Could this lower cave be another passage network that led to and from the palace? It wasn't all just nature; it had many human touches: cut stone, timber framework, leftover lumber. What if these were emerald mines? Colombia was famous for the precious gem. I just didn't know if we were in the right part of the country. If we were, maybe Pérez made his fortune by robbing other ships, but this was the primary source of his wealth and the reason for keeping it so secretive.

The moan, then shuffling behind me, made me turn. Brie slowly approached me. Her light brown pants were torn at her thigh, and her blouse had a gaping hole around her right boob. She wore a lacy bra. I wouldn't wear these kinds of bras unless it was a special occasion or cold weather so I could hide the unevenness of the fabric.

"I don't want to stay here alone."

One of her front teeth has broken off in half. Dirt covered her face, and her blond hair stuck out in different directions. I winced and held in a laugh.

She scowled at me. "What is that face for?"

"I cannot be held responsible for what my face does when you're talking." I ran my tongue over my teeth. My appearance wasn't any better, but at least all my teeth were whole.

"Seriously," she snapped. "Why are you looking at me like that? You look like shit too."

I pulled a smile and pointed at my mouth. "You're missing something."

Her mean expression dropped, and her tongue touched the broken tooth. She sank to the ground, and the sound she released nearly burst my eardrums. She was an ugly crier. With every passing second, the question of what Andrew had seen in her pounded harder in my brain.

"I hate this," she wailed. "I hate Richard. He made me come on this trip!" Brie patted her face and looked at me with huge Puss in Boots eyes. "Do I look horrible?"

Something moved in my heart. Pity? I had to admit—as much as I hated it—she was still pretty, but her character ruined her beauty. Right now, she looked like a sad and tired teenager.

I shook my head. "No. You can fix that tooth when you're back in London." Would it have killed me to say more to make her feel better? Yes. I didn't like her and wasn't trying to become friends.

Leaving Brie to collect herself, I searched for a rock that I could use to leave markings in the tunnels. I picked up a smooth, large pebble and scraped it on the wall. It left a faint streak. I dropped it and chose a stone with sharper edges. It wouldn't fit into my pocket, but it left a fat mark when I ran it over the surface.

"What are you doing?" Brie's voice came not far behind me.

"We should indicate which way we came from so we won't get lost if we need to return. It also ensures that we aren't making an infinitive loop. Try to find a good rock or two."

To my surprise, after several minutes, Brie returned with three stones. "I'm thirsty."

Until she said that, I hadn't realized I was, too. And I needed to pee. "Maybe we'll come across an underground spring. Excuse me for a second."

Brie stood by the door when I came back. "Were you not going to tell me about this door?"

"I assumed you weren't blind and saw it yourself."

"Where does it lead?"

"What am I, Google Maps?"

"You're the one who said you knew the way around here."

"I knew the way around at the level above us." Saying I knew was a stretch, but I'd not give her the satisfaction of knowing that. My torn sleeve hung over my wrist. I ripped it off and stuffed it into my back pocket. "Ready?"

"Don't you want to check this first?" Her hand went to the handle.

"Brie, don't."

She yanked on the iron ring, and it ripped off, sending her back on her ass. The bowed door burst, releasing a flood of boulders and dirt. Fear and anger rushed through me as I watched Brie scrambling backward like a crab in horror. The rockslide stopped shy of her boots. Thank goodness. The last thing I needed was for her to get more hurt and slow me down. My heart insisted Andrew and William were alive, and I was determined to find my way out of this and find my men. I wanted to hug William, and I needed to feel Andrew's warmth.

"There, now you know!" I snapped. "It's a dead end. You can follow me or try to dig your way through that."

I was expecting her to say something snarky, but instead, she got up and dusted her butt off as if that could make her pants any cleaner. "Fine."

Our footprints left a trail behind as we followed the cave vein, leaving marks at every turn. Every so often, we passed lanterns, which meant someone had used these tunnels before. Twice, we came through the same intersection. It was our only stopping point to rest before continuing into a different passage. After some time, we came to an open space with trickling water on one side. My mouth turned cotton-dry at the sight. I rushed to it and pressed my hands into the cold wetness, then without thought, I brought my lips to it. Water ran down my chin, neck, and chest, soaking my clothes.

"What if it's bad?" Brie yanked on my arm. "You can die."

I didn't care. This unfiltered, full of earth minerals—and maybe some bacteria—water was the best thing I'd ever tasted, better than the complex Opus One cabernet.

"God, this is good." I wiped my face. "Drink. This might be your last chance."

Brie wrinkled her nose and shook her head. I shrugged. Cupping my hands, I washed my face and neck, feeling the earlier pain and fatigue wane. It was like coming home after a long, strenuous day at work and taking a lukewarm shower.

Rejuvenated, I stepped back, not bothering to wipe the water drops off my skin. "You don't know what you're missing."

"Can we continue now?" Brie jerked her chin at the path.

I pulled my flashlight from my back pocket where I'd stuffed it earlier. "Okay."

The route went straight for a while, and then we rounded four bends. After another turn, we entered a deep passageway with a neck-breaking vaulted ceiling. A foot-wide fissure in the ground divided the path. Neither Brie nor I would fit through to fall to our death, but the issue was the further the pathway went, the wider the crack became, separating the walkway into two paths hugging the rock.

"Look at that," Brie said, her voice echoed off the surrounding rock.

I turned and looked where she was pointing above my head.

A stone lantern was built into the wall. From it, a chiseled-in half pipe ran along the path on both sides. It was like old-fashioned runway landing lights. I cautiously lifted my hand

382

and touched inside. I rubbed my fingers together, they were covered in a blackish fine powder mixed with grit and dust. This must have been some burning goo they used to light the way.

"This is so cool." I wiped my hand on my pants. "This has got to be the right way."

"Can we light it up?"

I arched an eyebrow. "Do you have a lighter?"

I doubted the flaming compound would burn after hundreds of years even if she did.

"No. Do you?"

"I'm not Inspector Gadget. Besides this," I raised my flashlight, "I've got nothing."

"Why are you so sardonic all the time? Either say nothing or give a valid answer." Her lips went into a flat line.

"Around you, sarcasm is all I know." I turned my focus onto which side to pick.

"Which way do you think we should go?" I asked, not sure why.

Brie hummed. "Left."

I went right.

"Oh my god." She threw her hands up. "Why ask if you weren't going to take my advice?"

"I tried to be nice and hoped you'd say right, so you'd think it was your decision."

First, we walked side by side, but soon Brie shuffled behind me. The gap in the ravine grew the deeper we went, and the path narrower.

"How long have you known Andy?" she asked. I rolled my eyes at the way she used that nickname again. She did it to irritate me, but I wouldn't give her the satisfaction to see it bothered me.

"Feels like my whole life," I said honestly.

A yearning unwrapped in my aching heart. Andrew and I had been together just shy of two weeks, but I was sure he was my soulmate. I could no longer deny that I was in love with him. I had to tell him that. And I had to tell him I would move to the South Pole as long as we could be together.

"You can stop your pretense that you're married. You aren't even engaged to him."

I haltered but then kept going. How did she know it?

"Why would you think that?" I said, cautiously navigating a new turn. By now, the paths ran parallel, a six-foot, dark, deep gap splitting them.

"Andy said he would propose with his grandmama's engagement ring. It's some old Victorian junk."

My stomach hardened with jealousy that Andrew had spoken to her about engagement. I also couldn't believe she called it junk. Then a swell of tenderness expanded in my chest. I was sure it was beautiful, and I wouldn't expect anything less of Andrew. He'd ask for marriage with a ring that was special to him.

"Why would you even pretend?" Brie said. "It's so stupid."

"What does it matter to you?" What I wanted to ask was why he'd even told her. Had he been thinking of marrying her?

"Just curious. Are you engaged to someone else?"

"No." I am not a cheater like you. "This is my man repellent."

The vertigo-inducing pathway narrowed to the point I wasn't comfortable walking without my shoulder grazing the cliff. One misstep could plunge me into the cleft. I pressed my back against the cold stone and shuffled my feet sideways, my left-hand fingers clinging to every crevice and cranny.

"Does it work?"

"When a man is a pig, nothing can stop him."

"That's so true."

Who would have guessed that we'd agree on something? It didn't mean we were BFFs, but it gave me a boost to ask something that had bugged me for a while. "Why did you leave Andrew for Richard?" Out of all the men you had to pick from, I wanted to add.

Brie was silent for a while as we carefully navigated. Was she coming up with a great excuse? Or did she know there weren't any.

"I was lonely," she finally said. "His parents had died, and he was sad for months. Yes, it sucked, but I thought he'd get better after a while. And then Charlotte gave birth and he moved her and her daughter into his house. He also gave up his inheritance to some educational charity." She sighed dramatically. "Do you know how much money that was?"

"I don't care," I said with a bitter tone. My leg ached to trip Brie and let the dark ravine swallow her.

"Well, it was a lot. I was already getting tired of his gallantry. Gifting that money was the last straw for me. I was angry with him and went to a pub. Richard was there. And one thing led to another."

Regret for asking stabbed in my gut because I hated this woman more than I did five minutes ago. And I was afraid I would find a way to hurt her.

I made another turn and haltered to a stop. "Shit."

A treacherous wooden walkway haphazardly pieced together out of planks replaced our granite path for several feet. There was no way to cross it in one move.

"What is it?" Brie asked, most likely afraid to lean in and look around me. I didn't blame her.

"It's a bridge. About six feet long."

"What?"

Could it hold us?

Pressing my body hard into the stone, I bent my shaky knees and slid down into a squat. I probed the planks with the hard edge of my flashlight. It felt solid. My hands changed the hold of the torch and shook the bridge with my hand.

"Can we walk on it?"

"We'll find out." I gradually straightened. My heart beat dangerously hard. I tapped with my right foot lightly on the bridge, then pushed harder. The bridge held together. Good start. "If I die and you make it, please tell Andrew and William I love them. And tell Andrew I'd move to England."

"So, you're not only sarcastic, you're also a pessimist?"

"I'm a realist."

I scrutinized the bridge once more. Slow or fast? Or did it even matter? Was it all about the weight? If I moved fast, there was a better chance I could cross to the other side before it collapsed. I studied the wood planks for a while, then turned off my flashlight and secured it into my bra.

"Are you crazy?" Brie hissed. "You can't see."

"I feel better if I have free hands. Shine your torch so I can see where to step."

Sweat soaked into the back of my shirt as I made the first step with my right foot. The bridge groaned but didn't tremble.

My feet, however, did—a lot. I placed my left foot on it and held my breath, my palms flat against the wall, fingers digging into narrow cracks.

Okay. Now. Move faster.

Right foot. Left foot. Right foot. The plank cracked.

"Fuck," I screamed, adrenaline propelling me to do a broad side jump. My body molded into the wall, and my chest heaved.

With trembling fingers, I pulled out my flashlight and turned it on.

"Your turn," I said, my voice shaking.

"If I die, it will be on your conscience," Brie muttered, stuffing her flashlight between her boobs.

"Nobody asked you to follow me," I said hoarsely between breaths.

"I said we should pick the left side."

"You're welcome to go back."

"Fuck you."

I laughed, but inside of me, everything trembled, and I wanted to cry.

Facing the ravine, Brie first shimmied slowly, then more quickly.

Right foot. Left foot. Right foot ... straight through the wood.

Her high-pitched scream ricocheted off the walls. She bent forward and her flashlight flew out into the ravine. I grabbed her forearm and yanked her backward, hot pain piercing through my shoulder. She stumbled but pulled her leg out and landed on the edge of the stone path, throwing her head and back into the wall.

"This place is a death trap," Brie said when she caught her breath.

"No shit."

A nervous laugh bubbled up in me. Brie started laughing too. Like idiots, we laughed until tears streamed down our cheeks. I wiped my nose. She wiped hers, too. If Brie and I became friends, we could reminisce about this adventure over tequila shots in years to come. But it would never happen.

Several minutes passed before we felt ready to move forward. After another few feet, luck smiled upon us, and the footpath widened to where we could walk normally. Me leading. Her following. The pathway on the other side dead-ended into a wall. I took pleasure in pointing that out with the flashlight. Brie flipped me off. The passage became at least three yards wide, but we stayed close to the wall.

After a turn, a distant babel reached my ears. I froze, closed my eyes, and concentrated. The thrill expanded in my ribcage to the point it hurt. I could distinguish Andrews's voice. My heart raced faster than when I had to cross the goddam wooden walkway.

"Do you hear that?" I whispered.

"I do," Brie said, her voice for once laced with enthusiasm. "Where are they?"

My eyes darted everywhere, following the light of my flashlight, searching for any open space where they could be, but finding nothing.

"Maybe it is further down?" I charged ahead, just barely restraining myself from skipping and jumping and doing a cartwheel. There would be time for it later—I hoped—when we were on solid ground. Excitement at the possibility of soon being in my brother's presence and feeling Andrew's embrace moved my legs at a rapid pace.

A cool breeze caught me off guard when I came across a hole in the wall large enough for an adult to climb freely into. Their voices traveled out much clearer, but so did another uproar. A rush of water. A river. A waterfall. I couldn't understand what they were saying, but it didn't matter. They were alive. And they were somewhere up this crawling tunnel.

I stuck my head into the hole and called their names at the top of my lungs. I yelled again and again until my throat hurt. Then I listened. Blood pulsated in my ears. My stomach turned into knots. No response. But it was them. I was certain. I pushed inside.

Chapter Thirty-One

I'd forever be grateful for my knees pressing into the seat in front in economy class, for most pants being too short, for every "how's the weather up there" joke kids made in middle school, because right now my long legs were propelling me upward one step at a time. Breathless Brie, with her petite frame, lagged way below me. For every push I did, she had to do two.

After entering the opening in the wall, we had crawled on all fours several yards before it took a ninety-degree turn and went up. It was tricky to hold the flashlight and creep up, spreading all four limbs, my boots constantly sliding down smooth surfaces. Halfway up, my shoulder screamed bloody murder from the weight I was putting on it. Every minute, I had to take a break, but the further I went, the closer and more visible the opening at the end became, and the louder the sound of water grew. In my gut, I knew that it was the waterfall from Augustine's sketch. Involuntary bursts of laughter escaped me.

I'd found it.

We'd found it.

Because of the loud rush of water, I couldn't hear anyone's voice, but I hoped—I begged—Andrew and William were up there.

With another push, my hands gripped the edge of the opening and the flashlight clattered onto the stone floor. I pulled myself over, belly crawled out, and rolled onto my back. Cool droplets gently beaded on my skin. Catching my breath, I willed my heart to slow down. Another dark cave but hopefully at the same level as Andrew and William.

I'd made it.

Hot tears ran down my face. God, I was tired.

"Can you help me?" Brie called out. "I can barely hold on."

Did I have to?

I kneeled near the hole. If I leaned in, she would be within arm's reach.

"Stop staring at me and help me."

Fuck her.

I scooted away. I didn't want to be a nice person to Brie. She didn't deserve it. She was mean the entire time, she dragged my brother here, and she broke Andrew's heart when he was at his most vulnerable. I should have let her dig her way through that door.

"Please," she said with a whimper.

Clamping my eyes shut, I cursed, then rolled on my stomach and held my good arm out to her. Her cold palm pressed into mine, and my long fingers gripped her hand. I pulled her out, and she collapsed on the floor. I shifted away from her, back leaning against the wall.

After several minutes, I picked up the flashlight and studied the large underground chamber with a tall single waterfall plunging into a sizeable pool. I grinned until my cheeks hurt. Across the body of water, one corridor led to a possible way out. There were no guarantees though.

A feeling of fatigue penetrated deep into my bone marrow, but I had to find Andrew and William. I had to keep going.

"I don't think I can move," Brie moaned.

"You know six languages, but you can't say thank you in any of them?" I grumbled.

"Thank you," she said, with so much scorn I was better off without it.

I scoffed and shook my head. Perhaps spending time alone with Brie was my karma's best joke.

"I think you and Richard are a perfect pair," I said. "I wish you two life-long happiness so you can spare other people from ever getting involved with either of you." She wrinkled her forehead, showing deep creases in her skin. She needed to invest in Botox. Because once her looks faded, what would be left of her?

The tunnel began to glow with flickering lights. I inhaled a sharp breath and staggered up on my feet. My heart twisted uncomfortably, not knowing who was about to walk out. I was sure I'd heard Andrew's voice, but it could have been a prank of my fatigued mind.

The time seemed to drag on, suffocating me.

A tall, broad figure wearing a Fedora emerged from the tunnel.

"Andrew!" I yelled, waving my hands. Even though I could hardly see his eyes in the darkness, I felt our gazes connect.

"Adriana." He threw his backpack off and sprinted toward me around the water's edge.

Heart pounding, I wobbled to him, my knees shaky and my boots slipping and gliding on the slippery stone. Nothing could stop me. Every fiber in me wanted to feel Andrew against me. Hug him. Kiss him. Press my face into his neck. Tell him I would risk everything for him. Tell him I would move. Tell him that I loved him.

My body slammed into him, and his strong arms wrapped around my back, hoisting me. My legs circled his waist, and my arms looped tight around his neck. I buried my face in the side of his face, his stubble scratching against my skin. Warmth coursed through my bones and I let myself cry.

"You're safe," Andrew whispered, voice catching on words, his hold on me tightening. "I thought I'd lost you."

I shook my head, tears stringing down my face. "I found my way back to you."

"I don't ever want to be parted from you again. I'll move to Atlanta," he said, chest rising, his breath hot on my neck. "I'm in love with you."

I drew back and cradled his tired face with my hands. "And I'm in love with you."

My mouth covered his, and my tongue swept between his lips. I weaved my fingers into his thick hair. The raw, husky sound in his throat made me shudder in his arms. He angled his head to deepen the kiss. I moaned from delirious pleasure.

Andrew nibbled on my bottom lip before his hot mouth traveled to my jawline, down my neck, leaving a trail of kisses and shivers in their wake. I was as close as I could get to Andrew, and yet it was still not enough. I pressed myself harder into him. His heart hammered wildly in his chest. Mine was on the verge of exploding.

From somewhere behind Andrew, William's gentle voice dragged me into reality. "Adriana?"

My gaze landed on him and I was overcome with mixed feelings of relief he was okay and guilt that I hadn't noticed his slim figure earlier when my focus had zoomed to Andrew.

Andrew carefully released me to the ground, and I rushed to my beautiful, exhausted brother.

"Hi, handsome." I embraced him, pressing my head into his shoulder and relaxing into his warm brotherly hug. And I cried. Again.

Christ, I need to get my shit together.

William's chest shook. "I was so scared."

My nose ran. "Me too."

"I thought you were gone." He sniffled. "I thought, 'fuck, now I have to go over all her crap in my condo and see what I want to keep and what to donate.'"

I burst out laughing and looked at his dirty face, then kissed his gruff cheek. "Keep the wine. Donate the rest."

"Heavens to Betsy. You'd need a week's worth of facials to fix this." William circled my face with his finger.

"Pff. You should see yourself."

William rolled his eyes. "Oh, I know." His stare went over my shoulder. "Yech. I was hoping not to see her again."

I turned. With my flashlight in hand, Brie wobbled towards us. Her leg slipped when she was near Andrew. She swayed in his direction. He caught her arm and pushed her to stand straight.

"Thank you, Andy," she said breathlessly, her eyes hooded.

I cursed inwardly.

William leaned in. "She did it on pur—"

"I know," I whispered to him, clenching my fists.

Brie shuffled past us without making eye contact. Did I want to shove her? Hell yes. But I resisted.

Brie continued to where Richard sat on a rock, his head leaning against the wall. She sat on his lap and hugged him, pressing her forehead into his shoulder.

Brandon stood on the other side of the waterfall, studying its crest. Two people were noticeably absent. Not that I wanted to see them ever again.

"Where are Igor and Vitali?" My eyes ping-ponged between William and Andrew.

They exchanged glances, and Andrew cast his gaze to the ground, shaking his head.

"It was sad but also very touching," William said in a low voice. "Did you know they were brothers?"

I figured they were related. They had a similar ugliness to them.

"What happened?" I stared at Andrew, remembering his threat to Vitali that he wouldn't make it alive. My hand went to my throat. "You didn't…?"

"When you and Brie went down," Andrew said, "the floor under Igor's feet collapsed too, leaving him hanging on by his fingertips. Vitali rushed to him and tried to pull Igor up, and they just … fell over. We couldn't save them."

"You should look at this," Brandon called, standing behind the waterfall's curtain.

We walked to him and faced a large ship's steering wheel at the base of an elaborate pulley system that rose about fifty feet.

I craned my neck, my gaze following the thick cables that looped over massive beams and disappeared into the ceiling.

"It looks like ship parts." I ran my fingers over the helm.

"They used them because they knew they were corrosion resistant," Richard said, coming up behind us.

Andrew studied the complex network, then moved over to the right side of the helm. He gripped the handles and pushed on them. The wheel didn't move. Andrew blew out a breath and cut his eyes to Richard.

"For once, you can help."

"I don't do heavy lifting unless I'm asked." Richard stepped over to the other side. Together, they yanked harder on the wheel. They made two more attempts, each making inhuman groans, before the wheel whined, gave in, and rotated a few degrees. The pulleys returned to life with creaks and screeches. My sweaty hands clutched William's forearm, my muscles going tense all over, expecting the worst. Based on everything that had happened since we'd arrived at the ruins, I was allowed to think something was about to misfire.

Andrew and Richard continued turning the helm. The gush of the water over the crest of the waterfall lessened and soon turned into a dribble.

"Adriana," Andrew said, his voice strained. "See that rope?" He jerked his head to his left. "Pull it to me." I jumped into action, my feet slipping on the moist rock. I dragged the cable to him. "Loop it and tie it into a bowline knot."

I gave him a blank stare. "How would I know how to do that?"

"I'll do it." Brandon's hands quickly worked the rope around the wooden spoke. When he was done, he stepped back. Richard and Andrew let go of the wheel at once. The line strained, holding the helm in place.

"Now what?" I asked, my flashlight bouncing from wall to wall in search of a new portal or the reason for cutting off the water. Everything looked the same.

"I see it!" William shouted, pointing down into the pool. I scrambled to him, and my heart skipped a beat when multiple chests and crates came into view at the base of the pond.

"We found it!" I yelled, catching Andrew's eyes across the cave. He beamed, and I mirrored his grin.

"We split it fifty-fifty," Brie said, her voice chafing my raw nerves the wrong way.

The floor beneath us trembled, causing my breathing to cease.

"You feel that?" William turned to me, wide-eyed. I nodded.

The pond bubbled, gurgled, and rapidly dropped, exposing all of Augustine's loot. Gold bars in open crates reflected light from our flashlights. Chests were stacked three high.

Unblinking, I stared at the twenty or maybe thirty wooden trunks, the shock of it all rooting me to the ground. Were they all full of gold? If so, my goodness, the find was priceless.

When the water had finished draining, Dickhead slid on his ass to the bottom, whooping at the top of his lungs. William made a step towards the treasure, but I placed my hand on his shoulder, shaking my head.

"Don't," I said in a low voice.

I worried Richard could pull a last-minute dick move. He didn't seem to have his gun with him, but that didn't mean he didn't have a knife strapped to his ankle.

With the tail of his flashlight, Dickhead struck a padlock, then threw the lid open. He made another whooping cry, spreading his hands over the shimmering gold coins, then digging his fingers in. He threw open another chest, exposing gemstones and jewels. He placed an emerald tiara on his greasy head and looked up.

"Dr. Jones, I have a new proposition for you," he said. A creepy feeling rose inside of me. "Fuck the Russian billionaire. Forget the Octavian group. How about you and I keep it all? With my contacts, we can double our profit. No, we can triple it." Richard roared with laughter, looking like the Joker—minus the frightening make-up.

"I'd rather get kicked in my teeth by a horse than work with you," Andrew said, his hand on his hips.

"I have a question." I raised a finger. "How are we going to move all of this?"

"We leave it and return with a new crew," Brie said.

I threw her a skeptical look. "Like I'd trust you not to return on your own and steal it."

"You are welcome to stay and guard it." She sneered, baring her fractured smile.

"Your tooth is still broken."

Her mouth clamped tight.

A loud crash of stone reverberated in the cavern, sending a shock through me, and a surge of muddy water erupted from multiple directions overhead. Rocks and sharp stalactites showered us and as a stone graced my shoulder I cried out and stumbled backward.

"Find cover," Andrew shouted.

"Adriana, move." Brandon yanked on my arm and pulled

me to safety in the passage they'd come from, just as several chucks of the ceiling fell. William and Brie rushed to us too.

Andrew yelled again, but over the roaring chaos, Brie shrieking, and blood pounding in my ears, I couldn't hear what he'd said. Richard scrambled up onto a slithery rock, losing the emerald tiara in the process, and Andrew grabbed his hand and helped him out of the pool. They pressed their backs into the wall opposite us, near where Brie and I had entered the cavern earlier, shielding their heads with their arms.

Another crack thundered and an enormous ceiling slab caved and plummeted onto the chests. Daylight split the darkness. My eyes connected with Andrew's, and I saw fear in them for the first time. Hairs rippled down my back. What if it was about to entirely cave in and bury us all?

Chapter Thirty-Two

The water levels rose at a rapid speed. Andrew yelled something to Richard and jerked his head indicating they had to move. A whirlpool developed near the hole Brie and I had crawled out of and into the cavern. That wasn't good. If Andrew got sucked in, he would either drown or die when the flow spat him into the ravine at the other end.

Andrew and Richard edged in our direction, water beating down on their bodies. Andrew slipped, losing his hat, but he held on to the wall. When they neared the passage, I leaned out, throwing my arm to Andrew. William held on to my belt.

"Grab on, Andy." Brie also stuck out her hand while holding on to Brandon.

Ignoring her, Andrew grasped my outstretched arm, and I pulled him to safety. He brought me to him, and I shivered in his embrace. He cocooned me in his warmth, sheltering me from the devastation we'd most likely caused. Andrew kept whispering everything would be okay. I wanted to believe him.

The ground shook again, and the corridor crumbled several yards from us, blocking the passage. We were trapped wet rats.

"How do we get out of here?" I cried.

"That's our way out," Andrew shouted over the noise, pointing at a hole in the cavern ceiling where a fallen tree was sprawled across, the ends of four thick hanging vines swaying and writhing like snakes in chaotic waters.

The cold drops hit my head and face. I looked up to discover a large crack over our heads. We had to move.

I wiped my damped face with my arm. "What about William's foot?"

"I'll be fine," William said.

We'd have to climb up fifty feet to reach the opening. Fragility and hunger drained my adrenaline. I touched my aching shoulder. "I don't think I can do it. My arm is too weak."

Andrew's eyebrows pinched, and his eyes searched the space. He glanced at my brother and then at Brandon and Richard. "Take off your belts." He began unbuckling his own. "You too, Adriana."

Andrew took the belt out of his pants and secured it tight around his waist, then he collected our belts. Looping the first belt over his, he fastened it to the next one, then tied them in one knot to ensure they stayed together. He repeated the steps with the others.

"Raise your arms," Andrew told me, then circled the end of the assembled strap around my chest. "It will hurt, but I'll haul you up this way."

The water level was thigh-high now, and treading through

the rotating flow would take some strength which I didn't have.

Gold glimmered in the turbulent water. Here. There. Then, more and more, the pieces of treasure bubbled up. Dickhead jumped into the water and began snatching coins.

"Leave it. It isn't worth it," Andrew yelled, waving his hand.

Richard lost his footing. He tried to get up just to fall again. I watched in horror as an undertow dragged his body toward the dangerous vortex, his arms flapping in all directions, searching for something to grasp. At the last moment, he caught a stalagmite and held on to it, sheer panic on his face.

"Bloody asshole." Andrew undid his belt and leaped into the water. Panic ceased my breathing.

Battling the current, Andrew dug his fingers into the wall, his knuckles white. He waded close to Richard and stretched his long arm. He couldn't reach him.

I picked up the end of the belt cord and shoved it into Brandon's hands. "Put it on."

"Adriana, no," William cried into my ear, grabbing my arm. "I need to help."

Brandon secured the other end of the belts around his waist. "I'm ready."

"You're crazy!" William let go of me.

I stepped into the water, the undercurrent rapidly pulling at my feet.

"Adriana, get back," Andrew commanded.

"Don't tell me what to do."

Digging my nails into the wall, I strained my leg muscles and edged towards Andrew.

"Grip the belt and reach for the dumbass," I said, fighting not to lose my footing and slam into Andrew.

He shook his head. "Go. Back."

"Not without you." I braced my boot on a rock.

Andrew's nostrils flared, and his jaw clenched. With another shake of his head, his fingers curled around the belt near my breastbone. He completely let go of the wall, yanking me slightly forward. His body slid closer to Richard. They grasped hands.

The pull on my back strained, and we moved slowly backward until we reached the corridor. Brandon and William helped us get back in. Five of us slumped against the wall and slid to the floor, our chests heaving. Brandon disconnected himself from me and passed the belt to Andrew.

Brie was missing. My stomach clutched at the thought she'd fallen into the swell, but then I saw her. Like a monkey, Brie had climbed up the vine, reached the top, and was slipping through the tree branches. The skinny jerk didn't even try to rescue her husband.

Giving ourselves a moment to catch our breath, we crossed the water one by one and began ascending using different vines. Andrew climbed, tugging me with him. Each time I had to use my right arm to pull up, a hot pain sliced like a blade through my shoulder. I clenched my teeth and pushed down a scream.

William and Brandon reached the top first and helped Andrew and me to get out. Richard was the last one to climb out of the hellhole. Crawling several yards from the gaping hole, we crashed on the soft grassy ground.

I unbuckled the belt from around my chest and took a deep

breath, letting my lungs expand, staring up at the glorious blue sky. It was beautiful. From now on it was my favorite hue.

Thank you, Lord. We were out. I would cry, but I was too tired.

Andrew's hand found mine and tugged on it. I rolled on my left side and rested my head in the crook of his shoulder.

"We're okay," he breathed out. His arm circled my waist. "We're okay now," he repeated.

In the distance, the thrum of a helicopter thudded through the air. Andrew cursed under his breath. Even I knew that the only person involved in all of this with enough money to have a helicopter was Nicolai Kolesnikov. Of course, he would sweep in to claim his victory. My heart sank. All of our trouble had been for nothing.

Two large green helicopters flew over us. The treetops swayed from the gust the machines created. Brandon stood up and slogged to an open area, waving his hands.

The helicopters made another loop before settling down, flattening ferns and grass. The door opened in one of them, and a tall man, resembling a young Denzel Washington, dressed in a navy suit appeared. Ducking his head, the man jogged in our direction. He didn't look like a Russian oligarch at all.

Andrew cursed again, but then the corners of his lips curled up. He loosened his grip on me and got to his feet.

"You've got to be kidding me," Richard mumbled, dropping his head on the ground.

"Good to see you, Dr. Jones." The handsome man grinned and took off his sunglasses. He looked to be in his mid-fifties.

"Dr. Evans, glad to see you again." Andrew stretched out

his arm to the man. Dr. Evans shook it, placing his hand on Andrew's shoulder.

"You look like you've been through hell," Dr. Evans said, then his brown eyes cut to me. "Miss Jones." He gave me a curt nod.

What was going on? I ran sweaty palms over my hair, slightly embarrassed by my appearance. Who was this man, and why did he know me?

"How did you find us?" Andrew asked.

"Yesterday, we received a phone call from Mr. Pines providing us with the coordinates of Augustine Pérez's palace." Dr. Evans looked at Brandon. "He also urged us to bring a medical expert." He scrutinized Andrew and the rest of us. "And I can see why."

With a low grunt, Andrew turned to Brandon. "How did you know who to call?"

"I know Richard's phone passcode and found Dr. Evans in his contacts." Brandon shrugged one shoulder. "When William disclosed the location, I made a call before Richard went after you two."

A blond woman dressed in a black jumpsuit and carrying a red medical kit approached us.

"I'm Dr. Tiffany Yates," she said, stopping beside me. "Can you tell me where you hurt?"

"Do you mind checking on my brother first?" I pointed at William, Brandon kneeling at his side, holding William's hand, their foreheads pressed together. A swell of appreciation for Brandon's thoughtfulness towards my brother expanded inside me. I had a good feeling about them. A feeling that William might finally have found The One.

I dropped back down on the ground, grinned, and took a deep breath. We were finally safe. And the treasure was too. As the tension drained out of me, a sudden regret that our escapade had ended crashed upon me. What next? How could I go back to my boring, ordinary life?

Turning my head, I caught Andrew regarding me tenderly, the corners of his lips turned up. The way he looked at me set off an explosion in my chest. I had nothing to worry about. We had closed the chapter on the Colombian adventure, but *our* adventure had just begun.

jou·is·sance | ʒHōōēˈsäns |

NOUN: Physical or intellectual pleasure; chips and salsa; jeans that make an ass look great; Outlander, Season 1 Episode 7; Andrew's lips; sex; sex with Andrew; building a life with Andrew; Andrew.

ORIGIN: The Triton bar, Costa Rica, the moment I laid my eyes on Dr. Andrew Oliver Jones.

Later that day, wearing a white towel around his hips, Andrew came out of the bathroom, his face clean-shaven and his hair wet. Droplets of water clung to his chest and left a happy trail between his defined abs. Bruises and red marks covered his torso and arms, but he looked sexier than ever.

And now I was wet.

I was also loopy from a painkiller Dr. Yates had given me to help with my strained shoulder.

For the next couple of days, while we waited on Octavian to help replace our lost passports, the Four Seasons in Bogotá was our residence. Brandon and William were also staying in the same hotel. Richard and Brie? I had no idea where they'd gone, nor did I care. When I asked Andrew what would happen to them, he said they would lick their wounds and continue working for anyone hiring them to find artifacts to stock the black market or someone's private collection. That was if Kolesnikov didn't turn them into fish food first for not getting him what he'd asked for.

Leaning my back against the headboard, I watched Andrew amble to the room service cart with the leftovers of our dinner. He plucked a green grape, popped it in his mouth, and then his hand went for a strawberry. His lips curved upward, and the tiny lines at the corners of his eyes deepened.

"You're staring." Andrew caught my gaze in the mirror.

"Yes, I am." I loosened my robe at my waist. I was sleep-deprived, and my right arm was in a sling—not super sexy—but I was up for a quickie. "I wouldn't mind if you gave me some of your tender loving."

Andrew sat on the edge of the bed next to me, and excitement buzzed all over me. He bit the tip of the strawberry and brought the berry to my lips. I opened my mouth but he gently brushed it over my lips instead. His beautiful eyes held mine while his fingers nudged my robe open, exposing my left breast. He rubbed the strawberry over my nipple, hardening it. Then he leaned in and drew my nipple into his mouth. He sucked on it until it was swollen, then he bit it, arousing me to the point of madness.

A cold droplet let go of his hair and dripped on my breast. He brought his face to mine. His hand cradled the back of my neck, his fingers sliding into my hair.

"I love you, Adriana Jones," he said, his lips brushing mine.

"I love you, Andrew Jones." I nudged his nose with mine, smiling.

Andrew's eyes searched mine, a question burning in them. "I need to ask you something."

My heart stuttered, and a warm sensation flooded me. He wasn't about to ask me what I thought he was going to ask me, was he? Too soon. What would I say? Oh my god, should we pick late spring or early fall next year? England, for sure. It had spectacular venues. I always wanted to get married at a palace.

"Yes, I will," I whispered.

Andrew's eyebrow went up. "I didn't ask you a question yet."

"Oh." I breathed. "Sorry. Go ahead."

"Would you like to take a trip to Iceland this June?"

Huh?

"That was not what I was expecting."

Andrew leaned back with a confused expression. "What did you expect?"

Christ, of course. It was stupid to assume Andrew would ask me to marry him. We met ten days ago. What was I thinking? It was the drugs. I wasn't thinking clearly.

"Nothing. Why Iceland?"

"Dr. Evans mentioned new information has been found about a legendary Viking ship, and they want to make sure the right people find it first, and since you and I make an outstanding pair … we could…"

Now, it was my turn to pull away and narrow my eyes. "I thought you were done with treasure quests."

"Come on, just one last time…" Andrew smiled sheepishly.

"What about my store?" I peered at him, my lips tugging up at the corners.

"The trip should take a few days. A week tops."

I hated to admit it, but I had enjoyed the thrill of this trip—except for the pain, the fear of dying in a crypt, Richard, Brie, and having guns pointed at me. "As long as we can stay away from caves. And preferably avoid Dickhead, too."

"Is that a yes?"

"Yes." I kissed the word into his lips. And then I got my tender loving.

Twice.

Epilogue

NINE MONTHS LATER

WILLIAM

Did Andrew's new female stalker finally leave?

OMG! YES! 😵 She stayed thirty mins past closing

Did Andrew come out of hiding?

lol yes

Thank you for helping today

Anytime, hun. Your business is half mine. I need to help sometimes.

You're a silent partner. And as much as you talk, you are not very silent.

I snorted and put my phone down on the counter. Upon returning from Colombia, I'd dove into remodeling the building. I had enough money to renovate and purchase the necessary equipment, but I needed more to order the initial inventory. William and I had worked out a short-term partnership, and he'd cosigned with me on a small business credit line. With his support and with the help of some companies agreeing to supply products on credit, I soft opened the store the first week of October.

Tomorrow marked our two-month anniversary, and tonight, we were preparing everything for the grand opening with a ribbon-cutting ceremony and hopefully a few local news crews.

WILLIAM

You know she will be back tomorrow for the celebration. With Andrew around she'll be your number one customer.

no doubt 😐

The man's a money maker. We should start selling merchandise with Andrew's face on it. Cups, aprons, full-size cutouts, chocolate figurines.

12-month wall calendar

Now you're talking. Naked.

No. Shirtless.

in red speedo 😏

😈 NO!

😩

"What are you laughing about?" Andrew asked, carrying a stack of cookie boxes out of the storage/office room where he'd hid for thirty minutes, waiting for Ms. Kitty Brown, our *very* loyal customer—but only on the days when Andrew worked in the store—to decide between robust heart-healthy or mild olive oil. Which she'd already bought last week.

"William thinks the only way for our store to break even is by selling your hot body. Would you agree to that?"

"I would agree to anything you asked me to do as long as it made you happy." Andrew set the packages on the bar's granite top, leaned his hip against it, and crossed his arms. He wore the same clothes from this morning when he'd left for the university, gray dress pants and a blue shirt, with two top buttons now undone. "What's left for us to do here?"

While Andrew and I renovated a two-bedroom apartment above my store, we lived in a small Airbnb studio nearby. I had moved off William's couch in March, and Andrew had moved in with me at the end of April. This fall he'd started teaching an Archaeology course at Emory University in Atlanta, two days on campus and one day online. On the days he wasn't working, he was here helping me in the shop.

As Andrew promised, the expedition to Iceland had been his last job for Octavian Global. Dr. Evans had overseen Augustine Pérez's treasure excavation and relocated the artifacts to the University of Cambridge. It wouldn't be until the end of next year that the public could marvel at the priceless findings. The only trips Andrew made these days were to see Charlotte and Lulu in England. They also had come once to the States, and we'd gone on a family vacation to Disney World.

The moment I'd met Lulu, I'd fallen in love with her. Now she called me just as much as she called Andrew, if not more, because, you know, we had girl stuff to chat about. The more time I spent with her, the less self-doubt I had about my ability to be a good mother. Andrew's absolute love and respect for me gave me the emotional and personal stability I'd lacked and lessened my anxiety about having a family.

"I'm almost done with this. Then I need to set up the drinks table and sweep the floors." I put a medium-sized olive oil bottle next to a California Merlot in a gift basket for tomorrow's raffle, then adjusted a framed photo on the wall of Andrew and me with a research team in Iceland. We stood beside a Viking vessel sheltered deep inside a (*argh*) cave, literally frozen in time. Over a hundred valuables were recovered: gold jewelry, silver coins, weapons, and an agate-carved Roman vase.

"Should these cookies go into the refrigerator?" Andrew lifted the top box lid and peeked inside.

"They can stay there. They won't go bad. Plus, the fridge is filled to the brim."

He hummed. "You're a few short."

"William took some vegan cookies home for Brandon. He arrived from London this afternoon." I tightened the ribbon on the basket and cut it.

Brandon and William were in a serious long-distance relationship. They had been racking up their frequent flier miles each month by taking turns visiting each other. This time Brandon had flown twice in a row because he didn't want to miss the store's grand opening. I told him it wasn't that big of a deal, but he'd insisted. The more, the merrier. I loved spending time with him, and he was like a brother to me already. And the way things were going between those two, he should officially become my family soon.

Andrew disappeared into the office and returned with a broom. While he swept between the rows of the dark mahogany wood shelves with stainless fusti tanks and prefilled oil and vinegar bottles, I rearranged—for the fourth time—the table decorations and placed a jar for the raffle tickets next to two large gift baskets jam-packed with products from our store.

"Anything else we should do before we go home?" Andrew asked, coming up behind me, his body a solid wall against mine. I love the word *home* on his lips. He brushed his mouth over my exposed shoulder, his hands gripping my hips.

"Hmm." I closed my eyes and leaned into him. "I can think of a few things we could do, but I'd rather take a shower first. Let's go. We can finish the rest tomorrow morning."

Andrew kissed the crook of my neck. "By the way, there was a delivery earlier. I set the parcel by the register."

I didn't remember anybody bringing anything this afternoon, but I also didn't hear Ms. Kitty coming in while I was on the ladder counting wine bottles on the top shelf. In the past several months, deliveries to my store were non-stop, including an array of new products, office supplies, and vendor samples.

I stopped by the register and pulled a light brown package closer. It was light and the size of a thick book. "Oh, it could be the organic soap I've been waiting for."

I leaned over the countertop, fished out scissors from a pencil cup, and used the blade to open it.

"Did you check it had your name on it?" Andrew said with

a teasing tone, his voice somewhere near me. I rolled my eyes but then glanced at the label. The name was a bit smudged, but it was definitely for me.

Setting the scissors aside I lifted the carbon folds and inhaled the sweet rose aroma. Inside amongst the pink and red rose petals laid a notecard with the words:

Adriana Jones, will you go with me on the adventure of our lifetime?

With a surge of anticipation, I swirled around and gasped. Andrew kneeled on one knee and held out a platinum ring with a cushion-shaped green stone surrounded by diamonds.

I forgot how to breathe.

"The secret of a happy marriage is finding the right person," Andrew said, his eyes glinting in the light. "I'm grateful that the universe conspired to help me find you by sending you the package with the bracelet. I love you, Adriana Jones. You are the greatest treasure I have found, and I would be forever grateful if you would agree to spend the rest of our lives together. Will you marry me?"

Tears filled my eyes as I practically shouted, "Yes!" Smiling wide, I allowed him to slip the ring on my left-hand ring finger. My hand was trembling, or maybe it was his.

Andrew got up, and I looped my arms around his neck and smashed my mouth against his. I moaned at the warmth of his lips, and the way his tongue moved against mine. "Yes, a million times," I said, coming up for a breath.

"This is my grandmother's Edwardian ring. If you don't like it, we can pick you a different one." Andrew ran his thumb over my cheek, wiping a tear. I relaxed against his chest, feeling his fast heartbeat.

"It's beautiful. I love it."

And then I kissed Andrew again and again, climbing on him, wrapping my legs around his waist.

"Let's go home," he said, his hot breath in my ear.

"Too far. Carry me to the storage room."

His smile told me it was the right choice of location. "Your wish is my command."

Acknowledgments

Becoming a published author has been my dream since middle school, and it took me thirty-plus years to finally become one. Some might say a combination of English as a second language and dyslexia is not ideal for an author, but it didn't stop me from writing this novel. As soon as an idea about an antique bracelet delivered to the wrong hotel room hit me, the story poured out of me. Did it have a gazillion missing *the* and *a* articles and words with misplaced letters? Of course, but those were easy to fix *(hmm, my critique partners might use a different word than easy* 🙂*)*.

A publishing journey is a mighty cocktail made with equal parts delight and anxiety. While it is primarily a lonely process, it takes a village to create a book. During my journey, I met many talented, wonderful, and kind people, some of whom are now my friends. The writing community is one of the most supportive and generous communities, and I'll be forever grateful for all the support I receive from it.

My critique partners know that I'm an echo word police, but the next passages are full of the echo phrase "Thank you" because I'm fortunate to have numerous people to acknowledge.

I'll start with enormous gratitude to my exceptional superstar agent, Helen Lane. Helen, without you, this novel would still be a manuscript file on my laptop. Thank you for inviting me to be part of your Hel's Angels team. Thank you for loving my characters and their adventure just as much as I do, and for helping shape this novel into what it is now. I'm much obliged *(see what I did here? I looked up how to avoid an echo "thank you."* 🙂*) to you* for steering me through the complicated publishing process, always quickly replying to my text messages and emails, and ensuring I'm okay and not lying under my desk during hard times.

I'm hugely thankful to my brilliant editor, Jennie Rothwell, for falling in love with *Digging Dr Jones* and convincing HarperCollins to give romance lovers worldwide a chance to read it. Thank you to Charlotte Ledger, Kara Daniel, and other wonderful One More Chapter team members who worked on this book. Thank you to Federica Leonardis, Caroline Scott-Bowden, and Laura McCallen for going over the novel with a fine-tooth comb to ensure all the *the's* and *a's* are in the right places and the sentences make sense.

I'm forever indebted to Lucy Bennet and Leni Kauffman for creating a mouthwatering cover. I receive the cutest DMs from strangers letting me know they have fallen in love with the sexy illustration of Dr. Andrew Jones.

My deepest gratitude to my friends, critique partners, and writer friends: Christine Kelly, Tanya Agler, Gina Banks, Toni Bellon, Naomi Blass, Kim Catanzarite, Lauren Connolly, Kim Conrey, Kathy Hamdy-Swink, Joanna Jelen, Kristine Laco, Tricia LaRochelle, Jeremy Logan, Kelly Mowry, Megan Benoit Ratcliff, Branda Sevick, John Sheffield, Kristen Terrette, entire AWC Romance Critique Group, and Atlanta Writer's Club. I'm worried I might have forgotten to mention someone, and if I did, please forgive me and know I'm forever thankful to you and the support you offered.

Thank you, Susan, for meeting me early in the morning before you had to open Leaning Ladder and letting me bug you with questions about what it takes to build a premium olive oil and vinegar store from the ground up.

Huge thank you to Bianca Marais, Carly Watters, and CeCe Lyra at The Shit No One Tells You About Writing podcast. Without your excellent guidance, I wouldn't have learned how to polish my query letter and manuscript.

Thank you to my incredible family and friends for their endless encouragement and cheerleading. To my mom and dad, I apologize in advance for whatever Google Translator translates to you when you try to read my book. *(Yes, I did mean to use that word during spicy scenes.)*

Thank you to my parents-in-law for reading early drafts, and a special thank you to my father-in-law, Olin, for going with me *(because I was too scared to go alone)* to my first critique meeting at Roswell Library.

My favorite part of writing this book was working with my son, Alexander. Alexander, thank you for helping me find ways out of plot holes and for always being eager to listen or ask questions about my book. To my daughter, Catherine, thank you for your lovely handwritten notes before or after my writing meetings, for spending hours with me crafting author swags, and for being my talented Canva helper. I love you both very much.

Most importantly, thank you to the love interest in my own love story, Burke, my husband. Our love story is my favorite because it's like an oak tree that started as a couple of nuts who stood their ground. Burke, I'm forever grateful for your endless support of my dream. Thank you for not minding participating in my *I-need-to-figure-out-if-it-is-physically-possible-in-a-scene* moments. 😊 Let's be honest, you enjoyed some of them. Thank you for going to all bookish events with me (sometimes dragging a printer from our house to a hotel just in case I needed it, carrying my heavy bags with books, and always getting me a glass of wine at the end of a long day.). There aren't enough words in any language to describe how much I love you.

And last, a sincere thank you to you, my dearest reader, for spending your precious time with my debut novel. Thank you for picking it up and reading it. I hope you found joy searching for the lost treasure with Adriana Jones and Dr. Andrew Oliver Jones.

The author and One More Chapter would like to thank everyone
who contributed to the publication of this story...

Analytics
James Brackin
Abigail Fryer

Audio
Fionnuala Barrett
Ciara Briggs

Contracts
Laura Amos
Laura Evans

Design
Lucy Bennett
Fiona Greenway
Liane Payne
Dean Russell

Digital Sales
Laura Daley
Lydia Grainge
Hannah Lismore

eCommerce
Laura Carpenter
Madeline ODonovan
Charlotte Stevens
Christina Storey
Jo Surman
Rachel Ward

Editorial
Kara Daniel
Charlotte Ledger
Federica Leonardis
Laura McCallen
Ajebowale Roberts
Jennie Rothwell
Caroline Scott-Bowden
Helen Williams

Harper360
Jennifer Dee
Emily Gerbner
Ariana Juarez
Jean Marie Kelly
emma sullivan
Sophia Wilhelm

International Sales
Peter Borcsok
Ruth Burrow
Colleen Simpson
Ben Wright

Inventory
Sarah Callaghan
Kirsty Norman

Marketing & Publicity
Chloe Cummings
Grace Edwards
Emma Petfield

Operations
Melissa Okusanya
Hannah Stamp

Production
Denis Manson
Simon Moore
Francesca Tuzzeo

Rights
Helena Font Brillas
Ashton Mucha
Zoe Shine
Aisling Smyth
Lucy Vanderbilt

Trade Marketing
Ben Hurd
Eleanor Slater

**The HarperCollins
Distribution Team**

**The HarperCollins
Finance & Royalties
Team**

**The HarperCollins
Legal Team**

**The HarperCollins
Technology Team**

UK Sales
Isabel Coburn
Jay Cochrane
Sabina Lewis
Holly Martin
Harriet Williams
Leah Woods

**And every other
essential link in the
chain from delivery
drivers to booksellers
to librarians and
beyond!**

ONE MORE CHAPTER

One More Chapter is an
award-winning global
division of HarperCollins.

Subscribe to our newsletter to get our
latest eBook deals and stay up to date
with all our new releases!

signup.harpercollins.co.uk/
join/signup-omc

Meet the team at
www.onemorechapter.com

Follow us!

 @OneMoreChapter_

 @onemorechapterhc

 @onemorechapterhc

@onemorechapterhc

Do you write unputdownable fiction?
We love to hear from new voices.
Find out how to submit your novel at
www.onemorechapter.com/submissions